ret·ri·bu·tion
A Marcus Clemens Novel
(Book Two)

James E. Anderson

This book is dedicated to the memory of the one true love of my life, my best friend and wife, Sharon. Though you are no longer here with me, your love and inspiration will remain forever.
Until I can hold you again....

Table of Contents

Prologue

His hair and clothes were still soaking wet as he lay quietly sprawled, engulfed by the unkept grass along the gently sloping incline, his feet near but not more than a yard from the water's edge. He had managed to crawl this meager distance before collapsing in the throes of sheer exhaustion, rolling onto his back, arms extended to either side. The day was typical summer Missouri hot, temperature hovering just below the 100° threshold, the sun bearing down mercilessly. The heat was so intense in the late afternoon that, even with his eyes closed, the inside of his eyelids appeared to him as blood red; the sunlight almost seemed to throb, it felt as though the sun's rays were penetrating right through the lids. He struggled to take in deep, calming breaths. He had been through the routine many times; in through the nose, holding each breath for five seconds, and then slowly and purposely releasing through the same orifice. He was attempting to relieve the stress and anxiety that was threatening his ability to breathe at all. He had been professionally trained in the methods of relaxation and the relief of tension, nervousness, and anxiety. He was totally confident his heart rate would slow to a normal pace and the muscle fatigue he was feeling eventually would subside.

Although lasting only a few brief moments, it had been a violent confrontation and he had experienced intense seconds which drove his adrenaline production levels through the roof. There is no doubt that he was fortunate to have been able to claw his way from the water and up onto the bank. Continuing the deep-breathing exercises, and with eyes still closed, he drew a mental picture of the physical surroundings he had noticed in the minutes prior to the encounter. His memory recalled thick woods consisting primarily of pine trees and covering at least two-thirds, if not a full three-quarters of the land immediately encircling the pond. The remaining cleared area was relatively flat with a dense growth of Indiangrass nearly three feet tall. There was a beaten down corridor through the Indiangrass, the same passage he had taken when arriving for this rendezvous. The pathway had been worn in the Indiangrass by numerous vehicles driven by locals who sporadically visited the pond to angle for smallmouth bass or carp. The oblong shaped pond itself was fairly large in size, measuring roughly 200' in length and approximately 120' across, but the water's surface dimensions had been reduced by an early summer drought which had lowered the level by a minimum of a foot. Even though the water level had dropped, it was still deep for a midwestern pond. Having just been in the water, he was certain it had to have a midpoint depth easily exceeding ten feet and likely nearing fifteen.

As a mathematical and analytical type of person, he visualized his position in a geometric fashion. Vertically, from the surface of the water to top of the bank, the measurement must have been six to seven feet. Accounting for the angle at which his body felt to be resting, he estimated the diagonal distance at about twelve feet from water's edge to the top of the bank of the pond. The top of the bank was a foot or so higher than the surrounding terrain and when considered in conjunction with the distance from the top of the bank down to the water's surface, there should have been no possibility that anyone could have witnessed what had just occurred in the pond.

Fifteen minutes had now passed, and his hair and clothes were beginning to dry in the scorching July sun. Breathing had become much easier, and his heart rate seemed to have returned to a normal range. Even though sweat beads had now replaced the pond water on his face, he felt a relative degree of relaxation. The tension had eased; calmness seemed to have settled over him, replacing the anxiety he'd suffered just twenty minutes or so prior. There was no breeze, the only sounds breaking the afternoon silence were the lyrical humming noises produced in unison by thousands of katydids somewhere out there in the vast reaches of the Indiangrass. He was beginning to truly relax when his peacefulness was interrupted, first by what seemed to have been a dog's barking. Then, without warning, a voice calling to him, conversation that was but a blur now, and intense pain. Eyes closed, unseeing, he wondered if he were having a heart attack. He had no idea what was transpiring. The pain in his chest was unbearable, he could not think clearly. Rapidly, he was being drug back into the murky pond, mouth and throat suddenly violated by muddy, silt-filled water. There was no possibility of inflating the lungs, no time to even gasp and attempt to hold his breath before going under. Inexplicably, the final thought passing through his mind before giving in to the inevitable was not one of imminent demise, but rather *'that stupid damned dog."*

Haunting Encounter

The squeaking brakes cried in protest as Mrs. Dennison gently attempted to apply them, slowing to drop eight high school passengers at the corner of Fernwood Drive and Driftwood Avenue. The date was May 18, 1967, and Jackie Dennison was glad the school year was nearing an end and the menacing brake screeching finally would be addressed during summer vacation. She was also thankful that this year she had been hauling high school students rather than the elementary and junior high children she had chauffeured for the past six years. Apart from a rare but occasional fight she was expected to break up (and there had been only two all year), she found the teenage passengers much more pleasant to deal with than the younger children. Elementary and junior high school students tended to be far more boisterous, unruly, and just plain louder than the older, more mature crowd she was now transporting. The 1966-67 school year had been by far the most satisfying and least stressful of her seven-year bus driving career.

1966-67 had also been by far the most enjoyable school year to date for a pair of love-struck fifteen-year-old ninth grade students at Lewis and Clark High School in Lewis County, Missouri. Marcus Clemens and Cassandra (Cassie) Worthington had been a steady item, essentially since their "chance meeting" at Franklin's Five and Dime four years prior. It was the spring of 1963, back when both were students in the fifth grade. Of course, as Marcus had quickly learned, the "chance meeting" had been prearranged, at the behest of Cassie and in cahoots with his best friend, Denny Wallace. It was not as if the two had been previously unacquainted. Marcus had carried an unrequited crush on Cassie for quite a while. He had been silently pining for her for more than two years. Cassie however, had only developed an interest in Marcus a few months prior to the preplanned "chance" encounter. Although they were in different classrooms, she would often spot him on the playground at recess or during lunch in the cafeteria. She had been too shy to approach Marcus, but when a mutual friend of both her and Denny had mentioned to Cassie that Denny had confided Marcus' secret affection toward her, she had decided to spring into action. She first confronted Denny with questions about Marcus and had learned that Marcus was enthralled with Cassie. So much so, according to Denny, that he would rush to the front doors of Roosevelt Elementary at the end of each school day just to admire her as she boarded her bus. Cassie and Denny had then hatched a plan for a rendezvous at the Five and Dime, and as they say, the rest was history.

Of course, much had changed since 1963. While the events of that year had been devastating to both Marcus and Cassie, what could easily have resulted in a deterioration of their burgeoning relationship had in many ways strengthened and reinforced their bond. Both of their lives had been threatened, and Marcus and Cassie had been forced to face demons that could never have been foreseen. The seeds of distrust that were sown toward those in whom they had placed their utmost confidence made for a difficult season of soul searching. The appearance of - and their reliance upon - an otherworldly presence had been difficult for two intelligent and realistic adolescents to fully comprehend and digest. Being completely aware of the ramifications that would have resulted had they revealed to anyone the existence and apparent mission of their mysterious friend, Marcus and Cassie had determined to remain totally mum on the subject. This shared secret further enhanced their commitment to one another and they remained steadfast in their mutual affection and admiration. In fact, their relationship had only blossomed and evolved in intensity.

Through the four years, Marcus had grown nearly a foot yet had gained no more than ten pounds over that timeframe. Gone was the childhood "baby fat" that had caused for him so much personal doubt and consternation. His build had become noticeably more sculpted, and as a result, his athleticism had improved dramatically. He had earned a school letter at LCHS in Junior Varsity football in the fall of 1966 and had embarked upon a mild workout regimen in hopes of gaining more weight and strength for his sophomore season.

Cassie, meanwhile, had grown only a couple of inches and had put on just enough weight to fill out what had been a somewhat spindly preadolescent shape. She was beginning to take the form of an attractive young woman. Although Marcus encouraged her to try out as a school cheerleader, Cassie had no interest in such endeavors, and was more gratified by her involvement in debate, drama, and student government. During their freshman year, she had served as class treasurer and prided herself on her fiscal abilities. Both stayed extremely busy with their school activities, and both had become quite popular on the campus of Lewis and Clark High.

Denny and Marcus had remained best friends, despite Marcus' busy schedule; seemingly he was always balancing between his school endeavors and paying adequate attention to Cassie. No longer was there an unlimited amount of time to spend with Denny. They still visited the banks of the Mississippi River to idly cast for catfish once or twice a month, and every now and again found a little time to play some catch and hang out on weekends. Occasionally, during the past couple of summers, they would float out to a sandbar a couple of miles downstream on a homemade raft they had fashioned from downed tree limbs and twisted manila rope. This was generally a "Tom Sawyer and Huckleberry Finn" weekend camping adventure. Invariably, Cassie would angle to join them (knowing full well that her parents would never have allowed her to tag along), and Marcus each time would recite all the reasons – and especially highlighting the dangerous and frightening ones - that "Becky Thatcher" could never camp with "Tom and Huck". The float trip banter had become a running gag, and Denny loved playing the antagonist in the mini drama.

In the fall of 1966, Denny had taken a part-time job as an usher at the Meridian Theater on Main Street, generally working Thursday, Friday, and Saturday nights. Due to his penchant for being a funny guy at school, his job at the theater was a Godsend as it enabled him to memorize jokes and one-liners uttered by some the grandest comedians, most vile villains, and heroic champions of the mid-sixties silver screen. Jerry Lewis, John Wayne, Sean Connery, Clint Eastwood, Steve McQueen – all were fair game, and none were safe from the copycat humor, satire, and amateur impressions that Denny so enjoyed.

As Mrs. Dennison brought the ear-piercing, screeching bus to a halt, Marcus stood in the aisle with both his and Cassie's books, politely stepping back momentarily to allow Cassie to precede him to the door. Disembarking the bus, Marcus reached with his right arm to take Cassie's left hand, as had become customary when they walked anywhere that was not on school property. On campus, such expressions of affection were frowned upon. Per the district school board, public displays of affection were unacceptable when on school grounds. Walking just a few feet after stepping off the bus, and before he could even begin to initiate conversation, Marcus was somewhat startled to see the Ford sedan parked at the curb thirty or so feet down Fernwood Drive. Though he hadn't seen the car since the fateful October night in 1963, Marcus recognized it and knew immediately who was sitting behind the wheel. Opening the driver side door and stepping out with cigarette dangling from his lips was Ellis Compton.

As Marcus and Cassie neared, Ellis took three steps forward. Dropping the cigarette, and extinguishing it beneath his black leather boot, Ellis extended his right hand toward the approaching Marcus. "Hello Marcus." Ellis smiled as he waited for Marcus to respond.

Marcus had not seen Ellis since the frenzied night at the house of Ellis' adoptive father, Oliver Compton. The unforgettable night during which Marcus feared his friend, Deputy Mitch Daniels, was going to be killed by Ellis and Ollie. In a matter of seconds, waves of horrifying memories flooded through Marcus' mind. It is amazing how much information the mind can process in just a fraction of a second. Before making any type of reaction toward Ellis' outstretched hand, Marcus glanced at Cassie. With his hand resting on her shoulder, he could immediately feel her muscles tense. She instinctively registered a visage of utter shock and disbelief. Her mind's eye instantaneously focused on the memory of Ellis preparing milkshakes for them as she and Marcus had sat on swivel stools at the soda fountain counter at Franklin's Five and Dime. Delivering their shakes, he had been rude and disrespectful, and it was at that precise moment she had realized that Ellis possibly had been the camouflage wearing figure that had attempted to attack her and Marcus in the dank, dark mausoleum at Forest Park Cemetery. And Cassie also knew that after all the facts had become known, Ellis had been revealed as the biological son of Marcus' only blood relative, Cousin Judy. This revelation meant Ellis was a second cousin to Marcus. As fate would have it, Ellis was the only person in the entire world, aside from Cousin Judy, who was from the same bloodline as Marcus.

Ellis Compton had served two years at the Missouri Training School for Boys, a juvenile detention center located in the small west central Missouri town of Boonville. The facility was home to notoriously bad apples from across the state. Upon his release from the reformatory, Ellis was now serving probation for his involvement in the crimes for which Ollie Compton currently resided on death row in the state penitentiary in Jefferson City, Missouri. After his release, Ellis had moved back home with his mother Alicia, in Fulton. Alicia Compton had relocated from Alexandria, moving to Fulton in the summer of 1964 - soon after Ellis had been incarcerated - in order to remain close enough to visit. So far as Marcus was aware, Ellis was still serving under house arrest well over one hundred miles away. Marcus had not seen him since he had been released from detention and the only reports he had received were by way of Cousin Judy, Jude Allensworth. Just as he had promised, Cousin Judy had maintained contact with Ellis. Although it was a

*one-hundred-and-fifty-mile drive from his new home
and job in St. Louis, Cousin Judy had seemed quite
earnest in wanting to develop a strong parental
relationship with his recently found son. Cousin Judy
also tried to visit once every couple of months with
Marcus and his stepmother Margaret, despite it being
a six-hour roundtrip drive.*

Marcus was forced to think fast. Less than two
seconds had elapsed since Ellis had extended his right
hand. Sensing Cassie's reaction, Marcus had quickly
stepped in front of her in a defensive maneuver, and
in the same motion had brought up his right arm to
take Ellis' hand in his. With minimal conviction,
Marcus shook hands with Ellis. Unsure exactly what
he should say, Marcus hesitantly muttered, "Ellis,
why are you here?"

"Marcus, I'm here because I owe you and your
girl an apology." Ellis spoke softly, with a tone of
hesitancy.

*It all came flooding back and raced through
Marcus' mind. Ellis had been his and Cassie's worst
nightmare. It was Ellis, dressed in camouflage clothing
and wearing a red ski mask, who had wielded the
machete in the Forest Park Cemetery mausoleum. Had
it not been for the timely interference of a mangy and
mysterious dog, God only knows what would have
been the fate of Marcus and Cassie. It had been Ellis
who had gotten into Marcus' apartment and stolen his
father's monogrammed red handkerchiefs in an
unsuccessful attempt to frame Marcus. And it had been
Ellis who had intended, along with Ollie, to kill Marcus'
friend Deputy Daniels.*

12

"What are you talking about Ellis?" Marcus felt the hair on the back of his neck standing up, just as the fur of an angered feline. "You tried to kill us and now you want to *apologize*?" Marcus' voice increased in volume and intensity. "I'm sorry, but what kind of crap is that Ellis?" Marcus knew his face had probably turned twelve shades of red, his anger boiling over in just an instant. His eyes felt as if they were bulging out of their sockets as he stared deeply into and possibly straight through Ellis' pupils, directly into what Marcus was sure was his empty soul.

Yes, Oliver Compton had been convicted of two murders and currently sat on death row. But while Ellis had not technically committed any murders, he had been convicted as Ollie's willing accomplice. Only sixteen-years-old at the time of the crimes, he was remarkably fortunate that a compassionate and lenient court system had allowed him to be tried as a juvenile. While Ellis was found guilty of aiding and abetting, and ultimately admitted to taking part in, and of being an integral cog in, the heinous crimes, an equally compassionate and lenient judge had sentenced him to only two years at The Missouri Training School for Boys. The prevailing opinion amongst locals who had any knowledge of the case was that Ellis was far more responsible for the deaths of the two young women than the resultant punishment would have indicated. It was no doubt good fortune for Ellis that he no longer lived in the vicinity of Lewis County.

As Marcus stared with disdain into the depth of Ellis' eyes, he noticed the cloudy wetness of formulating tears, with one seeming to slowly roll down Ellis' left cheek. While he did not drop his guard, Marcus did wonder how such a cold-hearted monster could show any degree of emotion.

"I *am* truly sorry, Marcus. And I *am* truly sorry to you too, Cassie." Ellis seemed on the verge of completely breaking down. "I have been beating myself up for three years now. I have spent the last three years feeling guilt and remorse and reliving the horrors that I was involved in. I know there is nothing I can do to bring those poor girls back. Nothing I could possibly do will ease the pain that their parents will have to live with every day of their lives. I can't do anything but sympathize with how you must feel about me. But Marcus, I know now that you are my family, and I've been thinking about that a lot. Except for my real dad, *your* cousin Judy, you are all I have. And I guess in a way, Cassie is now part of my family, too. All I can do is my best to make amends to you two for the evil I displayed, the hurt that I caused. If it takes the rest of my life, I will never stop trying to earn your forgiveness. I pray every night Marcus, that you and God will forgive me for what I did. I could try to make up a million excuses for all that happened, but not one of them would fly. All I can do is pray that you'll find it in your heart someday to forgive me, Marcus. You're my family, and believe it or not, I love you."

Marcus was taken back by the emotional words that Ellis had delivered. He had never actually considered the day that he would eventually have a face-to-face encounter with Ellis. Before Marcus could even begin to offer a response, Ellis turned away and hurried back toward his car, jumping in, starting it, and speeding away. Looking down at the sidewalk, Marcus thought he felt tears forming in his own eyes.

* * * *

The teens sat quietly on the wooden swing beneath the oak tree in Cassie's front yard. Seeking comfort, Cassie rested her head on Marcus' left shoulder as he stared blankly at the Worthington's manicured flower garden, the irises waving gently in the slight spring breeze. His hands rested in his lap, alternately tensing into tight fists then relaxing. Marcus rubbed his palms uneasily on the thighs of his Levi jeans. The past three years had been quite idyllic. There had been no distractions, nothing out of the ordinary. No drama, no mystery, nothing to cause any undue stress or worry. Their lives had been those of normal midwestern teenagers. Their existence had been relaxing and peaceful, listening to the antics of the DJs and rock and roll music offered up by 50,000-watt mega-station WLS broadcasting from Chicago. They had enjoyed the sounds and stylings of homegrown and traditional American rock, as well as its new challengers, the fresh and innovative British Invasion that was sweeping the nation. But today all that had changed.

Glancing down at the soft red hair of his girlfriend, Marcus gently stroked her bangs. Cassie looked up at him with red, swollen eyes.

"Marcus, how could we have assumed we would never see Ellis again?" she asked. During the two years that Ellis had been in juvenile detention, the

15

pain and heartache he had evoked in Marcus and Cassie had subsided into a subtle yet horrific memory. The effects of his actions had diminished with time. Never to completely go away, but less fresh, less noticeably severe. His release from detention and the subsequent house arrest and counseling had been cause for some consternation. The knowledge that a potentially dangerous predator was in such close proximity had been a bit unnerving. But with each passing day that Ellis remained in Fulton with his mother, subconscious confidence grew that he would remain out of their lives.

"I don't know," Marcus replied as he gently wiped a tear from beneath Cassie's left eye. "I guess we had just gotten comfortable with the idea that he would not be stupid enough to show his face. I mean, how could he possibly think he could just show up and say 'Hey, I'm sorry'. The gall of that guy!"

"Marcus, I was scared." Tears began building in Cassie's eyes once again. "I mean, what if he'd pulled a knife? Or even a gun? What would we have done?"

"I'm not sure…" Marcus paused. "I'd have done something, though."

"Marcus, do you think Opa would have been there if that happened?"

Opa was the nickname Cassie had affectionately given the mangy dog that had been their savior in the cemetery and the mausoleum. She had been insistent upon the dog having a name, and through her research had discovered that Opa was the informal German word for grandfather. Of course, they had learned that the mysterious mutt with the power of telepathic communication had in fact been Marcus' long-deceased grandfather. John Clemens had returned from the grave to serve as Marcus' guardian angel. Three years had passed since the last time Opa had spoken from the brush at the edge of the parking lot at the *Red Roof Lodge*. Oh, to be sure, his presence had still been felt. He had not gone away. He had often made himself known, occasionally appearing at the crest of a hill, or sometimes when Marcus visited the graves of his parents, skirting between headstones at Forest Park Cemetery. And he certainly had a penchant for presenting himself through the dreams of both Marcus and Cassie. With the passage of time, however, they both found themselves sometimes wondering if the occurrences of his miracle behavior had even actually happened, or possibly even been imagined. Neither had admitted this to the other. But they were fifteen now, and the voice heard only by Cassie became a small subject of doubt to Marcus. The miracles had occurred before they were even teens, while they were still just kids. The few times that Opa had spoken Marcus' name even became an issue with him. Self-doubt crept in and he wondered if it had merely been his imagination.

Cassie also sometimes wondered if Opa's heroics had possibly been a figment of her imagination. She had read of shared hallucinations or delusions and bore a fear that she and Marcus had been victims of this psychosis. In her reading, she had discovered that one person could have delusions

– such as hearing voices – and a secondary person could be led into accepting the same belief. Even though she felt certain the heroism displayed in the mausoleum by Opa was beyond any doubt real, the fact that Marcus witnessed those same events from a different perspective from hers was extremely puzzling.

"I'm quite sure Opa was there watching it all unfold, Cassie," Marcus replied as he gently pulled her close.

The Dump

Striking the wooden kitchen match against the black cast-iron hide of the unused potbelly stove, Jeremiah Paige proceeded to light the homegrown tobacco he'd just stuffed into his corncob pipe. Within a few quick staccato puffs, the tobacco glowed red, and he inhaled a deep draw of the coarse mixture. Exhaling and shaking the match briskly to extinguish the flame, Jeremiah deposited the burnt stick into the Folgers coffee can that ably served double duty as both a trash can and spittoon. Leaning back in his ancient wooden rocker, he gazed across the acres of trash that mounded on both sides of the gravel roadway that snaked for nearly half a mile.

Known simply as *The Dump* to locals, the trash disposal site was properly named the Lewis County East Trash Facility. Jeremiah Paige had been employed as day watchman since the spring of 1964. His prior employment had been as a general laborer in a rock quarry east of the Mississippi River near Quincy, Illinois. He had retired at the age of 62 and moved back to Missouri, into rural Lewis County during the first spring thaw of 1963. After a summer mostly spent fishing, and a winter of freezing boredom in the one-bedroom shanty in which he had been raised, Jeremiah had grown weary of retirement. He had been fortunate to have noticed the *Help Wanted* sign at all. Perhaps the sign had caught Jeremiah's eye because of the haphazard way it had been hung on the locked gate at the entrance to the dump. Jeremiah was a bit of a neatness freak, and when seen in his peripheral vision, the out of kilter mounting had drawn his attention. Properly affixed, the sign no doubt would have gone unseen. He had spied the notice on a sunny late spring morning of 1964 as he was driving toward town. He had planned on whiling away the morning in his customary manner, sitting on a wooden bench just outside Franklin's Five and Dime. From this vantage point he would leisurely watch the sparse traffic on White Street as it flowed to and from the flashing red light at the intersection with the two-lane U.S. Highway 61. This was where Jeremiah spent most of his sunny weekday mornings since retiring. He normally sat observing, both people and things, until the noon whistle blew at the small battery assembly plant located two blocks away and just off of North 4th Street. At the sound of the noon whistle, Jeremiah would treat himself to a small sack lunch and thermos of coffee he always brought along. Old habits die hard, and Jeremiah had cultivated his lunchtime routine through more than twenty years at the rock quarry. He found solace in continuing his noon ritual, even in retirement. The observance of a structured lunch break coinciding with the lunch whistle of the battery plant seemed to bring him a sense of order and purpose. On this sunny day, as Jeremiah sipped from his thermos cup, he noticed a scruffy stray mutt with matted fur sitting to his right, alongside the bench and staring straight ahead as if to mimic Jeremiah. Placing his right hand at the back of the dog's head and continuing to gaze toward the passing cars, Jeremiah said, "Yeah boy, it's pretty boring sittin' here ain't it? Whatchu think boy? Ought I go and apply for that job?" The dog stood, shook off some dust and lose hair, and began trotting westward on White Street. "Now what kinda answer is that boy?" Screwing the cup back onto the thermos he continued to sit, contemplating, until the whistle blew ending his lunch break. Still visualizing the dog sauntering away, Jeremiah shook his head and got up from the bench, first stretching, and then grabbing his thermos and sack lunch in each hand and walking to his parked car.

He had only driven a few blocks when Jeremiah had decided to park his well-maintained 1946 Hudson Super 8 sedan near the payphone at Walt's Tire and Auto Repair. The red two-door model was his pride and joy, always kept in pristine condition. As he had approached Walt McMurphy's shop, Jeremiah had concluded that the question he had presented to the stray dog at the wooden bench had indeed been answered. A religious man, Jeremiah had determined that God had sent the stray to show him direction, and because the dog had walked away in a generally westward path, toward the dump, he saw that as an omen. Jeremiah dialed the operator and after requesting the number and dropping his dime, was soon connected with the personnel department of Lewis County Government. County Personnel

Supervisor Scott Niemeier seemed to have no problem filling Jeremiah in on the reasoning behind the *Help Wanted* sign at the dump. Jeremiah learned that Old Bill Lechner had been the day watchman at *The Dump* since before World War II, but now in his eighties, his health had deteriorated to the point that showing up for work had become an uneven proposition. It seemed the dump was closed nearly as often as it was open, and the time had come to recruit Old Bill's replacement. Jeremiah decided the job sounded like a perfect opportunity. The day watchman had no physical duties to speak of. He merely was expected to greet incoming vehicles and have the drivers sign-in and complete a brief form on a clipboard. The information on the form was nothing more than a rough declaration of items being dumped, such as refrigerator, lawn mower, tree limbs or household trash. He then was expected to direct them to the appropriate location. It was amazingly simple, practically mindless work, paying right at the minimum wage of $1.25 per hour. The dump was open Monday through Saturday, but the hours were relatively short, 10 a.m. to 5 p.m. weekdays. And it was closed for lunch from 12:30 to 1:30 each afternoon, which would provide Jeremiah with a comfortable daily siesta. On Saturdays it was only open three hours, 10 a.m. to 1 p.m. After the fifty-to-sixty-hour workweeks at the quarry, thirty-three hours per week sounded like a walk in the park, especially without the physicality he had grown accustomed to enduring. As a bonus, the $41.25 a week gross pay provided a great deal more income than his $92 a month social security benefit. Jeremiah filled out a job application that same afternoon, and on Monday April 20, 1964, found himself with a worn, but new to him, set of keys in hand and unlocking the dump's gate at 9:45 a.m.

* * * *

It was now late in the afternoon on the 18th day of May in 1967 as Jeremiah sat in his rocker chewing the stem of his corncob pipe and gazing idly out the open front door of the ten feet by ten feet shack that he deemed 'his office'. With the sound of spewing gravel demanding his attention, Jeremiah diverted his eyes to the small window to his left and recognized a familiar orange Chevrolet Sportsvan, turning off from Missouri Highway 16 onto the river rock and shell entry to the dump. Rising from his chair and gently placing the spent pipe onto the lid of the stove, Jeremiah hitched up his overalls, picked up his cane and ambled out of the shack and to the far side of roadway. The van approached in a dust cloud and haphazardly skidded to a stop in the loose stone. The driver's window lowered, and Jeremiah was the first to speak.

"You know boys, one day they gonna be puttin' up cameras out here and ya'll ain't gonna be comin' in here no more without signin' in."

"We'll worry about that when the time comes old man. You'll be long dead before that ever happens anyhow. You got the keys? You seen us comin', I know. You got them eagle eyes, don't miss nothin'," bellowed the overweight driver with pencil thin mustache and slicked back main of oily hair.

23

"And hurry up old man, we got a long ride to go yet today. Gotta get to St. Louis before sundown." The long-haired, bearded companion added his two cents worth, as he normally did when he was tagging along.

"Here," said Jeremiah, "take the whole ring, but make sure you bring 'em back. Last time, you fools left 'em in the lock and I hadsta walk all that way to go get 'em."

"Shut up, you old fart. It was rainin' and I was in a hurry." The driver wagged his finger at Jeremiah and popped the clutch, spraying gravel and dust in his wake.

Jeremiah shook his head and yelled after them, "I know it was rainin' ya damn fool, I hadsta walk a half a mile in it!"

Jeremiah limped back into his office and resumed his position in the rocking chair. He repacked the corncob pipe, and striking another match, relit it. Closing his eyes, he thought back almost three years to the first time he had been approached by Tony Mancini. Tony had not been as heavy then, although his overall look was basically the same as now. It had been shortly after Jeremiah had taken over for Old Bill Lechner in the spring of 1964. Jeremiah had taken his new job seriously and had a sense of pride in his little 10' x 10' office. He had added a screen door that he had salvaged from the dump and patched up. He had replaced a broken window and had scavenged some left-over paint and spruced the little building up a bit. He recovered the old rocking chair when it had been discarded one quiet afternoon, and just generally tried adding touches to make the place more comfortable.

It was during the late summer of the renovation period that Tony Mancini had first appeared. He had originally dealt with Old Bill Lechner, but Bill's reliability had diminished to the point that Tony had been forced to move his business elsewhere. Unfortunately for Tony, he had run into insurmountable problems with his "elsewhere" and had now found himself once again parked outside the watchman's shack at the Lewis County East Trash Facility. He immediately noticed the changes that were taking place and sensed that Old Bill may no longer be the man with whom he would be dealing. Seeing no one at the shack, Tony stepped out of his orange van. As he approached the day watchman's shack and reached for the screen door handle, he was startled by the door of the nearby outhouse swinging open and a tall black gentleman with a slight limp approaching.

"Can I help you mister?" Jeremiah asked.

Still a bit startled and somewhat confused, Tony replied, "Yeah, maybe so. I was looking for Bill Lechner."

"Old Bill ain't here no more. My name's Jeremiah Paige. I'm the new watchman. What can I help you with?"

"Well sir, I used to deal with Old Bill. I got a big storage box there in the back of my van. I used to keep it here in the dump, Bill had arranged a kind of like *hiding* place for it," Tony explained, using air quotation marks to emphasize the word *hiding*.

"Hidin' place? What the Sam Hill you talkin' 'bout Mister? This here's a dump, it ain't no damned bank with safety deposit boxes to be hidin' stuff in. And who the hell are you anyways?" Jeremiah asked, "I told you my name, what's yours?"

"Oh, sorry. My name's Tony Mancini. And like I said, I used to do business with Bill."

"What kind of business? I'm guessing you paid Old Bill to let you hide that box of yours here, right?"

"Yeah, that's right Mr. Paige."

Jeremiah sensed opportunity knocking. "And just how much was you paying Old Bill to keep that box hid, Mister Mancini?"

"Ten dollars a month Mr. Paige. Would you be interested in continuing that business relationship? Of course, the county or the cops can't know anything about, I uh, I imagine it would be illegal for you to accept cash to store something on county property, right?"

Jeremiah saw the dollar signs flashing now. Most certainly Mancini was involved in something illegal here, but how could Jeremiah be tied in with it? He wouldn't be handling whatever was going into that box. He wouldn't have any involvement whatsoever. If he insisted on cash payment, there would be no link to Mancini's business at all. "You can call me Jeremiah, Mr. Mancini. You would have to pay me in cash, weekly, and in advance."

"You'd expect me to drive out here every week to bring you two dollars and fifty cents? I come all the way from St. Louis, Mr. Paige! It would take more than that in gas money just to drive out here."

"I didn't say two dollar and fifty cent Mr. Mancini. I'm gonna need five dollar a week. Inflation, ain't that what it's called?"

"That's ridiculous Mr. Paige. I can't pay that much. That's twenty dollars a month. And twenty-five in months that have five weeks! I'm sorry Mr. Paige, but no. No deal."

"Okay, Mr. Mancini. I guess you can take that box of yours somewheres else then." Tony Mancini wore a dumbfounded look. Jeremiah paused for a few appropriate seconds and then offered, "Whats say I come down to a flat twenty dollar a month instead of by the week, and ya only pay me up front on your first visit each month. Twenty dollar a month, first week every month. Whatcha say Mr. Mancini?"

"Alright, Mr. Paige, you win," Tony reluctantly agreed.

"It's Jeremiah, Mr. Mancini. And payments start today."

* * * *

Going on three years now that Tony Mancini had been showing up at the dump, at first on a basic once or twice a week schedule. But over the past few months, visits had increased to three and sometimes four times a week; occasionally he would return multiple times in a single day. Tony had always been regular with his payments, and even though Jeremiah had correctly surmised that increased visits indicated that business was booming and had shrewdly demanded his fee increase to twenty-five dollars a month, Tony had continued to be punctual with his payments, and always in the form of crisp twenty- and five-dollar bills. The extra money had allowed Jeremiah to buy himself a portable television with built-in rabbit ears for his house as well as a small space heater for his shack at the dump, which in conjunction with the pot belly stove, made the winter far more bearable.

Jeremiah rose from the rocking chair, picked up his cane and started toward the open door, expecting Tony to drop off the key ring. Tony had never given Jeremiah a viable reason for why he never kept the keys to his storage himself, he always insisted that Jeremiah keep them on his ring of keys. Jeremiah suspected that Tony didn't trust the associates he'd usually have in tow when he visited the dump. And the people he brought along were quite a variety of characters. Usually young white men, occasionally black men, Hispanic men a few times, and in more than one instance a peculiar Arab man, complete with turban.

Tony's visit today was stretching on longer than was the norm. Jeremiah stepped over to a wicker chair under a maple tree, just off the gravel road. He had only just eased into the chair when the unmistakable sound of two gunshots rang out in the late afternoon peacefulness. At the echoing sound, Jeremiah stood from his chair, instinctively looking to his left. Racing toward him at breakneck speed was the orange van. The first thing that crossed Jeremiah's mind was *"Fool's gonna leave with my keys, how am I gonna lock up here and get in my house?"*

The van slowed slightly, but obviously was not going to stop as it approached the watchman's shack. Jeremiah's eyes widened as he didn't see Tony in the van, but did recognize the driver as the long-haired, bearded passenger from earlier. As the van slowed, Jeremiah's eyes widened, realizing a handgun was aimed toward him. He briefly saw a flash and heard the unmistakable sounds of the gunshot and shattering glass as he was driven backwards. By the time Jeremiah had knocked over the wicker chair and sprawled onto the ground, all sight and sound had ceased.

* * * *

When Jeremiah awakened, he could not see at all, everything was dark; his first thought being that it was well past sundown, that he had been out for hours. His head ached; worse than any headache he'd ever had. Reaching up with his right hand, Jeremiah realized the right side of his forehead had been gashed, and he could detect small fragments of glass embedded primarily on the right side of his face. His fingers told him that his eyelids were sealed in a closed position by dried blood. Carefully rubbing his eyes with the palm heels of both hands, Jeremiah eventually managed to pry open his eyes and regain some of his vision. Managing to sit up, and realizing the sun was still visible toward the western horizon, Jeremiah struggled to regain his senses. Through blurred vision he detected an old friend's sad and concerned eyes staring back into his.

"Is that you John?" Jeremiah asked.

"It's me Jeremiah," came the reply, although John somehow spoke without uttering a sound.

"Am I still alive John?"

"Yes, you are Jeremiah. But I can't say the same for your associate, the one you call Tony. I brought your keyring, I found it near his body. And Tony's storage box is empty. I'm sorry I could not do anything to prevent this."

Jeremiah was stunned, both by his wound and the news that Tony Mancini was dead. Having provided a safe haven for Tony's storage box, and always suspecting the legality of Tony's "business", Jeremiah had never questioned him about it and had never even considered the occurrence of an event such as this. His head ached terribly, and Jeremiah struggled to think clearly. *"How will I explain any of this?"* he thought. Tony Mancini had not signed in when he'd arrived, how could his presence at the dump be justified? Struggling to concentrate and despite grappling with mental fog, Jeremiah realized he was going to have to sign Tony's name on the log and list the storage box as the trash that he had intended to drop off. Jeremiah had recognized the bearded man with Tony from previous visits but had never been introduced to him. Although something in the back of his mind told him that Tony might have referred to him as 'Billy Boy'. He decided that not knowing the man's identity was probably a good thing. If necessary, he could give a reasonable description of the man, and maintain a bit of honesty in denying any knowledge of who he was. His description would be so generic in this age of unkempt grooming and poor individual hygiene in the burgeoning hippie culture in America, that it would implicate half of the young American male population. Still sitting, and holding a bandana against his forehead, Jeremiah turned to his right to seek John's opinion of his strategy. But his furry four-legged friend was already two hundred yards down the gravel and shell road, almost all the way to Highway 16.

James E. Anderson

Reporting A Crime

It was nearly five p.m. and Marcus and Cassie were still sitting on the wooden swing. Despite sharing a somber mood, they were trying to enjoy the warm spring breeze. The conversation had managed to detour from the unnerving encounter with Ellis and, teased by the promise of enjoying Cassie's mother's pot roast for dinner, they waited impatiently for Cassie's father to arrive home from work. While both harbored thoughts and concerns over the appearance of Ellis, each were doing their utmost to brighten the mood of the other.

Four years had now passed since Jack Worthington had endured the most disastrous period of his life. He had been put thoroughly through the proverbial wringer, initially finding himself as a 'person of interest' in the tragic murder of the teenaged polka dancer, Zofia Wozniak, in the spring of 1963. The fact that his daughter and her friend Marcus had the misfortune of discovering the girl's corpse on the west bank of the Mississippi River made for extreme parental anguish. The nightmare of the summer of '63 was further compounded by multiple visits to his home by detectives from neighboring Iowa. At the time, Jack had been employed as an accountant in Keokuk, Iowa, some thirty-odd miles north of his home. To Jack's chagrin, suspicions had arisen concerning his possible involvement in the murder of a young woman with whom he had been acquainted. His familiarity with the victim, along with hazy circumstantial evidence, and in conjunction with the fact that the crime had occurred near his place of employment were enough to spotlight him as a viable suspect. The distasteful situation in which Jack found himself had resulted in severe conflict with Cassie's mother, Debbie. Even after being unequivocally exonerated, the unfortunate circumstances ultimately resulted in Jack securing employment in Hannibal, Missouri. His new job location was a bit further from home, but far removed from his previous job in Keokuk, both logistically and emotionally. Though ultimately being cleared of suspicion in the case, the Worthington's summer was further shattered by Cassie's abduction by the crazed murderer Oliver Compton. The brave actions of Deputy Daniels, Cassie's friend Marcus, and Marcus' father's cousin Jude Allensworth, had resulted in the safe return of his daughter, but not before anxious and desperate moments.

As they relaxed on the swing awaiting Jack's arrival, Marcus playfully brushed back Cassie's bangs. It was a Thursday, and as their relationship had grown, it had become customary for Marcus to visit Cassie and have dinner on Thursdays with the Worthingtons. Tuesday night dinners were shared by the youngsters at Marcus' apartment with his stepmother Margaret hosting. As they continued to steer the conversation beyond the encounter with Ellis, Marcus and Cassie had explored alternate subjects. The topic had turned to the movie they were planning to see on Friday night. *Casino Royale* was set to debut at the Meridian and who could resist the prospect of David Niven portraying a retired James Bond, not to mention the hilarious Peter Sellers also being in the cast? For at least the tenth time since they'd been sitting on the swing, Marcus brushed back Cassie's bangs, and then he surprised her with an unusual request,

"Cassie, I love the freckles on your forehead. Why don't you let your bangs grow out, part your hair in the middle and brush it to the sides? I've seen that style a lot in the magazines. I think you'd look cool."

Cassie blushed and said, "Yeah Marcus, I've thought about that. But what I've really been thinking of doing is parting my hair on one side and getting a pixie haircut, you know, like Twiggy? She's the most famous model ever, and I think I'd really like that hairstyle. What do you think?"

Hesitantly, Marcus responded, "Yeah, that would look good. But you wouldn't be able to put your hair up in a ponytail anymore, or even the pigtails you always used to wear if it were that short, would you?"

"Well, no, but I'd like to try something drastically different, you know? I think I'd like to go short." Cassie looked up to try to gauge Marcus' opinion through his facial expressions. "I can always grow it back out you know."

35

Marcus knew Cassie was trying to read his mind and struggled to express himself without showing his displeasure at her suggestion. "I think that would look really swell, Cassie. But gosh, I would sure miss your ponytail." When Cassie didn't immediately respond, Marcus put his foot deeper into his mouth. "Aren't you afraid you'd look like a boy if you cut your hair that short?"

"What?" Cassie's eyes threw daggers in Marcus' direction. "Marcus Twain Clemens! Are you kidding me? You think I'd look like a boy?" Judging by her bright red cheeks, Marcus had obviously lit a scorching fire beneath his girlfriend. "Don't you ever watch any television? Don't you realize what kinds of things are in style nowadays?"

"Now Cassie, you know I watch television. And yes, I know that haircut is in style. But that's in places like New York and stuff. Those people are weirdos!"

"Good God, Marcus! I know we live in the Midwest, but I guess I never realized what a country bumpkin you were!"

"I'm not a country bumpkin! I hardly even listen to country and western music at all."

"Liar! You listen to Johnny Cash and Merle Haggard all the time Marcus Bumpkin!"

"That's not true. You know I listen to the Beatles and the Kinks and other rock and roll bands. That's all that Mama listens to." Marcus was right in that assessment. Margaret had gone all-in on the British invasion.

"Whatever you say, Marcus. I'm going to ask mother to take me to Dottie's beauty shop Saturday to get the pixie cut. You'd better get used to the idea real quick mister, or you'll be eating dinner next Tuesday night all by your lonesome!"

"Oh now, come on Cassie. You know darn well..."

"Sshhh. Quiet Marcus!" Cassie interrupted holding her hand up in Marcus' face. "Quiet, listen."

"Listen to what, Cassie? What are you..."

"Shut up, Marcus. It's Opa. He's talking to me."

"What?" Marcus saw Cassie looking at the ground to her left, next to the swing. Opa stood in the exact spot he had always occupied when communicating with Cassie four years before. He was shocked that Opa had approached Cassie after so much time had passed.

"Cassie, tell Marcus to call Deputy Daniels. It's my friend, Jeremiah Paige. He's been shot and needs help. He's at the dump out west of town. I just found him. Tell Marcus to hurry."

"When did this happen, Opa?" Cassie asked.

"I just now found him, but there's no time to talk. I'll explain later." Opa's voice echoed in her head. Cassie hadn't heard the voice since the parking lot at *The Red Roof Lodge* in the spring of 1964. Almost exactly three years ago. But she had immediately recognized the voice and wondered if any of the old mystery had changed.

"Did you hear what he said, Marcus?"

37

"No Cassie, don't you remember? He only communicates with you. What did he say? Where has he been? He hasn't contacted us in three years. What's going on?

"Marcus, he wants you to call Deputy Daniels. Someone has been shot over at the dump. You sure you didn't hear anything?" Cassie was disappointed that Marcus could still not hear Opa's voice for himself.

"No, Cassie."

Jumping from the swing and grabbing at Marcus' hand, Cassie said, "Come on, you can use our phone. Do you remember Mitch's number?"

"No, I don't have it memorized. It's in my address book at home. We'll just have to call the Sheriff's Department."

Running across the front yard and into Cassie's house, Marcus asked, "Do you know who got shot? I know the old guy that works there, was it him?"

Reaching the parlor, an excited and mildly confused Cassie said, "How would I know Marcus? Opa didn't tell me that... No, wait, yes he did! He did say it was his friend. Um, Jeremiah Paige was the name."

"Ah Jeez, Cassie. That's him, Jeremiah Paige. He knew my dad, he used to work with him at the quarry. You've met him at Franklin's before, I'm sure."

Picking up the receiver, Marcus hurriedly dialed "0".

"Operator, how may I direct your call?" the woman's voice answered politely, but nonchalantly.

"Get me with the Lewis County Sheriff's Office, please. It's an emergency," Marcus blurted breathlessly.

"One moment, please," came the almost robotic response.

A brief dial tone droned through the earpiece of the receiver, followed by two ring tones and then a woman's voice, "Sheriff's Department, how can I help you?"

"I need a deputy and an ambulance sent to the trash dump out on Highway 16 right away. Someone has been shot," Marcus almost shouted.

"Is that the county's east side trash facility?" the dispatcher asked.

"Yes," said Marcus, frustrated by the question. "Can you send Deputy Daniels?"

"We will send the closest available deputy, sir. Give me a moment to dispatch an ambulance and deputy. Stay on the line, I'll need to get some information from you." The dispatcher placed Marcus on hold.

Marcus took a deep breath and looked at Cassie. They both instinctively knew what the other was thinking.

"What am I going to tell her, Cassie?" Marcus was scared and wasn't sure if he should even stay on the line until the dispatcher returned.

"I don't know Marcus. We've kept Opa a secret since the fifth grade. We can't tell anybody now. No one would believe us anyway. They'd think we were crazy."

"I know, but what can I tell her?"

"Tell her someone was driving down White Street and saw you and told you to call the police, so you raced home on your bike and called."

"Okay, Cassie. Gosh I sure hope she bel...."

"Hello, sir?

"Yes, ma'am," Marcus turned his attention back to the dispatcher.

"Sir, help is on its way. Are you at the scene now, sir? Did you see the incident?" the dispatcher asked.

"No ma'am. I'm not there, I didn't see anything," Marcus replied, trying to say as little as possible.

"Where are you calling from, sir?"

This line of questioning was killing Marcus and he wanted it to end before he was asked something that he couldn't readily respond to. "I'm calling from my girlfriend's house."

"What is phone number at your location, sir?"

"Fairview 7-6964."

"And your name, sir?"

"My name is Marcus Clemens."

"Do you know the person who was shot?"

Marcus would have done anything to be able to hang up the phone. "I believe his name might be Jeremiah Paige," he hesitantly answered.

"Sir, I'm a little confused. If you are not at the scene, may I ask how you could have an idea of the victim's name?"

Marcus paused momentarily, thinking and taking a deep breath before continuing, "Yes, ma'am. I was told that there was a shooting at the dump, and

I know that Jeremiah Paige is the watchman there. I know him and he's the only person that is usually there, most of the time."

"So you were not at the scene, Mr. Clemens? You were merely told the incident had occurred? Can you tell me who provided you with the information that there had been a shooting?"

"I don't know his name, ma'am. I was riding my bike on White Street and a man pulled up next to me, put down his window, and told me to call the police and an ambulance, and that a man had been shot at the trash dump."

"Okay, Mr. Clemens. Deputy Martin has responded to the scene and the ambulance is in route. Is there any further information you might be able to provide?"

"No, ma'am. I don't know anything else." Marcus breathed a huge sigh of relief, recognizing the conversation was about to end.

"Just one more thing, Mr. Clemens. We're going to need to have a deputy contact you for an official interview and statement. Would there be a convenient time for you to conduct this interview?"

The dispatcher's question caught Marcus off guard. He had thought he had done his duty and hadn't anticipated the prospect of enduring an interview and giving a statement beyond what he had offered already. "I guess I should be back home about 7:30 or 8:00 tonight." Marcus apprehensively told her.

"Would you prefer conducting the interview here at the station, Mr. Clemens? If we could expedite the interview, it could be beneficial to the investigation. If you'd like to stop here on your drive home, that would be fine."

"No, ma'am, I can't do that. I don't drive yet. I'm only fifteen."

"Oh, I see, Mr. Clemens. Then can I send a deputy to your home about 8:00 this evening. Would that work for you?"

"Yes ma'am, I think so." Marcus answered.

"Mr. Clemens, you had asked earlier for Deputy Daniels. Do you know Deputy Daniels personally?"

"Yes ma'am. We've known each other for a few years. Mitch....I mean Deputy Daniels; he knows just where I live."

"Okay, Mr. Clemens. Let me just get your address for the record." Marcus recited his address and apartment number to the dispatcher. After verifying by reading it back to Marcus, she said, "I'll have Deputy Daniels stop by at eight p.m. to get your statement. Thank you for your cooperation today. The Sheriff's Department is always pleased when citizens voluntarily perform their civic duty. Goodbye, Mr. Clemens."

"Yes ma'am. Goodbye."

Placing the receiver back into its cradle, Marcus gave Cassie a look that could only be described as panicky.

"Are you alright, Marcus?" Cassie asked.

"Yeah, but I wasn't planning on having to go through this conversation a second time. And especially with Mitch Daniels. I don't want to have to lie to him about Opa. Do you think maybe I should just tell Mitch about him?"

"No way, Marcus! Opa has been kept a secret for four years now. Who knows how much longer he will be looking out for you? We can't tell anyone about him. Deputy Mitch would never believe you anyway."

"I wonder if Opa is still outside?" Marcus wondered aloud.

"I don't know," Cassie said, "He did say he would explain later....so, maybe?"

They hurriedly reversed their earlier path and raced out through the front door, across the front yard, and back to the old wooden swing. Opa dutifully awaited, sitting on his haunches, in anticipation of their return and questions.

Cassie offered up the first query, "Opa, how did you know someone had been shot at the dump?"

"As on most afternoons, I had gone to visit my friend Jeremiah, and unfortunately I discovered him wounded." Opa's words drifted through and settled into Cassie's mind.

Cassie quickly relayed his response to Marcus, and then refocused her attention to Opa. "I don't understand, Opa. You told me earlier that it had just happened, but the dump is at least five miles from here, well out of town. It would have to take you at least half an hour to walk here to tell us. So, you couldn't have like, just found him, right?"

"Cassie, I don't know if you can understand, if you can accept the concept."

"What concept is that Opa?" she asked. Marcus, not knowing what Opa had said, had opened his mouth to speak but Cassie had instinctively held up her hand to silence him before he could utter a sound. She looked deeply into Opa's eyes, anxiously awaiting his reply.

"It will be difficult for you two to comprehend. Cassie, I am not bound by constraints such as time and space like you and all other human beings. I have the unlimited freedom to transport myself through time and space at any given instant."

"What are you saying?" Cassie was incredulous. Not in all her schooling and reading had she ever heard such an idea. Never in her wildest dreams had she considered such an impossibility. This premise was so ridiculous that it could only have been broached in some fantastic science fiction movie or television show.

"I'm trying to explain to you, my dear, that I can transport myself to any location that I care to, at any given earthly time. To further confuse your quite capable mind, I am also gifted with the ability to visit two, three or more locations at essentially the same time with only a slight earthly time variation of perhaps a few seconds. It is quite the empowerment with which I have been bestowed."

"The whole idea you're suggesting is amazing, Opa." Cassie gushed. "It is beyond anything I've ever dreamt of. So, you are saying that you saw this man shot, and then immediately appeared here, coming to us to call for help?"

"Exactly, Cassie. Just as I disarmed your attacker in the mausoleum those years ago and yet stood by your side the entire time."

"You saved my life, Opa." Cassie said solemnly.

"No, Cassie. Don't allow yourself to be misled. My mission is to protect Marcus. I am his guardian angel, not yours. Any benefit you derive from my presence is directly attributed to, and as a result of, my protection of Marcus."

"Opa. I have one more question. Why don't I have a guardian angel of my own?" Cassie earnestly wondered why she was seemingly being slighted.

"It is not for me to say, my dear. Someone, somewhere, perhaps must feel that Marcus has a calling beyond common members of society, and therefore deserves divine protection. I cannot venture any opinion in excess of that."

Cassie turned around to look at Marcus, who was still standing, arms hanging limply at his sides and looking totally confused. He was completely at a loss regarding the conversation that had transpired, with him privy only to one side of the discourse – only the words Cassie had uttered. Her mind racing, Cassie's curiosity peaked, she needed to learn more about Marcus' future. Why was he so special that he merited a guardian angel? She pivoted her attention back to Opa, hoping for more information. But Cassie faced only disappointment, realizing Opa was no longer there, as if he'd disappeared into thin air. She stood confounded by both his disappearance and the amazing details Opa had imparted.

"Cassie, what did my grandfather tell you? What were you talking about concepts and guardian angels and all that? What did he say?"

"He said you were one special guy, Marcus," Cassie's lips curled into a faint, knowing smile as she pondered the unknown significance of Opa's words.

"Huh?" Marcus felt a smidge flattered but was totally confused.

Cassie explained to Marcus how it was possible for Opa to know about the shooting at the dump and immediately be able to tell them about it. She told him Opa's description of manipulating time and space to be anywhere at any time. She reminded him of Opa attacking the mysterious machete man at the mausoleum and helped Marcus to comprehend why they both could have had differing views of what had exactly happened that day. Cassie began to realize just how immense were the powers that Opa possessed. She became aware, for the first time, that Opa had altered her perception of what had occurred. She had witnessed Marcus tackling the attacker, but now saw that Opa had forced that vision into her mind. Just as Marcus had maintained, she realized that Opa had intervened in order to save her boyfriend's life.

After detailing to Marcus her entire conversation with Opa, Cassie was prepared for a multitude of questions. But the only question Marcus asked was not one she was prepared to answer.

"Cassie, why would it be that if Opa is *my* guardian angel, that he is looking out for Jeremiah Paige?"

Wrapping Up The Day

The orange van pulled into the weed-infested parking lot of the *Bar None Saloon*, just over six miles west of LaGrange and an eighteen-minute drive from the Lewis County East Trash Facility. The van crept through the sparsely populated lot, parking clumsily near the right-hand corner of the building. It sat idling, driver side window down in front of a pay phone booth located just a few feet from the side steps of the Arcadian style porch that stretched across the entire forty-foot frontage of the antiquated building. The man behind the steering wheel slowly and gently stroked his beard as he contemplated the next step in his master plan. Turning slightly in his seat, he glanced back to briefly admire his freshly loaded cargo. *"This is just the beginning,"* he thought to himself, with no small measure of pride and with supreme satisfaction in his accomplishment.

The van continued to idle in the late afternoon sun as more traffic began trickling into the lot. The seedy establishment was a home away from home for a gaggle of roughneck Hell's Angels wannabes who frequently traveled north from the Hannibal area for weekend drinking and misadventure. The loosely organized fraternity of leather-clad rowdies referred to themselves as *The Brood*. The group's origin had been inspired in the mid 1950's by a circle of young men who had been heavily influenced by characters portrayed in the 1953 biker film, *The Wild One*. The film had featured a pair of young actors and future stars named Marlon Brando and Lee Marvin. The movie had depicted a motorcycle gang conducting a reign of terror over a small town. *The Brood* motorcycle club, thanks to their rowdy behavior, had earned a well-deserved reputation in both northeastern Missouri and across the Mississippi River into western Illinois. Numerous clashes with several rival gangs had taken place on both sides of the river, many right here at the *Bar None*. Battles waged, both inside the saloon and outside in the parking lot, had led to scores of broken bones and missing teeth. At least four known deaths were attributed to fights occurring on the property. But this was a Thursday, and the truly rowdy crowd wouldn't arrive until Friday night. This afternoon, the lot began filling with trucks and cars belonging to locals. Farmers, ranch hands, workers from the area's few small industries and retail establishments made up the demographic of the normal weekday clientele.

The long-haired former companion of Tony Mancini stepped from the van, keys in hand, and made his way to the payphone. Dropping in a shiny FDR dime, he proceeded to dial the seven-digit number. After three rings, a familiar voice came onto the line, "Schofield's Body Shop and Auto Repair. Max speaking."

"Max, it's Bill Lohman. The deed's done and the cargo is secure. I need the cash and a new ride quick."

"Are you at the *Bar None*?" Max asked.

"That's the rendezvous point, ain't it Max? You need to hurry. I don't know how long it's gonna take them to find Tony, but I need to get away from this van."

"What's the rush? It might take them days to find him." Max didn't understand why Bill sounded so skittish. It should have been a simple in and out. "What's wrong? There ain't be no heat, right?"

"No, not exactly....I don't think. I don't know....there could be heat, I guess it's possible," Bill stumbled with his words.

"What are you talking about? That place is far enough out of town, nobody could've heard the gun....Bill, there weren't no witnesses, was there?"

"Not exactly. There was that old man, the watchman at the shack. I didn't trust him. He seemed like he gave me the evil eye. I think he might could have ID'd me, you know?"

"Oh, crap Bill, what did you do?" Max was growing irritated.

"I had to put him down, Max."

"What?" Max felt exasperated. If Bill had killed the old man...killing the old watchman wasn't part of the plan. "Come on Bill. That old man's half blind, he probably never even noticed you."

"Maybe, but I had to look out for myself, Max. Tony was a fool, I'm not. He trusted me. But I won't take chances like he did, Max. I'll never trust anyone, and I guarantee I'll never need anybody to help me. I'm not like Tony, I can handle my own heavy lifting, take care of my own dirty work. And that's exactly what I did."

Max Schofield squeezed his temples with his thumb and forefinger. This should have been a simple project. Mancini had become a liability and needed to be eliminated. He had been pressuring Max for more money and had begun making threats. Max felt it was time to change donkeys, and Bill Lohman seemed like a natural. Perhaps Max had made an error in judgement.

"I'll be there in twenty minutes with your ride and your money. When you get back to St. Louis, park the car on the riverfront, in the lot for the *Admiral*. You know, the boat that does the river excursions?"

"Yeah, I know what the *Admiral* is. Hurry up, I'm waiting."

Hanging up the phone, Max thought for a just moment before again picking up the receiver and dialing. When the call was answered, Max was brief, "Hey, it's Max. Is the Thor there?"

"No," the woman's voice responded. "He out running errands. Should be back by nightfall though."

"You think he's ready for a promotion?"

"That's what I been trying to tell you, ain't it?" The woman asked.

"Good, tell him to stop by my office about 10:00 tomorrow morning. I'll show him how to access a company vehicle and explain his new duties."

* * * *

Deputy Martin turned off Highway 16 at the Lewis County East Trash Facility and started down the nearly half mile dusty gravel road that dissected the trash dump. He radioed dispatch at precisely 5:19 p.m. to report his arrival on scene. Lyle Martin had been hired as a deputy in Lewis County right out of the army in 1962. After graduating from Lewis and Clark High School in 1960, he had immediately enlisted in the army, where he had spent two years. He had been stationed in Panama and served as a Military Police officer there for just over a year. Upon his discharge and return home, Lyle wasted no time applying and being hired for a position with the Lewis County Sheriff's Department. In just over a month, June 25 being the anniversary date, Deputy Martin would mark the completion of his fifth year of duty.

Upon parking next to the watchman's shack, Deputy Martin's attention was immediately drawn to a bloodied black gentleman sitting in a wicker chair beneath a maple tree. As the deputy approached the apparent victim, he could hear the wailing siren of the approaching ambulance.

"Sir, I'm Deputy Martin from Lewis County. Can you hear me alright sir? How badly are you injured?"

"I'll be fine Deputy, just need a few stitches." Still holding the now soaked bandana to his head, Jeremiah was beginning to regain his senses.

Pulling out his notepad to jot down the victim's statement, Deputy Martin asked, "Can you tell me your name, sir?"

"It's Jeremiah Paige. I'm the day watchman here. How'd you get here so fast? Ain't nobody been here I know of and nobody ain't gonna pay no attention to a gunshot out here. What, did you just happen to come along?"

Looking up from his notepad, Deputy Martin responded, "Why no, I was called by dispatch to respond to a shooting here. Someone must have called it in."

"John called you, didn't he? I knowed he would help me. Couldn't understand why he just up and walked away like that. Now I know, he wents to get you."

Deputy Martin looked at Jeremiah quizzically, "Who is John, Mr. Paige? I thought you said no one has been here?"

"John ain't exactly a person, least not no more."

The ambulance pulled up next to the Lewis County Cruiser and two attendants stepped out, one with black medical bag in hand. As the attendants approached the old man in the wicker chair, Deputy Martin leaned a little closer to Jeremiah and practically whispered, "What do you mean, Mr. Paige? Not exactly a person?"

"Used to be, now he's just a filthy little mutt. But, oh yeah, it's my friend John, yessiree he is."

Deputy Martin stepped back to allow the medic to tend to the victim. He thought long and hard about what the man had just said. He ran the gist of what

Jeremiah Paige had just uttered repeatedly through his mind. *"Used to be a man, but now he's a dog, he's my friend John"*. *The man must be delusional. He just had a bullet graze his head and took a nasty fall. He's probably concussed and doesn't know what he's saying.* Lyle Martin determined that the strange things the man had said were nonsense and decided to exclude that part of Mr. Paige's statement from his report.

After consulting with the medical attendant to gain a grasp of Mr. Paige's condition, Deputy Martin decided to discontinue the interview until after the man had been treated at County Hospital. Upon the victim's being loaded into the ambulance, Deputy Martin walked over and leaned into the vehicle saying, "I'll talk to you again a little later, at the hospital, Mr. Paige."

Jeremiah strained to raise his head and with some difficulty said "Listen Boo, follow the road down to the end. On the left you'll see two big shipping containers. My key ring is out there where you found me, by the wicker chair. There's a key on it that'll open the locked container, the first one. You'll find another smaller container or cabinet inside. I don't know what's in it, but I think it's somethin' bad. John said Tony Mancini's back there, too. Says he's deader than a doornail. I ain't been down there, but John wouldn'ta lied to me."

* * * *

Hanging up the receiver and leaving the phone booth, Bill Lohman noticed a scrawny mutt sitting on the edge of the porch. The dog's eyes seemed to follow

53

Bill as he strode back to the van. Reaching for the door handle, Bill looked back at the dog and noticed the animal seemed to be baring its teeth. Releasing the handle, he began walking back toward the canine that seemed to wreak with animosity. As he approached cautiously. Bill detected the low guttural growl.

"What's your problem, mutt?" Bill stammered as he stopped and stood looking at the snarling, deformed snout. He noticed saliva dripping from the corners of the angry dog's mouth. Fearing the animal might be rabid and on the verge of attacking, Bill Lohman began a cautious and backward retreat, never taking his eyes off the crazed mongrel. Stepping up into the van, and taking his seat safely at the wheel, Bill looked down once again at the dog and thought back an hour or so to when he had taken care of business with Tony. It dawned on him that after he'd pulled the trigger, moved the body, and had loaded his cargo, this same ugly mutt had been standing across the road. The dog had sat, teeth bared, just as it was doing now. The sight of the animal's teeth had angered Bill at the dump, and he had thrown the watchman's keyring, hitting the dog. Hearing the animal's immediate and intensified growl, he knew he had made a mistake by throwing the keys, it would be insane to attempt to retrieve them. But then it occurred to him that he wouldn't be needing them anymore.

There was no doubt in his mind that the dog at the dump was the same dog that stood before him now. As unlikely and impossible as it seemed, that dog had somehow transported itself from the dump to here. It had taken Bill almost twenty minutes to drive here and there was no way that dog had walked here that quickly.

"I don't know what your story is Fido, but you freak me out." Bill Lohman continued staring at the dog with growing disdain. "I hate you and sure hope I never see you again. But I promise you this, if our paths ever cross again, I'll kill you."

* * * *

As Jeremiah Paige had requested, Lyle Martin drove nearly to the end of the road, easing the cruiser to a halt a good twenty feet short of reaching the shipping containers. Opening the door, he withdrew his service revolver from its holster and stood, legs spread, with both arms resting on the top of the door frame aiming the revolver at the nearest container. Both doors stood open. Assessing the scene before him, Deputy Martin could determine from his vantage point that the second container's doors were closed and did not appear to have a lock on the handle. After waiting a moment and thoroughly considering the situation and surveying his surroundings, the officer slowly stepped away from his vehicle and cautiously approached the open container. Standing behind the open left door, Deputy Martin slowly hazarded a peek inside the container. He immediately noticed a gray storage type cabinet with both of its doors open. The cabinet stood about six-feet tall, three to four-feet wide and likely had a depth of eighteen to twenty-four inches. As he slowly approached, the deputy saw that the cabinet appeared to be empty. As Deputy Martin slowly began to circle around the cabinet, he noticed what looked like blood smeared on the metal floor. Taking another step and craning his neck only slightly, Lyle Martin discovered the body of Tony Mancini.

* * * *

Jack Worthington had arrived home from work just before 5:30 p.m. After exiting his new green Chevrolet Bel-Air, Cassie and Marcus had approached and greeted him on the front lawn. After hugging Cassie and chitchatting for a moment, Jack strode toward the back yard to see Cassie's brother, Charlie. Cassie and Marcus had returned to the swing, plotting exactly how they would explain the day's events to her parents. Through their previous experiences, they had developed a proficiency in lying in order to protect the existence of Opa. And now, several years later they were going to have to reinstitute that talent. After giving her mother and father ample time to greet one another and conclude their normal pre-dinner discussion, they decided it was time to face the music.

Jack, with tie and jacket removed and collar opened comfortably, had collapsed into his easy chair, feet up on the hassock. Debbie had prepared and served him with his customary before dinner cocktail and she sat on the loveseat diagonally to his left, near the console television and facing the fireplace.

Marcus and Cassie came in through the front door and took seats on the couch, to Jack's right, next to the fireplace, directly facing the currently unused television console.

"How was school today, kids?" Debbie asked, initiating conversation in the customary Thursday night manner.

"It was good," Cassie replied with a smile. She had anticipated these exact words being spoken, but now was preparing to deviate from the usual script. "But mom, dad," she added, "the last two hours have been a total nightmare."

Debbie's face displayed obvious concern and Jack instantly looked up from the *Newsweek* magazine that lay open across his lap. "What's been a nightmare, Cassie?" he asked.

Cassie looked to Marcus, hoping he would take charge, but he sat silently, hands folded. Marcus felt it was wise to let Cassie take the lead here, they were after all, her parents. Perhaps he could learn something for when he made the same pronouncement to Margaret. When Marcus didn't respond, Cassie continued, "When we got off the bus this afternoon, Ellis Compton was waiting on the sidewalk."

"Ellis Compton?" Debbie wailed. "What was doing here. Isn't he still in jail or on probation or something?"

"No Debbie. He's been out of jail, or detention I guess it was called, for a year or so," Jack answered. "Isn't he on house arrest or something, Marcus? Never mind, that's not important. Cassie, what did he want? What did he say to you two?"

"He wanted to apologize, Daddy."

"Apologize? That takes some gall. He's killed people, he made you kids' lives a living hell! And *now* he wants to *apologize*?"

Marcus couldn't remain silent, "That's what I said too, Mr. Worthington.
I thought that was a brazen thing to say."

Debbie stepped into the conversation, "Well, I certainly hope you didn't accept his apology!"

"No ma'am, Mrs. Worthington. No way in heck," Marcus said.

"But you know the strangest thing? I think he really meant it," Cassie offered her intuitive opinion. "I could feel it in his voice, he sounded sincerely emotional. I think he really does feel guilty. He even said I was part of his family now and that he loved us both, and I think that when he left, he was crying."

"I don't buy it," Jack said. "I think he's full of it. No offense Marcus, I know he's your cousin and all, but I just don't believe he's all there. You know, in the head? He spent all those years with that nutcase Oliver Compton. I'm certainly not a psychiatrist, but I think that guy's craziness rubbed off on Ellis. How could it not of? A person is the product of his environment, that's what I think. Don't you agree, Debbie?"

"I'm sure you're right, Jack," his wife agreed wholeheartedly.

Jack took a sip of his drink, attempting to calm himself, but continued, "And that place he was at, that 'School for Boys', that's probably the worst place they could have sent him. Why, thirty years ago that place was named the worst juvenile facility in the whole damned country! Debbie, do you remember a while back a couple of boys were murdered in that 'school'."

"Yes, Jack. I do remember reading that," Debbie said. "I guess I'm a little surprised it's still operating."

Cassie looked to Marcus for support before adding to the conversation.

"Well, that's not all that happened today." Cassie continued with her description of the afternoon. "There was a shooting out at the dump this afternoon and now we're sort of involved in that, too."

"A shooting at the dump? What does that have to do with you two? How could you have any involvement in that?" Jack was startled by Cassie's news. "Cassie, you didn't even go with me when I took the old box spring out there last summer. You've never even been out there, have you.?"

Staring down at the shag carpeting, Marcus could feel all four eyes of Cassie's parents on him, sensing the accusatory stares, as if he had taken Cassie to the dump.

"No, I've never been there, but it's kind of crazy, daddy," Cassie tried her best to come up with a believable tale that would explain their involvement without revealing the whole truth. "Right after Ellis drove off, this guy pulls up in an old pickup truck and tells us to call the police and an ambulance. He said somebody got shot out at the dump. So, we came in the house and Marcus called the sheriff and told them. Now they have a deputy coming to Marcus' house tonight to get his statement and everything."

"I didn't hear you kids come in the house and use the phone." Debbie had been preparing dinner and had not heard anything.

"I guess you were busy in the kitchen, mother. Or maybe you were out back checking on Charlie."

"I have to say, Cassie, that story sounds a wee bit fishy," said Jack.

Cassie felt her face blush, hoping her father wouldn't notice a difference from her normal rosy complexion. She felt guilty telling him an outright lie and should have known he would see right through it. Marcus now sat wide-eyed, realizing he would have to face Margaret and stick with the same suspicious sounding lie.

"That guy in the truck, why would he be telling you kids about something that happened that far away? Driving all the way over here to tell a pair of teenagers to call the cops? That's insane! I'm no detective, but why would he do that? Unless he's the guy that did it. He must have left the scene and started feeling guilty or something." Jack thought for a moment before continuing, "Or maybe it was just an accident and he panicked and ran, and then realized he had to report it so told you two to do it. He was probably afraid to let the police know about it himself because even if it *was* an accident, he could get into some real hot water. I'm sure that's it. Poor guy was surely scared to death. Wow."

"Maybe. I never thought of all those possibilities." Cassie responded absent-mindedly while thinking about the fact that she and Marcus would now have to agree on descriptions of the pickup truck and its driver.

With dinner concluded, Cassie walked Marcus out the door and onto the front porch where they paused. "Marcus, why haven't you called Margaret yet? She needs to know about what happened today before the deputy gets to your apartment."

"I know, but I didn't want to bother her at work, and I knew it would be hard to explain without mentioning Opa. Besides, I'd rather tell her in person than over the phone."

"I guess I can understand that. I'm glad you were with me to tell my parents Marcus," she said before mildly chastising him, "although you didn't offer much help there at first."

"Cassie, you're a lot smarter than me. You were the star of the debate team, remember? You've always been able to think fast, a lot better than me. I figured I would let you come up with the story and I would just follow along." Marcus wasn't joking at all. He knew full well that he would have stumbled all over his words and was far better off to follow Cassie's lead.

* * * *

Margaret had returned home from her relatively new job just after seven p.m. She had purchased a used 1962 Chevrolet Impala in the spring of 1966, and with her newfound mobility had been able to expand her horizons. She was now employed at *The Goldmine*, an upscale, newly opened steakhouse in LaGrange. Her earnings had increased dramatically over her previous job at the diner, and even though she was working a bit further from home, driving to and from the restaurant was so much faster and easier than the walking she did when working at the diner. When Margaret had arrived home and as she partook of leftover steak and salad from her hurried lunch at *The Goldmine*, Marcus informed her of the day's happenings. First, he told her of the confrontation with Ellis which, of course, required no embellishment. He then was careful to relate details of the shooting, piece-by-piece, and exactly as Cassie had told her parents. Surprisingly, Margaret seemed to take everything in relative stride. In a way, Marcus was glad that he had told the story to Margaret and that she had calmly taken it all in. He regarded it as a rehearsal to the important performance he was about to present to his friend Mitch.

As promised, the doorbell chimed precisely at eight p.m. Margaret Clemens, accompanied by Marcus, opened the door to greet Deputy Mitch Daniels and his partner, Deputy Helen Wilcox. Marcus was surprised to see Deputy Wilcox; he'd assumed that Mitch would be visiting alone. Everyone entered the living room where Margaret offered them seats. Because she viewed Mitch as a friend, Margaret had wanted to make him feel at home and had therefore prepared a pitcher of sweet tea. With her guests seated, Margaret retreated to the kitchen to retrieve the refreshments. After she had returned and placed the tea and glasses on the coffee table, Deputy Daniels pointed out to both Marcus and Margaret that this was an official visit. He further explained that Deputy Wilcox would be conducting the interview while he would be taking notes. At the conclusion of the interview, he would have Marcus prepare a written statement to include in his report.

Deputy Wilcox began by asking Marcus to explain simply what had occurred to prompt him to call the Sherriff's Office. Marcus calmly repeated the story, verbatim, that he had related to Margaret. Deputy Daniels diligently took notes, pausing occasionally to ask a question of his own. Marcus made it clear that he had never seen the driver of the pickup truck before today. As he and Cassie had agreed, the truck was described as black, with no obvious dents or identifiable damage to it. He told them he hadn't noticed the make; it could have been a Ford, Chevrolet or even a Dodge, he didn't know. It did have a Missouri license plate, but it had been crusted with mud and the plate number indistinguishable. The driver was generically described as a white male, clean-shaven with short dark, almost black hair. In retrospect, the description that Cassie had conjured, and that they'd agreed upon, was basically that of her own father. Marcus was forced to suppress a smile when that realization crossed his mind. Deputy Wilcox seemed to be near the end of the interview. She had stopped asking questions and she and Deputy Daniels sat in a whispered conference as they looked through a stack of papers.

"Marcus, I have one more question about something that troubles me a little bit." Deputy Wilcox said. "You just told us that this man drove up to you in Forest Grove Estates, right by the

Worthington's house, asking you to call the police. Isn't that correct?"

"Yes, ma'am," Marcus answered.

"Well then, Marcus." Deputy Wilcox went on, "The story you told the dispatcher matches up perfectly with what you've told us tonight, makes perfect sense. Except for one thing. Can you explain to me why you told us the man came up to you on Fernwood Drive and you told the dispatcher the man came up to you on White Street?"

Marcus froze, caught in a lie. If he admits to lying, what forms of consequences will follow? He heard the question arise in his mind, '*What would you say, Cassie?*' Marcus suddenly was overcome by a sense of calm.

"Yes ma'am. I was nervous and didn't want to involve Cassie and her family, so I fibbed a little and told the lady I had been on White Street."

Mitchell Daniels had been looking down at his papers as Marcus was answering. Raising his head from the papers and directing his attention solely on Marcus, he said, "Marcus, look me in the eye and tell me this story you've told is the honest to God's truth."

Marcus was tempted to break down and tell Mitch the honest to goodness truth. The pressure felt enormous. Mitch was his friend. But Marcus knew that his grandfather had saved his and Cassie's lives and was his guardian angel. He could not betray Ópa.

Trust

Cassie stood silently to the right of Marcus as he placed a handpicked bouquet of yellow chrysanthemums on the graves of his grandparents, John Stuart Clemens and Anna Claire Allensworth Clemens. After learning that the mysterious harelipped dog (now known to be his guardian angel) was in fact a reincarnation of his father's father, Marcus had visited the Forest Grove Cemetery office to pinpoint the exact location of his grandparents' graves. Prior to the information provided by Cousin Judy, Marcus had been totally unaware of their existence, or of the fact that they were buried only a few hundred feet west of the graves of his parents, Elijah and Betty Jo. It had never occurred to Marcus on that life altering Sunday evening in 1963, when Opa had made his initial appearance, that he had sought refuge behind the tombstone of his own uncle, Harold Lee Clemens. Reading the name in the dim light of that early evening, while in mortal fear, he had realized the Clemens name matched his own. But, while consciously shrugging it off as coincidence, Marcus had felt an underlying suspicion that it was some sort of eerie premonition. And now, thanks to Cousin Judy and Opa, he knew the previously hidden truths about his family. And he became aware that Uncle Harold was buried side by side with his father and mother, John and Anna.

"I don't know why I never thought much about it, Marcus," Cassie wondered aloud, "but I wonder if there is a casket buried here for your grandfather?"

"I guess that's a good question, Cassie. I'd never given that any thought either." Marcus replied. "But, seeing as how his body was never recovered from the river, I doubt it. Probably they just put his name on the tombstone. Why would anyone go to the expense of putting an empty coffin in the ground? Next time I see Mr. Porter from the funeral home, I'll ask him."

"Better yet, why don't we just ask Opa?" Cassie couldn't suppress a smile. "He would be the authority, wouldn't he?" Nor could she hold back a reluctant giggle.

"Yeah, I suppose he would," Marcus said while stifling a smile of his own. "Hey, we'd better get a move-on if we're going to make it to the Meridian before seven. I've got to get my Sweetarts and popcorn before the previews reel starts and Denny gets bribed into giving away our seats in the back to some of those junior and senior neckers."

"And don't forget my Jujyfruits!" Cassie squealed as she began running down the path toward the cemetery entrance.

* * * *

"It's about time you got home, Thor." Alicia said in a scolding manner. "How did your meeting go with Max?"

"It was fine Mom," he answered.

"That's all, it was just fine?"

"Yes, Mom. It was fine."

"Well, what do you think? The job doesn't seem too difficult, does it?" Alicia was ecstatic that Max had called offering the new position to her son. "It can't be much more than your dad had been doing, can it?"

"Mom, I wish you'd stop calling Ollie my dad," he said. "He's not my dad. Yeah, he raised me, but he did one heck of a crappy job. I spent two years locked up and a year under house arrest because of him. And would you please stop calling me Thor? I hate that name."

"Why Ellis Compton, I think that's a sweet nickname." His mother thought Thor was a masculine and authoritative name that commanded respect.

"Mom, I've explained it to you umpteen times. The name is an insult. They called me that because of my fear of thunder and lightning. It was a joke to everybody at that stupid institution."

"Maybe it was a joke there Ellis, but in the line of business you're getting involved in it's a domineering, tough name. You'll earn far more respect with Thor than you could with *Ellis*," Alicia whined in a mocking manner.

"Mom, I went through a year of unsuccessful therapy trying to overcome that fear. And maybe I could have overcome it if they hadn't constantly badgered me about it, and especially with that stupid nickname."

"Suck it up Ellis. You're a grown man now, you'll soon be twenty years old." Alicia had no sympathy for her son's problems. "When do you start the new job?"

"Monday. I go to St. Louis Monday morning and meet up with a guy they call Bossman. He's supposed to have a load ready for me to deliver to Hannibal to some biker bunch called *The Brood*."

"Whoa," Alicia followed the exclamation with a long whistle. "Max is getting your feet wet quick. *The Brood* ain't small potatoes. I know. I've been doing his books a long time. Those guys are heavy hitters."

"Ah, come on Mom," Ellis said without looking up from the television as he switched through the dial in vain, struggling to find *The Three Stooges* reruns. "What are you trying to make me nervous or something?"

"No, no Ellis, not at all. I just kind of thought he'd start you off easy, moving a little weed. I didn't expect he'd start you right off in the big leagues, that's all."

"I wish I wasn't doing this at all. I didn't mind hauling auto parts for Max. I mean, he might be dirty, but at least that's legitimate work. I'm not so comfortable basically being a mule for these guys. What if I get caught?"

Alicia could only laugh at his concern, "You're not gonna get caught. Your dad never would have got caught if he hadn't let his childhood fantasies get the best of him. Him and his stupid attraction to little

68

redheads. If you two don't kidnap that little girl, he never gets caught much less convicted of murder."

"Would you please stop calling him my dad?" Ellis bristled each time Alicia referenced him.

"He is your dad, just like I'm your mom. We adopted you or you'd have ended up in a whole string of scummy foster homes."

"He is not my dad. *My* dad visited me at the Training School. He writes to me. He wants me to succeed, he cares about me. I've been thinking about getting my name legally changed to Jude Urban Allensworth, Junior when I'm twenty-one. I mean, that is the name I was born with you know."

"You ungrateful little ass. Don't you even think about changing your name and disrespecting the parents who raised you and gave you everything. If Judy cares so much, how come you never heard a peep out of him until after you got arrested?" Alicia was defiant in her words to Ellis. "And don't forget, he's the one you can thank for that scar on the back of your head. He's the one, Ellis, who slammed that trunk lid down on your head. And he's the one responsible for Ollie being on death row."

"And he's the one that's responsible for me being born, *Alicia*," for the first time in his life, Ellis called her by her given name rather than Mom. "Him and my real mother!"

Alicia slapped Ellis with all she could muster. "You better be in St. Louis Monday, and be on time. You have a lot to learn mister!"

* * * *

Max Schofield sat in his black 1966 Ford Mustang GT with its dual white racing stripes flowing from the car's grill, across the roof and down to the rear bumper. There were definite advantages to owning a body shop when it came to customizing one's vehicle. And a side business such as the endeavor Max was involved in provided the disposable income to purchase and enhance the value of the toys that he found irresistible. Relaxed, with windows rolled down, Max drummed his fingers on the bottom of the steering wheel, matching the intensity of Charlie Watts' base drum pounding out the foundation of The Rolling Stones hit, *Paint It Black*. The factory installed eight-track tape player had been a three-hundred-dollar option on the car, and it had been worth every dime. No longer constrained by the whims of radio disc jockeys, Max was now free to listen to whatever music his mood desired. And right now, his mood dictated hard driving intensity as he impatiently waited for Bill Lohman to arrive for the meeting that had been prearranged the day before. As he had told Bill he would, Max had met him Thursday afternoon in the parking lot of the *Bar None Saloon*. He had brought along duct tape and cardboard, to patch the passenger side window of the van, and had arrived in a pedestrian looking red with white trim 1965 Dodge D100 pickup truck. What Max had failed to do was bring Bill's money. They had agreed on a fee of $500 for the elimination of Tony Mancini. Tony had been an inconvenience, for sure, but Max had overestimated his confidence in Bill Lohman as a replacement. All it had taken was Bill's phone call on

Thursday, which included the admission that he had also shot the watchman at the dump. Max learned through a contact at the Lewis County Hospital that the watchman had survived the shooting. The news of his survival meant that there was a witness who could possibly identify Tony Mancini's killer, which in turn could serve to jeopardize Max Schofield's entire operation. As a domino effect of own his thoughtless actions, Bill Lohman had unwittingly sealed his very own fate.

Bill was running late for the meeting, and although perturbed by the tardiness, Max's mood had mellowed somewhat. He had ejected the tape, switched back to AM radio, and was calmly singing along with Petula Clark's *Don't Sleep in The Subway* when he noticed in his rearview mirror the rooster tail of dust on the beaten down path leading up behind him. Bill Lohman approached rapidly but slowed the Dodge pickup truck considerably as he eased around Max's Mustang, no doubt attempting to minimize the amount of dust he was depositing on his employer's prized vehicle. He parked the Dodge and climbed out slowly. Max remained in the Mustang, watching Bill closely. Confident that his employee was unarmed, Max opened his door and exited the vehicle. He immediately walked to the back of the car, unlocking, and opening the trunk.

Bill Lohman's internal radar seemed to home in on the back of the Mustang. He was almost directly in front of the car, leaning against the tailgate of the truck and had a severely obstructed view of what Max was up to. *Yeah, I'm late, but surely, he's not going to pull something on me,* Bill thought to himself. Right away he regretted that he had agreed to meet up with Max in the middle of nowhere. Not to mention that he had been stupid enough to come unarmed. Then it dawned on him that Max probably just had the cash stashed in the trunk and was merely getting it out. Or so he hoped.

Suddenly, the trunk lid slammed shut and Max emerged from the back of the car with two Garcia rods and reels in one hand, a fair-sized tackle box in the other, and a manila envelope tucked under his armpit. As he approached Bill Lohman, Max set down the tackle box next to the pickup's rear bumper and with his free hand pulled the envelope from under his arm.

"I figured if we're gonna be working together, we might as well socialize a bit, too. A little fishing is a good way to get to know somebody better, don't you think, Bill?" Max extended the envelope toward Bill. "Here's your cash. Count it if you want, it's all there. Sorry I couldn't get it together yesterday afternoon. Like I told you, the bookkeeper had a family emergency and had to leave early. She's the only one with a key to the petty cash box. Ain't that the shits? She's good though, been with me a long time. I trust her. I trust all my employees."

"That's how a good business should be Max. I agree a hundred per cent." Bill breathed a sigh of relief as he peeked into the envelope.

"Come on, just over this little hump up ahead is bass heaven. I pay a pretty penny to keep this little pond stocked to the gills, so to speak."

They strode up the small incline, and cresting its peak, looked down upon a large, somewhat murky midwestern nirvana. Bill wondered if the pond was a natural phenomenon or if it had been manmade. It was surrounded almost completely by a stand of tall pine trees and the only real blemish to the water's glassy smoothness were a scattering of reeds and cattails, grouped mostly at the southern-most edge, along its bank.

Both lines baited, the pair stood less than ten feet apart, alternately casting and recasting, searching for that perfect spot where the smallmouth bass would be searching for food. Max asked questions about Bill's upbringing, learning quite a bit about his family's roots in Kentucky. Feeling quite at ease with his boss, Bill inquired about Max's life and his road to success in both the auto body business and his extracurricular enterprises. Max had been more than happy to relate his story. He explained to Bill that he'd gotten his start in the army. He had done relatively well grade-wise in high school, and after graduation he'd enlisted in the army in 1951. He had taken a series of tests and had scored extremely high in mechanical aptitude. The army being the army, Max had soon found himself deployed and classified as an orderly in a field hospital behind the lines in no man's land, Korea. He was there all of 1952 and part of 1953. Max served eighteen months in Korea, and to his surprise learned a great deal, not only about medicine, but also the psychological effects of war. He saw first-hand the pressures and stresses faced by American soldiers. He also saw how those stresses and pressures were sometimes handled by some of the soldiers. Max witnessed intermittent drug use and realized how the drugs could potentially alleviate not just pain but also the mental anguish of many.

Upon returning home, Max used his mechanical skills to learn auto repair and body work, and by 1957 had opened his own shop.

"But that was only the beginning Billy Boy," Max explained. "I also remembered the drug use I'd witnessed and realized the weaknesses of the American male. And I decided to capitalize on it. A few trips into St. Louis, and I discovered the underbelly of the industry. And I claimed my stake in it."

"Wow, you got an amazing story, Max. I hope someday I can follow in your footsteps," Bill gushed. "I'd like to be ab....whoa, whoa....I think I got one Max!"

"Set the hook quick and reel him in Bill!"

Max tossed his own pole to the side and ran over toward Bill, grabbing the tackle box on his way. "Reel him in, reel him in!"

Bill brought the large carp he'd hooked nearer to the bank. "Ah crap Bill, it's only a carp. Reach down and grab him so you can unhook him and throw him back in. We're only here for bass today."

Bill stepped to the water's edge and lifted the carp from the pond. As he leaned forward, preparing to dislodge the hook, the face of a three-pound ball peen hammer drove into the base of his skull. Knocked senseless, Bill Lohman fell face first into the murky water. Without hesitation, Max Schofield landed his 187 pounds squarely onto Bill's back and using both hands pushed down on the bloodied mush of the back of his head. Within moments there was absolutely no resistance from Bill Lohman's now lifeless corpse.

Striding up from the water and taking a seat on the bank, Max waited nearly ten minutes to make sure there was no movement from Bill's body. When he was fully satisfied the deed was done, Max drug Bill's carcass from the water. Retreating to the pickup, Max unloaded the wheelbarrow and shovel from the back of the truck. Bill had failed to even notice that Max had stashed the items in the bed of the Dodge pickup truck before it had been delivered to him at the *Bar None* yesterday. Using extreme care not to strain his back, Max slowly drug Bill's body up the bank, over its crest, and proceeded to hoist it haphazardly onto the wheelbarrow. He rolled the wheelbarrow and its contents deep into the Indiangrass, where he proceeded to dig a shallow but sufficient grave. Dumping the Bill's body into the hole and rapidly tossing the excavated dirt over it, Max had soon completed his task. Returning to the pickup, he replaced the wheelbarrow and shovel into the bed. Retrieving the rods and reels, tackle box, and cash containing manila envelope, Max once again ascended the bank. When he had reached the crest, Max stopped and looked back at the pond, surveying the area for anything he might possibly have forgotten or misplaced. Everything seemed to be ship shape and just as it had been when he had arrived. As he started to turn away to return to the truck (he'd be driving the

Dodge, he wasn't about to soil his Mustang with the wet, muddy clothes he was wearing), Max noticed the mangy mutt on the far bank of the pond, sitting on its haunches. The sight of the animal forced a shiver down his spine. Yes, Max was wet, but it was a warm Friday afternoon, and he wasn't at all cold. The shiver was a creepy type of shiver, and the stupid dog made him feel uneasy. It almost felt like the dog was staring at him, accusingly. Max continued toward the truck. Leaning against the driver side door, he looked at his watch, noting the time as 4:17 p.m. Timing was everything and he had estimated well. Sixteen minutes later (three minutes late, but acceptably so), Hondo and Mooch, two of his buddies from *The Brood* would arrive. One of them would drive the Mustang back to the shop for him, while he took the pickup home, caught a bath, and then brought the truck back to his office.

Mooch took the keys from Max and fired up the Mustang. He simultaneously popped the clutch and hit the gas, leaving a cloud of dust as he raced away. With an acknowledged nod toward Max, Hondo revved the Harley that had brought them there and raced off in pursuit. Max started the Dodge, but before engaging the gearshift, couldn't resist glancing back once again toward the pond. Eerily sitting, still staring, was that stupid dog.

* * * *

The Timex on his wrist told him it was almost ten p.m., but Marcus was having too much fun to care that Cassie's father was late picking them up. He and Cassie had stepped out of the Meridian just before

9:30 and had been waiting on the sidewalk for his arrival. They had just seen *Casino Royale*, and while totally confused by the plot, were enormously entertained by the performances in the film. They had tried to keep track of the numbers of actors they recognized but had been forced to give up the fruitless attempt. They both loved David Niven as the retired James Bond and laughed hysterically at Woody Allen's portrayal of both the evil Dr. Noah and Bond's nephew Jimmy Bond. They were amazed that an actor the caliber of Orson Welles could have been cast in the comedy, and of course they loved Peter Sellers. Denny had joined them after fulfilling his duties as usher by helping to sweep the theater. And, as usual, he already had a good number of the comedic lines memorized. He would be working both the matinee and evening showings on Saturday and Sunday, so by Monday morning at school he should be prepared to recite ninety per cent of the dialogue. Just past ten p.m. (10:06 to be precise, according to Marcus' watch) Jack Worthington arrived at the curb. After the car came to a stop, Marcus and Cassie got into the back seat while Denny hopped in front with Cassie's father. Jack Worthington expressed his regret for making them wait so long (punctuality, especially when it came to his daughter's safety and well-being, was one of his virtues). Debbie had been under the weather and gone to bed early and as luck would have it, Jack had dozed while watching television. Fortunately for Cassie and her friends, Debbie had awoken and gone to the kitchen for a glass of water. Thankfully, she had seen Jack sprawled on his easy chair and quickly gotten him up and on his way (offering some choice *words of encouragement* as he slipped on his loafers).

Denny was first to be dropped at his house on Jamison, and then Marcus was delivered to his apartment west of town. Stepping from the car and preparing to head toward his apartment, Marcus heard Cassie whisper to him, "I'll call you when I get home." Marcus found that a bit out of the ordinary; Cassie always called him when she got home after Friday movie night. Why would she make a point of telling him she'd call?

Less than twenty minutes after he'd stepped into his apartment, greeted Margaret, and given a brief synopsis of *Casino* Royale, the telephone rang.

"Hello," Marcus answered, knowing that it would be Cassie.

Cassie was whispering, but couldn't seem to get the words out fast enough, "Marcus, did you hear him, or see him?"

"Who? What are you talking about?"

"Opa, Marcus. Did you hear him? Did you see him?"

"Where, when? What's going on, Cassie?" Marcus felt a smidge of budding excitement mixed with dread. If Opa spoke, something was going on. And it usually was not something good.

Obviously, Cassie didn't want to be overheard by her parents as she continued in a soft but animated whisper. "Oh, Marcus. I've been holding this in ever since we came out of the Meridian."

"Okay, Cassie. Just slow down, okay. What have you been holding in? Did you see Opa at the theater?" Marcus asked.

"No, I didn't see him. I just heard him. I hoped that maybe you saw him. I don't know where he was, I heard him, but I couldn't see him."

Marcus thought for a second, visualizing the scene, trying to remember if he might have seen anything outside, on or near the sidewalk after the movie. Him, Cassie and Denny. There were some other kids milling around, but no Opa. "Why didn't you say something then, Cassie? We could have looked for him."

"I couldn't, Marcus. I couldn't say anything in front of that blabbermouth Denny! He couldn't keep a secret if his life depended on it."

"You're right, Cassie," Marcus wholeheartedly agreed with her assessment. "Denny *is* the absolute last person we could ever tell about Opa."

"Tell me about it," she replied.

"Okay, so Cassie, what did Opa say to you?"

"He scared me, Marcus. A lot."

"What, Cassie, what did he say?"

"He said it's starting again. He said evil is afoot. And this really sounded scary to me, he said to be careful who you trust." Cassie paused a bit before adding, "Marcus, I'm scared."

"Cassie, don't worry, I would never, ever let anything happen to you. Never again," Marcus promised.

"No, Marcus. I'm not scared for me; I'm scared for you. You know you're the one they're after. It's that stupid document, that inheritance or whatever it is," Cassie said with disdain.

"Cassie, Oliver Compton is in prison. He can't hurt us. He can't do anything to anybody, ever again." Marcus wanted desperately to alleviate Cassie's fears.

"Don't be so thick headed, Marcus. Sometimes I wonder about you!" Cassie was frustrated with Marcus and found it difficult to keep her voice down. "Who were we standing face-to-face with, right here, right here by my house, yesterday, Marcus? Ellis Compton, Marcus, that's who!"

"No, Cassie. I don't want to believe that. I've been thinking about that a lot, ever since yesterday. I think I want to believe he was being truthful. I want to believe he was sincere. He's my cousin, Cassie. I've decided that I've got to give him a chance."

"Don't be stupid, Marcus." Cassie was adamant, "Opa specifically said *be careful who you trust* and you know just as well as I do, he was talking about Ellis Compton. He sure as heck wasn't talking about me, or my parents, or Margaret. Use your common sense, Marcus. Believe me, you cannot, under any circumstances, ever trust Ellis!"

Friendship

Within moments of the blaring sound of the air horn, relative silence gradually fell across the massive work site spanning the entire width of the Mississippi River. Workers on each side of the waterway scurried to make their way to the numerous burn barrels that were scattered up and down along the banks on both the Missouri and Illinois sides. It was lunchtime and several hundred men were scrambling, seeking the warmth of the fires on this chilly Tuesday in early December of 1934. The air was crisp with a persistent biting breeze emanating from the west. Outdoors it was hovering in the upper thirties, but when the temperature, along with the river's dampness and humidity, joined forces with an unyielding wind, even the hardiest and most seasoned of the heavily clad construction hands were miserable and chilled to the core. Thus, the lunchtime gravitational pull of the burn barrels. Lock and Dam Number 20, being built by the U.S. Army Corps of Engineers, shadowed over the last remnants of the one-time busy river town of Tully, Missouri. The project had been underway for just over two years now. Expectations were that the lock and dam would reach completion sometime late in 1935.

A thirty-three-year-old general laborer by the name of Jeremiah Paige took a seat on a log in the 'colored' grouping of burn barrels and, after a brief silent prayer, opened his pocketknife in preparation of cutting into and slicing open a can of pork and beans. Because Jeremiah's destiny was that of being born black just after the turn of the century, in early 1901, he had spent his entire lifetime, from birth and on into adulthood, dealing daily with the indignities associated with his lot in life. One such example, on this cold December day, was the relegation of the burn barrels and 'colored' lunch area to the furthest reaches of the jobsite, well separated from the white workers.

Jeremiah was in deep concentration, struggling to gain access to the pork and beans, when he glimpsed the muddy boots approaching from his right and instantly recognized the sound of the familiar nasally voice.

"Hi Miah," came the grunted, distorted greeting.

"Hi, John. Come, sit," Jeremiah motioned with his left hand to the space on the log next to him, a few inches closer to the warmth of the fire.

Nodding in appreciation, John sat and, after wiping his hands on his britches, began unwrapping his sandwich. Silently, and in deep thought, he took the first bite and chewed slowly. John regularly found himself alone at lunchtime; on most days he would walk the extra few hundred feet in order to take his noon meal with his friend, Jeremiah. The direct result of being cursed by a cleft palate was John spending a lot of his time alone. A vast majority of his fellow carpenters found it convenient just to shy away from him. Most of them flat out refused to work with him simply because the difficulty in understanding his speech was too much of a discomfort for them to handle. Nearly every day, John would stay busy building temporary handrails all by his lonesome. Most workers chose not to associate with John, but more than one knew they owed their survival to him. Several men had been saved from falling into the swift current of the mighty Mississippi thanks to the sturdy and efficient safety rails John had fashioned with little to no assistance.

"Having a good day?" Jeremiah asked, as he finally solved the challenge of the bean can. "Cold out over that water today, ain't it John?"

John absent-mindedly nodded in the affirmative.

"I miss them hot summers out on the raft, when we was young, don't you?" Jeremiah spooned a couple of bites of beans. With no response coming from John, Jeremiah set his spoon and can down and studied John's somber face. They had been friends since childhood, been through scores of tough times together. Yes, Jeremiah was black and John white, but they had never seen one another in terms of color. John was almost three years Jeremiah's junior, but just as with their color, neither saw age as an obstacle to their friendship. They had grown up together and endured years of bonding experiences, shared trials and tribulations, and had embarked on many exciting adventures. Through the years, they had developed a relationship truly bordering on brotherhood.

John had always been different from everyone else. He had been born with a cleft palate and was commonly referred to by most as a harelip. With time, the sight of his malady was something that most people managed to grow accustomed to and managed to overlook. Unfortunately, his speech impediment was a totally different matter. Speaking had been difficult for John, ever since he first had begun trying to form words. His voice had the tone of someone pinching their nose shut while speaking, and the annunciation of words was a nearly futile endeavor. The word 'you' sounded like it would have been spelled beginning with an 'N', and to the uninitiated listener, sounded like a grunted 'nyuh'. As he grew older, John found it most convenient to just nod his head, point a finger, or use his eyes and facial expressions to communicate. However, there were some folks who did have the uncanny ability to decipher his mumblings and understand him quite well. John's wife Anna, and especially his sister Mary, were two who thankfully shared that proficiency. His sons Elijah and Harold were not as talented despite having heard his style of speech since birth. Surprisingly, another person with the exceptional capability was John's friend, Jeremiah Paige.

"John, are you alright? You sick or something', feelin' okay?" Jeremiah was concerned by John's silence.

"Miah," John could never say the full word 'Jeremiah', and therefore shortened it to the much easier to say, *'Miah'*. "Con dyu it. Howld. Ah my fauht."

"Whatchu mean, you can't do it, John? Harold is not your fault. It was an accident. 'Twern't nobody's fault. 'Twern't yours, 'twern't Elijah's, 'twern't nobody's. Damned accident, and that's all there is to it. You hears me?" Jeremiah had talked John through these depressive episodes a number of times in the past several months. In July of this year, John had taken his two sons fishing on the banks of the Mississippi. The youngest, three-year-old Harold had managed to wander off, unbeknownst to John or his older brother, Elijah. Harold had soon been bitten by several copperhead snakes and had died a scant two days later. In Missouri, death by snakebite was not a terribly unusual event. There was normally a death from copperhead bites at least once every couple of years somewhere in the state. But, rare or not, tragedies are vastly different when they hit home. This tragedy had only happened in July, just less than six months ago. In the aftermath, John had struggled mightily with feelings of remorse and guilt over Harold's death.

After slowly nodding in acknowledgement of Jeremiah's words, John stood up and tossed his unfinished sandwich into the burn barrel. Turning, he took two steps toward Jeremiah and patted his left shoulder as a form of appreciative thanks. "I know id naut," he grunted and trudged back toward the dam to continue pounding nails.

* * * *

"Get up, stupid," one of the boys shouted.

"Say your name... you can at least say that, can't you, dummy?" chimed in a second boy. The three of them had formed a semi-circle around the younger boy, who now found himself sprawled on the cool moist dirt where he had just been forcibly deposited. He lay just next to the wooden rear wheel of an empty feed wagon. It was a mildly chilly but damp afternoon, Tuesday, September 6, 1910, and the targeted youngster was, of course, justifiably frightened. The boy was barely two months removed from his seventh birthday. His father had told him on that celebratory day that he was now a big boy, old enough to start helping with the chores on the farm. But he didn't feel like a big boy right now. Less than twenty minutes into his walk, taking a shortcut through Mr. Hemsath's property on his return home from school, he had been confronted by the three ruffians. His tormenters today were all at least two to three years his senior, and obviously enjoying themselves immensely.

"Get up harelip, don't be so scared," added the third. "We just want to know if you can talk or not."

"Yeah, we just want to find out if you're retarded or just plain stupid or what!"

Thinking of his father's words, calling him a 'big boy', and wanting desperately to put on a brave face, young John Clemens defiantly climbed back to his feet.

"Say broccoli, stupid," came the order. Despite the involuntary, but instinctive impulse for tears to form in his eyes, an embarrassed but determined young John fought back against his instincts. Standing now with renewed resolve, he looked firmly at the three and slowly shook his head no, appearing to dare them to react to his defiance. In reality, he knew he was too afraid to attempt to say the word, knowing full well that his garbled effort would only lead to further, and possibly more severe, ridicule. Despite his bravery, John, once again, found himself pushed to the ground.

An unamused bystander silently observed the scene unfolding next to the feed wagon. Accustomed to the same type of bullying and discriminatory rhetoric, he watched with great interest to see how the young boy would react to the abusive treatment. Impressed by the child's bravado and mildly angered by the boy being knocked to the ground, he decided it was time to initiate an intervention.

"Leave him alone." The voice came from behind them, causing a temporary distraction from their prone target. The three of them turned simultaneously, refocusing their attention to a tall, somewhat imposing young black who was nonchalantly leaning back, propped on an elbow against the half-door of Otis Hemsath's barn.

"And just who do you think you are?" the biggest, and likely oldest, of the boys asked.

"I'm the man's gonna beat the dog crap out of you three, if'n you don't leave that boy go, that's who I am," he calmly responded.

"Hey boy, do you know how much trouble you'd be in if you so much as touched one of us?"

Shrugging, he retorted, "I don't know, why's don't we find out," the tall black youngster began walking toward the three, arms dangling to his sides, and with both fists clenched.

Without hesitation, nor exception, the boys apparently no longer felt confrontational and scattered like cockroaches, hurrying on down the trail. The imposing young man continued in John's direction. "Are you alright, boy?"

"Nyea, Ine awri," John mumbled.

"Good, come on. I'll walk with you."

The two walked in silence a few hundred yards before John's rescuer spoke, "My name's Jeremiah, what's yours?"

"Jhan."

"Good to meet you, John," Jeremiah said before asking in an easy, matter-of-fact manner, "So, you're a harelip, huh?"

John nodded in the affirmative.

"Don't let it bother you none, my cousin gots one, too," Jeremiah continued, using a comforting tone. "That's why I know 'zactly what you're saying. I growed up with him, so's I got the gift of listening."

John glanced over and upward at Jeremiah and smiled broadly.

* * * *

They had nothing obviously in common, but somehow Jeremiah and John seemed to have been destined to find one another. Both considered themselves relative outcasts, and perhaps that was the common denominator they shared. John Clemens lived on a small farm, roughly eight miles east of

Monticello, Missouri. It was only about four miles from the homestead to the banks of the mighty Mississippi River, a distance easily covered by either horseback or horse drawn buggy or wagon. When John's father made the trip every other week to gather supplies, the wagon was the practical choice. Perhaps one Sunday a month, assuming nice weather, Ma and Pa Clemens would pile John and his younger sister Mary into the buggy, and they would attend church services in Monticello. Beginning in 1911, but generally only during the summer months, John would either borrow his father's old mare, or he and Jeremiah would make the trek on foot to the river to do some fishing or partake in other adventurous activities. When it seemed more feasible to stay closer to home, there were several ponds in the vicinity where fishing could prove fruitful as well.

Jeremiah Paige lived with his father on a small plot of land, less than an acre, and roughly a mile removed from the western-most border of the Clemens farm. Unfortunately, Jeremiah's mother had perished during a difficult, unsuccessful childbirth back in 1905. His baby sister had survived, but only for a short time, succumbing just a few days after her mother. In the wake of the loss of his mother and sister, it was only Jeremiah and his father sharing the one bedroom, less than five hundred square foot abode that sat on the southeastern corner of the property. Jeremiah's father, Clarence, had just enough land that he was able to annually produce a garden sufficient to fulfill the needs of two, and had a pen in which he raised a small brood of chickens, providing a necessary protein supply in the form of eggs. Occasionally they feasted on a roasted hen to supplement the fish they caught and nearby wildlife they were able to trap or kill.

The two youngsters' paths had never previously crossed, so far as either was aware. But, ever since the day Jeremiah had come to John's rescue, the two had become inseparable. They spent time together fishing, trapping rabbits, turtle hunting (Jeremiah's father was most proficient at preparing snapping turtle stew), and exploring nearby forests. They had even developed an unusual hobby - collecting snakeskins. The boys had first garnered interest in snakeskins when they happened across the discarded skin of a king snake. Jeremiah's father had explained to them that snakes molt, or shed their skin, several times a year. Rural northeastern Missouri, to Jeremiah's and John's delight, was a fertile hunting ground for interesting and varied species of snakes. Their shared collection contained the skins of a king snake, black rat, copperhead, cottonmouth, timber rattlesnake, and banded water snake. A typically glorious summer day for them might consist of a morning of picking and snacking on wild blackberries or elderberries, a lunch consisting of wild apples or pears (and sometimes the fruits of walnut or pecan trees), and an afternoon spend exploring the numerous creeks in the area. Often times a successful afternoon of fishing would result in a nice fried surprise for supper.

As years passed, and both boys matured, their adventures grew ever more bold and increasingly precarious. John's father spent spare time performing carpentry duties for neighboring families in need of his assistance. His work was normally voluntary, but now and again he would barter for needed goods. He was good at his secondary trade and wanting John to have options when he reached adulthood, taught him all he could of the trade. John was a good study, a natural at carpentry. He had scant interest in farming but knew that when his father got older, it would have to become his primary occupation. At an early age, John had determined that as long as his father was able to maintain the operation of the farm, he was going to pursue a career in carpentry. To that end, John concluded that he needed to come up with a project that would prove his skill in design and construction. In the early summer of 1918, bragging of his abilities and expertise in woodworking and with the promise of the adventure of a lifetime, John was able to convince and enlist Jeremiah to join him in undertaking the greatest commitment of their young lives.

The two spent nearly a month scouring the area forests for downed tree limbs and heavy branches, eventually securing enough wood to begin sawing, trimming, shaping, and fitting the lumber. Almost three months from the harvest of their first scrap of wood, and after much trial and error, Jeremiah and John loaded their eight-foot by twelve-foot raft onto John's father's wagon. The results of the project had to be tested. They had big plans for this raft, and if their three months of planning and building were to be in vain, better that the failure occur under controllable circumstances rather than in a more severe and dangerous environment. John hitched up his father's old mare, Myrtle, and with Jeremiah's aid, they transported the raft to the nearest large pond. They needed a large surface in order to practice navigation and experiment with John's sail design. The chosen pond was a little-known fishing hole, much larger in comparison to others in the area. A tall stand of pine trees nearly encircled the oblong pond, blocking some of the late afternoon sunlight. The location of the pond itself was nearly obscured by the tall, wild, and naturally grown Indiangrass, some reaching higher than John's head. Old Myrtle made her way slowly through the growth, finally delivering the wagon and its bounty to within a few feet of the incline leading up and then downward to the water's edge. It was quite the chore, and an exhausting endeavor, but John and his friend finally managed to finagle the raft (largely in thanks to the amazing strength of the now seventeen-year-old Jeremiah), from the wagon and to the edge of the pond. With the assistance of Jeremiah's steadying hand, John affixed the six-foot-tall mast, and its attached twin three-foot cross members, to the bracing on the floor of the raft. He then attached the rolled-up sail that had been fashioned from one of his mother's worn-out bedsheets, to the top crossmember. The craft seemed ready for its maiden voyage. Both teens silently prayed that it would not sink under their combined weight.

Walking into the brownish water along either side and gently pushing the raft into the water, both teenagers managed to crawl onto the homemade craft. Carefully, they both stood, somewhat thankful that the raft had not sunk under the strain of their weight. Each bent down carefully to pick up his respective oar which would help to maintain balance. They had done their absolute best to build a safe and sturdy raft. The oars were each secured by large eyelets so that they could not fall overboard and be lost. With John standing to the front right and Jeremiah to the left rear, they cautiously began navigating the barely rippling water. They practiced diligently, knowing that when they took the raft out for real there would be little margin for error. Thirty minutes later, both were fairly satisfied that the raft was seaworthy and felt confident they had successfully mastered the art of both rowing and steering. The only thing left to test was the mast and sail, and while the sail was not a necessity, John's inquisitiveness couldn't be denied. He could not suppress the need to prove or disprove his theory. If they could rely on wind propulsion, it would save a good deal of energy that, upon reaching their ultimate destination, could be more fruitfully expended on further adventure. The prevailing breeze was quite weak as Jeremiah unfurled the small sail, securely fastening it to the three-foot-wide lower crossbar on John's rudimentary mast. The old bedsheet serving as a sail was slight in surface area, less than three-feet wide and barely two-feet high but reinforced by double thickness. At first, with no discernible indication of any wind, the sail hung limply. But, after a few moments, an unsteady gust began to intermittently create some billowing of the sail. It wasn't much, but it was enough to allow the raft to inch forward a few feet. John took the uneven forward motion as a sign of success. He had purposefully designed the sail to be small. He feared a larger surface might collect too much of a strong wind and therefore provide a substantial amount of thrust which could make the raft totally uncontrollable or possibly even cause it to capsize. All things considered, John and Jeremiah were ecstatic with the results of the test run, mutually satisfied that the vessel was ready to be launched on its maiden adventure.

* * * *

Jeremiah had never had formal schooling, although Clarence had used his rudimentary skills in reading and writing to try to pass along to his son what he did know. What Jeremiah had learned from his father provided a foundation on which John had built, sharing with Jeremiah some of what he learned in school. Jeremiah's knowledge expanded, to the extent that he could satisfactorily read and write and gained a fair understanding of history. Jeremiah sometimes would ride along on horseback with Clarence to Monticello, where he would help his father out when he periodically worked performing odd jobs.

John had to return to the classroom after Labor Day. His parents were adamant that even though he dreaded attending school, he should complete his basic education. They were first-hand witnesses to the difficulties John faced because of his speech problems, both in school and in his limited exposure to the public. They had every hope that his life would be spent working on his father's farm, eventually taken over ownership and operation. John, however, had a bullheaded desire to pursue carpentry as a vocation. If that indeed were to be his life's passion, he was going to need every advantage he could muster, and a solid education was the most important building block he could acquire.

With the test run for the raft successfully completed, the next step was to finalize plans for their ultimate adventure. The teens had developed definitive ideas of exactly where they wanted to go and what they wanted to explore, but with school looming for John, they had to be selective in choosing the dates to carry out their excursion. The boys agreed that they couldn't afford to delay the adventure for long. They would have to go in September before there was the risk of cooler weather. No one would want to be on the water in chilly temperatures. In consultation with the trusted Farmer's Almanac, John and Jeremiah decided which weekend would offer the most favorable weather conditions. They planned to ask John's father to drive the wagon carrying their raft to the river's edge after school on Friday, September 13. About two miles downstream from the clearing from which they would usually fish, was a large sandbar on which they planned to establish a weekend base camp. There were plenty of neighboring areas to explore, specifically a small number of shale caves that reportedly existed a few miles south of the sandbar on the Illinois side of the river.

As a bit of a surprise, the suggestion of the river adventure was met by practically no resistance from their parents. Approval almost seemed too easy to obtain. Plans were finalized and the equipment necessary for two days of survival was gathered. John and Jeremiah determined they would return to their launching site by mid-afternoon on Sunday, stash and secure the raft for future use, and be able to make the walk home and, considering their probable level of exhaustion, be in bed by nightfall. The anticipation and building excitement over the course of the next two weeks were going to prove to be sheer agony for the two friends, and they would wish many times over they had chosen a different departure date. September 13 could not possibly arrive soon enough.

A Weekend To Remember

John Clemens was fortunate to have had two people, that beyond any shadow of a doubt, were the best friends he could ever have hoped to find. Jeremiah Paige had stepped into his world at a critical point in his life. By the time of the fateful day when Jeremiah had interrupted the bullying on the Hemsath property, saving him from a possible beating, John had already reached unimaginable emotional depths at the tender young age of seven. He had been starting just his second year of formal education in the two-room schoolhouse located a four-mile walk from his home. One room contained a total of twenty-seven students, ranging from grades one through six. The second housed a varying number of students, the youngest being eight seventh graders, with the remaining being scattered through the high school grades of nine through twelve. While the planned total number of students assigned to the upper-level classroom was nineteen, there were scant few days that lofty attendance level was reached. Most of the area homesteads were farms and, as a direct result of the demographic, when children entered their teenaged years, it sometimes became far more incumbent that they provide labor at home. Immediate need, and possibly even survival, carried far more weight than the questionable value of their education. It was rare that anyone managed to attend school for the full twelve years.

At the time of meeting Jeremiah, John had just begun his second year at the schoolhouse, and he had already neared his fill of teasing and bullying by the older students. The forming of a friendship with Jeremiah had been quite paramount in John staying the course that his father had projected for him. His father, David Clemens, had done all in his power to prepare John for the ridicule that he was going to endure as a result of his unfortunate and unavoidable fate. David was fully aware of the discrimination John would face as he struggled to fit into society as a person living with a severe physical deformity. David had also grown up suffering the same deformation that demonized his son. He had literally been on his own since early childhood, about as long as he could consciously remember. David had no recollection of a father, and nothing but faded memories of a mother whom he had watched agonizingly perish from some wretched fever when he was still very small. He could hazily recall a rainy and dismal winter's day; his mother had become completely unresponsive, exceptionally cold to the touch, and he had run to get help. But when he could only watch as a few of the distant neighbors came and simply carried his mother out into the woods for a hurried burial, David suddenly found himself with no one. Seen by those neighbors as but a useless outcast, no doubt infected by the same plague or fever that had taken his mother, David was left to fend for himself, abandoned and alone.

But he had managed to persevere and had somehow survived. As he aged, he grew more skilled and accomplished with each passing year. David began to flourish in his adolescence and, as he entered into adulthood, found he was able to carve out a meager but sufficient lifestyle. He was well into his thirties, when finally, he met and married Kathryn and, in a short while, they had brought two children, John and Mary into the world. Dismayed that his son had inherited the curse of his own harelip, David was determined to make it his life's work to teach John as much as he could, and to do everything humanly possible to ensure his future success. He impressed mightily on John the need for education. The world was changing, he would repeatedly remind him, and with the approaching change would also come opportunity. But that opportunity could be taken advantage of only by those who had prepared. And in order to be prepared, David warned, John had to be educated. As the years passed, David had taught John every survival skill that he had been forced to master out of sheer necessity. David had taught himself the craft of carpentry, and by carefully teaching and passing along every iota of knowledge that he possessed, his efforts allowed John to also became a proficient carpenter. David and John not only had a solid father-son bond, but as John advanced through his early teens, they had developed an unusually strong camaraderie.

The day of the river adventure had finally arrived. On his way home from school, and as they had previously planned, John met up with Jeremiah at their usual rendezvous point along Snake Creek Road. The two of them split up the equipment Jeremiah had brought for the weekend trip. Each shouldering an equal burden for the rest of the nearly two-mile walk, they finally arrived at John's house. Together the teens pulled John's father's wagon from the barn, parked it beneath the shade of an oak tree and began loading up the bounty that Jeremiah had provided. They then went into the Clemens house, hastily snatching up the provisions and canteens that John had prepared on Thursday night in anticipation of the glorious weekend and proceeded back through the screen door, placing them into the wagon. With all their supplies satisfactorily stashed away, the boys went to the side of the barn and gingerly carried the raft out to the wagon. Having previously loaded it onto the wagon by hand for their trial run, they were more prepared today and tried to heed one of John's father's adages – 'work smarter, not harder'. They carefully stood the raft on edge, leaning the bottom against the side of the wagon. John went back into the barn and harnessed Myrtle before bringing her from her stall. Once outside and near the wagon, John attached a thick rope to her harness. He then slung the rope across a tree limb that hung parallel to and above the wagon. Jeremiah caught the end of the rope and pulled it to the side of the wagon, tying it to the top edge of the leaning raft. John slowly walked Myrtle away from the wagon and Jeremiah helped lift as the rope, being pulled across the tree limb, slowly hoisted the raft as it gently slid up the side of the wagon. When the bottom of the raft was nearly three feet off the ground, Jeremiah whistled for John to stop. Concentrating, trying to keep the rope taut, John turned Myrtle and very slowly eased her back toward the wagon. As she approached, the rope began backtracking on the limb, allowing the high end of the raft to gradually lower. Jeremiah continued lifting so the raft wouldn't slide back to the ground. He was very careful to control the position of the raft as it moved, keeping it square to the wagon and gently leveling it out to avoid it making a sudden and drastic drop as it came down. Once the raft had completely settled, and the rope removed from her harness, Myrtle was brought around to the front and hitched to the wagon. After using the same rope to safely secure the raft to the wagon, the first phase of heavy work was finished. The two sat on a pair of hay bales waiting for David to arrive and drive the wagon. To occupy their time, John and Jeremiah talked their way through a mental checklist, making absolutely sure they weren't forgetting anything.

They hadn't a long wait before John's father strode from the back of the barn where he had been adding to the compost pile. It occurred to John that this was the type of setting in which he was most happy. Him, his father, and Jeremiah. These were among the few times John could feel comfortable speaking. Both he and his father's speech were unintelligible in the opinion of most people, but of course, they understood one another perfectly. And Jeremiah, having grown up around a cousin who also spoke in the same manner, had no problem with it whatsoever. The three of them spoke amongst themselves no differently than any other gathering of friends would nonchalantly chat. John, his father, and Jeremiah climbed up onto the wagon's bench seat. David, sitting in the middle, picked up the reins, and glancing to either side, first to John and then Jeremiah, smiled and said, "Here we go boys!"

Less than an hour later the wagon had been strategically placed at the river's edge, in the same gravelly clearing where they would normally start a day's fishing trip. David and John gently guided Myrtle as she stepped back a few feet, enough to submerge the very rear of the wagon. Satisfied with the positioning, Jeremiah attached the loose end of a twenty-foot rope to the raft and reaching back, tugged to verify that the other end was securely tied to the wagon. Once it was pushed into the water, they could not take a chance that a swift current would carry the raft away. Odds were slim that could happen this close to the bank, but there had been too much time and effort put into this project to risk their handiwork being lost.

"Ready John?" Jeremiah hollered down to his friend, who stood at the water's edge with one hand on the rope, prepared to provide assistance when the raft hit the river's surface.

Smiling broadly, John looked up and yelled back, "Let her fly, Miah!"

Bracing himself against the back of wagon's bench seat, Jeremiah mustered all he had, pushing with his feet as the raft slowly began inching off the back of the wagon.

"Need any help up there?" David asked as Jeremiah continued pushing, keeping the raft slowly moving.

"No sir, I gots it Mr. David."

Breaking from the support of the wagon, the raft teetered before splashing heavily into the water, immediately leveling out and floating splendidly. They all had secretly feared that when the edge of the raft hit it would nosedive into the water and submerge, never to resurface. But the gods had apparently were looking down favorably today, and the successful unloading indicated that this was going to be a blessed weekend.

"Congratulations boys! She floats!" Called David from the front of the wagon where he still had a hand on Myrtle's harness.

Jeremiah and John hooted with excitement. They hurriedly began transferring their supplies from the wagon to the raft. It quickly became apparent that the raft was going to be a bit cramped. John and Jeremiah had each brought two bedrolls apiece, they had carried along a canvas tarpaulin measuring eight-foot by eight-foot with which they planned to construct a tent in the event of rain, they had brought eight canteens of water, several small bags of beef jerky, cooking and eating utensils, a bag of wax paper wrapped lard, and two sacks of bread and cornbread. They also had brought along two .22 caliber rifles, a box of ammo, and two bamboo fishing poles. John and Jeremiah both were excellent shots, and they had every intention of shooting and cooking one or two meals over the course of the weekend. They also fully intended to pull in some catfish to round out their weekend food supply.

With everything loaded, both boys hugged David, thanking him for transporting them, the raft, and their supplies.

"Good luck boys. Happy hunting. If you end up with too much, we can always have a fry Sunday night," David joked as he swelled with pride in his son and Jeremiah. This was a big step forward for John along his path to manhood.

"Thank you for all your help, and all you've taught me Father." John hugged David once more before wading into the water and crawling up and onto his position at the front of the raft. He unfastened his end of the rope, and when Jeremiah untied the other end from the wagon, John rapidly began pulling and coiling it into a loop around his hand and elbow. Jeremiah jumped down from the back of the wagon into the water and climbed onto the back of the raft. Slowly and cautiously, unsure how their vessel would behave in the current of the river, the boys began rowing away from shore.

David made his way back onto the wagon but waited, turning to watch as the boys carefully paddled away. He continued watching, until the raft had drifted all but out of sight, heading south on the mighty Mississippi. He felt a slight warmth in his eyes thinking about how much his son had matured.

* * * *

Neither of them had ever ventured this far south along the banks of the river. The sandbar had been spotted very easily, but the boys were quite surprised to discover its actual size. From the distant view of it that they had glimpsed only once, months before, it had appeared to have been a somewhat large sandbar, supporting a wealth of greenery. Approaching on the raft, they came to the realization that this was not really a sandbar per se, but more of an island. The greenery that they thought they could see from a distance had turned out to be fully grown trees. This presumed tuft of sand that had only figured into their plans as a campsite, had turned out to be at least a quarter of a mile long and several hundred feet wide, and was definitely more island than sandbar. They quickly realized that the first adventure of Saturday morning would be to explore the unknown on this island.

Upon reaching their weekend home, and with less than an hour of daylight remaining, John and Jeremiah had made haste in pulling the raft out of the water and onto shore. They tied it securely to a pale looking birch tree and began setting up their campsite. Not sure if wildlife inhabited the island, they had determined that food and anything else needing to be protected from possible disturbance should be packed and wrapped up in the tarpaulin. Satisfied with the completion of their preparations, and as darkness began to fall, John and Jeremiah sat next to the campfire they had stoked.

"I never thought this sandbar would be so big, Miah," John commented as he chewed on a piece of jerky.

"Me neither. Ain't never heard tell of no island in a river before."

"Makes me wonder, with all the river traffic and steamboats and all, people probably been here hundreds of times," John thought of the thousands of times boats had sailed past this island.

"I betcha a whole slew of bandits done hid out here, John," Jeremiah suggested. "I say we go and explore this thing in the mornin', see if there's anything here to be found. Maybe we'll find us some buried treasure."

The boys agreed to walk the island in the morning, before embarking on their exploration of the Illinois side of the river. Pulling out their bedrolls, they prepared to call it a night. A cooling breeze rolled in off the water that lapped rhythmically against the sandy shoreline, and a nearly full moon shown down from the star-filled sky overhead. The environment was ideal for a relaxing and comforting night's sleep. But somehow, neither were able to drift away from their conscious state.

"Ever wonder what's up there, Miah?" John asked as he stared at the sparkling multitude of stars above.

"Not for us to know, John," Jeremiah answered as he lay on the sand, also mesmerized by the enormity of the twinkling expanse that stretched as far as one could care to imagine. "That be God's world up there, we gots no business even wonderin' what goes on up there. We'll all find out soon 'nuff, I reckon."

"I think you're right, Miah," John concurred before rolling to his side and closing his eyes.

* * * *

Jeremiah rose with the sun on Saturday morning, wiping the sleep from his eyes just as the sun was cresting the eastern horizon. After going into the nearby brush to relieve himself and rinsing his mouth with water from one of the canteens, he had restoked the fire and then immediately retrieved a bamboo pole, baiting it with a slice of beef jerky. Within ten minutes he had landed a medium-sized channel catfish and was hoping to haul in another before John awoke. He thought it would be an excellent start to the weekend if his friend could be awakened by the tantalizing smell of catfish frying over the open campfire. Thirty minutes or so later, his hope was realized as he hooked another, similarly sized channel cat. After cleaning them and tossing some lard into the frying pan, Jeremiah added the filleted catfish and commenced cooking their breakfast. He was amazed that John had managed to continue sleeping. Growing impatient, he called out to John, "Hey city boy, rise and shine! Lots to do today!"

There was no response coming from the neighboring bedroll. Jeremiah called out to his comrade once again, but still the only answer was eerie silence. Worried thoughts began racing through Jeremiah's mind. *Maybe we should have searched the area before going to sleep. What if there are snakes nearby? A rattlesnake? A water moccasin from the river? Or scorpions? Or black widow spiders?* Jeremiah set down the pan and hurried over to where his friend lay. Reaching down to shake John, the realization hit Jeremiah that he wasn't under the blankets. Jeremiah stood, eyes searching, looking in all directions; he didn't know if he felt relief or dread that John was gone.

Picking up and loading a .22 rifle, Jeremiah set off walking to the south, down the western edge of the island. Nearing the southern tip, it dawned on Jeremiah that it was a small island, and he began to shout John's name. The second time he yelled "John", the familiar voice responded. Stepping through the overgrowth less than thirty feet to Jeremiah's left came John, holding up a disappointingly small blue catfish and a carp.

"Where you been, John? You had me all worried and scared," Jeremiah admonished.

"Woke up before the sun and didn't want to wake you up, so I come down here to fish for breakfast," John offered apologetically. "I sure didn't mean to worry you none, Miah."

"Dang it, John! I caught two channel cats and done fried 'em up," Jeremiah said. "When I seen you weren't there, I set the pan down in the sand to come looking for ya. Ants and critters probably done got to 'em by now." Jeremiah was flustered but couldn't be mad at his best friend.

"That's alright, Miah. We'll start over with these," John said, holding up his fish and giving his best smile to Jeremiah.

* * * *

After breakfast, the two decided to take a quick tour of the island and then take the raft to the Illinois shore. It did indeed turn out to be a quick tour, it was a small area and there basically was nothing to see. The island was home to a lot of brush. They recognized sandbar willow, some growing well over the tops of their heads, and they also saw a fair amount of kudzu and honeysuckle. Scattered about were black willow and birch trees. Thirty minutes into the exploration, they had seen all there was to see.

Packing most of their gear back onto the raft, they shoved off for Illinois. The boys took their time cruising downstream. The friends had picked a good day as there was a little bit of floating traffic on the Mississippi. They were fortunate to share the river with one passenger steamboat, a paddle steamer called *The Island Queen,* which passed them as it made its way upstream. Just past noon, the boys paused for a cornbread and beef jerky lunch and were treated to something neither had ever seen. They got to watch a steam powered snag boat in action. The snag boat derived its name from exactly what it did. It snagged and removed debris from the river, hopefully before it had caused damage to any of the boats or steamships that navigated the waterway. Both boys were intrigued by the boat's use of cranes and winches to remove potentially hazardous 'snags' from the river. They witnessed as a huge fallen tree, probably weighing at least a thousand pounds, was lifted onto the deck of the boat and mechanically demolished.

By mid-afternoon John and Jeremiah had stumbled across the shale caves they had so hoped to find. Located at the base of a bluff, the cave entrance had been almost totally obscured. Jeremiah's uncle had found the cave by accident almost forty years ago, and while he had wanted desperately to explore it, was only able to go into the first chamber. He hadn't possessed a source of light, and so was unable to continue. And he never again had the opportunity return to the bluff. Before he had passed, he had told Jeremiah that there were three distinctly separate passages that branched off from the main chamber. John and Jeremiah, aware of what they had hoped to locate and explore, had the foresight to bring along kerosene fueled lamps. As they cleared a path through all the branches and debris that blocked the entrance, it occurred to John that everything seemed to have been placed there to purposely hide the entrance.

"Miah, I think somebody wanted to hide this cave," John opined, "I bet nobody has been in there since your uncle went in."

"You might be right Boo." For some reason that John never learned, whenever Jeremiah was nervous, shaken, or slightly scared, he would refer to whoever was with him as Boo.

The cave entrance was small, not very high, and the boys had to crawl through the opening. Once through and able to stand upright in the main chamber, John and Jeremiah lit their lanterns. The area was nearly circular, about ten to twelve feet in diameter. The uneven ceiling had a height of just about six feet, meaning John could stand fully upright, while the taller Jeremiah had to duck his head ever so slightly. Just as his uncle had reported, there were three separate passageways leading away from the chamber.

"Well Miah, ready?" John looked to his friend for affirmation.

"I think so," Jeremiah seemed hesitant.

"Miah, if it spooks you a little bit, it's okay, you know."

"I ain't scared of nuthin', Boo," Jeremiah replied. "I's just waitin' on you."

With a nod and a smile, John started toward the passage on the left. It quickly narrowed to just a couple of feet in width, and the ceiling began to lower. They continued for another fifty feet or so before the passage suddenly ended. They were facing a solid rock wall ahead. Forced to turn back, Jeremiah had to lead the single file return. When they reached the entrance chamber they had to decide if it was worth checking the other two passageways. After a brief discussion, they decided to try the middle one. John, displaying a higher tolerance for spiders and other such creepy crawlers, again took the lead. The middle passageway proved to be a nearly identical copy of the first, and after a few minutes they found themselves backtracking once again.

Back in the front chamber once again, Jeremiah expressed some frustration.

"Don't know why my uncle even told me 'bout this place," he said. "They ain't nuthin' to this cave. Waste of time, thas all."

111

"I don't know, Miah," John said as he scratched the top of his head in thought. "How long ago did you say he came here?"

"I think he said forty years maybe,"

"You know, it bothers me the way that entrance to the cave was camouflaged," John went on, thinking out loud. "When your uncle was here, that had to be around the 1870's or earlier and I don't think anybody has been here since."

"Well then, whatchu thinkin', John?" Jeremiah asked.

"I'm thinking it's probably a waste of time, but I want to look in that passage there, too," said John as he pointed to the one on the right.

Once again John, followed by Jeremiah went into one of the cave arteries. More than one hundred yards into a winding journey, the condition of the cave had remained unchanged. It had not narrowed; the ceiling had not lowered. The cave continued to twist and turn for another several hundred feet before it opened up slightly and dead-ended in a small chamber, with a roughly eight-foot ceiling.

"So, this is it? This is the end of the road?" John asked as if he were a lawyer questioning an imaginary witness.

"Waste of time," said Jeremiah.

"But it was an adventure," John commented as he held his lantern a little higher and walked around the edges of the chamber.

"Whatchu looking for John," Jeremiah asked as he too moved toward the opposite wall with his lantern.

John didn't answer as he continued examining the rock wall, now running his fingers along the surface. Seeing what John was doing, Jeremiah began his own hands-on inspection. Both boys continued to probe, when Jeremiah suddenly shouted, "John!"

John looked toward Jeremiah, allowing his eyes to adjust for the distance and uneven lighting. When the adjustment took hold, he could not believe what he was seeing. Jeremiah had apparently found a false spot in the wall. He had been able to push it slightly inward. John brought his lantern near, and with somewhat more intensified light, they both studied the wall carefully. Jeremiah was the first to notice the two slight edges cut into the stone. Just enough edge to lock the nails and fingertips of two fingers from each hand. Jeremiah assumed the grip with both hands and slowly was able to pull the stone outward. Once protruded an inch or so beyond the wall's surface, Jeremiah was able to grasp the stone and ease it out even further. When he had pulled it far enough to establish a firm grip, Jeremiah brought the stone all the way out and set it on the floor. John brought the lantern close enough to be able to see into the two-foot by two-foot hole. To his amazement, John counted twenty-two large gold bars hidden in the hollowed-out space. John stepped back so Jeremiah could see for himself.

In deep thought and amazement for a few moments, the two decided to regroup and take some time to make a sensible decision concerning their discovery. Jeremiah lifted the stone and replaced it in its original position. They picked up their lanterns and returned to the main chamber inside the cave's entrance. John paced while Jeremiah calmly sat on the stone floor and watched.

"I don't know, I really don't know," John said as he weighed thoughts, ideas, and options.

"Let's go back to the sandbar, eat supper and talk about it," Jeremiah suggested.

John agreed, and they left the cave, carefully replacing all the branches and camouflage they had removed. They reboarded the raft and began paddling north, against the current. Traveling against the current presented a challenge they knew was coming but hadn't realized would be quite so difficult. They attempted to stay in shallower water, close to shore in order to avoid the stronger mid-river current. They were only about three miles downstream from their campsite, but it took well over an hour for the exhausting return trip.

Back on the island, John and Jeremiah each manned a pole, but it was nearing nightfall, and nothing was biting. Standing fruitlessly at water's edge for what seemed an eternity, they remained empty-handed. River fishing could be quite fickle at times. But the idle time had provided them opportunity to discuss the day's earlier fantastic discovery. They had reached several conclusions while bouncing ideas and theories off one another. They concluded that there was no way for them to know or ever find out when or how the gold bars were hidden in the cave. It was widely known that the James Gang operated in Missouri around the 1870's, and the Younger Gang was also active in the same time period. The gold could have been the fruits of one of their heists. But, if that had been the case, why had no one returned for it? Obviously, Jeremiah's uncle had no knowledge of the existence of the gold, or he would have come back and claimed it long ago. Perhaps the gold bars had been the result of a more recent crime, in which case the owner may still be planning to come back and retrieve them. Another possibility they had pondered was that the bars were legitimately owned by someone who was old-fashioned and distrustful of banks. If that were the case, and they were to take the gold, it would be just plain robbery on their part.

The two friends took those thoughts to bed with them, to work through the possibilities, to allow their subconscious to weigh the options, to allow their dreams to recommend alternatives. In the end, a definitive decision would have to be made in the morning, a decision they would have to agree to live with for the rest of their lives.

Morning arrived carrying with it a cool mist and awaiting a life altering decision. Should they take the gold bars now, should they wait and come back sometime in the future to collect their fortune, or should they pretend they had never entered the cave nor seen the bounty that lay within? Perhaps as a sign of their absolute friendship, or maybe as a result of some divine intervention, both boys had awoken firmly convinced of the same logical and identical solution.

John and Jeremiah had agreed that to take the bars now would not be the best course of action. What if they did belong to an innocent and honest citizen. The removal of the gold would be criminal, and they both agreed that they could not live carrying that burden. Secondly, if they were to be caught in a robbery of that magnitude, they could end up spending the rest of their lives in a state penitentiary, which also would be too much to bear. Not knowing the origin nor rightful owner of the gold bars, they mutually decided that they could not ever return to the cave nor set eyes on the fortune it contained.

Neither of them knew, nor could ever hope to know, if the gold bars had been there forty years ago when Jeremiah's uncle had visited the cave. But John and Jeremiah had agreed that if the gold were still there forty or fifty years into the future, that whoever had put it there was quite likely no longer alive. With that probability in mind, John and Jeremiah agreed that if the gold bars did remain in their hiding place, they should be split evenly between their respective first-born grandsons. When the first-born grandson reached the age of eighteen, a map would be provided directing him to location of the treasure. He would then be required to hold half the gold for the other grandson who would ultimately collect his share when reaching the age of eighteen.

With the decision made and agreed upon, John and Jeremiah loaded all the food, equipment, and all the other provisions they had brought along, back onto the raft. Once again struggling against the swift current, the pair finally managed to complete the two-mile trip northward. The worn-out youngsters drug the raft back up onto the riverbank at a location that they had previously found and felt was sufficiently hidden away. Items that could be used on future adventures were packed and stored on the raft under the protection of the canvas tarpaulin. The hope was that everything could be kept safely there on a permanent basis, ready at moment's notice to embark on a new excursion.

Loaded down with the remainder of their equipment, the four-mile hike back to John's farm was arduous but in its own way satisfying. It had certainly been an eventful and exciting weekend that had served to further solidify the friendship between the two. Knowing they had agreed on a plan that would benefit their yet to be born descendants was reward enough to compensate for the riches they were bypassing in their own time. Reaching the Clemens farm just ahead of dusk, an exhausted Jeremiah was invited to spend Sunday night with John's family.

On Monday morning, although still physically worn out and emotionally spent, the two of them walked together toward John's school. Jeremiah turned off Snake Creek Road at their normal rendezvous spot, the same place where they had met on Friday afternoon. From there, Jeremiah would be home in another twenty minutes. Meanwhile, John continued the trek to his schoolhouse. Upon arrival, he managed to avoid his teacher's attention while successfully getting away with neglecting his assigned studies. He was working feverishly to draw a map of the sandbar/island and the neighboring cave and its arteries. He wanted to get all the details down on paper while his memories were still fresh. When it came time for his grandson to someday use the map as a reference and guide to claim his fortune, John wanted it to reflect pinpoint accuracy.

The Future, The Past

The time was swiftly getting away from her on this Saturday morning. Margaret Clemens had just finished cleaning up the kitchen following a delicious breakfast of cinnamon sprinkled, slow cooked Quaker oatmeal. The sweet and satisfying oatmeal had been accompanied by homemade biscuits slathered in sausage gravy. Her gravy was a source of pride for Margaret; it was prepared from a secret recipe, that so far as she knew, had been revealed only to her by Buster Finkel, the extraordinary short order cook employed by the *River's Edge Diner*. Margaret had worked with Buster for nigh on six years, her entire tenure at the popular local establishment. Buster had been a good friend to Margaret, often a proverbial life saver.

During the time she had known Buster, Margaret had not possessed a car of her own. The family car, one that Elijah had purchased during his ill-fated previous marriage to Betty Jo (Marcus' deceased mother), had been sold back in early 1960, a few months following Elijah's accident. In the aftermath of her husband's death, Margaret's bills had accumulated rapidly. Advised by a big city attorney from Quincy (who had appeared, unannounced and unsolicited, on her doorstep two days after the funeral), she had filed a lawsuit asserting negligence on the part of the quarry where Elijah had been employed at the time of the tragedy. However, the jury in the case had sided with the defendant, finding the rock quarry free of culpability in the accident. As Elijah's beneficiary, Margaret was fortunate to have received a meager workers' compensation insurance payout. Elijah's small life insurance policy had provided enough for funeral expenses, but with little left to spare, Margaret thought it necessary to sell Elijah's prized but now twelve-year-old Studebaker Commander Deluxe. She had briefly considered relocating with Marcus to Texas and moving in with family. However, being a hardheaded, stubborn, and strong-willed woman, Margaret instead had opted to stand on her own, find a job and attempt to pursue a self-sufficient lifestyle. Having been a housewife from the onset her marriage to Elijah, the only immediate work alternative had been to return to her prior profession of waiting tables. Even after Margaret had secured her job at the diner, times continued to be difficult. Without the Studebaker, Margaret had dutifully walked to and from the diner every day. Buster had tried to help her whenever possible. Often, on days when their shifts coincided, Buster would drive Margaret home. It wasn't unusual, on poor weather days, for him to go out of his way to stay at the diner after concluding his shift, making sure she had a ride. He would also slip to her extra unneeded food, or items that were about to spoil, rather than letting them go to waste. He had been a good friend, and it had been difficult for her to say goodbye when she quit her job at the diner. By the spring of 1966, Margaret had finally saved enough to purchase a used 1962 Chevy Impala. Suddenly able to transport herself whenever and wherever she pleased, Margaret took advantage of opportunity and had been fortunate to land new and far better compensated employment at an upscale steakhouse, *The Goldmine.*

Margaret always attempted to arrive no later than eleven o'clock for her regularly scheduled shifts at *The Goldmine.* With her days slated to begin promptly at eleven-thirty, this allowed her half an hour to prepare for the noon rush that was always expected, particularly on Saturdays and Sundays. Margaret preferred getting to work thirty minutes early, especially so on the busy weekend shifts. The premature arrival allowed her time to sit with a cup of coffee, catching up on any gossip and memorizing the daily chef's specials.

Marcus stood staring, turning his head from side to side, admiring his handiwork in the bathroom mirror. He had just finished rinsing the shaving lather from his face, having completed a task that really had not even been necessary. His was not yet a coarse nor full set of whiskers, but with a job interview scheduled for ten-thirty, he wanted to look his best. He had never held a part-time job before, but he was certainly hoping to get started with the one for which he was applying this morning. Marcus aspired to be a tire-changer at Walt's Tire and Auto Repair but was unsure what other duties might be involved. His friend Denny Wallace had been working part-time at the *Meridian* movie theater for a few months now, and Marcus was jealous of the roll of dollar bills Denny always carried in his pocket. Gazing at the reflection in the mirror, he rubbed Brylcreem into his hair and began combing, deliberately. Marcus had known Walt McMurphy since he'd been old enough to get out on his bike alone and was somewhat confident that he would get hired. He and Cassie often sat at Walt's, chatting and sipping Coca-Colas purchased from Walt's perpetually well-stocked vending machine. Even before he had begun hanging out with Cassie, Marcus and his buddy Denny had frequented Walt's. The years had passed, but nothing much had changed at the shop. Just as it had been when Marcus was back in grade school, all the kids from Roosevelt Elementary who regularly traveled or passed by knew that Walt McMurphy had the coldest six-ounce Coca-Colas in this part of the county, or at least on White Street. Margaret's knocking on the bathroom door broke Marcus from his nostalgic trance.

"Marcus, are you about ready?" his stepmother asked. "I need to drop you off at the garage a little early so I can get to the restaurant by eleven."

"Yes ma'am, be right out Mama," he politely responded.

Marcus was glad that Margaret finally had a car. He had been silently worried about her for years. There were many evenings that he lay in bed, worrying that she would encounter problems walking home from the diner alone and so late at night. Rare it was that, when Margaret was working a late shift, that Marcus would fall asleep without knowing she was safely home.

* * * *

Arriving early for his appointment, Marcus was glad that his stepmother had dropped him off at Walt's and he hadn't shown up for the interview in full sweat mode from walking. Just as he had learned long ago from watching his father's example, Marcus had sparingly applied Elijah's old cologne, hoping the fragrance would help to project a more mature image. The bottle of Elijah's Old Spice was a possession that Marcus coveted, a nostalgic reminder of Elijah's distinct smell when he had received hugs from his father. He had only recently begun wearing the cologne and did so only when he thought it a necessity, saving it for important occasions such as Sunday morning church and Friday movies with Cassie. Although Marcus had arrived at the shop early, Walt was ready for him and promptly invited the nervous teen into his crowded and disheveled office.

Walt McMurphy was in his late fifties and his age and lifestyle were beginning to show. His grey hair, substantially thinned out, hung shaggily over the collar of his distinctive white work shirt. Walt's two full-time mechanics were outfitted in blue. The white shirt, which stretched reluctantly over his rather fleshy abdomen, was the obvious indicator to all who entered the establishment that Walt was the person in charge. The interview had been scheduled for ten-thirty, but its early beginning had moved things along rapidly. By ten-thirty Walt already had

123

suggested and Marcus, without the slightest hesitation, had happily agreed on a generous starting pay. Marcus followed his new boss out of the office, and Walt began the process of showing him around the shop and describing his duties. Just a few weeks prior, at the onset of spring, Walt had extended the shop's closing time from five to seven p.m. on weekdays. Rather than hire a third mechanic to help with the burden of the additional hours, Walt had opted to bring in a part-timer to relieve some of the workload and take over some of the more menial tasks. Marcus and he had settled on an after-school schedule of 4:30 to 7:30 on Mondays, Wednesdays, and Fridays and 1:00 to 5:00 on Saturday afternoons. Marcus had one worry alleviated when Walt had generously offered to alter his schedule during football season, in September and October. He had suggested to Marcus that he would allow him weekdays off so he could attend daily team practices. But as a trade-off, Walt expected him to work the same full ten-hour shift that the mechanics handled every Saturday, 7:00 a.m. to 5:30 p.m. with thirty minutes for lunch. Marcus was told that his initial duties would primarily consist of the end of day cleaning of the shop, tasks such as sweeping, wiping down and degreasing surfaces, putting tools and equipment away, and general clean-up and maintenance. When time allowed, the mechanics on duty would train him on some of the work they did, and eventually he would be expected to perform oil and tire changes. Just before 11:30, Walt extended his large, grease-stained hand, and instructed Marcus to report Monday afternoon at 4:30 prepared to get started.

After shaking hands and collecting his allotment of five blue work shirts emblazoned in red with his embroidered name (Walt knew Marcus well, and when the interview had been scheduled a week prior, he'd gone ahead and ordered shirts for him), Marcus had made a beeline for the payphone. Dropping in a dime, he hurriedly dialed Cassie's number. The line was busy, so Marcus stepped back out of the booth and took a familiar seat on a short stack of tires. Deciding to wait five minutes for the line to become available, he unwrapped a stick of Juicy Fruit gum, popped it into his mouth, and looked around the parking lot. His eyes fixated on the most intriguing vehicle he had ever seen. Opposite Marcus, on the other side of the lot, sat a beautiful, shiny turquoise and white Nash Metropolitan. It obviously didn't belong to one of Walt's patrons; it wasn't in one of the customer parking spaces. The car was out near the sidewalk bordering White Street, all alone at the outer edge of the property, as if on display. Feeling an irresistible attraction, Marcus got up and strode across the lot to get a better look. His heart skipped a quick beat as he approached and saw the two words written on the white piece of cardboard that was attached to the windshield – For Sale $450. Marcus was only three months shy of his sixteenth birthday, the milestone age at which a driver's license could be obtained. He stood admiring the car, fantasizing about driving it to Cassie's house, her seeing him sitting proudly behind the wheel. The mental vision of Cassie brought him out of his fantasy and back down to earth.

Marcus jogged back across the lot to the payphone, dropped a dime into the coin slot and dialed Cassie's number.

She had been expecting his call and hoped that the ringing phone was Marcus. Cassie hurried to the parlor and, in nervous anticipation, picked up the receiver.

At the sound of Cassie's hello, Marcus excitedly offered his joyous news.

"I got the job!" he proudly announced.

"That's wonderful, Marcus," Cassie was happy for Marcus, but at the same time a little bit disappointed that he'd been hired. With him about to start working, the amount of time they would be spending together was going to undergo a severe reduction.

Cassie's first question to Marcus concerned his expected work schedule. She wasn't elated that he would be working Friday nights until seven-thirty, for that meant there would be no more Friday movie night.

"But I only work until five-thirty on Saturday," he reminded Cassie. "We could still go to the *Meridian* on Saturday nights."

"Marcus, the movies are at seven, you wouldn't have time to go home, wash up and get back to the *Meridian*." At least Cassie was pragmatic.

"We'll figure it out, Cassie. We always have Sunday night; we could go then you know." Marcus did some mental calculations before adding, "We'll talk about it some more. What time is your hair appointment? I might have time to either come to your house and go with you, or just meet up with you at the beauty shop."

"It's at one-thirty, we'll probably leave a little after one." She answered. "I think you can get here in time for a sandwich with us, don't you?"

"For sure. I'll see you in a half hour or so."

* * * *

He revved the engine once more before switching off the ignition. What a glorious ride it had been, from St. Louis straight west almost one hundred miles on Interstate 70, then south on Highway A for another eleven. Flying down the divided interstate with the top down, sporadically able to hit speeds exceeding one hundred miles per hour, the sleek silver Chevy Corvette Stingray convertible was a dream cruise. Since leaving Interstate 70, it had almost been like a sprinter cooling down just past the finish line. Ease off the accelerator, wind it down, and catch your breath, both mechanically for the car and emotionally for the driver. With a little over the century mark in miles traveled and even including the reduced speed after leaving the main highway, the entire trip had only taken just under ninety minutes. The old blue El Camino had been a sweet ride, but with newfound business success and extra moolah burning a hole in his pocket, it had been a no-brainer to part with five grand and step up to this four-wheeled rocket ship. The driver stepped out and strode to the front door of the small two-bedroom rental that was currently inhabited by the attractive auburn-haired bookkeeper, Alicia Compton, and her son, Ellis.

"Dad!" Ellis exclaimed as he opened the door and saw Jude Allensworth standing on the stoop. Ellis stepped out and embraced his real father.

Jude, or Judy, as he was known to everyone, had been sure to keep his word regarding his biological son. Although he never was able to physically see him as Ellis grew from infant to adulthood, when they had been reunited, Judy had vowed to develop the father-son relationship that they had been unable to enjoy for Ellis' first sixteen years. Ellis Compton had spent the initial decade and a half of his life as the obedient son of his parents, Oliver 'Ollie' Compton and his wife Alicia. Ollie had been a locksmith in the community where the family had resided, a couple of hours north in Lewis County. The three had lived a calm and normal rural lifestyle until shortly after Ellis had turned fourteen years old. For reasons he didn't know at the time, his parent's marriage had suddenly dissolved. There had been no obvious signs of impending problems. Ellis had returned home from school one afternoon to find Ollie sitting at the kitchen table, idly rolling the empty cylinder of his .22 caliber wood handled High Standard 'Sentinel' revolver.

"What are you doing, Pop?" Ellis asked.

"Oh, nothing son," Ollie had absent-mindedly replied.

Normally, when he got home from school, his mother would be sitting at the table, busy with pencil in hand and journals strewn about. Ollie would either be working in his shop or out on a service call. Alicia had a bookkeeping job that she performed, working mornings at the office and the remainder of the day from home, for a local auto repair business. Ellis' arrival from school would act as Alicia's notification that her workday had ended. Like clockwork, she would gather her paperwork and relocate it to the small table that housed the breadbox, over near the door leading to the back porch. She would then proceed to the kitchen sink, wash her hands, and dutifully begin to prepare supper.

Not immediately seeing Alicia, Ellis glanced in the direction of the breadbox and noticed the lack of papers that should have been there.

"Pop, where's mom?" Ellis was feeling a touch of uneasiness.

"Trash got took out, Ellis," Ollie looked, eyes appearing slightly reddened.

"What do you mean?" Ellis looked at his father's sad eyes and then the revolver still in Ollie's hand.

The realization registered that he was holding his gun, and seeing the obvious concern on his son's face, Ollie tried to present a reassuring smile to Ellis.

"Now don't go jumping to conclusions," Ollie offered. "Your mom's fine, she just ain't here no more. She's left Ellis, and we ain't gonna be married no more."

"What?" Ellis asked disbelievingly. He found it inconceivable that his mother had up and left without so much as a goodbye.

It wasn't until months later that Ellis learned the disturbing truth about his parents. Ollie's demeaner had changed a great deal and he had begun drinking far more regularly. It was on one of his alcohol-fueled evenings that Ollie had decided that Ellis was old enough to know the truth. It was a relatively simple, cut and dried reason for divorce. Ollie explained to Ellis that he had found reason to suspect Alicia had been involved in a romance with her employer. When confronted by the evidence he'd uncovered, Alicia had nonchalantly admitted her wrongdoing, volunteered to leave, and had even suggested a divorce. She had moved to Alexandria and Ellis had split his time between their homes, although he maintained his official residence with Ollie.

Ollie had begun teaching Ellis the ins and outs of being a locksmith, planning for him to someday join in the family business. While the effort to ensure a fruitful future for his son had been commendable, he had also been a grossly irresponsible parent by introducing him to the numbing effects of beer, hard liquor, and marijuana. They often shared these vices as they held discussions at the kitchen table, sometimes well into the early morning hours. Obviously, Ollie's influences were wielding undesirable results. Fueled by the disruptive and denigrating environment provided by Ollie, Ellis began undergoing immense personality changes, developing a total disregard for authority. His demeanor devolved and became that of a crass and soulless young man. It was during the midst of a whiskey and cannabis induced haze that Ollie had thrown all caution to the wind and had told the truth of Ellis' own upbringing and past life. The truth was unloaded as Ellis was told about his birth, details surrounding his real parents, and his adoption by Ollie and Alicia. Most damaging perhaps was his relating to Ellis the wild story he had been carrying in the back of his head for years. Ollie told him about Marcus Clemens and the supposed relationship with, as well as the possibility of inheritance from, Mark Twain. It was not difficult for Ollie to enlist the loyal assistance of a vulnerable and easily persuaded Ellis. Over the course of a few days, plans were hatched and the effort to obtain Mark Twain's fortune, by whatever means necessary, was put into play.

Unfortunately for the father-son crime duo, their well-conceived plans had not unfolded as they had hoped. Now, four years later, Oliver Compton sat convicted of murder on death row in a Missouri penitentiary, awaiting execution. Fortunately for Ellis, after completing two years of incarceration and one year of probation, he had been gifted another shot at resurrecting his life. And Judy wanted to make sure that he did just that.

James E. Anderson

Building A Case

Ellis carefully parked the Stingray in the driveway of the house that he shared with his mother. Judy had allowed him to drive back home from the laughter filled afternoon they had spent further solidifying their relationship. The two of them had just enjoyed an afternoon at the *Strike and Snack*, a local combination bowling alley, pinball arcade and pizza parlor. Father and son had enjoyed pleasant conversation over a lunch of salad greens and pepperoni pizza. As usual, they initially spoke on a topic they often discussed during their times together. Judy was running out of details but did manage to relate a few previously untold tales about Ellis' birth mother, Paula. Ellis had a deep infatuation with all things Paula, and each time he saw Judy, would try to pry more information about her. When talk of Paula Sue Schaeffer had been exhausted, Judy turned the subject to Ellis.

"So, Ellis, how has the job been going?" Judy asked, actually quite interested in what Ellis had been up to.

"Oh, you know dad, it's okay," he answered.

Rolling and lighting at least his six or seventh cigarette, Judy squinted through the haze and pursued the topic.

"Still doing all that driving? I had kind of hoped you'd have found something local by now," Judy wasn't enthralled by the idea of Ellis driving all the way from Fulton to St. Louis and then north up through Bowling Green, Hannibal, LaGrange and all the way to Kahoka. Judy knew very well what Ellis was doing for a living. He would drive to a warehouse in northern St. Louis County, load his backseat and trunk with auto parts and make deliveries to auto repair and body shops northward along U.S. Highway 61 almost to the Iowa state line. He was paid well, but it was an extreme amount of time on the road. He was more than quite familiar with the man who employed Ellis. He had known Max Schofield for a long time and had never had much faith or trust in the man, but Judy didn't want to let Ellis know that he had ever associated with Max. Just as he did not want Max to know that Ellis was his son.

"Yeah, but it's not that bad. Max says he's going to give me a company car to use, so that'll be good." Since their reunion, Ellis had always been comfortable talking openly with Judy about his jobs. But now, knowing how drastically his responsibilities were about to change come Monday, he felt a little bit uneasy with the subject. Ellis was aware that Judy had lofty expectations for him. After the nightmare he had been through under Ollie's wing, Ellis knew Judy expected nothing less than hard work and honesty from him moving forward. The last thing he wanted was for his dad to know about the shady underworld he was about to enter. He did not want to disappoint Judy and felt guilty over the information he was holding back. In the back of his mind, he found himself considering whether to make a call to Max and turning down the job offer.

After lunch, the two had spent another three hours bowling and playing a multitude of pinball games, most notably Apollo, Surfside and TV Baseball. Judy had posted the high game bowling with a 227, while the best Ellis could muster was 172. But Ellis had dominated at pinball, winning fourteen games and dropping only five to his father. Judy enjoyed every moment spent with Ellis. Every time he was with him, Judy was sure he spotted more and more of himself. His unspoken hope was for Ellis to not have the same type of temper that had plagued him, causing so many problems in his youth. Before leaving, they paused for another thirty minutes at the snack bar listening to the Wurlitzer jukebox. Judy didn't totally understand the appeal of the popular acts like The Beatles, Rolling Stones and The Supremes, and Ellis had tried to explain to him the virtues of the even more modern music that was evolving, and what created young people's interest in newer groups like Procol Harum, The Hollies, The Lovin' Spoonful, and The Doors.

* * * *

Ellis had a blast driving the 'Vette from the bowling alley back home. As they were re-entering the house, Ellis excused himself to make a phone call. When Judy had arrived earlier, Alicia had been out

135

grocery shopping. But now she was home, sitting on the couch watching an old Tarzan movie. She invited Judy to sit and visit for a while and went to the kitchen to put on a pot of coffee. Ellis returned from his bedroom and approached Judy apprehensively.

"Dad, I hope you don't mind, but I just talked to my new girl, and she was kind of expecting to go to the movies tonight. I probably should've already been at her house," Ellis sounded sincerely apologetic, largely because he truly was. He'd had a blast and enjoyed the day with his real father. Due to Judy's busy schedule, they only were able to get together occasionally, about once or twice a month. Ellis would love to have spent more time today with Judy and his mother, but he had only recently met Becca and felt obligated to her.

"No, hey Ellis, don't be stupid. Of course, you go on and see to your squeeze. What's the lucky girl's name?" Judy asked.

"It's Becca, Becca Honeycutt,"

"You'd like her Judy, she's from Tennessee, got the cutest southern accent," Alicia said bringing a cup of coffee in each hand. "You still take it black, don't you?"

"Yeah, thanks Alicia," Judy said as he reached for the steaming cup she had extended toward him. "You be good to that girl, you hear me, Ellis? You know you've got to be on your best behavior all the time."

"I know dad. I won't do nothing wrong," Ellis promised.

"Make sure, son. Take it from someone who's crossed the line and learned from it, okay," Judy was no expert but was trying to offer good fatherly advice to Ellis. Judy stood and took Ellis by the shoulders, "I know you won't do nothing wrong. You need a few bucks?" Judy asked as he reached into his pocket.

"No, dad, I'm good," Ellis smiled as he held his hands up, palms facing toward his dad. "I'm good, I'm working now, remember? Besides dad, you paid for everything today. Thanks." Ellis reached out and patted Judy's shoulder.

"Okay son, have fun at the movie," Judy said as Ellis smiled and headed out the door.

"Alicia, do you care if I smoke, or do I need to go outside?" Judy asked.

"I think you know that answer Judy," Alicia said as she reached for her pack of Pall Malls that lay on the end table.

Judy looked down at the coffee table in concentration as he finished rolling. He picked up the cigarette, carefully moistening with his tongue to seal the paper. He rolled the tips, popped it into his mouth, flipped open his Zippo and lit up.

After taking a deep drag, Judy pulled a flake of tobacco from the tip of his tongue and exhaled. He squinted at Alicia through a cloud of smoke, and with an irritated rasp in his voice, asked, "Why did you have Max hire him?"

"What do you mean? He needed a job. Look, I moved all the way down here to be able to visit and take care of him while he was at that stupid reform school," Alicia shot back at Judy.

"I sacrificed a lot for that boy," she said. "When he got out and the probation and house arrest was up, I couldn't just let him sit around the house all day anymore, could I?"

"No Alicia, I get all that, but couldn't you just let him keep bagging at that IGA store, for God's sake?" Judy asked in an aggravated tone.

"No wise guy, I couldn't," Alicia snapped back. "They was only payin' him a buck an hour! He wasn't even bringing home fifteen dollars a week on the hours they was giving him. I needed more help than that."

"I'm sure there were other jobs around here he could've taken, wasn't there, Alish?" Judy was not satisfied with either Alicia's answer or her attitude. But then again, that was just Alicia being Alicia.

"No, there wasn't."

"I'd rather he be bagging groceries than working for that ass, Schofield. You know, I ain't never trusted that man. Nothing good can come out of Ellis working for him," Judy continued to voice his irritation. "You know how he makes his money Alicia! You're his bookkeeper for Pete's sake!"

"I know perfectly well how he makes his money, Judy. But all Ellis is doing is running car parts. What he's doing is above board. Ain't no harm in that." There was no need now for Judy to know the truth about what Ellis was really going to be doing for Max Schofield. No doubt, he would find out soon enough.

* * * *

The three Lewis County Sheriff Deputies sat in somber silence pouring over stacks of statements, medical reports from attending physicians, a preliminary autopsy report from the county coroner's office, and various other forms of information and possible evidence that had been gathered in the wake of the homicide that had occurred late on Thursday afternoon. The incident, which had taken place at the Lewis County East Trash Facility, had left one man dead and another superficially wounded. Deputies Martin, Daniels, and Wilcox had all had some involvement in the immediate investigation, and as a result had been summoned to a hastily called meeting in Interrogation Room Number 3 at the county facility. The only person not yet in attendance was the man in charge, the detective who had requested the meeting, Bryan Reynolds.

Detective Reynolds was a relative newcomer to the Sheriff's Department, having been brought on board some eight months prior, late in 1966. John Dykstra had been the previous detective in charge of more serious crimes, including homicide, but he had suffered a mild heart attack in the summer of '66 and had opted for retirement. Thus, the hiring of Detective Reynolds. Bryan Reynolds was a veteran, accumulating twenty-eight years of experience, first in Evansville, Illinois, and the past sixteen in Chicago. At the age of fifty-nine, he had decided to cut back on the unrelenting workload of the big city and ease into a relaxing, laid-back position in rural Missouri as he neared retirement himself.

When Detective Reynolds opened the door and entered the interrogation room, it was obvious that his was a presence that commanded attention and respect. Standing two inches above six feet tall, he was a broad man, almost a hulking figure. He had been a body builder in his younger days, scoring well in amateur competitions throughout Illinois and Michigan primarily. Deputies Martin, Wilcox and Daniels all were familiar with the detective, although none had been involved in any investigations with him. As often is the case in this type of situation, they were knowledgeable regarding him, but with the three of them basically being subordinates, he was less aware of their backgrounds or experience. Detective Reynolds took the seat that had been left open at the head of the table, setting his briefcase on the coffee and cigarette-stained surface. He didn't utter a word as he leaned forward and released the clasps of the briefcase. Without hesitation, he opened it and produced four manila folders, distributing three to the deputies and keeping one for himself. He removed red ink pens and yellow highlighting pens which he also handed to each deputy. Relocating the briefcase to the floor, the detective scooted his chair back, angling it a bit to the left. He clasped his hands in his lap and briefly studied the three officers. Lyle Martin sat to his right and Helen Wilcox immediately to his left, with Mitch Daniels at her left elbow. Clearing his throat, Detective Reynolds opened the meeting with a question.

"Who folks, was Tony Mancini?"

All three deputies were momentarily silent for a few seconds, unsure exactly what the detective was getting at.

"He was the victim, Detective Reynolds," Deputy Martin offered.

"Well, I have to say that's very obvious answer isn't it, Lyle?" Apparently, if he was going to be calling them by their first names, Detective Reynolds had done some homework regarding the deputies with which he would be working.

"Folks, if we're going to solve this case, we can't be satisfied with obvious or simple answers to our questions. We're going to have to dig deeper; we've got to think a little beyond the obvious. We might be looking into a shoebox, but I can tell you the answers probably aren't inside that shoebox. And when we're in a close setting like this, call me Bryan. Out in the station or in the field, it's Detective Reynolds. But just us, it's Bryan. Understood?"

All three deputies either nodded or softly answered in the affirmative.

"Okay, with that out of the way, here's the answer to my question about our victim. Tony Mancini was a drug mule. I don't know who he worked for, but I damn sure do plan   to find out," the detective said with confidence.

"I apologize if I overstep my bounds Bryan, but how do you know he was a drug mule?" asked Lyle Martin.

"Mostly, from experience, Lyle. Residue I found at the scene. I sent samples out, and the test results aren't back yet, but I worked in Chicago, and I know heroin when I taste it and I know pot seeds when I see them."

"I didn't notice any of that Bryan, but even if that was the case, it doesn't necessarily mean the guy was dealing, does it?" Lyle seemed to push for a bit more information or evidence.

"It's like this Lyle," the detective continued. "I know what I know about what I found there. I worked the phone for hours yesterday, talking to contacts up and down this side of the river. I've got contact with a few moles inside some of the biker outfits in Chicago who happen to be in cahoots with some of these guys over here. I got it on pretty good authority that this Mancini clown had been delivering at least weed, if not more, to this bunch they call *The Brood* that operates out of Hannibal."

"If that's the case Bryan, do we go on the assumption that these bikers are behind this? Do you think they shot him, with the intent maybe to steal the drugs?" The question came from Mitch Daniels.

"Maybe, but I doubt it. I don't really sniff their involvement in this," Reynolds responded to the deputy. "What sense did you get when you interviewed the other guy that was wounded, this Jeremiah Paige?" Reynolds asked, as he turned back to Lyle Martin.

"Well, the only thing he said that remotely sounded like biker involvement was in his description of the guy that had accompanied Mancini that day. Beard and long hair he said, but these guys in *The Brood*, I see them more like the redneck type, you know?" Lyle had come from a military background and was used to that regimented, clean-cut appearance. He had heard enough about *The Brood* to know that many of the tenured members had fought in Korea back in the day, and felt it a certainty that, as former soldiers, they weren't the type to be influenced by current and temporary trends.

"You might be right in that respect, deputy," the detective concurred.

"If I can interject, Detective," Helen Wilcox spoke up. "From what I read in Lyle's report of his interview with Mr. Paige, I'm not sure I would put a lot of stock in anything the man had to say. I mean, he had to have been in shock after being wounded and then going unconscious for God knows how long."

Mitch Daniels joined in the dialogue by adding his opinion. "You're right Helen, he could have been delirious and possibly even hallucinating."

"Definitely so my friends, you're both right in what you're saying," Lyle spoke in agreement. "Listen, when I was an M.P. in Panama back in '61, we had some rogue commie attack the base perimeter. He shot up a half dozen of our boys and I helped to treat some of the wounded soldiers. If any of us would know how a confused and delirious person acts after the trauma of a gunshot wound, it would be me. But, even beyond that, I really don't think the old man is all there. If you know what I mean," Lyle said as he twirled the first finger of his right hand next to his temple.

"Yeah, I read that in your report, Lyle," Mitch responded. "But I've known Jeremiah for a long time, and he has never impressed me as a fruitcake, pardon the expression."

"Perhaps you need to read a little closer, Mitchell," Lyle retorted, feeling Mitch had come across a bit confrontational. "The man told me that a damned dog had talked to him. He even called the dog John, which, by the way, is a strange name for a dog if you ask me. Anyway, he asked me if John had called and sent me. Sounds a little whacko to me, don't you agree?"

"To be fair, Lyle, the man was in shock and couldn't have been thinking clearly," said Detective Reynolds.

"Bryan is right." Helen said, looking through her papers. "It says right here in your report that Mr. Paige had recanted his remarks about this dog named John when you performed your follow-up interview and collected his written statement at the hospital three hours later. I'd guess that by that point he would have regained his senses. It's highly likely that he may have had an old friend named John, and it was probably quite common that a dog would wander around the piles of trash. In his state, I wouldn't think it to be out of the question for him to have been confused and had intermingled memories at the time you had initially responded."

"I know exactly what it says that he said, Miss Wilcox," Lyle said defensively. "But you weren't there, neither of you. I saw his face; I saw the look in his eyes. He might have recanted at the hospital, and he probably had realized how crazy he had sounded earlier, but I saw the smirk on his face, and I clearly saw in his eyes that he knew something. The man is either crazy or senile, or we've got a talking dog named John wandering around our county."

"Well, I advocate thinking that encompasses looking outside the norm, but I think I will discount

144

the third option you suggested, Lyle." Bryan chuckled softly and picked up his manila folder, motioning for the others to do the same.

"I gave you all red ink pens and highlighters so that you can mark up and make notes on the pages that I brought today," Detective Reynolds separated papers and photos enclosed in the folder and began explaining. "Here are the crime scene photos that I personally took. As you can see from the blood smears on the floor, Mancini's body had been moved as someone attempted to conceal it behind the cabinet. Now obviously, the person responsible had hoped that by hiding the corpse he could buy time to get as far away as possible. But I believe we are dealing here with an individual who did not, and I'll repeat, did not graduate at the top of his class."

"This guy made some pretty stupid and glaring mistakes," Reynolds continued. "First of all, he was not wearing gloves and left fingerprints that were simple to lift. If his prints are already on file, we'll have his name by Monday and we, or whatever agency who has jurisdiction where he lives, will pick him up. As dumb as he seems to be, it will surely be an easy task to get names from him. Secondly, this Einstein left the drug residue on the cabinet shelves and didn't even attempt to clean up at all."

Lyle Martin raised his hand to interrupt. "Excuse me sir, but what if this guy doesn't have fingerprints on file? How could we hope to find the supplier or source of the drugs without his cooperation?"

"It would be harder, no doubt. We would have to rely more on our embedded sources and informants," the detective answered. "But make no mistake Lyle, our primary job here is to solve Mancini's murder. I'm hopeful there are prints on the books and we can nab this idiot rather quickly. The likelihood is that this joker has dabbled in petty crime in the past and been previously arrested. Hopefully, that should make him relatively easy to find. When, and not if, we find him, then we'll pursue our secondary goal and bust this possible drug ring. I'd like to think this watchman from the dump is not involved in any of this, but you never know."

Mitch Daniels raised a finger to attract the detective's attention, "As I stated before, I've known Jeremiah for a long time. I'm darned confident he would never get wrapped up in any of this. He wouldn't have any interest in any drug use or selling; I know him well enough, and I know his conscious would never allow him any involvement in killing anyone, not for any reason."

"I'm sure you are right, Mitchell," elbow on the table and rubbing his forehead, Bryan Reynolds abruptly changed the subject. "Let me ask you something Daniels."

"Yes sir?"

"Talk to me about this Clemens kid. What do you make of his story?"

"Not much to it sir, he was approached by someone who asked him to call the department and report the shooting. It's all in my report, Detective."

146

"Oh, I know, I know," said the detective with a wave of his hand. "Does it bother you at all or do you find it odd that the boy's description of the man in the black mystery truck is just about diametrically opposite of the description that the old man gave? And the vehicle descriptions were about as different as night and day as well?"

"I hadn't thought too much about that sir, uh Bryan. I guess I'm just rolling with the assumption that somebody was perhaps driving by, or maybe just entering the dump and witnessed what happened and, I don't know, panicked and left." Mitchell shrugged as he struggled with the scenario he'd presented, even though he'd run it through his own mind a hundred times. "Maybe the guy drove around a while and wanted to report it but didn't want to get involved. He sees Marcus on the sidewalk and figures he's older and responsible enough, so he pulls up next to him and tells him. You know, just like Marcus said happened."

"Sounds fishy to me," Lyle Martin spoke up again. "I still don't get why he changed his story about where he even was at when this stranger suddenly comes into his life."

"He explained that when we interviewed him that night," Helen interjected in defense of Marcus. "The boy was a little scared and nervous and wanted to keep his girlfriend from getting involved."

"Yeah," Lyle came back again, "but the kid even knew the watchman that got shot, he identified him by name to the dispatcher."

Detective Reynolds sat back watching the exchange, enjoying the back and forth among his deputies. The discourse was healthy and demonstrated their engagement in the discussion.

Mitchell was beginning to be irritated by Lyle's seeming distrust of Marcus. "What are you suggesting Lyle? Is it your theory that Marcus, who doesn't even drive mind you, killed Tony Mancini and shot Jeremiah Paige? And of course, the wounded victim, who by the way *knows* your purported shooter, then describes him inaccurately to protect his identify."

Helen again joined in, "Yes, Lyle. And then do you suspect Marcus drove the orange van back to his girlfriend's house and called the police?"

"And where is the van, Lyle?" Mitch asked. "Did Marcus drape a huge black cloth over it, snap his fingers and make it disappear?"

Detective Reynolds cleared his throat to regain the deputy's attention. "You folks have brought up some interesting points, some of which deserve further attention. What if Mr. Paige purposely gave a false description of the shooter. Is it possible that Paige was involved with the drugs? He also could have given an inaccurate description due to the mental state he'd been in as a result of trauma. Perhaps young Marcus is indeed involved after all, giving the description of a man and pickup truck that don't seem to exist. It is odd that a teenaged boy could not differentiate between models of pickup trucks to the extent he could not even venture a wild guess as to Ford or Chevrolet or whatever. It also seems quite convenient that the truck's license plate was mud covered and the numbers illegible, isn't it?"

"I have to object Detective, in regard to the reputation of Marcus Clemens," Mitch said, upset that Marcus could receive even the slightest consideration of involvement in any of this.

"We're not in a court of law Michell," the detective said off-handedly. "You needn't object."

Mitch Daniels was mildly offended by the cavalier remark, perhaps an unwise stab at humor by the man who had been nothing short of professional up until now.

"Detective," Mitch began to explain. "You weren't here in 1963, when Marcus and his girlfriend stumbled across the body of a young woman who had been brutally murdered and her corpse, not only discarded, but posed on the bank of the river. Those kids were only eleven years old at the time. Then they themselves were brutally attacked. If not for the grace of God and some random dog that had miraculously saved them, they'd have been murdered by a machete wielding lunatic." Mitch paused momentarily but wasn't finished.

"We later found that Marcus had been the target of a pair of crazies that had come up with a bizarre idea that he was in line for a massive inheritance. And they somehow believed they could receive the inheritance by taking him out of the picture. Marcus was instrumental in breaking that case. Essentially, he saved his girlfriend's life and, in the end, that boy even saved my life. I know him, I trust him, and I know he has nothing to do with any of this." At this point, Mitchell felt he had probably said too much and fell silent.

After listening to Mitchell's heartfelt plea on behalf of Marcus, Detective Reynolds moved on with the business at hand. "I think it prudent, and in our best interest to keep tabs on some people, see if they may slip up and lead us to more substantial information or evidence, or perhaps even absolve themselves of all suspicion." At this point, however, Detective Reynolds was of no mind to remove anyone from his list of suspects.

"If I may, Bryan," Deputy Martin suggested, "I'd like to volunteer to be the officer to keep an eye on our young friend, Mr. Clemens. In deference to fairness and honesty, I don't think I'd be going out on a limb to suggest that both Mitchell and Helen have vested interest in the boy, and it may be difficult for them to conduct surveillance in an unbiased and prudent manner."

"I appreciate your candor Lyle, and I think I would have to agree with your assessment. Mitchell, I'd like for you to keep an eye on Mr. Paige and the trash facility. It is quite possible, and perhaps even likely, that someone involved in this, and maybe even higher up the ladder than Mr. Mancini, may return to the proverbial 'scene of the crime'. If they do, I'd like our eyes to be there to bear witness."

"Yes sir," Mitch responded. It wasn't that he didn't trust Lyle Martin with the task of surveilling Marcus, it had more to do with all that had happened in the summer of 1963. He'd have much preferred to take on the responsibility of keeping an eye on Marcus himself. He had grown close to Marcus and his stepmother, and in his own mind, regarded himself in some ways as a guardian angel to Marcus.

Reynolds turned to Helen Wilcox and said, "Helen, I'm not sure why, but I have an inkling this girlfriend of Marcus Clemens - her name is Cassie I believe – I think she could be a cog in this machinery somehow. Would you please try to keep tabs on her activities, just to ease my mind?"

"Yes Bryan, I will," she replied.

Detective Reynold stood, indicating the meeting was adjourned. He began repacking his briefcase, and as he was finishing and closing the lid, Mitch Daniels approached.

"I just want you to know, Detective, that no matter what directions this investigation may end up leading, I can assure you that Jeremiah Paige and Marcus Clemens will not bear any involvement whatsoever. I give you my solemn word."

"I surely hope you're right, Deputy Daniels. I sure do hope you're right."

James E. Anderson

Meaningful Conversations

The windshield wipers droned to a steady rhythm as he sat patiently, waiting for her to exit the apartment and leave for several hours, not to return until later in the evening. The morning had brought with it a steady drizzle, not the most ideal of weather conditions. His plans had been well thought out, very deliberately made, and he was hoping for the best. He had visited this complex, parked, and waited in this lot at least a dozen times over the course of the past six weeks. He wanted to be one hundred per cent sure of the daily schedule and routine of the attractive thirty something and her housemate. He had to be sure she would be gone and the young man alone. Sure enough, just as he'd expected, at five minutes past ten o'clock on this Sunday morning, she'd left the apartment. Holding a section of the morning newspaper protectively over her lovely hair and, to avoid slipping on the wet concrete, she had taken hurried but short staccato like steps across the sidewalk toward her green Chevrolet Impala. It was an unseasonably cool and damp Sunday morning, and most residents had either already left for church or were taking advantage of the weekend by sleeping in late. He watched as she started her car and cautiously pulled away from the curb. It was time.

It had taken a great deal of courage to finally convince himself to make the two-and-a-half-hour drive, knowing full well that there was a very strong likelihood that it would once again be but a wasted journey. He had tried this once before, just a short three days ago, and had headed back home disappointed. He had put a lot of work in, performing surveillance, learning the daily habits of the two residents of the apartment. He sometimes felt a little twang of guilt, to be surreptitiously watching people as he had been. But he consoled himself, and attempted to excuse his actions, by realizing how in the end, his soul and conscious would finally be cleared. Leaving the relative comfort of his black sedan, he walked slowly, gathering his thoughts, and attempting to prepare the words that would justify his actions. Hesitantly reaching up, his right fist produced a firm but not obtrusive rap-rap-rap on the apartment door, and he then stepped back, uneasily awaiting a response. A gruelingly long twenty seconds later, the door opened.

"Ellis?" Marcus both uttered and asked, unexpectedly surprised by the man standing before him. For the second time in less than a week, Marcus stood eye-to-eye, confronted by the person who had been the worst nightmare of his entire young life.

"Hello, Marcus," Ellis replied somewhat sheepishly. While Marcus was no doubt surprised and shaken to find himself looking out the door at his nemesis, Ellis was in his own right, extremely nervous. He had no idea how Marcus would react to his presence on the doorstep. When they had met on the street on Thursday, although he had obviously been in an understandably extreme state of agitation, Marcus had remained relatively calm. But the situation today was markedly different than what it had been on Thursday afternoon. On that day, Marcus had been in the company of his girlfriend, Cassie. Perhaps having her at his side had been a factor, helping him to control his emotions. Ellis had known that appearing so unexpectedly that afternoon, and almost directly in front of the girl's house not being the most ideal of locations, that confronting Marcus was going to be a daunting task. He had done a great deal of thinking while spending two long years at The Missouri Training School for Boys. Ellis had gone through extensive psychological therapy during his incarceration and had found himself inclined to do a great deal of inner reflection. He had grown to realize that he had allowed his adoptive father to influence his emotional state, to the point that he had become an unknowing but willing follower. He had lost the ability to have good judgement or to make sound decisions on his own, had become essentially 'brainwashed' by Oliver Compton. Upon the completion of his sentence, Ellis had vowed that he would one day make amends to both Marcus and Cassie and would do whatever was necessary for him to be accepted into the Clemens family. And so it was that, after the first unsuccessful attempt, Ellis had carefully planned today's encounter, making sure that

Marcus' stepmother would not be home. He felt it imperative that he meet with Marcus in a one-on-one setting, free from any outside influences.

Both stood, momentarily in silence, as each searched for the proper words. To be sure, the situation was terribly awkward.

Finally, Ellis spoke, trying to use the words that he had practiced, but generally stumbled over during several attempted rehearsals.

"I know it was hard for you to look me in the eye and listen to what I tried to tell you and Cassie a few days ago. And I thank you for at least letting me get it out. I can also completely understand why it would be just about impossible for you to accept what I was trying to say. But I did mean everything that I said to you, Marcus."

"Why, Ellis?" Marcus felt much as he had on Thursday. "First of all, why did you try to kill us? Why would you want to? What demon could have possessed you to do something like that? Can you really think I could just forget everything and accept your apology and pretend that we suddenly have a relationship that is just hunky-dory? Excuse me if I sound a little perturbed, but I don't see where you get off, Ellis."

"You're right Marcus, and I can't blame you at all for feeling like you do. You know, I'd feel the exact same way if I was in your shoes." Marcus had not yet slammed the door in his face and Ellis hoped he might be making some inroads with him. "Marcus, I've been struggling for more than two years with how to talk to you. Trying to figure out what words I could use to convince you that the guy you saw that summer wasn't me, wasn't the real Ellis. I really feel kind of like I've been reborn, that I'm a new me. I was just hoping for a chance to explain things to you, maybe tell you some of what I learned the last couple of years. I'm just asking for a chance, Marcus. Please give me a chance to talk to you and prove myself."

Marcus stepped back from the door, a bit out of the way, and looking downward, averting his eyes away from Ellis said, "Make sure you wipe your feet, Mama hates it when I track in wet leaves and stuff." Marcus paused a few seconds as Ellis entered before asking, "Want a Pepsi? Usually we got Coke, but Pepsi was on sale at Dempsey's, and she likes to change it up sometimes."

"Yeah, Marcus, a Pepsi would be great." Ellis was surprised to have been invited in and was quite grateful to have been offered a soda. After wiping his feet carefully, he took a seat on the couch.

Marcus yelled to him from the kitchen, "Want a glass, Ellis?"

"No thanks, bottle is good."

Marcus returned with two freshly opened bottles of Pepsi, handing one to Ellis and taking a seat of his own in the easy chair, catty corner from the couch. They both sipped, and an uneasy silence ensued.

Speaking first, Ellis opened with a question, "How much do you know, Marcus? I gotta figure out just where to start."

"I don't know, Ellis. All I much know is what I got from Deputy Daniels and my cousin, Judy. I guess first thing is that we found out Judy is your real dad and you got adopted by Ollie and his wife."

"Ex-wife, Marcus. Him and her got divorced when I was like thirteen, fourteen years old."

"Okay, that makes sense since Ollie lived in Monticello and I guess your mom, sorry, I forget her name, was in Alexandria." Marcus didn't know much about Ellis' mother, as she apparently had not been involved in the events that had transpired.

"Alicia, her name's Alicia." Ellis told Marcus. "Anyways, mostly I was raised by Ollie. I never even knew that I had been adopted until the summer that Ollie hatched his stupid plan. That's when I first found out that Judy was my real dad, too."

"Yeah, Judy told us he's been going to visit you while you were locked up," Marcus had a sort of guilty feeling when using the term 'locked up', but then again, he was only speaking the truth.

"Thank God for him, Marcus. Getting to meet my real dad has been a major turning point in my life. He's given me a lot of support and has helped me a lot. He just came to see me in Fulton yesterday. We always have a great time when we're together." Ellis was overcome with relief that Marcus was even sitting here with him, having this conversation. "He thinks a lot you too, Marcus. He says you're a swell kid, and he likes your stepmom a lot, too." With a small laugh he added, "Dad says she's a good cook and a looker, too."

Marcus took the last remark in stride. He had wondered quite a bit, a couple of years back, if there might have been sparks between Margaret and Judy.

For a while Judy had come around every other weekend or so, but the visits had tailed off after a few months. Perhaps the irregularity in visits were due in part to the frequency with which Judy had begun making trips to see Ellis in Boonville, where he had been serving his sentence. At any rate, if anything had been 'cooking', it had cooled off considerably. Cassie had even brought up to Marcus the possibility that Cousin Judy and Margaret could someday marry, which in turn would result in Ellis ending up as Marcus' stepbrother. The scenario was an appalling thought to Marcus, and for a long time had been the subject of his prayers during silent devotion at church.

"Yeah, Judy is a really cool guy, Ellis. I fell in love with that little blue pickup truck he drives." Marcus thought back to memories of the El Camino sitting at the curb with the familiar smoke rings floating out of the driver's window. "I'd always get excited when I'd come home, and it would be parked out front."

"Oh, he doesn't have that anymore, Marcus. He's got this smokin' Corvette Stingray now. It's silver, and so cool." Ellis was elated to be telling Marcus about Judy's new ride. "He even let me drive it yesterday. It is so unbelievable, just so cool. You hit the gas, that thing jumps, it like lurches forward," Ellis said, motioning with his hand. "Just wait 'til you see it, it's really awesome."

Ellis and Marcus were sharing cordial conversation, with some rather 'feel good' moments, discussing someone who was important to both their lives. But eventually, and inevitably, the conversation turned back to the events of the summer of '63.

"I know it's gotta be hard for you to understand what I was going through, Marcus. I didn't know it then, but Ollie was really an ass. They told me in therapy that I was brainwashed, you know, just like in the war movies." Ellis had decided to try to explain to Marcus what the root cause of his behavior had been, attempting to not exactly make excuses, but get him to understand how an impressionable person can have their thought processes and even their behavior altered. He told Marcus about the supposed Mark Twain will, and Ollie's insane plan to frame Marcus and get him arrested so that the inheritance would instead fall to Ellis.

Oliver Compton had been his father, his sole authority figure, the person who had been the one to instill all concept of right and wrong into Ellis' life. His mother, Alicia, had her own problems altogether. She had a job to which she was dedicated, and as Ellis had neared adolescence, she'd had essentially no time for him nor interest in his upbringing. He had grown up with a proverbial chip on his shoulder. Ollie had taught him that as he would grow older, he would basically be a target for society, destined to be attacked. It was constantly ingrained that he was a Compton, through and through, and as a birthright of that name, he was better than most. But also, that by being born a Compton, people would be envious of him. He was taught to accept that, as a result of people's jealousy, and their bitterness toward him, they would always be trying to take him down. Ellis, a direct product of Ollie's teaching, had grown into his teenage years having developed a severely narcissistic personality. A further byproduct of his personality had been a total lack of any sense of either sympathy or empathy. If someone were hurt or troubled, Ellis did not even have the capability to care. Fortunately for his own well-being, after Ollie and Ellis had been caught, Ellis had received almost two years of extensive psychotherapy. When he had served his time and been released, he had returned home with a completely changed personality and totally new outlook on life.

"So, tell me again Ellis, how did your dad learn about this inheritance I was supposed to be getting?" Marcus had found it difficult to follow the progression of relatives from Samuel Clemens (Mark Twain) down through his grandfather and father.

"Okay, I'll start again," and Ellis repeated his words. "Ollie claimed that Mark Twain's brother had a son, his name was David, David Clemens. Now, he had two kids. One was your grandfather and the other was my grandmother, my dad Judy's mother. So, then there was my dad and your dad, and they were cousins. And then comes you and me, but see, my last name ain't Clemens."

"Okay, I got it now," Marcus had finally seen it all sink in. "It's supposed to go to our generation, to the last surviving Clemens, and that's me."

"Right, right," said Ellis.

"It couldn't be you, cause your last name is Compton, since you're adopted. But even if you weren't adopted, your name would be Allensworth, not

Clemens." Marcus considered what had been the motivation for Ollie to come up with his bizarre scheme. "I guess, in a way, your dad was kind of smart to put all that together and figure out how to set you up for the inheritance."

"Yeah, I guess, but I'm glad we got caught. I couldn't have lived with myself, even with that fortune." Ellis paused before asking, "Marcus, would you do me a favor and not refer to Ollie as my dad? I don't consider him my dad anymore, haven't for a couple of years. Judy is my dad, from now on."

"Sure, Ellis, no problem. So, I guess we're cousins now, huh?"

"If it's okay with you, Marcus, I'd like that a lot." Ellis smiled for the first time during the visit. But his mood sobered quickly. "You know, Marcus, Ollie gets executed in July."

"No, well, I guess I knew, but I didn't remember that. Gosh, I'm really sorry, Ellis."

"Nah, it's okay. I guess it bothers me some, but really, I mean he's got it coming, don't he?" Ellis decided to quickly change the subject. "Hey Marcus, tell me more about my dad, you know, Judy."

"Not a whole lot to tell," Marcus replied. "I mean I didn't know him at all until one day, out of the blue, he just showed up on the doorstep. Said he'd been living in Georgia. He was on his way to a business meeting and decided to stop and pay a visit to his long-lost family. He ended up moving up to Iowa for his job and then when you went to the reform school that you were at, we didn't see a whole lot of him anymore. Sometimes he stops by when he's on his way back from visiting you."

"Wait, he stops to see you after he sees me?" Ellis asked. "No offense, Marcus, but that's kind of strange that he'd go that far out of his way to see you and your stepmom. I make that drive all the time. That's a long way from Boonville, or Fulton for that matter, up to here and then back to St. Louis."

"St. Louis?" Marcus asked. "Why would Judy drive from here to St. Louis? If he had to go to St. Louis, I would think he'd go there first after seeing you, and then come here on his way back to Iowa."

"What do you mean, back to Iowa?"

"Back to Iowa, where he lives, Ellis," said Marcus.

"I thought that's what you said earlier, but I figured I misunderstood. I don't think he's ever lived in Iowa, has he? He told me he lived in St. Louis, but I got to admit, I've never been to his house, so I'm not so sure." Ellis was a tiny bit concerned by the confusion about where his father even lived.

"I don't know Ellis, there's always been something a little strange about Judy." Marcus confessed. "Me and Mama, we've never seen his house neither."

"Weird," Ellis responded to Marcus' revelation. "Man, I wish I knew more about dad. And mom too, for that matter."

"Ellis," the thoughts running through Marcus' mind were daunting. "How much do you really want to know?"

"Everything I could learn," he said, throwing a concerned, eyebrow furrowing look toward Marcus. "Is there more you're not telling me? Dad hasn't been in like, prison or nothing has he?"

"No, not exactly," Marcus realized he had already let too much slip. Essentially, the cat was out of the bag. "Can you handle a little bit of unpleasant news? I mean, Judy is a great guy, but he does have a little bit of a shady past."

"I can handle a little bit of shady, Marcus." Now Ellis had to know the truth about his father. "I mean, look what I was raised by. Dad can't possibly be worse, can he?"

"No, he can't," Marcus said. "Give me a minute."

Marcus went into Margaret's closet, removed the stack of comforters and pulled out the green footlocker. He hadn't touched it in four years, had last opened it when he and Cassie had read his father's and grandfather's notes. It had been four years and Marcus had grown quite a bit. The footlocker did not feel nearly as heavy as it had been in 1963. He had only planned to open it and dig out the newspaper clippings concerning Judy. He was still considering whether to show Ellis the copies of the clippings he had acquired of his mother Paula's murder and the subsequent trial. Marcus' instinct was to withhold that information for now. He did not know what Judy might already have told Ellis about his mother, didn't know what Ollie might have told him. But evidently, from what Ellis had disclosed so far, he had no idea that his birth mother had been murdered. Marcus was afraid to risk telling Ellis too much, or anything for that matter about his mother, and in the back of his mind feared Judy's reaction when he found out that Marcus had been the one to spill the beans. Ultimately, he decided that since he had already committed to revealing what he knew about Judy, things couldn't end up too much worse if he let him know the truth about Paula. Marcus picked up the footlocker and carried it into the living room. Ellis looked inquisitively at the green box as Marcus awkwardly entered the room.

Setting it down carefully in front of the couch, not wanting to scratch Margaret's immaculately polished wood floor, Marcus raised the lid. Reaching inside he pulled out the clippings that his own father, Elijah, had preserved. Most pertained to Judy's youthful and unsavory history spanning both sides of the Mississippi River. Taking nearly twenty minutes to read and digest the information, Ellis raised his head and looked at Marcus. "It looks like my real dad was an ass too, doesn't it Marcus?"

"Oh, I don't know, he was young," offered Marcus, trying to sound apologetic for Judy's wild and irresponsible youth. "I guess sometimes young people do some crazy things, right? I mean, times were different back then, you know?"

"Yeah, well maybe I came by some of my stupidity naturally then, huh?" Ellis figured perhaps some of the behavioral tendencies he'd been treated for in his psychotherapy had come about naturally, through his genetic make-up. Maybe Ollie hadn't been solely to blame, maybe the onset of his psychological problems had not been brought on totally by environmental circumstances after all.

"Nah, probably not, Ellis. I mean, yeah, Judy was a little bit of a troublemaker when he was young but look at how he ended up. He's a successful businessman and look how much attention he pays to you." Marcus felt a might strange trying to encourage Ellis. After all, he wasn't yet sixteen and Ellis was nineteen or twenty years old, Marcus didn't even know for sure. "He's told Mama and me a bunch of times that he was gonna do all he could to help you grow up right. He's got big plans for you, Ellis."

"Yep, you're right, Marcus. He does try awful hard to help me. And he definitely did get his life straightened out. Gee, just look at that Vette that he drives. You don't get something like that by accident, do you?"

"For sure, for sure," Marcus said with a smile.

"Okay Marcus, what else you got? Anything in that footlocker about my mom?" Ellis was anxious to know if Marcus had any information on her whereabouts, where she might have gone. "I'm gonna find her someday, I want her to know that I made it through, that I'm alive and kicking!"

The choice of Ellis' last few words hit Marcus right square in the gut. How was he supposed tq tell Ellis the truth about Paula Sue Schaeffer?

Taking a deep breath, Marcus began, "You already know your real mother's name is Paula Sue Schaeffer."

"Yeah, yeah, I know her name, Marcus," Ellis said, repeating what he already was certain of. "And

166

I know that after I was born, she wasn't ready for a kid, and she put me up for adoption. And then she disappeared, vanished. Do you know where she ended up, Marcus?"

"Yes, Ellis, I do. She is…"

"Where, Marcus, where? I gotta find her. Man, I gotta meet her!"

"No, Ellis, I'm sorry, but it's not that easy." Marcus didn't know how to break it to Ellis, so he decided to be blunt. "Ellis, your mother is dead. Paula Sue Schaeffer died about a year after you were born."

"What? Oh man, how Marcus? What happened to her?"

"She got murdered, Ellis," Marcus felt terrible. He couldn't imagine what Ellis had to be feeling right now. "I'm really sorry to have to tell you like this."

Ellis' eyes immediately dampened. "I never got to see her, never even met my mom, Marcus."

Marcus placed a hand on Ellis' shoulder. "I know, I'm really sorry, Ellis."

"I guess you got newspaper clippings on what happened to her too, right Marcus?"

"Yeah. Actually, I've got Xerox copies from the library. I got the stories off of microfiche at the school library." Marcus thought he'd better offer them to Ellis. "Do you want to read them, Ellis? You're welcome to."

"Can I?" He asked.

Marcus handed him the newspaper stories concerning her death, the arrest of the drifter Winslow, his trial and execution.

167

After reading everything that Marcus could provide, Ellis said, "A least that bastard got what was coming to him. Now I know how the families of those two girls that Ollie killed must feel. I'll bet they will be celebrating when Ollie is finally dead, too."

Ellis took a couple of deep breaths, and asked Marcus a favor, "Man, I'm spent, and my mouth is really dry. Marcus, can you spare another Pepsi or a glass of water?"

"Sure, there's more Pepsi in the fridge, I'll be right back." Marcus got up from the floor and went to the kitchen to retrieve two more sodas. While he was gone, Ellis glimpsed curiously into the footlocker, wondering if Marcus had any other information that he still planned to share.

Marcus came back into the living room and handed Ellis his drink, "Here you go, Ellis."

"Thanks," Ellis took a deep swallow, and emitted a small belch. "Sorry about that Marcus. My mom gets on me when I don't excuse myself." He laughed lightly at what he'd just said. "After learning all this about my real mom, it seems kind of funny to call Alicia my mom."

Ellis took another sip, then asked Marcus, "Anything else for me, Marcus? Any more revelations that I should be aware of?"

"No, I think that's about it." Marcus said. "I was kind of worried about if I should tell you what I did know. Judy will probably be mad as a hornet when he finds out what I just told you."

"Don't worry, Marcus. If you don't tell him, I won't neither. It's our secret. I'll just wait him out.

I'm sure one of these days he'll tell me about everything, and if he don't, oh well. Thanks to you, at least I know. This means a lot to me, Marcus, thank you."

"You're welcome, Ellis, I guess I'm glad I could help you out."

"I'm curious though, Marcus. What's that old binder I saw in there? Is that all your old history, family tree or something, on your side of the family?"

Not sure how to respond, cautious about what to say, Marcus opted for honesty. "You want the truth, Ellis? If I tell you the truth, will it bother you?"

"Why would it bother me? We've been honest with each other since I got here." Ellis was curious why Marcus would ask such a question. "No, unless it's even worse news about my mom or dad, no. Whatever's in there ain't gonna bother me."

"What's in there Ellis, there was a time you'd have killed for it," Marcus told him, honestly.

"What's that supposed to mean, Marcus?"

Marcus just sat looking at Ellis. A minute or two passed before Ellis exclaimed, "Oh my God, Marcus, is that your inheritance? Holy crap, I don't think I ever really thought that story was even true."

"Well, don't get too excited, Ellis. Maybe it is and maybe it ain't, I don't even know." Marcus actually did not know for sure. The binder had never been opened.

"Are you kidding?" Ellis asked. "You mean to tell me you never have looked in there to see? Why not?"

"Because there's a letter that comes with it that says it can't be opened until I'm eighteen, and it has to be opened in front of a certified lawyer, that's why." Marcus didn't think it would be that hard for Ellis to understand.

"I can't believe you haven't looked inside! Why not?" Ellis could not see why Marcus wouldn't at least want to take a peek at what the binder contained.

"Because I can't open it Ellis, it's locked."

"Well, who has the key then? Somebody has to have it. Is it that lawyer you're talking about?"

"No, Ellis, nobody has the key," Marcus and Ellis perhaps had buried the hatchet to an extent, but Marcus most definitely did not feel secure enough with Ellis to admit that he possessed the key to the binder. "The lawyer has a sealed envelope that has the key in it. The envelope can't be opened until I'm eighteen and in front of the lawyer. Then I can open the envelope and access the key, and then I can open the binder and see what's in it."

"Oh, okay, I get the picture now," said Ellis. "Wow, Marcus, I can't wait until you turn eighteen. How long is that, two more years? That is so neat. Man, I can't wait."

"Yeah, me too. I've been waiting for a long time to find out just what is in it." Marcus had not really been thinking about it too much. His eighteenth birthday was still a long way off, and it wasn't worth getting wound up over just yet.

"Hey Marcus. I have an idea if you're interested."

"What's that, Ellis?" Marcus asked, wondering what Ellis was thinking.

"Marcus, I've only been trained by an expert in one trade, and I'm pretty darned good at it." Ellis gave Marcus a wink.

Confused at what Ellis was getting at, Marcus asked, "What Ellis? Are you telling me you're a trained carpenter, a dentist? I'm no good at charades, what are you talking about?"

"Ollie was a locksmith, Marcus. He taught me, he had always planned on me joining the business. Listen, I've got picks and stuff out in my car." Now Marcus saw what Ellis had been alluding to.

"Are you saying you can open that lock without having the key, and we can look inside?

"Exactly, Marcus! You can see just what your inheritance is. You don't have to take it out, just get a look so you'll know what you got coming in a couple of years." The idea was very tempting. "I know just what you're wondering about too, Marcus. Yes, I can lock it back and no one will ever know it had been opened."

"Oh man, I don't know Ellis. That would be wrong, so wrong."

"I'll tell you what, Marcus. I don't even want to know what's in there. I owe it to you for what I put you through." Ellis sounded sincere, but Marcus was so hesitant to let him open the binder. "Marcus, I'll unlock it for you and then I'll just go outside while you look. When you think you've seen enough, close it up, call me and I'll lock it back for you, okay?"

"Let me think a minute," Marcus said.

"I'll go to the car and get my tools, give you time to decide, alright?" Ellis stood and walked toward the door. "If you don't want to, that's fine, no problem. But if you do, we'll be ready." Ellis opened the door and headed toward his car, leaving Marcus to think.

Five minutes later, Ellis tapped on the door and opened it. As he re-entered the living room he said, "Well?"

"Okay, but we have to hurry," was Marcus' reply.

"What's the hurry, Marcus?" Ellis asked.

"Cassie and her family are probably back from lunch. They go to LaGrange for lunch after church every Sunday. I need to get over to her house. Even when I don't go with them, I still go see her in the afternoon, you know, after they get back."

"Okay, no problem, my friend." Ellis then suggested, "Tell you what, Marcus. After we're all done, I'll give you a ride to her house. I need to go to my boss' house when I leave here, it won't be out of the way or nothing."

"That's great, Ellis, thanks."

"S'okay," said Ellis as he worked to pick the lock. Ten seconds later he said, "There you go, Marcus. I'll step outside while you check it out. Call me when you're ready to lock it back up, okay?"

Marcus waited until Ellis was safely outside and the door was closed, then slowly raised the flap on the binder. His first observation was that there was no cash inside, only papers. He pulled the contents out and the first item he noticed was a handwritten note that Marcus confidently recognized as being in his grandfather's penmanship.

To My Fortunate Descendent,

In 1909, when I was but six years of age, my father David had decided to find out, once and for all, if our family tree did indeed reach up to the noted author, Samuel Langhorne Clemens, who you will know better as Mark Twain. My father traveled east, where he was unable to secure an audience with Mr. Clemens at his Connecticut mansion. However, he was successful in making an appointment with Mr. Clemens' personal attorney, Malcolm J. Witherspoon. Speculation had been round that Samuel's brother, Orion had sired an illegitimate son, who possibly could have been my father, David. Orion had passed some twelve years prior; the truth had gone to the grave with him. My father therefore had traveled, planning to meet with Samuel, to ascertain the facts of the matter. Mr. Witherspoon denied in no uncertain terms, that his client's brother had produced any out of wedlock children. But, in the interest of fairness and to be absolutely certain, as my father waited, Witherspoon took a carriage to the nearby Clemens residence, to received absolute verification. He returned, holding steadfast to the denial. Strangely though, out of pity for my father, or perhaps just having been in the Christmas spirit, Mr. Clemens had ordered his lawyer, Mr. Witherspoon, to produce paperwork (of which you are now obviously in possession), dated December 14, 1909, in which 100 shares of the Detmeyer Drydock and Machine Company of St. Louis would be willed to the last surviving male descendent of the David Clemens bloodline. This offer was very generous of Mr. Clemens, and perhaps was an underhanded admission of the possibility of a familial connection. There is absolutely no way of predicting how many generations will pass before this inheritance is received. If our family is fruitful, the opening of this binder may never occur. Whoever my fortunate descendent shall end up reading this letter, you will also find in this binder a map, hand drawn by myself, of a treasure that I had discovered, along with my great friend, Jeremiah Paige in the year 1918. If you follow the directions precisely as drawn, you are sure to be richly rewarded.

    Sincerely,

    John Clemens

Marcus was flabbergasted by the discovery of the note and the accompanying papers. The speculation had proven true, there actually was an inheritance, and he truly was going to be the beneficiary. Now Marcus was faced with a decision. Should he trust Ellis with the truth of what was in the binder? He already knew of the binder's existence and what was supposed to be in it, so Marcus could hardly pretend it contained nothing of importance. The answer Marcus settled on was to split the difference. He was going to return the stocks and the legal papers prepared by the Esquire Witherspoon almost sixty years ago to the binder, but he kept out the letter and map that his grandfather had prepared. For the time being he slipped them behind Margaret's Zenith console radio, thinking they would be safe there until he returned from Cassie's later in the evening. This way, even if Ellis did prove to be untrustworthy (which Marcus had to admit was a distinct possibility), and somehow managed to come back to the apartment and steal the footlocker (he was, Marcus now knew, a skilled locksmith), he would still maintain possession of the treasure map, which he suspected might be the most valuable of the binder's contents.

Marcus repacked and relocked the footlocker. He went to the front door and called out to Ellis, who was leaned against the front fender of his sedan, nonchalantly drawing down on his cigarette. "Hey, Ellis, all done in here." Ellis discarded the smoke and jogged back to the apartment, dying to know what Marcus had found.

Ellis came in, again carefully wiping his feet before retaking his seat on the couch. As he sat, Marcus was picking up the footlocker.

"Be right back Ellis, got to put this thing away," Marcus said as he carried the footlocker back to Margaret's bedroom.

Marcus returned, collapsing back onto the easy chair.

"Well?" Ellis asked excitedly, "Is it a fortune like Ollie suspected?"

"Nope. Hardly. You saw how narrow the document binder is. Wasn't anything there but paper," Marcus laughed out loud. "No jewels, no diamonds, not even any money."

"Seriously?" Ellis asked. He also couldn't help but to laugh. "Man, Ollie would have bet his house that you were going to inherit a fortune in gold or something." Ellis sat shaking his head for bit, then asked, "So what was in there? Had to be something valuable, right?"

"Mostly just paper, Ellis. There were some legal papers from Mark Twain's lawyer, and some stocks that I guess I will inherit."

"Wow, so you really are related to Mark Twain. Marcus, that's pretty awesome, even if you don't get a big inheritance. And hey, if you're lucky, those stocks might be worth a ton now, you know? It's possible."

"No, Ellis. The paperwork specifically says that none of my family is related to Samuel Clemens, and that nobody in my family can ever file any legal claims against his estate. And it just says that the stocks mentioned in there will go to the last surviving member of the David Clemens bloodline. Yeah, I hope they're worth a lot, but I'll have to just wait and see, I guess"

"That's still pretty cool that you're getting something, even if it might not a big deal. Congratulations, Marcus." Ellis seemed genuinely happy for Marcus. "Hey, are you about ready to go? I'll drop you off at your girl's place before I go to Monticello."

"Sure, Ellis. And thanks," Marcus said.

"No problem. Thank you for letting me spend some time with you, had good time and I learned a lot."

As they walked to Ellis' car, Marcus got an uneasy feeling when he spotted the scraggly dog sniffing around the nearby the trash dumpster. The dog seemed to be minding its own business, but

Marcus knew the four-legged scavenger was watching them as they strode toward the sedan. The animal appeared to go unnoticed by Ellis, but if he'd seen it, Marcus was sure that he would have said something. A few summers may have now come and gone, but Marcus had seen that Ellis still carried a scar. There was no way Ellis could possibly have forgotten Opa.

* * * *

Twenty-five minutes later, Ellis was pulling into the driveway of the house he used to call home. His father, Ollie, had been an employee of Max Schofield, and Max was always known to take care of his people. In return for Ollie leaving any word about Max and his drug business out of the case against him, Max had paid above market value to purchase the Compton homestead. That windfall had allowed Ollie the necessary cash to hire a pair of expensive big city lawyers to fight his case and, he had hoped, save him from the death penalty. Unfortunately for Ollie, their expertise had not been enough to convince the judge to be lenient and only pronounce the lesser punishment they had sought, a life sentence. It would have to be conceded that Oliver Compton had been a man of his word, as he had left Max unmentioned. He had maintained during the trial that the marijuana found in his workshop was all his, something that he cultivated in his spare time and for his personal use. Under the circumstances, Ollie had attempted to do all he could to care for his family. Among other conditions of Ollie's silence was the solemn promise from Max that he would continue to provide lucrative employment for Alicia and Ellis for as long as they wanted.

Ellis approached the front door, but before he could even raise a hand to knock it was opened wide and Max, with a can of beer in his hand, motioned for him to come in. "Heard you coming up the drive," Max said. Driving on the gravel driveway created a distinctive sound, and when a person grew accustomed to that sound, it could be picked up instantly.

"So, what brings you all the way up here on a Sunday, Ellis?" Max casually asked, with a touch of earnest curiosity.

"Well, two things actually, Max," he answered.

"Okay then, let's start with number one. You're not here to ask for a raise already, are you?" Max was an authoritative figure, and his words carried weight. "You do a good job with the parts delivery, but you got to put in a couple of satisfactory weeks with your new duties before we talk about the next step in pay. And it'll be there, okay?"

"Oh yeah, of course Max. I'm not concerned about money, I'm plenty happy with my pay."

"Good, Ellis, glad to hear that," Max said.

"Max, what I'm kind of worried about is what I'm going to be doing. I mean, I was in jail for two years and I just got off probation. I don't want to have to go back."

"Relax Ellis. Your pop worked for me for what, nine or ten years? Never had a problem, never got caught holding." Max had been quite satisfied with Ollie's performance in transporting marijuana, there had never been an issue in that regard. "Your dad ran into his trouble because he didn't know how to develop a sound plan, and the weak plan he did develop, well, he didn't know how to execute it properly. That, and he couldn't control his urges, especially that stupid thing he had for young redheaded girls. The girls were his downfall, Ellis. And then he dragged you down with him. Trust me, Ellis, you are better off without him. You'll be under my wing now; I'll teach you right. And you, my friend, will end up a rich man, wait and see."

"Gee, I hope you're right, Max," said Ellis.

"Oh, I am Ellis, I am. So, what was the second thing you said brought you up here?"

"I went to see my cousin, Marcus Clemens," Ellis told him.

"Oh brother, I bet that went swimmingly, didn't it?" Max asked in a markedly sarcastic tone.

"Well, I went first a few days ago and tried to talk to him and his girlfriend," Ellis explained. "And yeah, I got rebuked, I guess is the word for the response I got from them."

"Not surprising is it, Ellis?" Max could certainly have predicted the reception that could have been expected. "Same thing again today, I would suspect, right?"

"No, last time he was with his girlfriend. I made sure to talk to him alone today, and that worked out a lot better. We spent about three hours together. We really had a good and meaningful conversation."

"How so?"

"Marcus told me a lot of great information about my real mother and father. I didn't know anything at all about my mother. And I really didn't know very much about my father, even though he's been visiting regularly the past couple of years. He's just never really said much about himself to me, I guess." Ellis had no idea if Max had any knowledge of his birth parents. Alicia had been his bookkeeper for years, and Ollie had told Ellis about the romance she'd had with Max that had caused their divorce. So, Ellis thought there was at least a likelihood that she'd had conversations with Max about the facts surrounding Ellis' adoption. Assuming that had been a possibility, it would also follow that she might have told him about Ellis' birth parents, as well. After learning of the divorce, Ellis couldn't understand how Ollie had continued working for Max while being fully aware of their relationship. But then again, he never knew Ollie and Alicia to act very romantic with one another during their marriage. Maybe their whole relationship had been a loveless sham.

"What kind of things did he tell you about your real parents, Ellis, and how or why would Marcus Clemens have any information about your family?" Max wasn't exactly connecting dots here. "I wouldn't have thought he'd known you from Adam before Ollie's scheme went haywire."

"I don't know, Max. He's got a whole green box, you know, like the army guys keep stuff in. It's full of all kinds of stuff." Ellis innocently told a suddenly very interested Max Schofield.

"Okay, Ellis, so what do you mean stuff, exactly?" Max asked.

"I don't know, like newspaper clippings and documents and stuff, I guess," Ellis sensed the level of interest Max was showing and decided perhaps he needed to reel back a little on what he was divulging.

"I was just having a thought, Ellis," Max said, the wheels turning in his head. "Your dad, Ollie, he might have actually been on to something. By any chance, is your real father's last name Allensworth?"

"Yeah, why Max?" Ellis wondered aloud.

"By God, you might just be in line to get that Mark Twain inheritance that Ollie used to ramble about, after all. I always thought he was nuts, but he might have been right all along." Max took a deep swig of beer, draining the can.

"Tell you what, Ellis, I got some thinking to do." Reaching down into the cooler by his feet, Max pulled out another Budweiser and smiled at Ellis. "I think you're gonna work out fine kid. Make sure you show up on time in St. Louie tomorrow to pick up your company car."

Max got up to show Ellis the way out. As he opened the door for him, he said, "Ellis, when you get home tonight, tell your ma that Max said to open the books and raise your starting pay to five bucks an hour. Good night, kid."

James E. Anderson

Deep Secrets

Cassie opened the front door and greeted Marcus with her normal peck to his right cheek. Marcus drew her into a brief hug, and they entered the parlor where Jack and Debbie had been deep into a game of *Parcheesi* with Cassie and her young brother Charlie. With Marcus occupying a side chair, Cassie retook her seat and the game continued.

"I've never played this game, Twigs. You've got to teach it to me someday," Marcus said as he looked toward Cassie. She gave Marcus a sideways smirk of a smile. He actually thought the pixie cut was cute on Cassie, it seemed to bring out her freckles more, but she knew that he couldn't wait until it grew back to its normal length.

"Twigs?" Jack asked, slightly amused at the name Marcus had directed toward his daughter.

"It's her new haircut, Jack," Debbie clarified for him. "It's the same style as that model Twiggy wears. When we left the beauty parlor yesterday, Marcus informed Cassie that Twigs was her new nickname until she was able to wear a ponytail again."

"Oh, I see," Jack acknowledged that the nickname seemed appropriate enough. He, personally, didn't care for the cut and therefore announced that he too would be using the new moniker for Cassie, at least for the time being.

After the completion of the game (which of course, she had won), Cassie excused herself from the game table and she and Marcus headed outside to their familiar perch on the front yard wooden swing. On the way out, Cassie had snagged a pair of used bath towels to dry the swing of leftover moisture from the morning's drizzle. Upon arrival, Cassie had made quick work of wiping down its smooth varnished surface. Satisfied with her handiwork, she and Marcus took their seats just as the sun began to peek through the dissipating cloud cover. Having maintained an uneasy silence as they had walked across the front yard, Cassie now drew a deep breath and slowly exhaled as she turned to face Marcus.

"Exactly how do you explain this, Marcus?" Cassie asked, not without an intonation of her pent-up anger. "I saw who dropped you off. What's that all about? Where did *he* come from? Please, can you give me some kind of a reason that you could be in a car with him?"

Marcus had assumed that Cassie would have been unaware that Ellis had brought him to her house. He had no idea that she had happened a glance out the parlor window just as Ellis had parked to let Marcus out in front of her house. He would have preferred that the subject of Ellis' visit would have been a conversation that he could have initiated, not one that Cassie would begin by forcing him onto the defensive.

"It's hard to explain Cassie. Things just kind of happened." Marcus knew better than to use the new nickname when addressing his girlfriend when she was in this type of mood.

"Where did he even come from, Marcus? Did he just pick you up on your way here?" Cassie was at a loss. "How could you get in his car? How could you trust him?"

"He showed up at my apartment this morning, right after Mama had left for work," Marcus began. "There was a knock at the door, I answered, and there he was."

"And what did you do, Marcus?" Cassie thought that he would have told Ellis in no uncertain terms to hit the bricks. "You didn't tell him to get lost?"

"I started to, but I couldn't do it." Marcus tried to explain to her, make her see what he had been faced with. "He was so sincere, he tried to tell me again what he had said out here on the sidewalk after school the other day. Cassie, it was hurting him to talk to me."

"Marcus, if it hadn't been for Opa, he would have killed us in the mausoleum!" Cassie was incredulous. "And then he helped his dad kidnap me! Who knows what might have happened to me the next day if you and Deputy Daniels wouldn't have showed up that night."

"I know, Cassie, and you're one hundred per cent right about all that. But after talking to him, hearing everything he had to say, I feel pretty confident that he has changed, that he told me the truth about that he had been brainwashed and didn't understand what he was doing."

On the one hand, it felt wrong to be trying to defend Ellis from the evil he had perpetrated, but on the other hand, he was sympathetic to the upbringing that Ellis had endured. He tried to relate to her the stories Ellis had shared concerning Oliver Compton, how he was raised, the learning of his adoption. Marcus tried to share with Cassie the empathy he felt toward Ellis, who had grown practically into manhood before learning about his real father and mother. He tried to impress upon Cassie the devastating emotions that Ellis had to have suffered, first to learn that he had a different birth mother from the one he had grown up with, and then to be told that she had abandoned him after birth, putting him up for adoption.

Cassie was not particularly receptive to the forgiving attitude Marcus was presenting to her on behalf of Ellis.

"Don't you dare put him before me, Marcus Clemens."

"I would never do that, Cassie, never. Not in a million years." Marcus desperately wanted Cassie to know that she was his everything in life. Though he had felt it for a long, long while, Marcus had never been able to bring himself to admit to Cassie what was truly in his heart. "I love you, Cassie. And I always have. Aside from God himself, I will never put anyone before or above you."

His words brought moisture to her eyes and comfort to her heart, but even as she received a reassuring hug from Marcus, they still did not eliminate the feelings of fear and foreboding associated with Ellis Compton.

"I believe you Marcus and thank you for saying that. But I still can't trust him" she said. "I hope you understand."

"I do, but I still want you to know more about Ellis. Maybe the more I tell you, the more you can see why I have relaxed my guard toward him." Marcus went on to explain opening the footlocker and the sharing with Ellis of all of the information that it included. He told Cassie about Ellis reading the newspaper clippings about Judy and Paula Sue Schaeffer. Marcus told Cassie how he had nearly choked up when Ellis had read the truth about his real mother, and the fact that until today he'd believed she had abandoned him after birth. Cassie seemed to have begun to relent a bit when Marcus dropped the biggest bombshell.

"Cassie, I opened the document binder."

"What? Are you serious Marcus? You took the key from the envelope?" Cassie was utterly surprised by this revelation.

"No. The key is still in the envelope. Everything is still intact. It can still be taken to a lawyer, and everything done properly, by the book."

"Then how did you open it?" Cassie naturally wanted to know.

"Ellis. His dad was a locksmith and taught him the trade. He picked the lock for me." Marcus explained. "But don't worry, no one will know. It's all locked back up and I put everything back in Mama's closet."

"Marcus, why would you let him do that? Now he knows what was in the binder, now he knows about your inheritance!" Cassie only needed a second's thought before asking, "Was there an inheritance? What was in it, Marcus?"

"Well, first of all, Ellis picked the lock on the binder, but he went outside while I opened it and looked inside."

"And?" Now Cassie's curiosity had come to the forefront of her attention.

"What was inside was a document giving me one hundred shares of a boat company in St. Louis. Detmeyer Drydock and Machine Company was the name. Maybe, if we're lucky it will be worth something." Marcus was hopeful, but not overly ecstatic.

"I wonder how old those stocks are? They could be worth a lot by now, right?" Cassie asked quizzically.

"I don't know. The letter in there says they were given by Mark Twain in 1909, so, I don't know, maybe."

"Wait, Marcus, does Ellis know, did he see the stocks?" Cassie's female intuition kicked in and detected cause for concern.

"Well, yes and no. He didn't see what was in it. I already had the footlocker packed and locked when he came back inside." Before Marcus could continue, Cassie had stepped back in.

"Okay, he didn't see in the binder, so that's the no part. What's the yes?"

"He did ask what was in it, and I told him some papers and documents," Marcus related. "When he asked what kind of documents, I guess I kind of admitted there were some stocks."

"Oh, Marcus, you shouldn't have told him that. What if he comes back and steals the footlocker?" Cassie clearly did not trust Ellis at all.

"I don't think so Cassie. He didn't even seem that interested." Marcus thought back to this morning a little more carefully. "He was happy for me; he didn't even ask what kind of stocks they were. I think he said he hoped they were worth something after this long."

"Oh my gosh, Marcus!" Cassie suddenly exclaimed.

"What?" Marcus said, surprised at Cassie's outburst.

"Marcus, Friday, after the movie, remember Opa was there?"

"Yeah, so what?"

"Marcus, Opa said it's starting again. Don't you remember?" She could distinctly hear Opa's voice, or more accurately, remember feeling it in her mind. 'Evil is afoot. Be careful who you trust.' The thought caused her to shudder. She repeated Opa's words to Marcus.

"And you think he's referring to Ellis?" He asked.

"Well, it can't be Ollie, he's on death row now, isn't he?" Cassie asked with a touch of sarcasm.

"Who else could it be? They were the only ones involved. Who else knows about the inheritance?"

"Honestly, Cassie?" Marcus was surprised that Cassie could so drastically limit her list of possible suspects. "Mitch Daniels and half the County Sheriff's Department, Cousin Judy, and just about anybody that happened to go into the courtroom during Ollie Compton's trial, probably know something about it, I'm sure. Not to mention people that Ellis or Ollie might have talked to in jail or wherever. There are probably hundreds of people in this state that know that I might have an inheritance coming from the great Mark Twain."

"Wow," Cassie had to admit, "maybe I'm being a little shortsighted about everybody that could know something about it, but for my money, I'd bet the only person to worry about is Ellis."

"You could be right Twigs, but I hedged my bet on that, too."

Marcus proceeded to tell Cassie about the more important news. He gave her a synopsis of the letter his grandfather had surreptitiously inserted into the document binder. It had been placed there sometime well after it had been put under lock and the key had been put inside of the still securely sealed envelope. And more importantly, he gave a brief description of the treasure map that his grandfather had carefully drawn in 1918.

"When I had replaced everything back into the footlocker and closed the combination lock, I kept the letter and map out for safe keeping." Marcus described the concern that he too had felt regarding

Ellis. "I probably wouldn't have even thought of it until Ellis had offered to open the lock on the document binder."

"Right, I see," said Cassie. "When you found out he was a locksmith, you realized he could break into your apartment, and the footlocker, and the document binder and then steal it all."

"That's right, Cassie." Marcus admitted. "My bet is that whatever treasure my grandfather and Jeremiah Paige found will be worth more than the stocks. Call it a hunch, but that's what I think."

"Whoa, whoa, whoa, Marcus. Your grandfather and Jeremiah Paige found this treasure?" Cassie was amazed that Marcus had skimmed right past the information he had just given to her. "Are you talking about the Jeremiah Paige that works at the dump? You mean the guy that got shot last week? You said you knew him, Marcus. How do you know him?"

"Well, Denny and I met him on our way to go fishing back in that summer of 1963." Marcus told Cassie some things that she had missed that summer. "Remember, when your parents were worried about there was a killer on the loose early that summer and they made you stay in the house all the time?"

Cassie nodded in the affirmative. Aside from nearly being killed in the mausoleum and having been kidnapped by the Comptons, her being held captive in her own home was one of the worst things she had ever experienced. She had hated feeling like a prisoner, being housebound during that period. Of course, she understood her parents' concern, but she and Marcus had only recently become girlfriend and boyfriend. As any normal kid would, she had longed to be able to get out and do things together with Marcus.

"Well, during that time, me and Denny would go to Franklin's, or just pass by going fishing or something, and this old guy would be sitting on that wooden bench in front of the store. He always brought a lunch sack and a thermos and was there every day."

"And Marcus, the kind young gentleman that you are, decided to stop and talk to him."

"Exactly. Almost every day that summer. Me and Denny found out his name and he told us that he had just retired. When I found out he used to work over at the rock quarry, I told him about my dad."

Marcus gave Cassie a short summary of what Jeremiah had said on that particular day. He'd thought of it many a time, often when visiting his parents' graves. His memory might even have captured it word for word.

"*Elijah Clemens, I remember him very well. He was a good'un, that man he was. I worked just as a general laborer out there. Your daddy, he drove all them big ol' machines, them graders, and back hoes, them big ol' things that done the diggin' and stuff. And course the bulldozers. Thas what kilt him right there. He was runnin' a tight track right there, edge of the pit. Them dozers, they's wide and heavy you know what I'm saying. Probably shouldn'ta been there doing that, but I bets they made him to do it, I think he probably knowed better, but what can you say. Damned thing slipped in the mud I reckon, went tumblin' down that pit wall. Good thing his daddy was long gone, ita been*"

192

real hard for him to handle that. I'd knowed him too. Good man he was too, just like your daddy. Your daddy was always good to me. You come from good stock young Marcus, yes you do boy. You make sure you keep up your line, just like them before you. Good people treat people good. You remember that son, you remember that."

"Well, gosh Marcus, no wonder you were worried about him when he got shot." Cassie was impressed that Jeremiah had known Elijah Clemens and taken the time to talk to Marcus the way he had, consoling him, and speaking kindly of his father.

"Well sure I was Cassie; he was my dad's friend and all." Marcus replied.

"Marcus, didn't you just say Jeremiah was with Opa when they found this treasure that your map is about?" Cassie had an epiphany and couldn't believe Marcus had not yet mentioned what she had realized.

"Yeah," Marcus was stuck in the past, still thinking about the words Jeremiah had spoken four years prior.

"Marcus, Jeremiah knows what the treasure is and exactly where it is located. We have to go see him and learn the answers."

"Cassie, he knew who I was when I first met him that summer. If he wanted me to know, he would have told me. There probably isn't any real treasure, probably nothing to it, or I'm sure he'd have mentioned it, right?"

"I don't know, but I think we should go see him." Cassie insisted.

"Well, the dump is closed today, and I have to start work tomorrow afternoon. I guess we could go see him Tuesday after school then."

"Sounds perfect, Marcus." Cassie was almost giddy with excitement, her mind was totally off of the subject of Ellis Compton, at least for the time being.

* * * *

Jude Allensworth sat patiently, elbows propped on the narrow desktop, his chin resting on his thumbs and interlaced fingers. A two-foot-tall, padded partition stood to both his left and right. They were designed to allow for some semblance of privacy as the guest spoke via telephone receiver with the inmate seated on the opposite side of the double pane bulletproof glass. Even though only the speech of the person on the guest side of the glass could reasonably have been expected to be heard by a neighboring visitor, the partitions did provide for an imaginary barrier and thusly a perceived sense of security. Judy was fully aware that much of what was perceived as 'high security' in this maximum-security facility was nothing much more than precisely that – a perception. The illusion was a necessity though, when it was recognized that that the Missouri State Penitentiary was located not more than a stone's throw from the State Capital's Rotunda. It was less than one mile and a five-minute drive (or twenty-minute walk) that separated, in Judy's opinion the workplace of legal criminals and the residence of convicted ones. But, Judy reasoned, was it really for him to judge? He had worked both sides of the fence, lived the straight and narrow, and sloughed with the hogs in his time. And so, he waited patiently and sat in silence.

More than twenty minutes behind schedule for the two p.m. visitor's session, Oliver Compton was ultimately brought, in handcuffs, to his seat across from Judy. One cuff was removed from his left hand and fastened to a steel eyelet that was firmly embedded in the floor. This allowed him to reach the phone receiver mounted to the partition on his left. Judy's receiver was to his right, positioning them in a mirror image, directly across the glass.

"I'm surprised they brought you in cuffed in front like that, Ollie, and not behind your back." Judy commented. "After all, you are a hardened and violent convict."

"Hardly, Judy," Ollie replied. "I'm a model citizen in here."

Neither spoke for nearly a minute. Finally, Ollie asked, "So what brings you all the way from St. Louis? I know you're not just here for a social visit. We haven't spoken for God knows how many years."

"I came out yesterday to see Ellis," Judy looked at Ollie with concerned eyes. "And I'm not sure I like what I'm seeing."

"What's that supposed to mean, Jude?" Ollie instinctively went on the defensive. "I don't even know the boy anymore. Thanks to you swooping in and playing *Daddy* all of a sudden, after nearly twenty years, he ain't got nothing to do with me anymore. Since he got out, he ain't come to visit, not even once. None, nada, zip. I raised that boy, gave him everything, taught him everything he knows, and he can't so much as come tell me hello. Haven't even seen a letter in nearly two years."

"What the hell do you expect, Ollie? You ruined his life. You're a damned albatross that Ellis will wear around his neck for the rest of his life!"

"Sir," the voice came from behind, that of a guard, from a distance of eight or ten feet. "Can you hold it down, and watch your language? It's Sunday, and there are ladies here visiting today."

"Sorry officer. Give the ladies my apologies, please." Judy said in a more composed and dignified manner. Pulling a pack of Camels and Zippo from his inner sport coat pocket, Judy lit up. After two calming drags, he again lifted the receiver, returning his attention to Ollie.

"Ollie, Ellis got an early release from his house arrest and probation, did you know that?"

"How would I, Jude? He don't talk to me remember?" On Ollie's side of the glass, there apparently was no protocol relating to curbing, the volume.

"Then I suppose you don't have a clue as to what he's doing to earn a paycheck then either, do you?" Judy asked.

"Of course, I do. Just like Alicia, he's working for Max, delivering auto parts."

"You know that he's working for Max Schofield?" This revelation angered Judy. "How did you know that?"

"Look, Jude, it was part of the deal I made with Max. We're both men of our words. I don't let the cat out of the bag about his side business, he keeps Alicia and Ellis on the payroll for as long as they want. Plus, I'm sure you know he bought my house so I could afford those worthless lawyers I hired. What a waste they were."

Judy sat shaking his head. "I can't believe you are so stupid, Ollie."

"What? What are getting at, Jude?" Ollie asked, wondering just what it was that made him appear stupid to Judy.

"Ollie, when is your execution supposed to be?"

"July 11th, why? What's that got to do with anything?" Surprisingly, Ollie wasn't even worried about the lethal injection he was facing. He was just glad that the gas chamber was no longer an option in the state.

"Ollie, after you're dead and buried, do you really think that scumbag Max Schofield is gonna give a rat's ass about Alicia, or Ellis for that matter? He might keep her around awhile, just because she's been there so long. But Ellis? Running parts? He can bring a monkey in to do that, he won't need Ellis!"

"Sure, he will. He'll keep them both around, he gave me his word."

"His word? Are you kidding me? Ollie, I bet you haven't heard about that guy he had running his dope up and down Highway 61 from St. Louis, have you?"

"That Italian guy? Tony something, yeah, I used to pick up from him, out of St. Louis, yeah. What about him?"

"Dead, Ollie, dead." Judy told Ollie what he had heard. "Got whacked, right there at the dump. Bam!"

"Oh, man, I knew that guy." Ollie sat shaking his head. "I knew that guy. He was okay. Wasn't nothing wrong with Tony. I wonder why? Who done it? Do they know?"

"Not yet. But you see what I'm getting at, Ollie?" Judy was trying to appeal to Ollie's rationale. "Don't you see the road that you've got Ellis heading down? Max is nothing but a dirtbag, he don't give a crap about anybody but himself and his bottom line. If he ends up using Ellis to run drugs or whatever and screwing up that boy's life, the blame's all gonna hang on you. I'll spit on your grave every opportunity I get, buddy. You better believe."

"Max wouldn't do that. He's got too much respect for Alicia to get Ellis involved in any of that crap. You'll see, mark my word." Ollie then hit Judy straight out of left field. "Just why are you getting so high and mighty anyway, Jude? I don't know who you think you are coming out here and giving me all this grief. Maybe you don't remember, or maybe you never even realized what all I done for you."

"What are you talking about, Ollie? Remember what? I don't remember anything you ever did for me!" Before he could get reprimanded again by the guard, Judy had lowered his irritated voice a few decibels.

"Twenty years ago, Jude, twenty years ago. Your girlfriend Paula. Don't you remember how I covered for you, how I testified against that drifter and got him convicted for killing her."

"Yeah, of course I remember your testimony. But are you crazy or something, Ollie! What's wrong with you? What do you mean you covered for *me*?" Judy couldn't believe Ollie was making such a wild accusation.

"You killed her, Jude. Have you forgotten? It's only been twenty years; how could you forget something like that?"

"What?" Judy was suddenly furious and finding it difficult to control himself. Oh, if he could only wrap his hands around Ollie's throat right now. Judy's jaw tightened as he gritted his teeth. "I did not kill Paula Sue. I loved that woman with all my heart. How could you possibly accuse me of something like that?"

"Because, Jude, I witnessed it." Ollie said matter-of-factly. "I guess you have completely wiped that horrible memory from your mind, haven't you?"

"You're crazy!"

"Am I? I saw the whole thing." Ollie continued nonchalantly. "She wouldn't agree to marry you and you refused to give up your son. You told her to give the baby to you to raise, and of course she said no. So, you hit her. First with an open palm, but the second time was a punch. When she fell to the ground, you pounced on her like a starving mountain lion on a gopher..."

"Shut up Ollie, shut up or so help me..."

"So help you what, Jude? So help you what?" Ollie asked mockingly. "What do you think you're gonna do, break that glass and come beat me up like when we were teenagers? The glass is bulletproof,

199

Jude. You can't touch me. I may be in prison, but I'm safe in here, safe from you."

"You're out of your mind, Ollie. You're a lunatic."

"Not really, Jude. I'm actually very sane, very calculating. Yeah, I just made all that up just to rile you, and it worked, didn't it?"

"Why Ollie, why would you do that?"

"Because I want you to know that I could tell that story to the cops anytime I'd like and they'd swallow it, hook, line and sinker. And do you know why, Jude? Take a guess why." Ollie paused, staring at Jude. "C'mon, Jude, take a guess why."

"I don't know Ollie, I don't know."

"Because I hate you, Jude, that's why. You had Paula Sue Schaeffer, and I wanted her. But when she had Ellis, and didn't want anything more to do with you, I swooped in and tried to be her knight in shining armor. But you know what? She still loved you. You don't know what you had, and you blew it. She loved you, but you were so immature, drinking all night, carousing, fighting, getting arrested. Paula was too good for all that, way too good for you."

"I don't know where you get off talking to me like this, you..." Judy was once again cut off by Ollie.

"Well, so see Jude, I'd had it with Alicia, and I wanted Paula, but she still loved you. So, I figured if I couldn't have her, maybe I'd have a part of her, through Ellis. If something were to happen to her, maybe, just maybe, Alicia and I could adopt him. See Alicia couldn't have kids, but we could always adopt, right?"

"You filthy little..." Judy was interrupted once again.

"That's why I can describe exactly what you did to her, because I witnessed it all. There are little secrets that the cops knew about but that no one else could know. Except the killer. Or a witness to the killing. So, you see Jude, until the day I'm executed, I'm a witness to Paula's murder. Because I'm the one who did it. But I'm already on death row, ain't I? But now, if I decide to rat you out, you'll be on this side of the glass, too."

"I'll kill you Ollie, I swear I will kill you!" Judy shouted into the receiver.

Ollie had hung up the phone, turned, and motioned to the guard that he was ready to return to his cell. Looking back through the glass at Judy, who was still screaming into the receiver as the guard on the visitor side was rapidly approaching, Ollie calmly picked up the receiver and said softly, "By the way, Jude, I killed your sister Elsie, too." As Ollie had gently hung the receiver back into the cradle, Judy had flown into a rage and began beating on the glass with his fists, shattering the phone receiver in his grasp. As two penitentiary guards struggled to restrain him and pry loose the destroyed receiver from his now bleeding hands and knuckles, Judy continued screaming at the soundproof and now blood smeared glass.

James E. Anderson

Dealing With Details

Unhappily surveying the contents of his lunch tray, Marcus approached the table at which Cassie had already seated herself. Denny Wallace had taken up a position opposite Cassie, and he also appeared displeased as he poked at and shuffled his fork through the goulash on his plate. The dull, dry, and exceedingly bland, recipe served at the Lewis and Clark High School cafeteria was loaded with a variety of vegetables and a sparse portion of not very tender cubed beef. Cassie was relatively devoted to a healthy diet, and she actually enjoyed the vegetables, although she would also agree that the dish could use a touch of additional seasoning or flavoring. As Marcus took his chair, he couldn't resist registering his displeasure with Monday's menu selection.

"I'd rather be munching down on a bologna sandwich," he mumbled while opening his milk carton.

"Not that bad," said Denny, as he continued stirring through his serving. "At least we're using forks. When pigs eat their slop, they're doing it straight out of a trough."

"Don't be gross, Denny," Cassie scolded. "It's not that bad, and it's good for you."

"Maybe it is healthy, but it's still nasty, if you ask me." Denny was quite emphatic with his opinion. Looking from Cassie to Marcus, Denny asked, "So, aside from *Casino Royale* Friday night, how was your weekend?"

"Pretty crazy, really," Marcus said.

"Yeah, I'll say," Cassie interjected. Denny noted the furrow in her brow and worried expression worn on Cassie's face and turned to Marcus for further explanation.

"Ellis showed up unannounced on Sunday morning."

"No kidding?" Denny asked in earnest amazement. "What did he want? Same as the other day, begging your forgiveness? I hope you told him to take a hike." In Denny's opinion, Marcus should never, under any circumstances, even consider Ellis' apology. When he had told Denny on Friday about the Thursday afternoon encounter, Denny had been adamantly opposed to Marcus giving Ellis so much as the time of day.

"Come on, Denny," Cassie said, "You know Marcus as well as anybody. Of course, he gave in."

"Seriously, you caved?" Denny was surprised, but not taken totally off guard. They had been friends since first grade. He knew Marcus better than anyone, Cassie included. And he knew how soft-hearted his best buddy could sometimes be.

Marcus went on to explain everything that had transpired during the Sunday morning visit. The only things he conveniently failed to mention were the document binder, stocks, and treasure map. He was Marcus' best friend, but Denny had never been a person with whom to entrust a secret.

Denny seemed to be able to sympathize minimally with Ellis, but he was not totally convinced that Marcus had done the right thing by allowing him to gain a foothold.

"And Marcus got hired at Walt's," Cassie added proudly, attempting to lighten the mood by redirecting the conversation.

"Ah man, congratulations, Marcus!" Denny was truly happy for his buddy. "But I guess that's gonna mean even less time for us to hang out, huh?"

"Yeah, I guess so," Marcus replied.

"You're just going to have to get yourself a girlfriend, Denny Wallace," Cassie told him, emphasizing her point by using a sing-song childish voice.

"Fat chance of that!" Marcus said laughing heartily. "There aren't any blind girls in this school!" Even Denny had to smile at that cut down.

Near the end of the day, as they entered their shared sixth hour biology classroom, Cassie informed Marcus that after school she was going to call the information operator to see if she could get a telephone number for Detmeyer Drydock and Machine Company of St. Louis. She also told Marcus that he'd better be sure call her the minute he got home from his first day of work at Walt's Tire and Auto Repair.

Slipping uncomfortably into a new-fangled plastic combo desk, Marcus' unfortunate but reactionary response to her was, "Sure thing Twigs, right after I call Denny." The slap to his shoulder was stout enough for him to realize that his joke was ill received.

* * * *

Marcus reported for work at Walt's precisely fifteen minutes early, at 4:15 p.m. After years of walking to all his destinations, he had an excellent sense of how long it would take to get from any given point to another. Walt's Tire and Auto had been one of his favorite haunts for the past six or seven years, and his timing for the trip from his apartment had been right on the money. Walt McMurphy had been out running errands when Marcus arrived, but Chester Bernstein had been more than happy to show Marcus how to get clocked in and directed him to the shop's supply storage room that would be his domain for the immediate future. Marcus was delightfully surprised at how quickly his three-hour shift flew by and felt reasonably satisfied with his first day's production. As Walt killed the lights and locked the door, it dawned on him that Marcus did not yet drive and had already begun walking home. He got into his pickup and caught up with Marcus a mere half block away.

Pulling alongside him, Walt called through the open passenger side window, "Say Marcus, let me give you a ride."

"Ah, gee, thanks Walt, but I'm good," Marcus said. "I'm used to walking, it don't bother me none."

"Nah, I insist." Walt responded. "First day, you're probably tired. Besides, I wanted to talk to you."

Walt stopped in the middle of White Street and Marcus climbed into the truck. "How was the first day, kiddo?" Walt asked him.

"Oh, it was good, Walt. Thank you for asking and thanks for giving me the opportunity, I really appreciate it."

"You're welcome son," Walt said as he side-eyed Marcus. "You've been in and out of my place for what, about five years or so now? When you applied for the job, I knew I was gonna hire you, you know. I knew you were a responsible kid."

"Thanks, Walt." Marcus felt a little bit embarrassed; he wasn't accustomed to being praised.

"You're welcome, Marcus, just speaking the truth. Didn't you wonder why there were embroidered shirts already there waiting for you? I went ahead and ordered them when you scheduled your interview," he said.

"No sir, that never even occurred to me," Marcus answered honestly.

"Listen, Marcus," Walt said in measured tones. "Chester mentioned to me that you seemed to be interested in that Metropolitan that's been sitting out front."

"Yes sir, I did tell him I thought it was a neat car. I hope someday, after my birthday, I might be able to find something like that," Marcus confessed. "That is, if I could save up enough money."

"Well, I was thinking about that. When do you turn sixteen?"

"August 14," Marcus told him and then wondered aloud, "Why?"

"I was just thinking. Why don't you talk to your stepmother, Miss Margaret, about it. If you talk to her and you really think you want that car, maybe we can work something out."

"Really, you mean that, Walt?" Marcus felt a ripple of excitement coursing through his body.

"Yep. Tell you what Marcus. If you can find a way to put one hundred dollars down on that car, and pay me five dollars a week, or more if you can afford it, out of your paycheck each week, I'll park that car in the back and hold onto it for you. So long as you're paying me five bucks a week, I'll keep it for you. If you haven't missed any payments by your birthday, I'll knock fifty dollars off the price and I'll hold onto the title, but you can have the car. When you've paid a total of four hundred, I'll sign the title over to your stepmom and the car will be yours, free and clear. Sound good?"

"Wow, that really would be swell, Walt!" Marcus couldn't believe the deal he was being offered. But then the reality of the situation hit him. He only had thirty-seven dollars saved up in his savings sock in his dresser. He had some pocket change on him now, but not much. Where would he come up with another sixty-three dollars?

"Well, you talk it over with Miss Margaret and let me know when you come to work Wednesday, okay?"

"You betcha, Walt, I will." Marcus thought he was more excited now than when he had found the treasure map yesterday.

When Walt dropped him at his apartment, Marcus ran excitedly to the front door. As expected, he opened the door to find Margaret nestled on the couch in front of the old Philco Predicta watching the Monday night CBS lineup of shows. Monday was one of only two weeknights that she was off from her job at *The Goldmine,* and it was her favorite evening of the week. She had already watched *Gunsmoke,* and *The Lucy Show* was just concluding. *The Andy Griffith Show* was about to start, and the highlight of the evening would be *The Carol Burnett Show* at nine o'clock. After entering the apartment, Marcus had told Margaret hello and gone directly into the kitchen in search of the leftovers that Margaret had promised would be waiting. Marcus wasn't disappointed as a pot of beef stew simmered on the stovetop. After placing a folding TV tray in front of the easy chair, Marcus positioned his dinner and bottle of Pepsi on the tray and sat down. Having failed to munch on his customary after school snack before leaving for Walt's, and it being an hour past his normal dinner time, Marcus felt ravenous. He had just savored his first mouthwatering bite of dinner as *The Andy Griffith Show* took its first commercial break.

During the pause, Margaret asked Marcus how his first day as a working man had gone.

"Pretty good, Mama," he replied. "I met Chester Bernstein and Louie Dupree. Chester is a pretty neat guy. He showed me a lot. Louie is from Canada; he's really got a weird accent. He taught me to say a couple of things in French. Cassie and I had been thinking about taking Spanish in our sophomore year, but if I'm still working here, I think I'd rather take French because Louie be able to help me a bunch."

Margaret and Marcus continued to make small talk during commercial breaks, but when *Family Affair* began at eight-thirty, Marcus knew his opportunity had arrived. He had hurried to make sure he'd finish dinner before *Andy Griffith* had ended. *Family Affair* and its star Brian Keith were Margaret's least favorite on Monday night. He felt confident that he could use the whole of the next thirty minutes to talk to Margaret and feel her out regarding the subject of the Nash Metropolitan, as well as the deal that Walt had proposed. When he had secured Margaret's undivided attention and felt he had her cornered, Marcus proceeded to pull out all stops as he described the beautiful car and carefully laid out all the details, just as Walt had stated them.

"What do you think, Mama?" Marcus asked.

"Well, I guess I'd have to think about, Marcus," she replied.

"Well, Walt told me to let him know when I come to work Wednesday," Marcus told her. "So, I don't have much time to let him know."

Margaret pulled a tablet and pen from the drawer in the end table and began calculating. After a few moments, she had reached some conclusions.

Okay Marcus. The car is four hundred and fifty, minus one hundred for the deposit. That leaves three hundred and fifty. You will have eleven paydays before your birthday, so that is fifty-five dollars you'll pay it down, leaving two hundred and ninety-five. Now, you said he'd take off fifty if you don't miss a payment and, believe you me mister, I'll make sure you don't miss one. That will drop it to two hundred and forty-five if my arithmetic is correct. Right, Mr. Math Whiz?"

"I'm doing it in my head, but yes, I think that's right Mama."

"How much do you have saved right now, Marcus?"

"Thirty-seven dollars and eighty-six cents, exactly," Marcus reported.

"Forget the change," she said, still thinking. "That means you need another sixty-three dollars for the down payment, correct?"

"Yes ma'am." Marcus replied, cringing a bit when he realized he was asking Margaret for that much cash.

Margaret thought for a few moments and continued to perform scribbled calculations in her tablet. Finally, she looked up from her paper.

"Alright, I will loan it to you. And it is a loan mind you, Marcus." Margaret was going to help him but was also going to be sure that it was a valuable learning experience. "You will pay me back, and with a flat ten per cent interest added for the sole purpose of helping to teach you fiscal responsibility. I will loan you sixty-five dollars and you will pay me back that sixty-five plus six dollars and fifty cents in interest. That's a total of seventy-one dollars and fifty cents. Understood, Marcus?"

"Yes ma'am. Thank you, Mama."

Marcus was exceedingly pleased that Margaret had agreed to help him. It had been an eventful and memorable day for him. He'd started his first job and been offered a great deal on a beautiful car. And now to have Margaret promise her help and support, how much more could he ask for? Marcus could not seem to involve himself with *The Carol Burnett Show* tonight. By the time the second set of commercials rolled around, Marcus had excused himself and gone to his room. Lying on his bed, with one arm across his barely conscious eyes, Marcus was suddenly awakened by Margaret's voice.

"Marcus, Cassie is on the phone. Were you supposed to call her?"

Marcus felt terrible, he'd promised but had forgotten to call Cassie when he'd arrived home.

Picking up the phone, Marcus immediately apologized for not calling.

"I'm so sorry, Cassie. There was a lot going on and I forgot that I'd promised to call."

"How could you forget, Marcus? Do you how that makes me feel? I promised to do something for you, and I did it. But does my boyfriend call me? Like he promised? No, of course not." Marcus quickly sensed that Cassie was significantly miffed. Before he could stammer a reply, she continued, "It's my hair isn't it, Marcus? It's my hair, you didn't want me to cut it, but I insisted, and you hate it and now you don't like me. That's it isn't it, it's my haircut."

"Cassie, Cassie, settle down, please," Marcus felt desperate to calm his girlfriend's concerns, but was at a loss for the right words to say. "No, it's not your hair. I've been teasing you, but really, I love your haircut. You look beautiful with it like that."

"Really?"

"Yes, of course, I love it," he reassured her once again.

"Okay, if you really mean it." Cassie had calmed immensely.

Marcus was surprised that it had only taken a few seconds and a handful of soft, flattering words to diffuse the situation.

"Are you alright, Cassie? Is everything okay now?"

"Yes, Marcus, I'm fine," she said. Speaking in a more normal, relaxed cadence. "But why didn't you call when you got home. I was worried that you got hurt or something at the garage."

"I'm sorry, Cassie," Marcus was sincere. The last thing he would want would be to worry or upset Cassie. "I just got preoccupied talking to Mama, and there was some excitement, and I don't know, I just somehow forgot I was supposed to call you."

With Cassie's emotions back in check, Marcus began with what she was expecting to hear, by telling her about his new job. He described what he did and the people he worked with, Chester and Louie. Cassie was interested to learn that Louie was Canadian and spoke French. She agreed that it might be a good idea for Marcus to study French next year and take advantage of a free tutor. For herself, though, she professed that Spanish was the language that would probably be more useful and practical to master and use in the future.

With the subject of work exhausted, Marcus dropped the good news onto Cassie's lap. He told her about the Metro, as he had already begun calling it, bragging on the good deal Walt was giving him. Cassie was excited at the prospect of Marcus driving his own car in just a few months.

"That is wonderful that Margaret is helping you," Cassie and Margaret had a very good relationship, Cassie thought the absolute world of Marcus' stepmother. "If you do get your license and start driving right after your birthday, you'll be able to take me out for my birthday, won't you Marcus?"

Marcus knew, of course, that Cassie's birthday fell just twenty-nine days after his, on September 12.

"For sure, for sure, Cassie," Marcus replied. "And I'll be rolling in dough by your birthday, too!"

Marcus wasn't sure, but he thought that perhaps Cassie was more excited about the car than even he was.

Thirty minutes into the conversation, Cassie was finally able to tell Marcus that she had contacted the information operator for the greater St. Louis area. According to the operator, there were no listings for Detmeyer Drydock and Machine Company of St. Louis.

"Well, maybe the company isn't actually based in St. Louis at all," Marcus posited. "Isn't there like a Bay St. Louis in Mississippi or Louisiana or something? And I'm pretty sure there's an East St. Louis in Illinois too, I think."

214

"That's true," Cassie said. "Just because it said 'of St. Louis' doesn't mean it has to really be in St. Louis. That could just be something they threw into the name because somebody thought it sounded good."

"Right," Marcus said. "That's okay, we'll figure it out when the time comes, Cassie."

"Yeah, we will, absolutely," Cassie replied. "One more question Marcus. What did Denny have to say about your car?"

"Nothing."

"Nothing? I can't imagine Denny wouldn't have anything to say,"

"How could he, Cassie? He doesn't know about it," Marcus explained.

"So, you really didn't call him first, like you said you would, in biology class?" She asked him.

"Of course not, I'd never tell anyone something like that before you, Twigs." And Marcus wasn't exaggerating.

"Well thank you, Marcus. You are a wonderful boyfriend," she gushed. "So, are we going to the dump tomorrow to see your friend Jeremiah?" Cassie asked. "I think it would be amazing to hear what he has to say about the treasure, and the map, and especially I'd like to hear his recollections and memories of your dad and Opa. I'm really excited about going to see him."

"Me too, Twigs," Marcus had already gotten insight from Jeremiah on his father, but he was every bit as anxious and curious as Cassie was to learn about his real grandfather.

215

* * * *

It was just past three thirty in the afternoon, Alicia had finished up her paperwork, and had just settled on the couch with a can of beer. As she sipped, she contemplated following the beer up with a nap. However, her plans were interrupted by rapid and forceful knocking on the front door. Setting down her beer and placing her unlit cigarette in the adjacent ashtray, she crossed the small living room and opened the front door. Expecting to be addressed by a door-to-door salesman sporting a pencil thin mustache and slicked back greasy hair, Alicia was startled to see Jude Allensworth on the stoop.

"Back so soon?" She asked. "Weren't you just here on Saturday? What's the matter, Judy, you starting to find me irresistible, too?"

"No offense, but I gotta admit Alish, I find you quite resistible," Judy dug at her pride. "Not my type, sweetheart. But we do gotta talk."

"C'mon in," Alicia said as she crossed the living room and picked her cigarette back up and struck a match. "Want a Falstaff? I just cracked one for myself."

"No thanks."

Upon taking the first deep drag of her Pall Mall and exhaling, she said to her guest, "Okay, I'm a big catfish, I'll bite. What's up? What brings you back so quick, Judy?"

"First, where's Ellis?" Judy wanted to make sure he wasn't around to hear any of the conversation.

"Working, I suppose. Probably up around Palmyra, Hannibal, somewhere like that," she said.

"Why are you so concerned about that boy? He's a grown man, he don't need you stepping in here at his age and changing his diapers, for Pete's sake."

"He's my son and I care," Judy fired back. "I don't like who he's working for, and I want you to convince him to find something else to do.:

"Ain't gonna happen. He's gonna do whatever he wants, he's a big boy." Alicia studied Judy's face. "You didn't come here to harp on his job again anyway, Judy. You just did that Saturday. And if that's why you are here, I don't want to hear it, I ain't got time. So why are you here?" Alicia was not one to take guff or be talked down to. She had been hardened by being married to Ollie. She was demanding an answer from Judy.

"I went to see Ollie yesterday, Alish. He's lost his mind in that place,"

"Why do you say that Judy? I honestly thought he'd lost his mind years ago," Alicia offered her honest opinion on her ex-husband. "What kind of a sane man would have killed that poor teenaged girl and posed her body on the riverbank? He had to have been crazy to have done that wouldn't you think? What kind of a lunatic would kidnap a ten-year-old girl? He'd have probably killed her too, if y'all wouldn't have caught him that night."

"He's gotten worse Alish," Judy said.

"He can't get no worse. Look what he did to Ellis. He nearly ruined that boy's life getting Ellis to follow him, to help him," Alicia certainly exhibited no love lost for Ollie. "People don't know Judy, but he almost killed me. Don't you know why we adopted

Ellis? It's because I couldn't have one of my own, that's why. And that was Ollie. He literally beat the physical ability to have kids right out of me. That's the real reason why we got divorced. People think it was because of Max. No, it was all Ollie. He's always been crazy, Judy."

"I don't doubt what you're saying, Alish. I thought he was crazy when we were teenagers, but he's hit the bottom these days. He's delusional now," Judy told her.

"Okay, Judy," Alicia was ready for the story Judy was prepared to tell. "What's he saying now?"

"Now he's threatening to tell the cops that I killed Ellis' mother, Paula Sue Schaeffer," Judy said. "The lunatic says he can prove it."

"But they already executed somebody for that. Twenty years ago. Ollie testified against the guy, he testified that he saw him with the machete. You remember that don't you, Judy." Alicia thought that case was all said and done two decades ago. "How could he claim now that you did it?"

"Because he said he can testify that he lied before to protect me, and that he saw me do it, and he can describe it blow by blow, just the way it happened. He said only the cops know the truth. And he can give the detailed description that only the killer or a firsthand eyewitness could provide."

"Judy, did you do it?" Alicia asked.

"Of course not. That's what I'm trying to explain to you, that's why I know he's crazy. He's on death row, he doesn't have anything to lose."

"I don't understand, why would he do this to you?" Alicia couldn't comprehend Ollie's motive or a reason for his behavior.

"He claims it's because he hates me. Alicia, he told me that he was tired of you, that you couldn't have kids and that he wanted Paula," Judy told the story exactly as Ollie had told it to him. "His stories are crazy. He says when Paula wanted nothing to do with me, that he tried to win her over, but she wouldn't have nothing to do with him. He told me he killed Paula, so that you two would be able to adopt her baby. He flat out told me that he killed Paula."

"But he didn't kill her Judy, he couldn't have," Alicia was calm in her response. "That would have been impossible," Alicia looked Judy directly in the eye. "It's impossible."

"Why is it impossible, Alicia?" now Judy was not comprehending. "Ollie says he knows exactly what happened. He had to have done it."

"No Judy, I remember the story very distinctly," Alicia related what she remembered. "Paula had been missing for several days, maybe a week before they found her body. I remember because I got a phone call from a neighbor telling me about it."

"So, what does that have to do with Ollie?" Judy asked.

"He wasn't even here, Judy," Alicia went on with her explanation, shaking her head. "We'd been together for, I don't know, maybe two years, and we got married on May 8, 1948, and then we went on a honeymoon to California. We didn't even come back until Memorial Day weekend. I remember specifically being in San Francisco when Arlene called and told me about Paula."

Judy ran his hands through his hair thinking, trying to connect dots that didn't seem to even be on the same page. He was concentrating on scenarios and possibilities.

"And you know what else he said, Alish," Judy's anger began percolating with the memory of Ollie's smugness as he picked up the receiver for the last time yesterday.

"He told me he killed Elsie. He admitted that he killed my sister." Judy slammed his fist onto the top of the coffee table.

"I don't doubt it a bit," was Alicia's response.

They both sat in silence for nearly five long minutes.

"How is it possible, Alish?" Judy wondered aloud. "How could Ollie have testified against that guy if he wasn't here when it happened? If you're telling the truth about being in California, how could the cops have not known that?"

"I don't know, Judy." Alicia spoke softly, calmly. "I know he didn't kill Paula; he couldn't have. What was the first story he told you about testifying, when he tried to say you did it?"

"He said he did it to cover for me."

"Yeah, that's what he told me too, in 1948." Alicia smiled as Judy looked at her with red eyes and a worried face.

"I don't know, Judy," she said pensively. "Maybe he was covering for you. Maybe you did kill Paula."

Miah

The two barefoot young men, one black and one white, leisurely paddled the homemade raft, staying in close to the shore as they attempted to avoid the strong and powerful flow found near the middle of the river. The formidable current forced the muddy brown water rapidly downstream. Venturing that far from the bank would undoubtably bring tragic results were the raft to capsize out in the deepest part of the waterway. There is no question it would promptly be swept below the surface, along with its crew. Wisely, the friends stayed in tight. Their rowing didn't appear to require much effort, the sleepy current close to the bank did most of the work for them. What was at least a two-mile journey south on the Mississippi River had seemed to have gone by in a flash. It was as if the two teens had just shoved off, and here they were, already on the northwestern point of the sandbar, assembling firewood and preparing their campsite. The crooked smile of a crescent moon shone down upon them as their hastily built fire began to initiate the warming of the cool crisp autumn air.

There was no logical reason for them to go on a camping trip with the unseasonably low prevailing temperatures. Just as illogical was their choice of campsite, as they had settled on a desolate sandbar, a destination which would require a relatively treacherous river route to reach. The evening was not so cool that physical harm would be caused by the chill, as overnight temperatures would continue to remain well above the freezing threshold. However, it was going to be quite miserable during the pre-dawn hours. As midnight approached, the two continued taking turns stoking the flames, gradually expanding the size of the campfire to a near bonfire proportion. When both were satisfied that the size and heat production would be sufficient to last the night, they snuggled into multiple layers of bedrolls placed as close as reasonably possible to the warmth. An eagle's eye view of the campsite revealed a quietly serene and comforting scene. Two young men sleeping peacefully, well wrapped, and cozy next to a raging, yet pacifying fire. The river's current continued flowing smoothly past the campers as they slept, water lapping lazily against and gently advancing onto the sandy shore of the small island.

Just a couple of hours past midnight, and from the same eagle's eye viewpoint, movement seemed to occur. Several kerosene lanterns had been lit and were casually moving about on the southeastern most portion of the sandbar. An observant eagle would have taken note of the lanterns beginning to travel, single file and moving rather quickly along the eastern shore, in a northerly direction. Reaching the shore of the northernmost point of the sandbar, and well outside the tree line, four lantern bearing strangers began to circle back southward on the western side of the bar. From the high vantage point, it became painfully obvious that the destination would be the overly large campfire belonging to the two sleeping teens.

Suddenly awakened by the shouting of the intruders, the two youngsters jumped from their bedrolls and stood, without their blankets or any other type of covering. They were both disoriented and shivering in the dark, partially paralyzed by the brisk and slightly damp breeze. With the two held at gunpoint, the obvious leader of the foursome began shouting questions and demands.

"Where is it?" Either tell me now, or show me, and we'll let you go free."

The young black man spoke on behalf of them both, "Don't know what y'alls talkin' about, sir."

"We don't have all night, Jeremiah. Give us what we're looking for and we'll be gone before sunrise, and you two can finish up your little trip."

"But sir, we don't know whats you be talkin' about."

"Don't act stupid like this half-wit John Clemens. We know you two found a pirate's treasure and buried it right here on this sandbar somewhere. Tell us now where it is!""

"No sir, can't do that I'm afraid," Jeremiah responded.

"Well, you're a brave one, Jeremiah, I gotta say. But I wonder how brave you'll be when you see we're serious." The stranger raised his rifle, pointing the barrel toward the younger boy.

Jeremiah dove protectively in front of his friend, his left hand pushing John Clemens away, forcing him to fall down onto the sand just as the trigger was being squeezed.

The entire scene was momentarily devoid of any sound as the next few seconds were conducted as if in a vacuum, silently and in slow motion. A single inaudible shot was fired with a discernible flash at the barrel's muzzle, and Jeremiah Paige's body spun in a wildly contortive manner, landing clumsily in a heap on the ground, dangerously close to the fire's edge, face down and motionless.

"Miah!" shouted John as he jumped to his feet and ran to his fallen best friend. Two of the intruders grabbed young John, one on each arm and pulled him back before he could reach Jeremiah. The leader of the group pointed his rifle in John's direction.

"I guess now it's up to you to spill the beans, Clemens. You know where the treasure is?"

Despite the obvious defiance in his eyes, John slowly nodded his head in the affirmative.

Relieved, the leader lowered his rifle. "Glad one of you had some sense. Now do you want to tell me?"

John hacked up and launched a large glob of phlegm, landing a bullseye into the leader's right eye.

Upon retrieving a red bandanna from his back pocket, and slowly and deliberately wiping his face, John's tormenter now raised and aimed the rifle's barrel in John's direction. The motion was swiftly followed by the unmistakable sound of the rifle's hammer being clicked back. "You shouldn't have done that son."

The shattering, explosive sound instantly brought Marcus out of a deep and fitful sleep. He could hear Margaret's raised voice from the kitchen. He hurriedly threw back the thin and sweaty twin sized sheet he'd been sleeping under and raced into the kitchen. Margaret was on hands and knees, struggling to gather up the shards of broken glass while also trying to corral and contain the sticky brown liquid that had spread across the hard ceramic tile flooring. Marcus scurried to the pantry to retrieve a mop and bucket and quickly returned to aid Margaret in the clean-up.

"Marcus, how many times have I asked you to lay the soda pop bottles down on the bottom shelf of the refrigerator? You know how this thing wobbles. As soon I pulled the door open a bottle that you stood up on the top shelf came falling out."

"I'm sorry, Mama." Marcus felt embarrassed by his inconsideration. Of course, Margaret had told him time and again that because of the old Frigidaire's instability, that eventually something would fall out when the door was pulled open. It was a standing rule that nothing would be stored near the edge of the shelf, and particularly nothing made of glass. When gathering his dinner and drink last night, Marcus had taken the last chilled bottle of Pepsi. Another standing rule was that the person removing the last of anything from the refrigerator also bore responsibility to immediately restock the item. Marcus had taken a new six pack of Pepsi from the pantry, intending to fulfill his duty to replenish the supply. And yet when he had placed five bottles properly on the bottom shelf, he had carelessly stood the sixth upright on the top shelf. The sixth bottle should have been returned to the pantry.

"I did that last night; I don't know what I was thinking." Marcus' apology must have struck a chord with Margaret because she seemed to merely shrug her shoulders, indicating she was not terribly upset.

"It could have been much worse," Margaret smiled at Marcus, appreciative that he was helping with the mop. "If it had been a jar of pickles, or maybe ketchup, it would have been worse. We'll survive."

Marcus was thankful that he'd been blessed with such a wonderful stepmother. Margaret had always been somewhat strict, but in the past few years, she had seemed to mellow considerably. Marcus felt relieved that she was understanding and not angry with him. But as he continued to mop the kitchen floor, his mind began to return to the dream he had been abruptly pulled from. He wondered why had he dreamed about his grandfather and Jeremiah Paige? Was it because of the letter and map he had discovered in the footlocker? It just all seemed so strange. He knew of the sandbar he had seen in the dream and was very familiar with it. It was a popular campsite for many of the local kids. He and Denny had taken their homemade raft and Mr. Wallace's canoes on several float trips and camped there often during the past few summers. Marcus was curious why he saw Opa and Jeremiah in that setting. He wondered if they really had camped there when they were young. Had they built a raft similar to the one he saw in his dream? The unanswered questions made him even more excited to visit the dump after school today. It was quite likely that Jeremiah Paige not only could verify the treasure, but just might hold the key and answer to all the questions Marcus now had dancing through his mind.

* * * *

Jeremiah Paige had opened the gate, driven on down the gravel road to the watchman's shack and parked his Hudson. It was his second day back on the job and he was feeling a little more relaxed this morning. Opening the screen door to enter his office, Jeremiah paused to gaze on down the road, deeper into the dump. Before entering the shack yesterday morning, he had continued down the road to get a look at the container that had been so important to have cost Tony Mancini his life. There had not been very much to see. A wide-open container, an empty storage cabinet, and a blood-stained corrugated metal floor. Police crime scene tape had remained hanging, albeit somewhat loosely and sagging some four days later. The scene had been properly staged, but Jeremiah was curious regarding the competence, enthusiasm, and overall commitment of the county's crime investigation team.

It had drizzled overnight and was warm this morning. As a result, it was already getting muggy by mid-morning. Jeremiah flicked on the small window fan that he had installed just a few weeks prior, in anticipation of a warm summer. He had set the fan up to blow outward, therefore drawing air in through the screen door, creating a slight breeze across the position occupied by his rocking chair. Jeremiah prepped himself for a relaxing morning. Tuesdays were generally quiet during the early part of the day. He poured himself a cup of coffee from his trusty green thermos bottle. Dropping two envelopes of BC Powder into his mouth and chasing them with coffee, Jeremiah sat in his rocker. He slightly rubbed the bandage on the right side of his head, near the temple, and gently touched the two small Band-Aids on his right cheek. He had been fortunate to have only been winged on Thursday afternoon. Jeremiah had felt the burn of a direct hit back when still a teenager. A .22 caliber long shell had buried itself deep into his right hip, contributing mightily to his use of a cane in his golden years. Until a couple of summers ago, he had only been saddled with the inconvenience of a slight limp. But as he had aged and lower back pain had exacerbated matters, he'd found it a good deal easier, and far less agonizing, to rely on a cane or walking stick. Sitting comfortably, Jeremiah loaded his corncob pipe, struck a match against the pot-bellied stove, and lit up.

He had spent a lot of time yesterday, sitting and rocking in his chair, contemplating the events that had transpired last week. He never had the slightest interest in delving into Tony's activities, and actually had no idea of what he had been up to. So long as Tony came through with his cash, Jeremiah was a happy and satisfied camper. Through slight tidbits that he had picked up during the course of a series of interviews he had been subjected to, both in the hospital and over the weekend at home, Jeremiah had surmised that Tony had been associated with a local group of drug runners. That was fine and dandy with him. Jeremiah felt like the three little monkeys – see no evil, hear no evil, speak no evil. He was totally in the dark and had confidently repeated the same phrase time and again, "I don't know nothing."

Jeremiah hadn't seen hide nor hair of a customer all morning and had lightly dozed off in his rocker. He didn't hear the county cruiser when it had pulled up and parked in front of his shack. Jeremiah was awakened, though, by the sound of the car door slamming behind Deputy Lyle Martin, who had quickly entered through the screen door.

"Hello Deputy Martin. Come to ask more questions?" Jeremiah asked.

"Oh no, Mr. Paige," the deputy replied. "No sir, I've already submitted my report, gave all my statements, I'm all finished up with my part of the investigation. I was just in the area and thought I'd check in with you. I spoke to Deputy Daniels this morning and he said he had stopped by yesterday. He said he thought you still seemed a little dazed and confused, so I just wanted to, you know, follow up."

"Don't know why he'da said that. I'm doin' fine. Little bit of headache, but side a that I's good," Jeremiah assured Deputy Martin.

"Good, good. I'm glad to hear that, Mr. Paige." Deputy Martin did a quick visual survey of the shack. "I am a little curious about something, Mr. Paige. Meant to ask the other day. Not part of the investigation or nothing, just a personal question, if you don't mind. I was kind of wondering what kind of tobacco you smoke in that pipe of yours."

"Prince Albert mostly, why?" Jeremiah wondered what he was getting at.

"Nothing homegrown, Mr. Paige?" Deputy Martin seemed to be asking something that Jeremiah certainly hoped the deputy didn't mean as an implication that he was involved in Tony Mancini's business.

"No sir. Ain't never touch the stuff, if you sayin' what I thinks."

"Oh, no no no, Jeremiah, I don't mean to imply anything. It was just that the other day, there was a bit of an odd smell in here that I don't notice today." In Jeremiah's opinion, Lyle Martin certainly did seem to be implying something that slightly offended him.

"Well now that you mention it, Deputy I do's believe I mighta farted in here that day, pretty goodun if'n I remember right."

Deputy Martin nearly doubled over in laughter. "Oh, now that's a good one Mr. Paige, a good one." Catching his breath and shaking his head, he continued, "In all seriousness, Mr. Paige, my father smoked a pipe and I've smelled the aromas of lots of blends, you know like cherry and whatever. I never smelled anything like that before."

"It's a special mixed batch I found over by Quincy, when I worked to the quarry. What you was smellin' was cloves. They gets grounded up and mixed in," Jeremiah decided to be forthright with Deputy Martin. "Them cloves, they says they got some healin' power to 'em. Gonna make me live forever I hope."

"Cloves, huh? That's interesting, I'm going to research that. Maybe my old man will want to try that, too." Deputy Martin started to open the screen door, but then he stopped. "Oh, I almost forgot to tell you. There's another special detective that is going to stop by this afternoon to ask you a few more questions, try to clarify a few things, if it's okay with you."

"How many times I gotta talk to you folks? I done talked to you a buncha times. That Reynolds guy, he seen me at the hospital and then again at my house on Sunday," Jeremiah was perturbed by the thought of another interview. "Is it that same detective, that Reynolds guy again?"

"No, it will be a different one this time. He's like a boss to Detective Reynolds," explained a smiling Lyle Martin. "You'll like this guy."

The deputy let the screen door spring shut behind him as he made his way back to his cruiser.

Jeremiah resumed his position in the rocking chair, struck a match and relit his pipe. Thoughts passed through his mind, remembrances of the previous question and answer sessions with both Martin and Reynolds. He had to be sure he remained true to everything he had told them previously. He also wondered what types of new questions this detective could possibly have for him. Jeremiah felt confident he could breeze through another interrogation, perhaps his biggest concern was what time the man was going to show up. He had to lock up at five o'clock and he hated not leaving on time. The only thing worse than leaving late would be not leaving at all. He drew deeply on the pipe and smiled inwardly.

* * * *

As was customary, Marcus and Cassie sat across from Denny at their lunch table. They had things to discuss today but it was going to be difficult with a third wheel present. Marcus broke two crackers into his chili bowl as Cassie took a bite of her peanut butter sandwich. This was one of the few things they did not have in common. Marcus ate crackers in his chili, and always finished the bowl before even starting on the peanut butter sandwich. Cassie, on the other hand, ate the sandwich first because she preferred to let the chili cool before starting it. Denny, of course had his own method entirely. No crackers for him. Instead, he liked to fold the peanut butter sandwich and dunk it into the chili. There was always a red liquid trail from bowl to chin when this tasty meal was served. Undoubtably, Denny would be wearing a fair portion of chili drippings on the front of his shirt. Marcus felt especially gratified on days like today, when Denny had forgotten to consult the weekly lunch menu and had worn a white, or similarly light-colored shirt.

As Cassie neared the end of her sandwich, Marcus was compelled to ask a question. She had told him after second hour that Mrs. Mackey, her home economics teacher, was absent today.

"Who did you have for a sub in home ec today, Cassie?" Marcus asked.

"Nobody. The whole class showed up and then Miss Crabtree came running in a couple of minutes later and sent us all to the library for study hall," she told him gleefully.

"Good, were you able to get your homework done?"

"Sort of. I spent my time trying to find Detmeyer Drydock and Machine Company," Cassie said.

"Really? Did you find out anything? Are they a big famous company?" Marcus asked expectantly, hoping for good news, hoping the stocks actually would be worth a lot of money.

"Not exactly, Marcus. I'm not a hundred per cent sure, but I think they might be out of business."

Marcus was disappointed, but slightly encouraged that Cassie had said she wasn't one hundred per cent sure. He knew how thorough she could be when researching something, so he was confident that there was still a sliver of possibility that he could be holding something of value.

"Maybe we can find out more, but I went on microfiche and checked on the stock markets and found Detmeyer listed on the New York Stock Exchange in the early nineteen-forties, but then it just disappears," she explained.

"What are guys talking about? Stock exchanges?" Denny asked.

"Yeah, we're working on a project for social studies," Marcus offered up a feeble excuse, hoping it would be enough to pacify Denny. He surely did not want to disclose the whole real story surrounding the stocks to Denny.

"Oh man, how boring. I'm so glad I don't have to deal with these honors classes that you two have to put up with," Denny shook his head. "I don't know how you guys do it."

Marcus and Cassie both breathed sighs of relief, realizing that their conversation had flown well above Denny's head.

Sixth hour biology wrapped up a bit early and Mr. Cannon afforded the class five minutes to chat, provided they hold the volume down. Marcus and Cassie found themselves finalizing their plans to visit Jeremiah Paige. They had planned to ride together on the bus route to Marcus' apartment complex. From there, it was only about a twenty-minute walk. The dump was open until five, and they planned to be able to spend at least thirty minutes with Jeremiah. They hoped he could tell them just what the treasure map would lead them to and provide some insight into the mystery of Opa and the real life of John Clemens.

* * * *

The Lewis County East Trash Facility was closed for lunch from 12:30 until 1:30 p.m. on weekdays. Jeremiah had completed his meal and secured a short nap in plenty of time to drive halfway up the road, unlocking and reopening the gate. Upon returning to his office, he again had reclaimed his customary seat in the rocking chair and began perusing a *Car and Driver* magazine, mostly skimming through the photos and illustrations until his eyelids became heavy and he began to fade.

There had not been a single customer all day long. That was not a terribly unusual occurrence on weekdays. Most trash dumping occurred on Friday afternoons or Saturday mornings. Tony Mancini had been the only semi-regular visitor on weekdays. It was now almost four in the afternoon, and Jeremiah was once again wide awake. He had already begun considering what he might prepare for dinner in another hour and a half, when the calm and quiet was interrupted by the dump's first visitor of the day. A sharp looking black Mustang had turned off Highway 16 and now slowly crept down the gravel road. The driver was obviously trying to practice dust control as he cautiously approached. The sporty vehicle pulled in and parked on the far side of Jeremiah's Hudson. A well-dressed, mustachioed man, wearing black suit and tie, and oddly enough, accessorized by a black newsboy hat, emerged carrying a brown leather satchel. Jeremiah stood, looking through the screen door as the man leisurely walked toward the shack. He quickly surmised that by the way the man carried himself, and the professional demeaner that he seemed to project, were both indicators that this had to be the special detective that Deputy Martin had warned him would be coming this afternoon. Jeremiah greeted the visitor by pushing open the door as he arrived.

"Afternoon," Jeremiah said as he held the door open. "I's guessing you ain't droppin' no trash, is ya?"

"You would be guessing correct then wouldn't you, Mr. Paige?" The stranger smiled and offered his hand in greeting. "I'm Detective Perry Mason with the MDI, uh, the Missouri Department of Investigations." The man reached into his inner breast pocket, extracted, and quickly flashed open and closed, a pocket identification and badge holder. He just as swiftly replaced the credentials, back into the same pocket and proceeded to take a seat in a hardbacked wooden kitchen chair that sat diagonally across from a rocking chair in Jeremiah's small self-proclaimed 'office'. Setting down his satchel, he reached inside and pulled out a portable tape recorder that was, oddly enough, roughly the size of a bible or hymnal. The words *the whole truth, so help me God'* for some reason played through Jeremiah's mind. He had never seen such a recording device in person. In all the other instances in which he'd been questioned or asked for a statement, notes had been taken by hand and the statements had also been painstakingly handwritten. Jeremiah assumed that since this man was an employee of the state, that he was entitled to all the latest law enforcement equipment and technology available.

"Pleasure to meet you Mr. Mason," Jeremiah could not resist a smile when considering of the irony evoked by the detective's name.

"It's okay if you laugh at my name, Jeremiah. I hope you don't mind that I call you Jeremiah. I like to keep my interviews informal and light, as comfortable as possible, you understand." The detective seemed like a decent, down-to-earth person. When Jeremiah had been interviewed by Detective Reynolds, he had been very stoic and rather uptight. "I often get teased about my name, but believe me when I say, my parents made me a Perry Mason long before the *Perry Mason* television show had even been thought of."

"I understand that detective, but it is a might funny to hear, I gotsa say."

Detective Mason smiled knowingly and placed the tape recorder on the top of the pot-bellied stove. "Shall we get started, Jeremiah?"

The questions started innocuously enough, very simple and forthright, at first. But as the interview progressed, Jeremiah realized that this state investigator had really done his homework, and shown amazing insight into whatever it was that Tony Mancini had truly been involved in. Jeremiah almost felt he was more being lectured than questioned. Detective Mason most definitely had knowledge far beyond what Jeremiah could ever have imagined. It felt as if the detective was seeking more to corroborate than to obtain additional information.

Detective Mason let Jeremiah in on some of the suspicions that he had developed concerning Tony's motives, his operation, and the associations he had cultivated and established. He had explained to Jeremiah that Tony had been working for years for a local kingpin who had vigorously maintained a profitable territory, stretching from St. Louis northward, reaching all the way into southern Iowa. He explained how this man ultimately enlisted the aid of members of local biker gangs, and relied upon their nefarious behavior, to increase his distribution network deep into the northeastern interior of Missouri, and even across the river on into west central Illinois and northward. He posited that the mastermind who employed Tony had even set his sights on expanding his area of influence to include the massive potential underground market of Chicago.

Jeremiah took all this information in thirstily. While he personally disdained the use of drugs, had always felt they were the work of the devil, he still thought it fascinating that a single person could build such a network of distribution and eventually rule a small empire as this mystery person had seemingly done. He began thinking back to some tidbits of the brief conversations that had been shared and realized that Tony had confided more than he had probably ever intended. Most days, Tony had traveled with a partner, and on those days, he tended to be short and incommunicative with Jeremiah. But on days when he arrived alone, he was almost undoubtably more open and willing to make conversation. In retrospect, Jeremiah realized that Tony Mancini had been the type of personality that needed to talk, he had a need to brag about himself, his accomplishments, and endeavors. When he showed up at the dump with a passenger in his van, he already had someone to entertain, whose attention he could command, and was completely satisfied with his audience of one. Therefore, on those days, he would present himself as aloof and disinterested and had no real need to engage with Jeremiah.

"Jeremiah, you have stated that you did not recognize the man who was with Tony that day, the man who shot you. Is that correct?" Detective Mason brought Jeremiah out of his trance with the question.

"Yeah, das what I toldem," Jeremiah replied.

"I'm not so sure that's true, though, is it, Jeremiah?"

"Whatchu mean, I done toldem that, didn't I?" Jeremiah asked.

"Yes, I believe you did, Jeremiah. But let me try to refresh your memory. I can say for certain, without a shred of doubt, that man had accompanied Tony Mancini on numerous trips that were made here, to this facility. In fact, I know positively that his name was Bill Lohman. Are you sure you don't remember that man or his name from previous visits here?"

Jeremiah thought hard and deep, back to one of the days when Tony had arrived at the dump alone, and they had talked. It took a moment, but the buried memory began to resurface that Tony, on at least one occasion, had mentioned that the long-haired, bearded man's name was Bill Lohman. He wondered how that information could have managed to remain hidden in his subconscious. When talking to his interviewers, he had purposefully given a generic description of the man, but not because he was trying to withhold the shooter's identity. Even if he had remembered the name, he wouldn't have given it because he was trying to keep himself as far from suspicion as practicable. But now, with so much known information that Detective Mason had obviously garnered, there really was no reason to continue to deny the identity of the man who had shot at him. He felt secure that with all that Detective Mason knew, his own name had been removed from suspicion of any involvement in Tony's activities.

"You know, Mr. Mason, now that you say the name, I thinks I do 'member that hippie boy, yessiree. Billy *was* his name. I members Tony callin' him that. Yep, I do, now." Jeremiah felt a sense of relief by somewhat clearing what had been lurking in his subconscious.

"So, you did know who he was? Well, that's good to know Jeremiah," said Detective Mason.

"If'n you already knowed his name then, did you catch him already? I'd like to see that boy's hide behind bars, yeah I would," Jeremiah said.

"I have a feeling that fellow might have already faced his comeuppance." Detective Mason's reply seemed rather conclusive. "Since we now have established the shooter's identity, let me delve a little deeper into your memory bank, Jeremiah."

"We can surely try, sir." Jeremiah wondered what other memories might be sufficiently stirred.

"Did Tony Mancini ever mention who his boss was, you know the person behind everything? Did he ever give any indication who the brains of the operation were?" These were pretty direct questions, but unfortunately, they were questions that Jeremiah was ill-prepared to answer.

"No sir, he never told me nuthin' about who his boss man was or nuthin' like that."

"Well let me try and jog your memory a bit. It seemed to help you when I put a name to your shooter. Let's try us a few names, okay? Does Oliver Compton ring a bell? Did Tony ever mention him?"

"I knows the name, but not from nuthin' Tony told me. That's that man kilt that girl over on the riverbank a few years back. Lived right o'er here in Monticello I thinks didn't he?" Jeremiah knew of Ollie Compton; was sure he'd been a locksmith in the area for years.

"How about Stuart Metcalf? Ever heard Tony talk about him?"

"Can't say I ever heard that name, nope."

"Jude Allensworth ring a bell?"

"No sir, don't believe."

"What about Max Schofield? I bet Tony mentioned that name, didn't he?" Detective Mason, took off the newsboy hat that he somehow, strangely, had yet to remove while conducting the interview, and laid it next to the tape recorder. It wasn't until the hat was placed atop the stove, next to the tape recorder, that Jeremiah realized no buttons had ever been pushed on the device. Detective Mason had never turned it on, and up to this point the interview had not been recorded. How could the detective ever hope to recall everything that had been said, all the questions that had been answered, in the past half hour?

"Well, Jeremiah, did he ever mention Max Schofield?"

Jeremiah diverted his eyes from the stovetop back to his interviewer. His mind struggled to retrieve memories of past conversations with Tony Mancini. And a few old memories came rolling back in, like an ocean's tide.

"Schofield? He's the guy runs that body shop, fixes cars out in the county, out by Monticello ain't he?" Jeremiah asked. The detective made no effort to respond to the question, he just sat staring at Jeremiah, waiting for more, apparently.

"Yeah, took my car there one time when it was puttin' up a fit out there on Highway 16 and 511. Yeah, place is out there on double B. I member now."

Jeremiah thought a little more about what Tony had told him on one of the days when he had arrived at the dump alone.

"Yeah, yeah, I talked to that guy Max that day, matter of fact, seemed like a nice 'nuff fella." Jeremiah looked up and toward his right at the ceiling, thinking. "Tell you what, Detective, I'da never spected that man be a guy peddlin' drugs, no sir." When he lowered his eyes to look back at the detective, Jeremiah was surprised to find himself looking down the barrel of a cheap .25 caliber *Saturday Night Special* revolver, not exactly the type of firearm he would expect a police officer to be brandishing.

Detective Mason stood, gun held firmly in his left hand and trained steadily on its target, stepping forward and to Jeremiah's left.

"Well, then Jeremiah, it sounds as though our friend Tony did impart some useful information to you after all, didn't he?"

"You ain't no cop at all, are you, Mason? You done suckered me in just 'nuff to pull out what I'd knowed." Jeremiah studied the man carefully, beginning to make a realization. "I met you once before didn't I. I shoulda knowed, I shoulda knowed you looked familiar. Take away that mustache...dammit, thatsa fake mustache ain't it. I can't believe I got took like this."

* * * *

The two young high schoolers had gotten off the bus on the corner, just up the street from Marcus' apartment, and immediately made a beeline toward Highway 16 and the county dump. They somehow felt they were in a mild race against time.

Twenty minutes later they were finally nearing their planned destination.

"Told you," Marcus said consulting his watch as the pair had made their way from the highway and were headed north along the gravel road. "I knew we could make it before four-thirty."

"Lucky thing you had me along to make sure you kept up the pace, Marcus." Cassie retorted. "If you were by yourself, you'd have been kicking cans and stopping to throw rocks all the way, and it would have taken you twice as long."

More than halfway down the road from highway to the dump, Marcus spotted someone leaving the watchman's shack that Jeremiah fondly called his *office*. Holding out his arm in a motion to stop Cassie, Marcus paused as he saw the man walking toward Jeremiah's distinctive red car. Suddenly, Cassie grabbed awkwardly at his arm and said, "Marcus, hurry, into the cornfield."

"What?" Marcus initially resisted Cassie's tug, until he heard her words of warning. "Get into the cornfield, Marcus. Opa said to hurry and hide."

Marcus had been through enough with Cassie to know that if Opa had spoken to her, or warned her of something, that he'd best take heed. They ran across a small ditch next to the road, just off to their right, and into the nearby rows of corn. Because it was so early in the season, the stalks were barely two feet tall. They ran about three rows deep into the field where they found Opa on his haunches waiting for them. They attempted to hunker down as low as possible, hiding as best they could, hoping to make themselves invisible to whatever it was that Opa was warning them about.

They had only a moment to wait before they witnessed the black car, which Marcus instantly recognized as a Mustang GT, speed by and make a sharp right turn onto Highway 16. As soon as the car had passed, Opa had sprung from the field and begun racing toward the watchman's shack. Confident that the Mustang had completed its turn onto the blacktop and was speeding off in a westerly direction, Marcus and Cassie felt safe enough to vacate their hiding spot. They both ran to catch up with Opa, who now sat with his head hanging sadly, just outside the closed screen door. Arriving several steps before Cassie, Marcus opened the screen door with Opa scooting in past him. Marcus took a quick peek and promptly released the door, allowing it to slam shut. He turned just in time to stop Cassie who was approaching rapidly, panting and gasping to catch her breath.

Anxious to protect Cassie from what he had briefly seen, Marcus mercifully led his exhausted girlfriend across the road to Jeremiah's wicker chair that was still positioned beneath the maple tree. Marcus gently, if somewhat forcibly, pushed her down onto the seat. Only seconds earlier, Cassie had seen Opa hurry into the shack just as Marcus had opened the door.   Still struggling to regain her wind, she looked up at Marcus with her eyes expressing worry and tears beginning to form.   Wordlessly, Cassie sought answers to the questions that were swirling in her head.   She knew Marcus was unaware of the words being spoken by the voice that only she could hear.   Opa's sad and whimpering wail was sadly projected into her receptive mind, repeating the words over and over, "Oh Miah, oh Miah. I'm so sorry. Oh Miah."

James E. Anderson

Evidence

The three of them waited quietly across from the watchman's shack, sheltered under the shade of the maple tree. Cassie, sitting with drying tears in the wicker chair that Jeremiah had so loved to relax in on breezy summer afternoons, gently stroked the top of Opa's head as she stared expectantly, yet absent-mindedly to her right, up the road and toward the two-lane highway, awaiting the arrival of the authorities. Marcus seemed to wander about aimlessly just to Cassie's left. In actuality though, he was nervously pacing, deep in thought as he carefully considered what they should or should not feel free to tell the imminently arriving police officers. Marcus dreaded the thought, but knew that, when the authorities soon appeared, they would bear and present a multitude of queries that likely would keep them there until sunset. Marcus had so many questions of his own that now would remain unanswered. He'd already committed to memory a mental list that he had planned to present to Jeremiah; questions to which only Jeremiah could have provided answers. But now Marcus was faced with so many others. Why would anyone have wanted to do this to Jeremiah? Although Marcus did not really know him that well - after all, they weren't what would be termed *intimate friends* by any means – he did feel a strong attachment to Jeremiah. When he had learned that Jeremiah had known and previously worked alongside his father at the rock quarry, Marcus instantly felt magnetically drawn toward the older man, sensing a mystical connection. His interest was further piqued by the revelation that Jeremiah had been childhood friends with his grandfather. The realization that they had shared a long-ago friendship, coupled with the mystique surrounding the newly found map and promise of buried treasure, had only intensified Marcus' attraction to Jeremiah, compelling him to want to know more.

Still idly petting Opa, Cassie glanced over at Marcus, and it suddenly dawned on her that he was holding a strange looking hat in his hands. It looked vaguely familiar to her; she felt certain she had seen that style on television or perhaps on a newsreel at the Meridian.

"Where did you get that hat, Marcus?" She asked.

"It was in the shack, on the floor next to the stove. When I went back in to get Opa I saw it. I think I've seen Jeremiah wearing it before in town," he said, innocently.

"Do you think you should have taken it; I mean that could be evidence or something, couldn't it?"

"No, it's just his hat. I don't know exactly why I picked it up, just an urge, a spur of the moment thing, I guess. But anyway, I'm going to keep it for a memory of him."

Cassie gazed back down toward the highway, wondering where the responding police car was. It seemed they had been waiting an eternity, and it was a chilling thought to her that a dead man was inside the tiny shack less than thirty feet from them, separated only by the narrow gravel road.

"What do you think is taking so long, Marcus?"

He looked down at his watch to estimate how long they had been waiting.

"I don't know. I would imagine that when we stopped that car and asked the guy to call the police, that it took him as long to drive to a telephone as it took for us to walk back down to here. We've been back at least ten minutes, so I'm sure they'll be here pretty soon."

The words barely had time to settle on Cassie's ears when the first wailing siren broke the rural silence. Moments later, the scene was flooded with police cruisers. Marcus counted three from Lewis County, one Missouri Highway Patrol trooper's vehicle and another unmarked sedan with a flashing red light on the dashboard. Fortunately for Marcus and Cassie, two of the cruisers were piloted by familiar faces in Deputies Daniels and Wilcox. It was somewhat soothing to them that officers they knew and respected had responded. This would make it a good deal less stressful when answering questions and giving statements. Fortunately, the time they'd spent waiting for a response had allowed them opportunity to coordinate their stories. They had agreed on the fact that they had been on the scene merely to pay a visit to Jeremiah. He was an old friend that Marcus had met when Jeremiah would sit on a bench outside Franklin's Five and Dime a few tears back. They agreed they would admit that Jeremiah had worked with Elijah some ten years ago, which was initially the basis for their friendship. And they would report that they periodically visited with him while he worked his shift at the dump. But Marcus and Cassie had promised one another that there would be no mention of Opa, the inheritance, Jeremiah's friendship with Marcus' grandfather, or anything that could possibly create any type of close connection or relationship to Jeremiah or anything of his personal life beyond a casual friendship. They had pinky sworn, a childish, but solemn gesture of honor that sealed the most cherished of agreements between the very best of friends.

They remained under the maple tree while Deputy Martin and Detective Reynolds entered the shack. Deputy Daniels looked in their direction, and raised the pointer finger of his right hand, an indication that he would be over to speak to them momentarily. Cassie nervously reached down to once again pet Opa, but instinctively seemed to know he was no longer going to be there. She stood and walked a few feet, circling the chair and tree scouring the immediate area for him, but to no avail.

"Opa's gone, Marcus," she said.

"I figured as much," he replied. "You can always count on him when something terrible is happening, but when things start to settle back down, he's out like Flynn." Marcus had mangled Denny's 'in like Flynn' movie quote but somehow, under the circumstances, it had seemed appropriate.

The deputy and detective exited the shack, with Detective Reynolds carefully holding the retrieved firearm, which was wrapped in a white handkerchief, presumably to protect against the contamination of any potential fingerprints. Detective Reynolds placed the confiscated evidence in the front seat of his sedan and returned to the other four law officers. The five of them formed a tight circle and from their distance talked indistinctly. They weren't much more than twenty feet from Marcus and Cassie, but they spoke in hushed tones, and while some mumbling could be overheard, their conversation was largely indiscernible from where they currently stood.

After conducting what was to Marcus and Cassie an agonizingly long meeting, Deputies Daniels and Wilcox separated from the group and started across the road toward the teens. As they approached, Deputy Wilcox reached to take Cassie's hand and led her back to the wicker chair she had vacated only moments before. Deputy Daniels placed his left arm across Marcus' shoulders and gently nudged him down the road, a little deeper toward the dump's abandoned contents. They continued down the gravel roadway until Mitchell was sure they were out of earshot of both Cassie and the duo of Martin and Reynolds.

"This almost seems suspicious, Marcus," Deputy Daniels began. "Somebody comes to you, what was it, four, five days ago? And this guy tells

251

you this man has been shot at the dump outside town. You call the Sheriff's Department and report it, telling us you knew instinctively that Jeremiah Paige was the victim. Now, today, you and Cassandra happen to wander upon this scene, and once again, it's Jeremiah Paige that has been shot."

"I don't know anything about what might have happened, Mitchell. Trust me. We visit Jeremiah every once in a while, and today, well.....I don't know what happened, but it's terrible."

"Oh, I believe you, Marcus, I'm not accusing you of anything. It just seems so strange that's all. I mean, why you?" Mitch Daniels just could not draw a connection, much less come to any conclusion as to why Marcus seemed to always find himself embroiled in the few major criminal activities that occurred in Lewis County. "I mean, four years ago you two found yourselves involved in the first bona fide murder the county had witnessed in years. We catch the guy, but during the trial, facts are revealed, and we find out about his scheme to steal your inheritance."

"Yeah Mitchell, but that doesn't have anything to do with this," Marcus said in response. "I mean it couldn't, right? Jeremiah doesn't have anything to do with any of that."

"No, no, I'm sure there's no connection. It's just curious that you're the chosen one, the common link it seems, you know?" Mitchell seemed to be thinking out loud, or perhaps he was attempting to drop a keyword that would spark some subconscious reaction from Marcus. "Don't you think it's kind of weird that fellow chose you to talk to about the shooting last week? All the opportunity that he had to tell someone else, or to have just called it in himself, but instead he drove all that way and picked you to talk to. We still don't have any leads on that truck either, by the way."

Marcus had nothing to say; of course, they would never find a truck that doesn't exist. He'd done his best to put the story of the mystery man in the pickup truck out of his mind, but now the guilt of lying about the made up and non-existent character ate at his stomach. Marcus wondered if he might be developing an ulcer.

"Yeah," Deputy Daniels continued. "And now, today, it's you that's running out to the road, flagging down a car and reporting the shooting of the same person, at the same location. Just strange Marcus, just strange that's all."

Once again, Marcus had no reaction or response, there was no information that he could offer. There was no way he could ever mention the existence of Opa, that would be a fantasy far beyond belief. Even if he were to confess to Mitchell that Opa was the secret connection to Jeremiah Paige, there was no way he could prove Opa's very being. He showed up only when he wanted to be seen, he could not be called or conjured. He did not communicate with anyone but Cassie. Even if Mitchell could or would lay eyes upon him, Opa would appear just as any other dog, and a shaggy, mangy looking one at that.

"So, the statements you provided to Deputy Martin and then later to me and Deputy Wilcox last week, there is nothing there that needs changing or needs to be amended or added to, correct?"

"No, Mitchell, I told you all everything I knew and everything I said was the truth." Marcus had already explained to Deputies Martin, Wilcox and to Mitchell how he had met Jeremiah, that he had learned that Jeremiah had worked with his father, and the knowledge of that connection had been the basis of their casual friendship.

"Okay, Marcus, I appreciate your honesty," Mitchell patted him on the shoulder, turned and initiated a return toward Cassie and Deputy Wilcox. Only a handful of steps into their return, Mitchell paused for a moment, and turning to Marcus spoke softly, "I doubt that you're aware, Marcus, but when Mr. Paige was shot last week, we found the body of another man in a storage container near the very back of the property. We found evidence that indicated drugs had been stored back there and we can only assume that the shootings were somehow related to that discovery. I know you weren't really that in tune with Mr. Paige's personal life and didn't know him all that well, but did you know or even suspect that he might have been involved in the drug trade at all? Ever see or hear anything that, when looking back now, might have raised suspicion? Did he ever mention to you any names that maybe you weren't familiar with?"

"No sir, Mitchell. Jeremiah never really talked about anybody. We mostly just talked about things; you know?"

"Okay, Marcus, I can accept that. Why would he mention anything like that to a teenager, anyway?" Mitchell thought perhaps there had been a chance that Jeremiah Paige had attempted to enlist Marcus as a client, or perhaps a potential connection through which something like marijuana could have been sold to local high school students. "One more thing, Marcus. Did you ever notice anything, or is there anything at all that you can think of that might have caused him to want to take his own life?"

"Mitchell, do you think Jeremiah killed himself?" Marcus asked, somewhat surprised that his friend would suspect that possibility.

"Why yes, Marcus. It's obvious that Mr. Paige committed suicide. The weapon was lying on the floor right next to where he sat, and I'm fairly certain that when the basic investigation is completed, and testing is performed that his fingerprints will be found on the gun." Deputy Daniels carefully explained.

"No, that's not what happened, not at all," Marcus protested. "Somebody shot him, Mitchell. I thought you knew that."

"What would make you think I know that Marcus? This is a classic example of a suicide. The weapon lay at the victim's side and when results come back showing his prints on the weapon, the case will be cut and dried."

"Mitchell, when I looked in there, I saw the gun on the floor, too. But the more I think about it somebody put it there."

"And why do you think that Marcus?" the deputy asked.

255

"Mitch, I hadn't gotten to telling you it yet, but when we were almost here, I saw someone leaving. I saw him walk out of the shack, get in his car and leave. I didn't hear any gunshot, so I guess I thought....Oh God, Mitch. I don't know what I was thinking."

"You saw someone leave?" Mitchell grabbed Marcus' arms with both hands. "Are you telling me someone was here when this happened? Why didn't you tell me sooner?" Mitchell yelled to the group that still stood in a semi-circle, "Hey!" and waved his arms, motioning toward Detective Reynolds and Deputy Martin. "Come on, Marcus."

The two ran the nearly hundred and fifty feet back to where the cars were parked, and the group awaited.

"Detective Reynolds, Marcus here says there was someone here when the incident occurred." Deputy Daniels reported in a raspy, winded voice.

"Yes, we know Daniels, Deputy Wilcox already gave us a description of the man and the vehicle," the detective replied.

Mitchell's first thought was to wonder how Helen Wilcox had reported the information before he had even gotten it from Marcus, but it quickly occurred to him that she had been interviewing Cassie Worthington. He also briefly wondered why it had taken so long for Marcus to mention the man. However, it didn't take much thought for him to realize it was probably his own fault, that he had dominated their conversation by making the session more about Marcus and his strange coincidental involvement in this case. He had inadvertently forced Marcus to think about and explain himself, rather than effectively questioning him and extracting real and pertinent information.

Deputy Martin entered the conversation by offering his take on the presence of the mystery man and the black car. "This guy that the kids saw was probably here to drop off some piece of junk. He probably went into the shack here to sign in and found the victim. I'm sure he was freaked out and left in a hurry, in a panic. Luckily, the girl over here thinks she was able to remember the license plate number."

"Well, that's good news, Lyle," Deputy Daniels commented. "At least we can get a statement from him, verifying what he found."

"I hope Cassie got his plate number right, and I'm sure she did. She's got like a photographic memory." said Marcus to the gathered officers. "And I've got a feeling that the man that left in that car killed Jeremiah."

"Don't be stupid kid. The man shot himself, plain and simple. It's a pretty sure thing if you ask me." Deputy Martin strongly doubted Marcus' assumption.

"Why do you say that Deputy Martin," Marcus asked, taking a defiant step forward.

"Listen, Marcus. It's none of your business, but you seem like a pretty smart kid, so I'll explain. I say that because the guy that got killed here last week, his name was Tony Mancini, okay? Well, we're pretty sure Tony was dealing in marijuana. Good chance Mr. Paige here was working with him. Now, I suspect

Paige killed him and then winged himself to cover up the murder, make it look like somebody else did it. But he's worried, maybe he knows that we know about what Mancini was doing and he thinks he's going to get caught and decides to do himself in."

"That scenario doesn't work out, Lyle." Detective Reynolds interjected. "Paige had glass particles embedded in his face, so he was probably telling the truth about someone shooting through the window of a van. How else could they have gotten there? Plus, if he did shoot Mancini, then where's the vehicle he arrived in. He was signed in and the log showed he dropped something off in the dump, so he had to have been driving a car or truck or, voila, a van. He lived in Granite City, Illinois and the vehicle, a car by the way, registered to him was found in a parking garage in St. Louis. So, he had to have been here in another vehicle. If he was traveling alone, then where's the vehicle?"

"Okay then, second option." Deputy Martin delved into another possibility. "Mancini has a boss. The boss is upset with him, maybe he was skimming or something, so the boss kills him. Then to protect Paige from any suspicion of involvement, he wings him as a way of protecting him, keep him looking like an innocent bystander. But Paige is still worried about getting caught or worried the boss might come after him for something. So once again, he decides to do whack himself."

"Even a weaker assumption Deputy Martin," said Detective Reynolds. "That still doesn't explain the glass in his face, and there doesn't appear to be any reason for the supposed boss to be wanting to come after Mr. Paige. So, for what reason would he want to kill himself? There had to have been an outside motivation that led to this, and unfortunately that is something we will probably never know. In the meantime, Lyle, Trooper Forrester is pulling owner information on the tag number that the young lady provided. I'll want you to follow up on that plate and pay that man a visit as soon as possible."

"Yes, Detective, I'm on it," Deputy Martin accepted the assignment.

Tired of listening to a discussion that was going absolutely nowhere and wondering how these professionals could have overlooked such an obvious clue, Marcus spoke up.

"Can I say something?" Marcus asked. "I respect your experience and your theories, but I can tell you positively that Jeremiah did not shoot himself."

"And why do you think that son?" Deputy Martin asked with a slightly bemused look on his face.

"Well, number one, Jeremiah told me a couple of years ago that he had once been shot in the stomach or something, and almost died from it." Marcus said as he recalled the seriousness with which Jeremiah had related the story. "He told me he would never own a gun, and he said that if someone knew what it felt like to be shot, that they would never shoot another person, or even an animal for that matter. He said there was no need for a man to own a gun, aside from hunting for food, and that he preferred to do his hunting at a grocery or five and dime."

"But Marcus, the gun was laying right next to him, there can't be any doubt that he'd fired it and it had dropped to his side. And that's especially so if it turns out that it has his fingerprints on it." Deputy Martin laid out the indisputable facts for Marcus to digest.

"I know, sir. I saw the gun laying there myself," Marcus continued with his pleading. "But the gun was lying to Jeremiah's left, which would mean he shot it with his left hand, correct."

"Yeah, so? That's not unusual," said Deputy Martin.

"Well sir, I know for a fact that Jeremiah was right-handed, I don't believe he would have tried to shoot with his left hand," Marcus explained.

"Still doesn't mean anything Marcus, many a suicide has been committed by people shooting the gun with their off-hand." Lyle Martin brushed off the possibility that it couldn't have been done left-handed.

Cassie took a place at the edge of the circle and said, "Marcus is right, Jeremiah could not have done that to himself."

"Why Cassie?" Helen Wilcox asked as she stepped up unexpectedly behind her, placing her hands supportively on Cassie's shoulders.

"Look at Jeremiah's left hand," Cassie said. "His fingers are all gnarled up. I noticed it the first time I spoke to him, and I was afraid I'd hurt his feelings, but I went ahead and asked him anyway how they got like that. He said when he worked at the quarry a few years ago that he got his hand caught in some type of a rock crusher or pulving...or pelving... oh what was it, Marcus?"

"Pulverizer, Cassie, he called it a rock pulverizer," he answered.

"Yeah, yeah, that's it, a rock pulverizer," Cassie went on. "Anyway, he crushed most of the fingers on his hand and when they healed, they got all twisted up looking."

"And that's the third reason that I know Jeremiah didn't commit suicide," Marcus said. "It would have been almost impossible to have gotten his fingers into the trigger guard, much less be able to pull the trigger. And he certainly would not have reached all the way around to shoot himself in the left side of his head."

"Well now, that's certainly food for thought. We may have to reconsider and delve a little bit deeper." Detective Reynold was a little perturbed that neither he nor Deputy Martin had noticed the condition of Mr. Paige's hand while they had investigated and before the body had been removed. He pulled out his pad and jotted a note to himself to have the coroner photograph the hands of the victim.

"Daniels, Wilcox make sure to securely lockdown this little shack, before taking written statements from these two witnesses. You can do that here or back at the station, whatever you prefer. Just make sure you contact their parents as soon as possible. Then finish up with them and get them home. I believe they will be due in school tomorrow. I'm going to try to have a state crime scene investigator out here tomorrow, as early as possible. You can help me with that Trooper Forrester, can't you."

"Yes sir, I'll call a request in right away," he replied.

Cassie returned to the wicker chair, and Marcus took a seat in the grass next to her. They sat quietly as everyone but Deputies Daniels and Wilcox left.

"I feel terrible, Marcus. I liked Jeremiah."

"Me too, I'm going to miss him." Marcus hadn't felt this degree of sadness in a long time. He idly picked at blades of grass and gently tossed them into the air watching them flutter in the gentle breeze.

Cassie sat, staring solemnly at the screen door of the shack, thankful that she hadn't run as fast as Marcus, and that he had stopped her before she had looked into Jeremiah's office.

Despite her sadness, a strange calm came over her and Cassie could feel goosebumps forming on her forearms. She took a sideways glance at Marcus just as he shivered, an obvious chill running from his neck downward.

"Everything is fine. Miah is with his parents. He is happy," the words were whispered softly in Cassie's mind.

Looking Ahead

Jack and Debbie Worthington waited impatiently on their front porch for the arrival of the Lewis County Deputy's cruiser that would be safely returning their daughter. Debbie stood, in a decidedly nervous state, alternately wringing her hands and interlacing her fingers. The handwringing had been going on practically nonstop, ever since it had initiated just prior to dinner time. That was when it had occurred to her that Cassie was late. She had learned long ago not to fret when Cassie didn't always come home directly from school as she often would embark on mini excursions with Marcus. But the two were extremely trustworthy and could always be relied upon, without fail, to walk in and greet Debbie prior to five-thirty. It was not just rare for Cassie to be late; it was unprecedented. Fortunately, the telephone had rung at a quarter of six. Jack had only been home from work for five or ten minutes but had already begun preparing to go out looking for Cassie. Thankfully, the call from the Lewis County Sheriff's Department had come just as he was about to leave. Sadie, the dispatcher at the Sheriff's Office, was mildly surprised that Mr. Worthington had instantaneously recognized her voice and remembered her from the several occasions on which they had spoken back in 1963. It had been Sadie's duty, on this late afternoon, to call the parents of Cassie Worthington to inform them of the happenings at the county's easternmost trash facility. While the news was devastating for Cassie's parents, they were justifiably relieved that their daughter was fine, and pleased to know that she would be delivered to their doorstep no later than seven p.m. Debbie had been a nervous wreck, waiting for over an hour now; her fingers were actually beginning to hurt as a result of the intense pressure she had been exerting. In a sense, she was lucky that she had not rubbed or peeled off any skin from her fingers, hands or wrists.

The Worthington's were finally able to breathe a collective sigh of relief when they spotted Helen Wilcox's patrol car as it turned the corner and slowly cruised to the curb in front of the house. Deputy Wilcox got out, circled the car and opened the passenger side door, allowing for Cassie to step out. As soon as she had spied the car rounding the corner, Debbie, followed closely by her husband, had started to run across the front yard. Immediately upon Cassie's exit from the car, she was greeted on the sidewalk with a long, silent bear hug from her mother. Jack put his hand on Cassie's shoulder, and using Marcus' new nickname for her said, "Hey Twigs. Are you okay?"

"Yes daddy, I'm fine," she responded.

"Thank you, Deputy, for bringing her home safely," Debbie said with moist eyes and a slight tremble in her voice. Jack nodded toward Helen, wordlessly echoing Debbie's gratitude.

"My pleasure folks, I always enjoy seeing Cassie," Deputy Wilcox replied, winking at the teen. "I would just prefer it be happening under more pleasant circumstances."

Helen Wilcox walked back around her patrol car and returned to her position behind the wheel. After giving the family a waving gesture, to which Cassie responded, she put the gearshift into drive and pulled away.

Cassie led her parents back into the house, more than ready for the dinner that her mother had kept warm and was thankfully happy to serve.

* * * *

Marcus had told his friend Mitchell that a call need not be placed to Margaret. She was busy serving steak dinners at *The Goldmine* this evening, and he knew that the Sheriff's Office would make sure he was returned to his apartment well in advance of Margaret's arrival home from work. He had convinced Mitchell that a call placed to her at the restaurant would only serve to upset her and cause undo worry and stress. He wasn't hurt, everything was fine, and there was no reason to create a completely unnecessary situation. When all was said and done at the dump and Deputy Wilcox had driven Cassie away, Deputy Daniels gave Marcus a lift back to his apartment. It was a short trip, but on the way Mitchell commended Marcus on his keen-eyed detective work and sharp attention to detail.

"It's not a stretch at all to imagine Lyle Martin failing to notice the fact that Mr. Paige's left hand was mangled," Mitchell quipped with a slight smile, "but I am surprised that detail could have escaped the eagle eyes of Detective Reynolds. He was a big city investigator, used to working tough cases. He's got a lot of experience in things of this nature."

"Mitch, can I ask you a question?" Marcus asked politely enough, but he did not bother waiting for an affirmative response. "Why was Deputy Martin so dead set on the idea that Jeremiah had shot himself? Even when I offered him proof otherwise, he still wanted to try to push toward his idea that Jeremiah had done it himself. It was like he ignored me. Why did he act like that?"

"Well, honestly Marcus, Lyle Martin is a bird of another feather."

"What do you mean, Mitch?" Marcus didn't recall ever having heard that particular wording before.

"You never heard that expression before, Marcus?" Mitchell was a little surprised, he'd always pictured Margaret as the type to quote old sayings and adages. "Actually, the real saying is *birds of a feather flock together*. It's an old idiom that pretty much means that people who are similar are drawn to each other. You know, like you and Cassie and your other friend, Denny's his name, right?"

"Yeah, it's Denny. We've been friends since we were kids."

"Got news for you Marcus, you're still a kid." Mitchell advised. "But I digress. So, now that you're familiar with the original saying, when you say someone is from another feather, or of a different feather, it just means that they're not really like you, kind of like an oddball, or the odd man out. Follow what I'm saying?"

"Yeah, I got it. So really, my friend Denny is a bird of another feather, but Cassie and I accept him just the same, right?" Marcus asked.

"Yep, if you say so. I don't really know your friend Denny, but I trust your judgement." Mitchell wouldn't really have an opinion one way or another, he'd only seen Denny a few times. Although he did remember seeing Denny wandering the aisles of the Meridian Theater where he worked as an usher. He seemed to take pleasure in discouraging the teenaged neckers by spotlighting them with his flashlight and seemed to constantly be mumbling to himself like an actor practicing his lines.

The Deputy pulled his cruiser up to the curb in front of the apartment. As Marcus prepared to get out of the car, he absent-mindedly flipped Jeremiah's hat onto his head before reaching for the door handle. Opening the door, he thanked Mitchell for the ride home.

"Oh, you're welcome, Marcus," he replied. "Listen, Marcus. Try not to think about this too much. If somebody did shoot Mr. Paige, it's not your fault, you've got to know that. You couldn't have done anything to stop it, okay? I just want to make sure you don't go beating yourself up over it, alright?"

"Okay, I'll try to remember that. Thanks Mitch."

"You're welcome, Marcus." Marcus shut the door but, fortunately for Deputy Daniels, he had left the window down. "Hey Marcus," Mitchell called out to him. "I like your hat. My dad used to wear one like that when he hawked newspapers as a kid, over in Quincy."

"Thanks Mitch." Marcus waved and turned to head to his front door. He was so glad that he'd had the instinctive presence of mind to have bitten his tongue. When Mitchell had complimented his hat, Marcus very nearly had said something to the effect of *yeah thanks, it was Jeremiah's.* Slippage like that could have been disastrous.

* * * *

The hour was relatively late, the ten o'clock news had just kicked off with its lead story, a recap of the day's events in the southeast Asian mudhole known as Vietnam. Without a doubt, in terms of etiquette, it was definitely too late for a visitor to be calling. Occasionally there could still be that rare late-night caller pounding on the door, unaware that Oliver Compton, the locksmith, no longer inhabited the property. Max Schofield was about to drain his fifth Schlitz malt liquor and was considering a bathroom run to properly prepare for his sixth, when he detected the unmistakable sound of a car racing up the gravel driveway. Downing his final swig, he set the empty can on a coaster on the coffee table, rose and walked a bit unsteadily to the front door. There he mentally rehearsed a rude greeting to present to the unwelcome visitor. But when he realized that the person approaching was, in fact, a uniformed police officer speed walking toward him, Max managed to revert at once to what he hoped was a reasonable facsimile of full-scale sobriety.

Max had flipped on the porch light prior to the officer stepping up to the door and, as the man drew near, he recognized him as the lone Lewis County Deputy that Max held in his pocket.

"What brings you here this late at night?" Max opened the door wide, an unspoken invitation for his guest to enter. "You want a malt liquor? I was about to have the one on the coffee table, but I got another six-pack in the ice box if you want one."

"Sure, that sounds good. My shift is over, and I was about to head home to the missus. A cold one wouldn't hurt at the end of a long day."

Max fetched an ice-cold Schlitz and handed it to his minion, who had taken a seat on the worn red leather couch.

"How'd everything go today at the dump? Cut and dried suicide I'm assuming, shouldn't have been any glitches, right?" Max asked.

"Before we get into it too deep, Max, fill me in on a few things. It's kind of tough to try to run interference, when you're not really sure just where the play is being run, or for that matter, why it's even being run."

"Like what, Deputy Dawg?" Max didn't too much care to be questioned by his subordinates.

"Well, first of all like, why kill the old man, Mr. Paige? He wasn't involved in Tony's business, I'm pretty sure he didn't know any of his associates. From what I know, he didn't have any idea who Bill Lohman was, either. Just the whole thing has a smell to it you know?"

"The old man knew a lot more than you would have guessed," Max told him in explanation.

"No wait. Let's just back up to the beginning. What was Tony's transgression that he teed you off so bad to begin with. He's been running your product for years. Was he skimming off the top, copping product? What was his sin after all these years that made you want to have Billy whack him?"

"I think just the fact that I kept him around so long might have been the whole problem, in a nutshell." Max opened up to him about his personnel for the very first time. "He was getting too big for his britches. Started hammering for more money, a bigger cut of the action."

"Yeah, but that's kind of a normal progression you'd expect in any business isn't it Max?"

"Sure, to an extent. But regular raises weren't enough for Tony." Max took a sip of malt liquor, wiped his mouth with his forearm, and continued. "When he got up enough nerve to start making threats to me, that's when I knew it was time."

"What kind of threats?"

"Well, mostly it was about the big boys down in St. Louis. He started making noise about ratting me out to the brass, threatened to start dropping hints about the goods I was picking up from outside sources and was moving, you know, cutting into the territory that belongs to the hub down there." Max must have had one or two too many malt liquors to be revealing so much information to one of his underlings. "Imagine if they knew that I was selling somebody else's merchandise to their customers? I'd have been trying to swim the Mississippi while wearing cement boots, for sure."

"Okay, after hearing that, I guess I can see your motivation to act quickly and decisively on him."

"Should have been easy as pie. At that time, it was a simple matter of Billy taking care of business, but I guess I had way overestimated that guy. First of all, it wasn't supposed to be done at the dump." Now Max was admitting that his choice of Tony's replacement had been a major error in his judgement. "Should have been done over at the *Bar None Saloon*. Plenty of things like that have happened there over the years, wouldn't have been a big deal, just another biker crime, you know how that goes down. No suspects, no arrests, no nothing. Anyways, I explicitly told him that, to do it there in the bar parking lot. But no, the idiot misunderstood, he thought that's where I was supposed to meet up with him afterward. Damned fool. And then he goes and shoots at the old man. Wouldn't have been so bad if he'd have killed him, but again, no. The idiot leaves a witness."

"So, whatever happened to Bill Lohman? You send him back to St. Louis, tell them he was too green to do you any good anymore?"

"Yeah, something like that. Let's just say he's out of the picture and let it go at that." Max said. "So then, that brings us up to today. I go over there, pretend I'm a cop and start grilling him. And that's when I find out that I'm glad I got rid of Tony. The rat hadn't told the old man a whole lot, but just enough. And then, my stupid luck, the old man had brought his car to my shop a while back and I had talked to him. When he realized I was wearing a fake mustache, he fingered me. It was like a light bulb went off in his head and he put two and two together. I didn't have no choice by that time. So, like I asked you earlier, everybody bought into the suicide scenario, right?"

"Okay, about the suicide," Deputy Dawg then went into everything that had transpired the entire afternoon. He started at the beginning, explaining how Max's car had been seen leaving the scene by two teenagers, a boy and his girlfriend. He told him how the teenaged girl, her name was Cassie, had picked up on his license plate and given an accurate description of his car.

"Okay, I'm darned confused here already. I don't remember seeing any kids out there, nowhere," said Max, suddenly starting to sober up. Funny, isn't it, how a little bit of fear and sense of worry can sometimes erase the fog of a mild stupor?

"You were probably just in a hurry and didn't notice them. But Detective Reynolds will be waiting tomorrow for statements that need to be taken from you in the morning setting up your alibi and hopefully forcing doubt on the validity of the girl's recollection of your tag number."

"Okay, okay. Anything else I need to be aware of?"

"Did you wipe the gun clean of your prints?"

"Yeah, of course I did that, I'm not stupid you know," Max raised his voice near the end of the sentence.

"What about prints from Paige? Did you press the handle and trigger into his hand to establish his fingerprints?"

"No, I didn't." Now Max did feel stupid, how could he have forgotten anything so simple and basic?

Deputy Dawg was afraid that what Max had just said was exactly what was going to be the answer, the response he'd pretty much expected. After learning of the victim's injured left hand, he had assumed that it would have been difficult to stage a lifeless and mangled hand in order to force prints onto the weapon. The only real hope had been for Max to have used the right hand instead. The odds that a self-inflicted wound to the left side of the head could have been produced by a weapon held in the right hand of the victim would have been infinitely small, but the presence of such evidence would be sufficient to create at least a shred of doubt. He explained to Max the lack of any likelihood at all that the old man could have wounded himself.

"Think really, really hard, Max. Was there anything, anything at all that you carried into that watchman's shack with you that you did not bring out with you when you left? Anything?" The deputy was worried that with the mistakes Max had made that had already been uncovered, and considering either his stupidity or lack of understanding, that there could still exist a possibility that he might have left some identifying item or article behind.

Max was concentrating, taking inventory of exactly what he'd brought along in his effort to make himself look official. "I don't think so. I had the satchel, in it was a note pad, pen, tape recorder. No, I specifically remember taking it all out and placing it back in my desk in my office at the shop."

"Good, I sure hope you're right, Max. We can't afford any other blunders. It's bad enough that you allowed your car to be seen. I don't get it Max, all the cars at your disposal, interchangeable license plates, why would you take your very own vehicle?"

"I don't know. I had run a few errands earlier, just wasn't thinking, I guess."

"Well, I'll do all I can to try to clean this mess up for you. Try to lie low for a couple of weeks, will you?" Then something else occurred to him. "Oh, brother Max, with Tony and Billy both out of the picture, don't tell me you're running shipments out of St. Louis now. Please tell me you're not."

"No, I took care of that right away. I got Alicia's kid doing it."

"Alicia, who's Alicia?"

"She's my bookkeeper. Her and her boy, they live down in Fulton. The boy is never up here except for deliveries, so slim chance he'll ever get pulled over or anything. Good kid. Ollie Compton's boy, remember him?"

"Are you kidding me, Max. That kid is an ex-con. There's probably a good chance that if his tags get spotted, he'll get pulled right over just so somebody could have fun hassling him."

"Is that what you would do, Deputy Dawg?"

"If you hadn't of just told me he was working for you I would have, yeah."

"Well, nothing to worry about. He drives a Plain Jane company car that he picks up in St. Louis every morning. Gets switched out every few days. The Bossman down in the Lou, he's careful about that kind of stuff."

"Bossman, huh? Is he one of those mafia types? Wears a suit and a fedora, looking really uppity all the time?"

"No actually, he never wears a suit or a hat. He's more a blue jeans and tee shirt kind of guy." Max pictured the last time he'd seen the Bossman. "You know, now that I think of it, he drives a convertible and when he's got the top down, he does wear one of them sports car guy caps. You know the kind I'm talking about? They're kind of like those old newsboys' hats, you know. I got one of them I like to wear some........oh crap."

"Oh crap, what?" the deputy could almost hear the words that Max was preparing to utter.

"My hat, it fell on the floor, I knocked it off the stove and forget to get it. Ah, geez, I guess when I picked up the tape recorder, or maybe when I staged the gun, I don't remember."

Deputy Dawg suddenly remembered Marcus standing in the circle with the other police officers, twirling a newsboy hat in his hands.

"I'll see if I can sneak into the crime scene tonight on the way home." He remembered Detective Reynolds ordering the scene secured and locked down but didn't recall anything being said about having it manned or monitored. "If it's still there, I'll snatch it. If not, we'll just try to play if off as belonging to Mr. Paige."

"I hope you can get away with that." Max said rather hesitantly.

"Why do you say that? Don't tell me, you wrote your name inside, in the band and with a Magic Marker, so you wouldn't lose it?"

"Not exactly, but if the band gets flipped down, my initials are embroidered there."

* * * *

Marcus had not beaten Margaret home by very much. Arriving, he had gone directly to the bathroom and bathed, dressed, and gotten settled in front of the television. Dinner time had adjusted slightly with Margaret's new job. Mondays and Wednesdays were her off days and she had been cooking their normal seven p.m. dinner. But that had been forced to slide back one hour be this week with Marcus having begun working part-time and not getting home until the neighborhood of eight o'clock. Tuesdays and Thursdays Margaret normally arrived home from her job a shade past seven, which also resulted in an eight p.m. dinner. Friday, Saturday, and Sunday evenings Margaret worked until just past closing and generally didn't get in until the ten o'clock news was just finishing up. On those nights, Marcus would fend for himself, feast on leftovers, or occasionally have dinner at the Worthington's house.

Tonight, Margaret splayed across the table a dinner of fried chicken sided with macaroni and cheese. The food had been specially prepared by her friend Buster at her old haunt, *The River's Edge Diner*. As she continued setting out utensils, Marcus pulled up a chair and proceeded to tell her the sad news concerning his friend Jeremiah Paige. Margaret had never met Jeremiah but knew of him well enough through Marcus' stories and tales. She was aware that he had worked with Elijah at the rock quarry, and as such felt saddened by his passing. She strove to console Marcus, but there really wasn't much she could say to alleviate his grief. It would just require time for the healing to occur and she stressed that to Marcus.

Margaret was distraught when Marcus revealed that it was almost a certainty that Jeremiah had been murdered, and that once again he and Cassie were sitting right square in the middle of everything. There was a good bit of healthy back and forth between them, and Margaret urged him and Cassie to do everything in their power to distance themselves as much as possible from involvement. She was encouraged by the fact that, once again, Mitchell Daniels was part of the investigation. She had every confidence in his ability to ensure that Marcus would be kept safe and out of harm's way.

After dinner and dishes, Margaret and Marcus went to the living room to watch *The Red Skelton Show*, which was due to air on CBS at 8:30 p.m. It was still more than ten minutes until the show would begin, and too late to try to watch something that was about to end, like *Daktari*, so Marcus decided it would be a good time to tell Margaret about Sunday's visit with Ellis. When she had arrived home late on Sunday night, Marcus had already been in bed, asleep. The opportunity to discuss the topic last night had been naturally overshadowed by all the talk about his new job and the decision by Margaret to help Marcus in the purchase of the Nash Metropolitan from Walt McMurphy. This evening would have to be the time, Marcus couldn't continue to put it off.

Taking a deep breath, Marcus began spewing all the details to Margaret. He explained everything, from Ellis appearing on the doorstep right after she had left for work on Sunday morning and all the way through to opening the document binder. He conveniently failed to mention the letter from Opa or the treasure map. He also did not feel quite ready to share with Margaret the fact that Jeremiah and Elijah's father had been best friends in their youth. There just were some things that seemed best kept under wraps.

Marcus was careful to paint an exemplary picture of Ellis. He was categorically certain that Margaret would have absolutely no faith in Marcus' assumption and resulting confidence that Ellis had truly been rehabilitated. He was sure that, despite his contention that Ellis had been through two years of psychotherapy, nothing had essentially changed. Even as Marcus tried to assure her that Ellis had been able to see and understand the problems caused by his adoptive father, he feared that her opinion would remain unfettered and unchanged, that the person she had viewed in 1963 as a psychopath was still, in her eyes, nothing short of a monster.

Margaret mulled over all that Marcus had imparted and asked a few pointed questions. One thing she wanted to know was how he felt about Ellis being in the company of Cassie. Did he truly trust Ellis after what he had put them through? Marcus had to be honest with himself and with Margaret.

"I think so," he answered from the heart. "I do believe that Ellis was earnest with me. But at the same time, I would be cautious. Would I trust Ellis with her alone? Probably not yet. But in my company, yes."

"I think that is a good answer, Marcus," Margaret seemed to agree with him. "From what you have told me, it is a matter of trust that is going to have to grow and be nurtured amongst the three of you. Before you expose Cassie to his presence without adult supervision, here is what I propose Marcus. Have Ellis to come here for dinner one evening, let me meet him. Give me the opportunity to judge for myself. I didn't know him before, and I admit, I am somewhat apprehensive, but give me a chance to gauge his sincerity."

Marcus felt a bit sheepish, because he had felt so supremely confident on Sunday when Ellis had dropped him at Cassie's and left to go to Monticello.

"Will Thursday night be acceptable, Mama?" he asked.

"Thursday, Marcus? That's a bit of short notice, isn't it?" Margaret was taken off guard by Marcus' request.

"I can't be dishonest with you, Mama," Marcus said. "Sunday, when Ellis was here, I felt good. It was nice to be with someone who shares history and what's the word? Oh, oh, I have it, it's genealogy. We share those things. Just me, Ellis and Cousin Judy, nobody else. Anyway, I felt so good that I asked him then if he would come and have supper with us on Thursday."

"Marcus Clemens, how could you extend an invitation without consulting with me first?" Margaret asked him brusquely.

"I'm sorry Mama," Marcus felt his face redden with guilt. "I don't know, I just, I just felt so good and confident in the moment, I guess. I guess I just assumed you would be okay with it when I told you. And I meant to tell you before now, Mama."

"We've discussed the word assume before Marcus." Marcus knew that Margaret was about to remind him that it was one of Elijah's favorite sayings. "Your father always said that didn't he Marcus? Ass-U-Me. Please don't you ever make an ass out of me, Marcus."

"Yes, Mama."

"That said, when Ellis knocks on the door Thursday night, you can't just turn him away, can you?" It only took a second of thought before Margaret continued, "I'll bring steaks and baked potatoes home from *The Goldmine* and heat a can of green beans. Do you want to invite Cassie as well? I can drive her home after supper."

"Thanks, Mama."

What's Next?

Marcus let himself into the apartment, bypassing his normal detour to the kitchen, and instead heading straight to his room in order to strip off his school clothes and redress into his blue work shirt and pants. With it only being his second day of employment at Walt's, a new routine was going to take some time to grow accustomed to, especially having to sidestep his customary after school snack. Sitting in the now too-small chair belonging to the desk set that he had been gifted by his father and stepmom for his seventh birthday, Marcus slipped on and laced his new pair of black leather work boots. As he straightened back up, Marcus could not avoid noticing Jeremiah's hat. He had carefully placed it on top of his desk upon returning home last night, and seeing it now brought the gruesome vision of Jeremiah, slumped in a terribly uncomfortable looking fashion, in his beloved rocking chair. Marcus was so glad that he had reached the shack first and had been able to keep Cassie away, saving her from witnessing the horror that he had stumbled upon. He stood, taking one final look toward the hat and shook his head, telling himself not to wallow in self-pity. What was done was done, there was no point in thinking or worrying about it too much. Even though he felt certain that he had seen the man who had ended Jeremiah's life, matters were beyond any control he wielded. He had to convince himself that if Jeremiah had indeed been murdered, then Mitch Daniels and his law enforcement friends would have to be trusted to piece together the evidence and track down the culprit.

Marcus went into the kitchen to retrieve a glass of water before leaving for Walt's. Walking through the archway and past the table on the way to the sink, something in his peripheral vision caught his eye. An envelope was propped up against the napkin holder on the table. Neatly printed on it, in Margaret's unmistakable handwriting was his name – Marcus - with a smiling face drawn to the side. Marcus felt a sweeping flood of elation when he peered into the unsealed envelope. Inside were twenty-dollar bills, five in all when counted, that had been folded inside a piece of stationary from Margaret's tablet. The folded paper contained a short note penned by Margaret, telling him that she had run to the bank this morning and withdrawn enough cash for Marcus to give Mr. McMurphy for his required down payment. There were just absolutely some days that Marcus was so grateful that his father had married Margaret. He sometimes wondered what type of life he would be leading right now without the grace of her presence and guidance.

* * * *

On Thursday evening, Margaret walked carefully into the apartment carrying her purse and three paper bags that bore the name and logo of *The Goldmine*. Cassie jumped from the couch and, remarkably. was able to pull two of the bags from her grasp, helping to keep her from dropping them as she tried to close the door. Marcus and Ellis had not even managed to stir before Cassie had been able to save the day.

Margaret and Cassie carried the bags to the kitchen table and carefully unpacked them. Wiping her hands on a dish towel, Margaret, with Cassie following, re-entered the living room to welcome her guest. Ellis and Marcus both stood as Marcus made the introduction.

"Mama, this is Ellis Compton, Cousin Judy's son, and my second cousin. And Ellis this is Margaret Clemens. Technically, I guess she is my stepmom, but not really. This is my Mama, the best mom there is."

The two tentatively shook hands, with Margaret expressing her gratitude to Ellis for him showing the initiative to take the first step toward developing some semblance of a familial relationship with Marcus. Five minutes of small talk ensued, followed by Margaret requesting Cassie's assistance in the kitchen. Marcus and Ellis resumed watching the tail end of *Daniel Boone* on the television. Marcus had always enjoyed Fess Parker's portrayal of Daniel Boone and was surprised when Ellis told him that back when he was about eight years old that he was almost positive that the same actor had played Davy Crockett on television.

In the meantime, Cassie had placed the steaks and potatoes in casserole dishes and put them into the preheated oven for warming. Margaret opened and emptied two cans of sliced green beans into a medium sized saucepan, seasoned and began slowly heating them on the stovetop. As they worked to prepare the meal, the two talked in hushed, whispery tones.

"So please tell me, Cassie, what is your opinion of Ellis? Marcus swears to me that he has changed and is a different, better person. What do you think?" Margaret was aware than Cassie was none too pleased by the encounter with Ellis a week prior, but she had just been through a week of talking with Marcus and had now spent at least an hour or so with him here at the apartment. Her thoughts and feelings were important to hear. Margaret knew that Cassie was a thoughtful and insightful person, and she valued her opinion.

"Honestly? I trust and respect Marcus and what he feels, but I'm not as convinced as he seems to be. I don't view myself being as much of a forgiving person as Marcus." Cassie's answer was candid, and Margaret knew she was responding in an honest and forthright manner. "I still have nightmares about him at the mausoleum and of being tied up and gagged in his dad's car. I don't know Margaret. He does seem sincere and maybe Marcus is right, maybe he was brainwashed and the things he did weren't his idea or fault and maybe he truly is sorry for everything. But I just don't know if I'm really ready to forgive and forget. I don't sound too harsh, do I?"

"No, and I completely understand your point of view, Cassie," Margaret sympathized. She hadn't realized that even after four years, the trauma of Cassie's kidnapping had left such deep and enduring scars. "I feel for both of you, for going through that, and now having to deal with what happened Tuesday. I can only imagine the shock and emotional upheaval you went through that afternoon and night."

"Oh, we'll be okay, Margaret. Marcus and I have each other, he has you, and I've got my folks. In the end our family members will help us through, I'm sure of that." In that regard, Cassie was confident. And it helped her by knowing that Opa was always there looking out for Marcus.

As a matter of fact, Opa had been the subject of discussion for her and Marcus after school today, before Ellis had arrived. Cassie had brought that very matter up to Marcus when she had asked him why he thought Opa hadn't done anything to help Jeremiah. They had been best friends their entire lives on earth, and Opa obviously knew what was happening just down the road from where they had hidden in the cornfield. It was as if Opa had seen into the future. He had called to them to come hide amongst the cornstalks, in the nick of time. They had gotten down low and out of sight just as the man's car had sped by. What if they had been on the road when he passed? Would he have stopped? He might have decided they were witnesses to what had happened and could have decided to kill them as well. But, as Cassie had speculated all this to Marcus, the realization hit her that *Marcus* was the reason that

Opa had hailed them. Opa was Marcus' guardian angel, not Jeremiah's, and not hers. She was fortunate to have been with Marcus. As a result of him being protected, she had benefited from her proximity to him. If she had been walking the road alone, at the same time and same spot, and everything had happened along the same timeline, there would not have been a call from Opa. Cassie would have likely been considered an unfortunate witness to Jeremiah's murder, and there stood a reasonable chance that she too could have been eliminated. She was also reminded that in the mausoleum, it had been Marcus who had pushed her back and told her to run. Opa had not interfered until Marcus' life had been threatened, only then did he spring into action. And then later, in the very same location, when they had been attacked and rendered unconscious, Opa had been the entity that had pulled the sack off Marcus' head and probably saved his life. Cassie, in the meantime, had been kidnapped by Oliver and Ellis Compton. And Opa had done absolutely nothing to stop them, or to help her.

The sad fact had made itself known to her that as much as she loved and cared for Opa, his sole focus and obligation was to Marcus. He would not and could not save her, even if the situation came down to it. And now she fully understood and accepted why Opa was unable to do anything for Jeremiah. Not until it was too late, and as she had heard, all he could do at that point was stand by Jeremiah's side and apologize.

* * * *

The dinner had been an enjoyable experience for all four of them. The ribeye steaks were exceptional, even more so considering they were takeout from the restaurant and had required reheating. Conversation had been pleasant, and Margaret was delighted to learn many of the details of Ellis' life. He had not delved deeply into his mid-teenaged years, the time during which he had fallen inextricably under the influence of Oliver's twisted mind. But he had been more than happy to share with them regarding the marvelous relationship he now enjoyed with his real father, Judy. Ellis had raved about the attention and generosity of his dad, though not nearly so much as he did about the groovy Corvette that Judy drove. Marcus sensed that Margaret had warmed considerably to Ellis, and though he was sure she would have liked to have questioned him pointedly about the events for which he had spent time incarcerated, she had left that water unrippled, completely unmentioned and kept free from discussion. Looking ahead, in four more days it was Memorial Day. With it being a Monday, it was Margaret's normal day off anyway. She and Marcus had planned to spend the afternoon with Cassie's family. It had become a new tradition, having commenced in 1966, and over the past year Margaret was happy to have gotten to know Jack and Debbie better than ever. For the past four years, they had been spending some of the holidays together, and Margaret sometimes selfishly worried that one day Marcus and Cassie would have a falling out and hers and the Worthington's camaraderie would suddenly come to an end. Marcus had hoped to have Ellis join them for the Worthington barbeque, but when Cassie (at Marcus' insistence) had asked her parents, the request had been met with a resounding no. Certainly, not enough time had passed since Cassie's kidnapping and despite her pleading on Marcus' behalf to allow Ellis a chance, the answer remained firm.

The evening passed rapidly, and it was still a school night for Marcus and Cassie. As ten o'clock approached, Margaret decided that it was about time for Cassie to be driven home.

"Well unfortunately, I think it's time that all good things must come to an end," she said. "Marcus, would you please fetch my purse so that I can drive Cassie home?"

"Sure Mama," he replied as he began to rise from the couch.

Suddenly standing up, Ellis said, "Excuse me, Margaret, but I need to be leaving also. I could drop Cassie at her house, it wouldn't be out of the way for me."

Cassie hoped it wasn't obvious, but her eyes immediately darted nervously toward Marcus. She dearly hoped that he would intervene. Ellis had been charming all evening, but as she had told Margaret earlier, her trust was not yet there.

"That's very kind of you to offer, Ellis, but honestly, call me old fashioned if you will, but Cassie is Marcus' girlfriend and honestly, I really don't think that would look good nor be considered appropriate."

Cassie breathed a sigh of relief that Margaret had quickly derailed that plan.

"Well, I could ride along, Mama," Marcus offered. Cassie was dismayed that Marcus would make such an offer. Not that she wouldn't feel safe knowing Marcus was accompanying her, but Cassie had been relieved, feeling like she had just a dodged a bullet, and now Marcus was edging her back onto the firing line.

"That's a good idea, Marcus," Ellis said. "It'll give us a chance to talk a little more. We can take Cassie home, and I'll drop you back by here."

"Are you sure you don't mind, Ellis?" Margaret asked.

"No ma'am, not at all. It would be my pleasure."

"Okay then. Actually, that would probably help me out," Margaret was sort of relieved to have the extra few minutes alone. She had been on her feet since eleven this morning, was tired, and she still had the kitchen to clean up. She had put it off earlier because she knew time was short. It was a school night, and she had chosen to allot as much time as possible to conversation, to speak to and hear from Ellis Compton. The kitchen could wait until later when everyone had left, and it was just her and Marcus.

With the decision made that Ellis would drive Cassie home, she and Marcus had followed Ellis out to the Ford sedan. As they all piled into the front bench seat, Ellis apologized for the condition of the car. The seats had small tears and the dashboard was cracked. The car was almost twenty years old, nearly as old as Ellis, and it definitely had seen better times.

"I'm hoping it won't be too long until I can trade this in on something new," Ellis quipped as he started the car. Marcus hadn't thought much about it until he watched Ellis working his way through the gears on the column mounted gear shift, but he was soon going to have to learn how to drive with a stick shift transmission in the Metropolitan he had just placed a one hundred dollar down payment on. Margaret's car had an automatic transmission, and that is what he practiced in and would take his driving test with. But after he acquired his license, he was going to have to quickly learn how to master a manual transmission. He asked Ellis about the degree of difficulty in working the clutch and the gearshift at the same time.

"It's not that hard to learn, Marcus," Ellis said confidently. "It's just a matter of developing a little bit of coordination between your feet, your mind and your right hand. Whenever you're ready, you let me know and I will teach you with this car. It won't take long at all. We'll go to a parking lot, and I'll show you how to get comfortable with the clutch. It won't take no time at all."

"Gee, Ellis. Would you?" The thought that Ellis would help him was enough to put a huge smile on Marcus' face.

"What about you, Cassie? Will you be needing lessons?" Ellis asked her. Cassie was already a wee bit uncomfortable as she sat in the middle, between Ellis and Marcus, doing her utmost to turn ever so slightly away from Ellis and lean gently into Marcus.

Every time Ellis reached up for the gearshift, she worried that she was going to be hit with an elbow to the breast. But to his credit, Ellis was careful and had yet to make any contact with her.

"No Ellis, but thank you," Cassie said, perhaps a bit curtly. "I've already starting learning on my dad's car, and it has an automatic transmission, so it's been pretty easy."

"What kind of car are you looking to trade this one for, Ellis?" Marcus asked him, genuinely curious. Getting down to the last few months before getting his license, and now working part-time at Walt's, had served to intensify Marcus' interest in cars.

"Actually Marcus, I'm thinking real hard about getting a new Camaro when the '68 model comes out in September. A red hard top, I hope. I thought about a convertible, but dad's Stingray is a convertible, and I don't too much care for ragtops." Ellis had been studying magazines like *Motor Trend* and *Car and Driver* drooling over the new makes and models that were going to be coming out in the fall. "They're talking about the price tag might be close to $3,000, but I bet it's worth it."

"Wow, that's a lot of money for a car," Marcus whistled at the cost.

Cassie elbowed him sharply in the ribs. "Knock it off, Marcus."

"Ow, what's that for?" Marcus flinched, and Ellis had to look over curiously with Marcus wailing in pain. He too wondered what had drawn Cassie's ire.

"You whistled, you big lug, and it's after dark!" Considering Cassie's intelligence level - and she was

291

extremely smart – she was terribly superstitious and very aware of activities that she believed were bad omens. She feared breaking mirrors, walking under ladders, black cats crossing her path, the number thirteen, and even though it was basically a Chinese belief, she was especially concerned with whistling after dark. That was the one that had always been hard for Marcus to understand. He had always heard that whistling in a graveyard was bad luck, but to Cassie, whistling after dark was an invitation for ghosts to follow you home. Which again, confused Marcus because, after all was said and done, wasn't Opa a ghost?

"We don't need any more bad luck, Marcus. And I certainly don't want any ghosts around." The belief had been with her since her grandmother had instilled it in her when Cassie wasn't much more than a toddler. Excepting Opa, Cassie wanted nothing to do with any ghosts.

As they entered Cassie's subdivision, Marcus wanted to get back to the conversation they had been engaged in before Cassie's interruption.

"That Camaro, man Ellis, that's a lot of money," Marcus couldn't fathom paying that much for a car. He supposed $3,000 was more than he would make in an entire year at Walt's.

"It's not too terrible, Marcus. I hope by September I can maybe put down half and then dad has kind of promised me he would borrow me the rest."

"Wow, that would be so neat. I can't wait until you get that car, Ellis," Marcus actually found himself excited for him.

"Here's my house," Cassie had to interrupt, she thought Ellis was going to drive right by it.

The Ford eased to the curb and Marcus opened the door and stepped out, preparing to walk Cassie to her porch.

As she began to scoot toward the open door, Ellis touched Cassie ever so lightly on the shoulder. Surprised, she looked back at him as he spoke with a slight grin on his face.

"It was nice seeing you again, Cassie. Thank you for trusting me to bring you home." Ellis spoke in a soft tone. "I know you had reservations riding with me, even with Marcus along. And I understand that. I appreciate your faith."

"Oh, that's okay," she said, momentarily at a loss for words.

Marcus walked her to the front door, and they stood on the porch for a few seconds.

"Did you hear what Ellis said?" Cassie asked Marcus.

"Yeah, I did," he responded.

"That was nice of him, Marcus," she said softly. "He sounded like he really did appreciate my feelings and how uneasy I was. Maybe he has changed, Marcus. You believe it, don't you?"

"Yeah, Cassie. I do think so," Marcus said attempting to reinforce her thoughts.

"Tell him I said thank you for the ride, okay," Cassie said. "I should have, but I didn't." Cassie gave

Marcus a goodbye peck on the cheek and said, "Good night, Marcus." She turned the door handle and in five seconds was gone for the night.

On the drive back to Marcus' apartment, they were both relatively quiet.

"Ellis, Mama and I are going to Cassie's folks house on Monday afternoon for Memorial Day, you know, for a barbeque. I had Cassie ask her parents if I could bring you along," Marcus felt awkward trying to get the words out to express what their response had been. "But...."

"I know," Ellis said as he interrupted Marcus. He knew exactly where Marcus was going and wasn't surprised or upset. "I get it Marcus. Let's face it, they think I was going to kill their little girl, and I helped my dad, well Ollie. I try not to call him dad anymore. Her parents know for a fact I helped kidnap her. Marcus, I understand there's no way I would ever be invited to their house. And it's okay."

"Really?"

"Yeah, of course," Ellis said. "It's okay and I completely understand how they feel. Me and my therapist back at *The School,* we talked about it a lot. He explained how the first thing I had to do was to come to terms with myself. Kind of like being an alcoholic. You've got to admit to yourself what you are. Until you see that, you can't get better. And once you realize and recognize your errors, then you can start thinking about forgiving yourself. After you've gotten through that stage, then you start looking for ways to earn forgiveness from the people that you've wronged. Sometimes you find that forgiveness and sometimes you don't, sometimes it's impossible. I'm working on that with you and Cassie now and I hope eventually I'll get there. But Cassie's folks, that will be a lot tougher and there's a pretty good likelihood it'll never happen. If it doesn't, that's okay. As long as when I go to meet my maker, I can stand there proud and say, welp, by God, I tried."

"Wow, that's really something, Ellis," Marcus was drawn to the depth of what Ellis had said.

"Something else, Marcus," Ellis added. "Cassie and her parents may never believe what I'm going to tell you, but I swear it's the honest to God's truth. At the mausoleum that day, my head was really messed up, but - and this is the truth - I was only there for you. I wasn't there for her. I wouldn't have touched her, I swear. That's why I was wearing the ski mask, so Cassie could leave, and if she wasn't able to see my face, she couldn't identify me. I was going to let her go, I swear to God."

"What about at your house, after you had kidnapped her?" Marcus asked.

"I honestly don't know what Ollie's plan was, Marcus," Ellis responded with remorse in his voice. "I guess he was going to use her to try to get to you."

"Cousin Judy, your dad, told me back then that he thought you guys were going to kill her and try to frame me for it, Ellis," Marcus said allowing a little bit of anger to seep in. "I have to know, was that true?"

"No, absolutely not," Ellis said, but then he quickly amended what he'd just said. "No Marcus, I don't think so. Ollie is crazy, so I don't know for sure, maybe. But I can tell you this, if he was going to, I wouldn't have let him. She was an innocent kid; I would not have let that happen."

"What would you have done, Ellis?" Marcus wanted to know. "How could have stopped him."

"I would have killed him if I had to, Marcus," Ellis raised his hand, palm turned toward Marcus. "I swear, I would have killed him dead. Marcus, I had just found out he wasn't my real father, I was already mad at him. If he had laid a finger on Cassie to hurt her, that would have been it, I swear to you."

They had been parked in front of Marcus' apartment for at least five minutes, probably more. What a trying week this had been. Ellis, Jeremiah, the stress of his first job, and now today, what was going to be next?

"Listen, Ellis. We'll be busy on Monday on the holiday. What are you doing Sunday?" Marcus asked. "I go to church and then out to lunch with Cassie and her folks every other Sunday, and this is the week I go with them."

"I know, Marcus. I've been tracking you for a while so I could figure out when you got home from school so I could try to talk to you, like I did last Thursday. And when to I'd be able catch you home alone, like I did the other day." Marcus didn't know for sure if he should be mad at Ellis for following him so closely or commend him for putting in so much effort to try to make things right. "I know when you go to church, where you go to lunch and what time you get back to Cassie's house. I feel guilty Marcus, but I know your schedule pretty darned well."

"Okay then, Ellis," Marcus went on with his thought. "Do you like to fish? Do you want to go to the river and try for some catfish Sunday, in the afternoon?"

"I don't know Marcus," Ellis had an alternate idea. "You like smallmouth bass?"

"Yeah, that sounds pretty good," Marcus hadn't caught a bass since last summer. "Do you know a place?"

"Sure do, just the spot," Ellis said with a smile. "Ollie's old place, where I used to live. There's a good-sized pond, one of the deepest around here, and it used to be real well-stocked. The guy that bought it from Ollie and owns it now is my boss, so there's no problem getting out there I know for a fact he doesn't like to fish at all, so those bass ought to be huge by now."

"Yeah, that sounds nifty, Ellis," Marcus started to get a bit excited at the prospect of hauling in some bass.

"Good. I'll be at Cassie's house about two o'clock to pick you up, and I'll bring all the rods, reels and bait. You just bring yourself."

James E. Anderson

Rain and Gloom

The flags, both the American stars and stripes and the Missouri state flag, were being whipped about violently and haphazardly by the gusting early morning winds. Flapping defiantly in a westerly wind one moment, the obedient colors were wont to instantly change position and directional orientation, readily adhering to the imminent whim of Mother Nature. Leaving the post office and approaching his Corvette Stingray, Judy Allensworth angrily tried pulling down on the outer canopy, but to no avail. He struggled for a few miserable seconds to return the umbrella to its original configuration. A sudden gust had inverted the canopy, reversing the ribs, and Judy was now standing in a deluge, the umbrella rendered worthless to him. What had been a canopy under which he had safely stood, the umbrella had now quickly become nothing more than a bowl, collecting raindrops rather than deflecting them, a totally worthless apparatus that he inexplicably continued to hold in an upright position above his drenched head. Judy hastily cast it aside, dumping it in an abandoned heap on the sidewalk. Be it someone else's responsibility to either fix or dispose of it. Judy climbed into his silvery chariot and looked into the rearview mirror, thoroughly disgusted by his foul luck. He briskly wiped the dampness from his brow and ran his hands through his thinning gray hair. He hoped this umbrella malfunction had not been the harbinger of a disastrous day.

On the bright side of things, with the weather forecast being so bleak, it was surely going to be at least a two-hour drive to Fulton to visit Ellis. Perhaps that would be long enough to allow his clothes to reasonably dry. There was no point in hurrying. People tended to drive like beginners when they were faced with stormy weather. No one seemed to handle their vehicles with the degree of self-confidence and aplomb to which Judy was quite capable. If there were no traffic on Interstate 70, he would absolutely fly the entire distance. Rain is not that difficult to drive in, according to Judy's ego inflated opinion. The biggest fear of most is the possibility of hydroplaning, which Judy felt was really nothing to despair. As long as a driver knew the defensive maneuvers required to combat the temporary loss of control, there was nothing to dread. Judy had always been supremely confident in his driving ability. But in respect to other drivers, he fortunately did not that exude that confidence. The road was filled with too many who were inexperienced, unskilled, or just plain stupid for someone, even as talented as Judy, to trust enough to ensure with his own safety. As such, Judy knew it would be a long and tedious journey.

Just more than two hours later, about thirty minutes past the noon hour that he had confidently told Ellis would be his ETA, Judy arrived for his Saturday visit. It had been a long and tedious trip, with many a driver unwilling to exceed a grandmotherly highway speed of fifty-five miles per hour. On the upside, it had given Judy plenty of time to think. It had been a difficult week. There had been a multitude of rather serious problems on the job, he had employees with whom he had been unhappy and some who had failed to live up to expectations. There were others for whom he shared considerable concern. Judy had also encountered personal problems that had demanded immediate attention, and there had been assorted other items which had required painstaking and detailed planning and coordination. Judy was a very busy man from Monday morning through the end of every Friday. But the weekends were his.

Saturdays had become very special, the one day of every week or two that was set aside to kindle his relationship with Ellis. Judy looked forward to visiting his son, he saw so much of himself in Ellis. His looks, his personality. Ellis could flash the masculinity, the edginess that Judy knew he had inherited from the Allensworth genes. But sometimes, occasionally, he could sense Paula's softness and compassion. Judy hoped that Ellis would go through the rest of his life displaying the best of both worlds. He wanted nothing more than to see Ellis' confidence shine through, but he also was aware that owning some of Paula's inherent sensitivity would bode well for him and someday come in quite handy. Judy often wished that he had been gifted with some of that as he grew up, it certainly could have supplied a tempering to his troubled youth.

Ellis had been waiting impatiently for his father's arrival, and when he spied through the picture window Judy's sports car arriving at the curb, he jumped from the couch and hurried out the front door. A steady drizzle was continuing to fall as Ellis ran to and jumped into Judy's car.

"How are you doing, dad?" He asked.

"Good, how's everything with you, Junior?" Judy replied with a similar question. On the drive to Fulton, he had decided that if Ellis didn't object, he was going to start calling him Junior. Judy had never liked the name that Ollie and Alicia had given him post-adoption. Judy also felt that with the boy's original birth name having been Jude Allensworth, Junior, the moniker was morally, if not legally, correct. Perhaps at a later date, Judy might push to entice Ellis to legally reclaim his birth name.

Replying to Judy's question, Ellis answered with, "Great, dad. I'm taking Becca to see the Grass Roots tonight in Columbia, you know, at the auditorium at Mizzou. It's really going to be groovy; I think." Ellis seemed quite worked up about the concert. "I heard a bootleg of their next single, it's not out yet, but I think it's called *Let's Live for Today*. Neat song, I hope they play it."

Of course, Judy had never heard of the Grass Roots, but nonetheless, he was not about to let his 'squareness' be known.

302

"Yeah, that does sound great," he said enthusiastically.

As had become habit, Judy drove to the *Strike and Snack* for lunch, bowling, and arcade games. He envisioned how nice it would be in another year or so when Ellis turned twenty-one and they could enjoy a beer together. Judy thought he would have to make it a point to be here for Ellis' birthday, it would be a special memory for him to have his first beer with his dad. Judy was hopeful that by then Ellis would have gradually eased Ollie from his conscious mind and allowed him, his biological father, to be placed front and center.

The afternoon seemed to fly by, and Judy made a conscious effort to track the time. He didn't want to run Ellis short of time. He knew the boy would have to shower, change, pick up his girl and still hightail it to the campus for the concert. By four-thirty they were headed across the parking lot. The pavement was still wet, but the rain had stopped.

"Do I get to drive home?" Ellis asked in anticipation of handling the powerful Vette once again.

"I don't know, Junior, it's pretty damp out here and the streets are still wet. Dangerous combination, that car and wet streets." Under the circumstances, Judy was leery of allowing Ellis behind the wheel.

"Ah come on dad. I'll be careful, I promise." There was a nagging feeling that inclined Judy to have compassion for Ellis and ultimately forced him to reconsider, "Okay." Judy tossed the keys to his son and climbed into the passenger side.

Ellis did a fine job driving home, he was extremely cautious. Not a single time did he spin the tires taking off on the wet pavement, nor did he slow down for a stop sign or stoplight and hit the brakes so suddenly that he'd skidded. Judy was impressed with how carefully Ellis had handled the powerful vehicle.

They entered the house together. Alicia had not been home when Judy had first arrived, or so he had assumed since her car had not been parked in the driveway. Upon their return her car was outside, but she was nowhere to be seen. Judy sat in the living room while Ellis showered and otherwise prepared for his date. Just prior to Ellis emerging from his bedroom, Alicia had stepped out of hers. She had briefly glanced in Judy's direction and then gone ahead, without saying a word, into the kitchen. It seemed a bit strange to Judy that Alicia had not offered coffee, a Coca-Cola, or a bottle of beer. It was normally a customary offer, and since he had begun visiting, he did not recall it ever having not been made. When he came to see Ellis, and after they had returned from their outing, Judy habitually stayed around for a while. Even after Ellis had acquired his new girlfriend and begun leaving to see her after he and his dad had returned from their day together, Judy still would hang for thirty minutes or so. He wanted to use the time to discuss Ellis and what was going on in his life, as well as catching up with Alicia. When she passed back through on the return to her bedroom, Judy noticed she was carrying a glass that held what appeared to be a clear drink, vodka he had assumed. Alicia had not looked at all in his direction when leaving the kitchen. For no particular reason, Judy felt a slight sensation of heat flowing gradually from his upper back and rising through his neck.

Ellis emerged from his room, wearing a brightly and haphazardly designed colorful shirt, in stark contrast to his normal white tee-shirt. He glanced into the living room then walked to the kitchen. Not seeing Alicia, he asked Judy, "Where's mom? I saw her car out front."

"I think she's in her bedroom, son," Judy replied.

Ellis walked to Alicia's room, knocked, and tried the lever handle, which didn't budge, indicating that it was locked.

"Mom, you in there?" He asked.

"Yes, Ellis. Are you leaving for the show?" She replied.

"Yeah, I'm about to. Are you alright?"

"I'm fine, Ellis. Just a little under the weather. Probably just the monthly thing. I'm okay. You run along and have fun. Tell Becca I said hello." Alicia had effectively ended the conversation.

"Okay, I will. Bye. I'll be home late, so I'll see you in the morning." Ellis walked back up the short hallway into the living room where Judy sat, hands idly in his lap.

"I guess she's not feeling well, dad," Ellis said apologetically. "Are you going to leave now?"

"No, Junior. I think I'll stay a few minutes, make sure Alicia is okay, see if she needs anything. I can let myself out."

"Okay then. I probably should get a move on. Don't want to be late. Thanks for coming, I had a lot of fun today. See you again next Saturday, right?" Ellis asked as he sauntered toward the door.

"Oh yeah, for sure. Say, before you go, what's with that shirt you're wearing? Colorful, ain't it? Makes me feel drunk just looking at it." Judy quipped. Of course, he'd seen the style before, he just wanted to appear fatherly, he supposed.

"It's called a tie dye shirt. All the rage nowadays," Ellis laughed as he answered. "You need to get one, dad."

Ten minutes after Ellis had shut and locked the door, Alicia appeared once again from her bedroom. She walked purposefully to the living room, where she stood, arms folded tightly across her chest. Her hair was disheveled, her eyes were red, somewhat bloodshot and her bottom lip quivered ever so slightly as she cocked her head back and stared angrily at Judy.

"I'm surprised you're still here." She stammered. "Pretty ballsy of you."

Judy looked at Alicia, appearing dumbfounded. "What? Alish, I always stay and talk to you after I spend time with Ellis. You know that. Why is today any different? Are you alright? You don't look so hot."

"Oh no, Judy, I'm fine. I'm just jim-dandy, I am." Alicia was obviously upset about something, and Judy was pretty darned sure he was soon going to know why.

Alicia paced a few steps before stopping and screaming her question to Judy, "What the hell do I say to that boy Judy? You're jumping all around here wanting to play daddy to him, but where will you be when he gets home? Oh yeah, you'll be back in St. Louis, sitting your ass in some bar while I'm the one standing here in the middle of the night trying give him the news."

"Alish, calm down a little," Judy stood, trying to play a mind game. His ploy was this - he would be banking that his size, compared to her diminutive stature, would establish an aura of authority on his behalf. His hope was that would then force her into a subservient mindset, which in turn, would make her feel dependent upon him. His thought was that rather than showing anger toward him, that she would instead turn to him, relying upon him for support.

"Just ease off a bit and let me help you," Judy tried to play the part of the understanding therapist. "What is the problem? What happened that you are so upset?"

Unfortunately for Judy, Alicia was too strong willed, and his psychological maneuvering had not achieved its desired results. She had moved in closer to him, but not in any effort to seek comfort. As she approached, she began flailing with her fists against his chest, screaming, "You killed him, you killed him."

"Alicia, stop. Settle down." Judy grabbed at Alicia's forearms, first attempting to stop her furious punches from continuing, and then to get her to calm herself. "Here, sit down, tell me what you're talking about."

Alicia began sobbing as she fell back onto the loveseat. "Why Judy, why did you do it? You didn't have to. It was all going to be over soon enough."

"Alish, what the hell are you talking about?" Judy asked again. "Please calm yourself and start at the beginning."

"Judy, they came today, right after you and Ellis left, about one o'clock. They just showed up unannounced at the door." Alicia started sobbing all over again.

"They who, Alish? Who showed up?"

"The cops, Judy, the cops. They didn't beat around the bush, they just said *he's dead.* It was like they were just reporting the news on the tv. No emotion, no sympathy, nothing, just *he's dead*, that's it."

"Who are we talking about Alish? Who died? Your dad, brother, an uncle? Who are you talking abou...." Then it hit him. "Ollie, you're talking about Ollie? When. How? What happened?" Judy seemed astonished, taken by surprise.

"Damn you, Judy. Don't you even try to act like you didn't know," Alicia said belligerently. "You just told me less than a week ago. You said he threatened to turn you in for killing Paula Sue. I'm not stupid Judy. You couldn't take a chance that Ollie would turn you in, so you had to shut him up. I know you did it, Judy. I know it and you know it."

"Listen to what you're saying, Alish! For God's sake, Ollie was in a maximum-security prison. Like I could just walk in there and kill a man? For Pete's sake Alicia, just listen to what you're saying." Judy needed to learn more about what exactly had occurred at the prison. He needed details. "What happened Alicia? You've got to talk to me honestly so I can help. What happened? Was it suicide, heart attack, what?"

"Come on, Judy," she replied. "Acting like you don't know. You probably planned it. He got stabbed in the exercise yard, Judy. They let about six of the death row inmates out at once, and they got into a fight, all of them. It was a set-up; I know it was. He got killed by a shank, but to make it look good, two or three of them used saps, so several of them had cuts and lumps. I know it was all a set-up. There's no way for them to know who used the shank. He was the only one stabbed, everybody else, including Ollie got beat up with the saps."

"Okay, Alish, everybody knows a shank is a homemade knife, but what's a sap? I never heard of that before."

"God, Judy, why do you want to pretend to be stupid with me?" Alicia felt frustrated because she was sure Judy was feigning ignorance. "Judy, you spent time in jail. You know what a sap is."

"No, Alish, I don't."

"Christ, Judy. It's a rock or a padlock or something really hard in a sock. You swing it around like a club or something and, wham, you bop somebody on the head."

"That's sounds pretty primitive, like a caveman weapon or something." Judy winced, just thinking about how being hit by a sap might feel.

"Judy, you can't kid a kidder, alright," Alicia suddenly sat up a little straighter and spoke in a more affirmative tone. "You knew Ollie was going to rat you out, and even if you didn't kill Paula, you and your business couldn't afford to risk you getting arrested."

Judy sat stone-faced, listening attentively.

Alicia went on, "Let's face it Judy, you have the means, you have the connections inside, you've got the cash to have Ollie silenced for good. You couldn't risk waiting for his execution, you had to act in a hurry. You're no angel, Judy Allensworth. You did it."

"You're wrong about this, Alicia." Judy stood firm in his denial.

"Look, Ollie was going to die in a couple of months anyway. I was prepared for that. So, this doesn't bother me all that much, although I would have liked to have talk to him one more time, just to get a few final questions answered." Alicia took a deep breath and went on, "I'm mostly bothered the most because now I have to tell Ellis, and I can't tell him the whole truth, Judy. And that's your fault. Because you're his natural father and he loves you and looks up to you. Ollie raised him from an infant. He wasn't perfect by a longshot, but he raised him just the same. How can I tell him the truth?"

Judy sat, wordlessly staring into Alicia's determined, yet pleading eyes.

"How do I tell Ellis that his father killed his father?"

Alicia sat, matching Judy's steely stare momentarily, before rising from the loveseat and pointing toward the door.

"Get the hell out of my house."

Fishing

Ellis was rudely awakened by The Dave Clark Five and the ravaging drum beat of *Glad All Over*. He fumbled for the off switch on his clock radio, regretting that he had not adjusted the volume down slightly from the level at which he had been listening to his music yesterday morning while awaiting Judy's visit. The brief reminder of spending yesterday afternoon with Judy was enough to kick start his foggy, early morning brain into remembering the reason why he had even bothered to set the alarm for a Sunday morning. Normally, Sundays were reserved for sleeping in, they were days which were more or less optional in his youthful lifestyle. If he woke up feeling energetic, perhaps he would clean out and wash his car, and then just knock around the remainder day. On some Sunday mornings, Ellis lacked the energy to do much of anything, and would just lounge around the house, alternately napping and watching television. The past several weeks, since he had acquired a girlfriend, he had been presented a third option, one which usually relied upon the whims of Becca's family. They were regular church goers, very

311

family oriented, and at least twice a month enjoyed Sunday afternoon get-togethers and family outings with Becca and her two older sisters, one of whom was married with a daughter of her own.

As Ellis sat in his underwear on the edge of his bed, he thought ahead to the reason he had made sure to be up by nine o'clock this morning. His dad, Judy was coming by at ten so they could drive together to Marcus' apartment and from there, spend the afternoon fishing. He had asked Judy yesterday if he would like to tag along. He knew that his dad and Marcus had grown close during the infamous summer of Ellis' demise, but in the years since, Ellis had dominated Judy's time and attention. According to Marcus, the two hadn't seen much of one another the past couple of years, and Ellis thought it would be good for the three of them to share company. Despite the long drive, Judy had been receptive to seeing Marcus. He had always spoken fondly of him to Ellis, and it just seemed a good and natural thing for the three remaining Clemens clan blood relatives to spend some time together bonding.

Ellis showered, dressed, and went into the kitchen, where Alicia sat at the table sipping coffee. He poured himself a cup, stirred in two teaspoons of sugar and joined her. Nothing was said for a moment, but Alicia finally broke the silence by asking Ellis how he and Becca had enjoyed the show.

"Oh, it was really good, mom," Ellis reported. "Becca's favorite song was *Tip of My Tongue.*" He giggled bit before adding, "I think she's got a little crush on one of them. I think his name is Rob Grill."

"That's nice, Ellis." Alicia got up, and as she poured a fresh cup asked Ellis if he was still driving all that way today to go fishing with his cousin.

"Oh yeah, mom. It's going to be an awesome day," Ellis was looking forward to Judy's arrival at any moment now. "I didn't have a chance yesterday, did dad tell you that he's driving back out today and going with us?"

Alicia nearly dropped her coffee as she was walking back to the table. "Judy is coming here, today?" This was news she was not expecting to hear this morning. How much worse could the timing possibly be?

"Actually, he'll probably be here in another half hour or so, maybe less, he's usually early." Ellis told her. He thought she looked like somebody had stolen her puppy. "Are you okay?" Ellis was a bit concerned. He had forgotten that she had been feeling poorly last night. "Are you still sick from last night?"

"No, no Ellis, I'm fine." But Alicia was not fine. She was mad, she was angry, and she was hurt. Judy hadn't the decency to even tell her he was going with Ellis today. And now, here he was going to show up in thirty minutes or less and she still had not broken the news to Ellis about Ollie.

"Ellis, I've got something important to tell you that might make you want to cancel your fishing trip today." Alicia was trying to figure out exactly what to say to Ellis.

Ellis looked at Alicia with a dumbfounded look on his face. What in the world could she have to tell him that would make him want to stay home from going fishing, and especially after his dad would have driven this far?

"Ellis, your father died." Alicia opted to blurt out the words, but immediately realized her error.

"My dad? Mom, are talking about my real dad, Judy?" Ellis was confused and unsure what to think. "Or is it Ollie?"

"I'm sorry Ellis, it's Ollie. I'm sorry, I should have been more specific." Alicia wished she had thought more carefully and worded what she had said in a more delicate manner.

Ellis remained silently in his chair, stunned by the news. The urge was there to cry, but tears were not forming. He just sat staring into space, toward the dreary green wallpaper he had always so hated. Alicia waited, expecting that Ellis would break down and was, in some ways, disappointed that he had not.

"How? What happened?"

Alicia explained to Ellis about the fight in the prison exercise yard, about the saps and the shank, and the fact that they would never know which of the men had actually been the person who had performed the stabbing.

"Why did he do it? What could Ollie have done from a prison cell to cause somebody to kill him?" Ellis asked the question, his mind unable to conjure up a motive for an action so extreme.

"Who knows why any of those men on death row would do any of the things they have done? Them and people like them, who knows why they think like they do?" Alicia had a theory, a very strong theory, one that she believed from the bottom of her heart.

But, in deference to Ellis and his devotion to Judy, it was a theory that Alicia had determined would have to remain unspoken.

"Are you going to be alright, Ellis?" Alicia asked. "Can I get you anything?" Ellis didn't immediately respond, and after a few seconds she asked, "Do you want some fried eggs for breakfast? Pancakes, maybe?"

"No mom, but thank you. I'm really not hungry right now. When we get close to Marcus' girlfriend's house, that's where I'm picking him up, um, when we get close, dad said we'd go to the *A & W* for lunch. I'll be good 'til then."

Ellis got up from the table, rinsed his cup, leaving it in the dish drainer, and went outside to the shed. Ostensibly, he had gone to gather rods and reels and his tackle box which was loaded with lures, hooks, weights and other various and sundry fishing items. The visit to the shed actually served a dual purpose, as it gave him a few moments to think, reminisce on good times with Ollie, and to perhaps shed a few silent tears.

* * * *

The drive from Ellis' house outside of Fulton to the *A & W* parking lot had covered a total of 104.6 miles and taken a shade over two hours. Judy had napped a large part of the way; he had been up late on Saturday night and had already made the hour and a half drive from St. Louis to Fulton. The timing had been excellent. It was nearing twelve-thirty in the early afternoon, and they easily had an hour or more to enjoy lunch before meeting Marcus at Cassie's house. The road trip had been made in Ellis' Ford sedan. He would have preferred riding in his dad's Corvette Stingray, but it only seated two and there were going to be the three of them, plus gear.

After they had finished eating, and Judy had chain-smoked three stubby unfiltered Camels (he rarely bothered to roll his own these days), they got back in the sedan and cruised the short distance to Cassie's house. The family had not yet returned from their lunch at *The Red Roof Lodge* and so, with time on their hands and all four windows rolled down, Ellis and Judy sat and chatted.

"So, mom told you about Ollie last night then?" Ellis asked. They had touched briefly on the subject just after beginning the drive.

"Yeah, right after you left to go get your girl and head to your concert. How was it? Good band?" Judy didn't know The Grass Roots from The Zombies, but he was sure it wasn't the type of music that tripped his trigger.

"Oh, they were great, a really good show." Ellis recited to his dad the titles of some of the songs they had had played, but of course, Judy was familiar with none of them. A lull ensued for a few moments, until Ellis asked another question. "Dad, why do you think somebody killed Ollie? I wonder what he did that was so bad, and that it made someone so mad, that they felt like he needed to die for it?"

Judy did not know the extent or detail to which Alicia had gone with her description of Ollie's demise. He trusted that she had not ventured so far as to share with Ellis her suspicion that he had ordered or orchestrated Ollie's death. Alicia could be a vengeful and vindictive person, but he didn't picture her being so overboard that she would risk destroying Ellis' relationship with his biological father.

"I don't know, son," Judy responded with, what he felt, was a fairly honest assessment. "You never know what is on the minds of people like the ones he was locked up with. Something he might have said or done, maybe somebody had revealed some deep dark secret to him, and Ollie had tried to use it against him. Maybe he knew something from the past of one of those guys, and when they found out, they wanted to make sure he kept quiet. Who knows, strange things happen. There's like a code of honor among people like that, and the first rule is you never rat nobody out."

"Well anyway. I mean, everybody knew he was going to get executed, but I just wasn't ready, you know what I'm saying, dad?" Ellis couldn't hide the fact that he was deeply bothered by Ollie's death.

"Of course, I do Ellis. Look, I understand what you're feeling. I mean Ollie raised you, and he was the only dad you knew for what, sixteen years or something. Of course, losing him is going to bother you, it's going to hurt. But you'll get through it," Judy gave Ellis a reassuring smile and patted his shoulder. "I'll always be here, whatever you need, Junior. Always."

The Worthingtons had arrived home and Cassie, Charlie and Marcus had made a beeline for the house. Marcus needed to change clothes in a hurry, and Charlie was in dire need to use the bathroom. As the Worthingtons had gotten out of their car, they had seen and recognized Judy exiting the black sedan. Hand in hand, they strode across the lawn to greet him. Judy had taken a few steps forward, and when they met the two men had shaken hands. It had been a while since Judy had visited, he had he been a stranger for the better part of two years. Ellis remained in the car, but Judy called to him, insisting that he get out and say hello to Cassie's parents. Ellis opened the door and stood politely offering a shy wave. He was aware of their apprehension and felt it best not to come and physically greet them.

Judy smiled at Jack and Debbie and said, 'Ellis was kind enough to invite me to go fishing with him and Marc today. I haven't been bass fishing in years, plus I realized I haven't been here to see Marc in forever, so I thought what the heck, let's go for it."

"Well, I'm sure it'll be therapeutic for you, Judy. Getting to see Marcus, and not to mention the quality time spent with your son here." Jack nodded toward Ellis, as Debbie stood at his side, smiling dutifully.

It seemed a bit of a struggle to make small talk, it was painfully obvious that the presence of Ellis made Cassie's parents appear somewhat uncomfortable. Fortunately, Marcus and Cassie had reappeared, and the time had come for the boys to leave for their day of fishing. Marcus had wanted to invite Cassie along, and he knew Judy and Ellis would have welcomed her participation, but he owned enough common sense not to even make the suggestion to her parents. Marcus got into the backseat and with his wave and one from Judy, the black Ford sedan departed.

* * * *

As Ellis drove up the familiar driveway toward his old house, memories returned for all three of them. The thoughts for Ellis were varied. He had grown up in this house, played in this very yard. To his mild surprise, the old swing set from his childhood still sat, rusting though it was, off to the left side of the workshop. He had once broken his left wrist, when falling awkwardly while bravely – or so he thought at the time - jumping off the swing, way back when he was in second grade. He had made his first key in that workshop. And this house was the last place he had tasted freedom before being transported to the Lewis County Jail.

To Marcus, the memories were overwhelmingly sad. He remembered slamming this very car's trunk lid down on the back of Ellis' head. He vividly remembered trying to lift Ellis' limp unconscious body, before being rescued in the effort by the strength of Cousin Judy. The only good memory was that of seeing Cassie being freed from the back of the old cargo van by Mitch Daniels.

Judy briefly thought back to his dismay at having to play such a big part in Ollie's arrest. He would have preferred not to have been involved at all, but his worry and concern had been for Marcus, and helping him to reunite with his girlfriend. His concern right at the moment, however, was the sight if the Lewis County Deputy's Cruiser that was just leaving from the front of the old workshop. Judy was well

319

aware that Max Schofield was now the owner of the property. Judy was quite familiar with Max and his businesses. The fact that a deputy had just been visiting with him certainly piqued his interest. Judy strained his neck as the police vehicle passed on its way back to the main road, but due to the sun's glare, he was unable to identify the deputy inside the car.

Max had seen Ellis' approaching Ford while standing next to the deputy's car, just prior to its leaving. As a courtesy, Ellis had planned to stop and let his boss know that they would be fishing in his pond this afternoon, but Judy had suddenly nixed that plan. He insisted that Ellis simply drop him at the house, and he would tell Max. Judy said he had some things that he wanted to discuss with the man anyway, so they could just let him out. Judy pointed out the beaten down path, as if Ellis was not already familiar with it, that led to the treasured pond. Some of Ollie's old neighbors still liked to frequent the fishing hole, and thus there were always tire tracks and grooves where the sprawling Indiangrass was permanently bent over and flattened from the pickup trucks and tractors that carried fishermen out there.

Dropping Judy near the workshop entrance. Ellis proceeded off the gravel drive, through the side yard and into the field of Indiangrass. They needed travel only a few hundred yards until they had reached their destination. Stepping from the car, Marcus immediately suspected, and wondered if Ellis' boss was aware, that some young rowdies had possibly used the pond for a party or other wild gathering. There were a few scattered beer cans and obvious motorcycle tracks that had been made in the grass, having dug slight grooves into the soft ground. When Marcus noticed the tracks, he assumed they probably had been produced by gunning the throttle and popping the clutch, or so he guessed. He had seen Louie Dupree do that with his Ducati 250 back behind Walt's shop earlier this week. The bike's back tire would dig easily into the grass and soil, and Marcus wondered at the time if Walt didn't get mad at Louie for tearing up his grass.

It required two trips for Marcus and Ellis to get everything moved to the pond. First, they toted the actual fishing equipment, and on the second trip it took one on each side to carry the old metal Cronco cooler that, loaded with ice and Coca-Colas, felt as though it weighed a ton. They settled over to the left on the southern side of the pond near some reeds and cattails where Ellis hoped the bass might be lurking, hopefully looking for food. The water was warm and murky, so Ellis opted for spinnerbait lures. He had a few beetle spinners that he thought might do well under the mid-afternoon sun, near the vegetation that was in close to shore. If the water were more clear, perhaps he would have gone with a light green, nearly transparent topwater plug and tried fishing further away, more out toward the open areas of water.

While the two of them got everything prepped, Judy had carried on a discussion with Max Schofield. The first question on Judy's mind concerned the exact type of job duties Max had Ellis currently performing.

Max, of course, had no idea what information Ellis might have already fed to Judy, but he seriously doubted that he would have reported the actual truth. Why would any son confess to his father that he was delivering drug shipments for five dollars an hour? With that in mind, Max had decided to leave things where they had been a few weeks ago, and told Judy that Ellis was merely delivering auto parts, nothing more.

"Does a fine job, too," Max even added praise for good measure.

"Well, let's make sure we keep it that way, Maxie," Judy said in a very suggestive manner. "I'm trying to do my best to keep his nose clean, I don't want him following in Ollie's footsteps, turning out like he did. I want the boy to be something in life."

"Hey, no problem, boss man," Max promised. "I'll keep Ellis on the straight and narrow, don't you worry, you have my word on it."

"Good." Judy seemed satisfied with Max's promise. "Speaking of Ollie, did you hear the news?"

"About Ollie? No, what about him?" Max had to feign ignorance. His deputy friend had just brought the information to his attention moments before.

"Dead." Judy dropped the news like a sack of potatoes. "Got shanked in the prison yard Friday, one of the other inmates got to him"

"Ah man, that's too bad," Max shook his head. "How'd the boy take it? Seems like he's alright. If it was my old man, I doubt I'd feel like going fishing with my buddies."

"He acts like he's okay, but I got a feeling it's probably eating at him pretty good." Judy was sure Ellis was hurting inside, that was why he told him he understood his feelings. He had no problem with Ollie holding a place in Ellis' heart, the man had been his father for years.

"He's a good kid," Max said, offering encouragement. "Comes from good stock, and all said and done, Ollie raised him pretty good. He's strong, I'm sure he'll be fine."

"Yeah."

"Hey, speaking of buddies, who's that kid that he brought with him, is he that Clemens kid Ellis was telling me about?" Max asked. "That's the kid Ollie was trying to get to back then, isn't it? Isn't he Elijah's boy?"

"Yeah, that's him. Elijah's son, Marc." Judy verified who Marcus was, but wondered why Ellis had discussed him with Max. "What did Ellis have to say about him?"

"Oh, he was just saying something about the kid finding out he really is getting some big inheritance from Mark Twain," Max replied with what Ellis had told him. "I thought that was really something, everybody thought that story was hogwash back when Ollie tried to spread it, you know back then, around the time of his trial and everything."

Ellis had told Judy about it yesterday at the bowling alley. He had asked Judy to check up on an old boat company in St. Louis that he said Mark Twain had supposedly held some stock shares in. Ellis said he thought that all the stocks had been left to Marcus.

"Well, Maxie, who knows, maybe the family really did come from royalty, eh?" Judy said it with an outward laugh. But on the inside, he was left wondering. If what Ellis had said was true, then why in blue blazes would he blab about it to a character like Max Schofield?

Judy had other business he continued to discuss with Max. Another thirty minutes passed before they finally separated, and Max returned to his house with Judy beginning the long walk toward the pond. He spent the time thinking about Marcus' supposed stocks, the Detmeyer company, and he began to wonder himself if Marcus really was in line for a hefty windfall.

While waiting for Judy to catch up with them, Ellis had filled Marcus in on the news surrounding Ollie's death. Marcus expressed his sincere sympathy for both Ollie's death and the tragic circumstances involved. Marcus had experienced the devastation of losing his own father, although he had been much younger. For Marcus, today's memories were not as fresh and painful as they had been a few years ago. He tried to encourage Ellis by pointing out the fact that he still had Judy and his mother, Alicia. He tried to emphasize that he had a strong support system around him and that he would eventually make his way through the heartache that would come and go for years.

Judy made his way over the crest of the bank to find the boys laid back, chewing blades of grass and sipping Coca-Colas. He didn't see any sign of smallmouth bass on what appeared to be a pair of empty stringers lying casually at the water's edge.

"Not biting today?" Judy asked.

"Not even a nibble," Marcus replied.

"I don't know dad," Ellis said. "I wonder if this pond has been fished out. It was always loaded when I lived her. I remember one time a few years ago when Ollie paid to have it restocked. I figured they would have multiplied a good bit by now and it would be chock full of four and five pounders."

"Don't know son, I'm not that much of a fisherman. Maybe the neighbors have caught about everything." Judy grabbed a Coke from the cooler, picked up the rod that Ellis had prepared for him, and walked about eight or ten feet away. Guessing that he'd located just the right spot, he cast his line and took a seat in the grass. Lighting a cigarette, Judy relaxed and prepared to wait.

They all sat quietly, listening to the crickets and katydids. The afternoon sun bore down, and the temperature seemed to rise exponentially. There were plenty of pine trees circling all but about a quarter of the pond's circumference. Unfortunately, with the sun's positioning in the sky and the relative location of the trees, shade was not an available option. It was already hot today, and the promise was that it would be a scorcher of a summer. Tomorrow was Memorial Day and the county's swimming pools would be opening for the summer season offering residents some respite from the heat.

Every ten minutes or so Marcus would recast his line. He was looking forward to going to Cassie's tomorrow for the barbeque. And he wished that Cassie's parents would eventually come around to realize that Ellis had changed from the person that they thought they saw. It would have been nice to have had him there tomorrow, as part of his family.

Judy sat quietly, deep in thought, his head almost perpetually encircled by a cloud of smoke. His mind was occupied with thoughts about his business, Ollie's death, Ellis, and his future, and oddly enough he found himself thinking about Paula.

Ellis tried to focus attention on his rod, but his mind was far, far away. He was having visions and memories of his childhood racing through his head. He saw Ollie playing catch with him. He saw Ollie standing next to him, right here at this very pond, teaching him how to bait a hook. And he saw Ollie chopping with a machete at a teenaged girl wearing a brightly colored dress with bloodstains discoloring the whiteness of her top.

And to the northwest, partially obscured and unseen due to the background of pine trees, sat a dog, intently watching.

Food For Thought

Ellis sat at the table, the Thursday night dinner with Marcus, Cassie and Margaret having just been completed. With their new Thursday night meal tradition now in effect, and Margaret not getting in from work until past seven p.m., it was almost a necessity for her to bring home something from *The Goldmine* or pick up take-out meals from the *River's Edge* or *A & W*. She had considered slow cooking stews on the stovetop but was distrustful of leaving a hot electric burner unattended all day long. It was the second Thursday of June, and tonight Ellis had generously promised to surprise all by bringing a dinner choice that would appeal to everyone's taste. After his last delivery he had stopped on his way northward, just outside of Hannibal, and purchased two large sausage pizzas from the new *Pizza Hut* that had recently opened. They had kept the pizza pies warm in the oven, and by the time Margaret stepped through the door, the feast was spread and ready to be enjoyed.

Afterward, Margaret and Cassie had graciously cleared the table of plates and utensils while Marcus and Ellis had disposed of the emptied pizza boxes, hurriedly running them out to the community trash dumpster. Chores completed; they had reassembled at the kitchen table. Ellis had been saving his good news for after the meal's conclusion, until the others had all finished discussing the happenings of their individual days.

"Alicia decided this past weekend that she is going to move back to Alexandria, so I'll be living close by again. I hope that means I can spend more time with you all." Ellis couldn't contain his beaming smile.

"Well, that is wonderful news!" Margaret said. "It will be nice having you nearby, we'll be able to gather so much more often."

"That's great, Ellis." Marcus was ecstatic that Ellis was going to be back near the neighborhood again rather living two hours away. He knew what a strain the distance had to be for Ellis. He spent all day driving his route between here and St. Louis, and then after visiting Marcus on Thursday nights, he had the long drive back to St. Louis. Once there he would return the company car, retrieve his, and then have another two hours of driving back to Fulton. Marcus couldn't imagine how exhausted Ellis must feel on Friday mornings.

"It will be super swell having you around all the time," Cassie said. In the past few weeks, she had warmed up considerably to Ellis, but still felt a slight bit of edginess when he was nearby. She was not yet approaching the point that she felt totally comfortable in his presence.

As the talk of Ellis' move began to wane, Margaret noticed the time and tapped the table to get Cassie's attention, "*Peyton Place* starts in a few minutes, Cassie. Let's go grab our seats." The ladies went into the living room while Ellis and Marcus remained at the table.

"You know what Marcus?" Ellis asked, slowly shaking his head. "I don't think I can sit through a half hour of that soap opera."

"Yeah, me neither," Marcus agreed. "Want to go check out my room?"

"Sounds good to me." Ellis had been indoctrinated to *Peyton Place* last Thursday and was definitely not enthralled.

Marcus sat on his bed and Ellis took the small desk chair.

"I guess I should have showed you my room before now, huh?"

"Actually, Marcus. I've seen it before, remember?" Ellis tried to smile as he reminded Marcus that he had secretly visited the room a few years ago.

"Oh, yeah, I forgot." The reminder was stark. He had been sitting on the old toy box that, even today, remained in the same spot beneath the window. Cassie had been relaxed on the bed when Marcus had heard a noise outside the window. When he'd turned to investigate, he had seen someone running away. At the time, he had not recognized the fleeing figure as Ellis.

"I'm sorry, Marcus. I feel bad that I invaded your privacy like that," Ellis looked at him with obvious remorse. Marcus could not presume to have any comprehension of the guilt and embarrassment that must eat at Ellis every day of his life. Ellis had put forth so much effort to atone for his past transgressions, and, as a result, Marcus felt nothing short of respect for him.

"Wow, where did you get this old newsboy hat, Marcus?" Ellis picked up and admired the hat.

"That belonged to my friend, Jeremiah. I keep it as a remembrance."

"Oh, I see. Jeremiah, your friend that you told me about that died a few weeks ago. Gosh, I'm sorry Marcus," Ellis said. "That's sad."

"Yeah, too many people dying around here lately," Marcus mused. "The guy out at the trash dump, Jeremiah, your dad. Way too many people."

"What happened at the dump? I don't think I heard about that." Ellis asked.

Marcus told him the story of the guy named Tony that had gotten killed there and about Jeremiah being wounded.

"Wow, pretty amazing. Yeah, way too much all at once." Ellis sat thinking about the story Marcus had just told.

Silence ensued for a few moments before Ellis, still holding Jeremiah's hat, asked a question.

"Not to be nosy, but when did Jeremiah give you this hat, Marcus?"

"Oh, he didn't give it to me, I found it." Marcus explained.

"Gee, I wonder where he got it? Wonder if he got it at like a rummage sale or something." Ellis turned the hat over and peered once again at its underside.

"I don't know. Like I said, he didn't give it to me, I found it, inside his shack, the day, the day he got...you know." Marcus tried to avoid talking too much about what had happened to Jeremiah.

"Are you sure it was his, Marcus?"

"Well, I'm not positive," Marcus replied. "I mean, I saw it laying there by his stove and I remembered seeing him wearing one like it before, so I guess, I guess, I just assumed it was his. I'm pretty sure it is. Why?" For some reason, Margaret's reminder of one his father's sayings began repeating itself in his brain, *Ass-U-Me*.

"I don't know, something just makes me think, that's all." Ellis paused for a minute, gathering his thoughts, as he imagined a scenario that he didn't really want to consider, for his cousin's sake.

"Marcus, there are initials embroidered inside the flap on this hat. It says M.S. I know somebody with those initials that wears one of these old-style hats, too."

"Really?" Marcus asked, surprised to learn there was anything there on the inside. It had certainly not occurred to him to even look. "What made you even notice that? Who's the person you know that the initials match?"

"I don't know exactly why I looked, maybe because Ollie always wrote his name inside the flap of his hats, right behind the brim. Maybe I was checking for his name, I don't know," Ellis had to admit to himself, he still thought about Ollie, perhaps looking for signs from him. "And the initials are the same as my boss, Max Schofield. You saw him the other day when we went fishing. He lives in the house where I used to live, he's the guy my dad stayed behind to talk with that day."

Seeing the initials had really set the wheels spinning in his brain. Ellis knew that the man that had been his predecessor, who had previously worked for Max, had abandoned his job. Max had told him this guy he had called Tony, had just up and disappeared one day. When Marcus had mentioned that a guy named Tony had been killed at the dump and that Jeremiah had been wounded, it occurred to Ellis that perhaps the murderer had decided that Jeremiah had known too much or maybe was a witness. Marcus finding a hat, which happened to contain Max's initials, seemed terribly coincidental.

"So, you think this hat belongs to him? How do you think Jeremiah came to have it, then?" Marcus asked Ellis.

"I wish I had an answer," Ellis told him. Although he thought he might very well have the answer, Ellis wasn't about to share those suspicions with Marcus. If he did, he was afraid that he would be implicating himself, and the last thing he would want Marcus to know was that he was involved in drug distribution. He had worked far too hard to try to regain trust from his family to admit that he still was far from being an angel.

"I'm guessing that Jeremiah picked it up at a church bazaar or something." Ellis was ready to put the hat discussion in the rearview mirror.

"We need to think about another fishing trip, Marcus. Since the pond was a bust, maybe we try the river next time, what do you think?" Ellis thought the prospect of pulling in a gigantic blue catfish might be enticing.

"I'd been thinking about that myself, Ellis," Marcus was definitely agreeable to the suggestion. "My friend Denny's dad has a canoe that we could probably borrow. We take it two or three times every summer down to a sandbar a couple of miles downstream to camp out. We used to go on the weekends, but I'm working Saturdays now and he works weekend nights at the theater."

"That sounds like a good time, but when do you suppose we could go? I mean, we both have jobs to think about." Ellis was always free on weekends, but as Marcus had said, every Saturday he was at Walt's.

"With school out, Walt gave me more hours, but the shop isn't open on the Fourth of July and Walt already said he was closing at noon on Monday, the day before the Fourth." Marcus had already thought of the possibility of suggesting the trip, even before Ellis had mentioned it, but didn't know if it would fit Ellis' schedule.

"Yeah, that will work out fine, Marcus," Ellis knew he was going to be free on both days. "If you can borrow the canoe. we can probably tie it on top of my car and drive it to the river. How do you and your friend usually get it there?"

"We carry it," Marcus said laughing. "It takes two trips for the canoe and our supplies, but it's not that far, he lives right there on Jamison Street. It's only a half mile walk."

"We'll use the car. Work smarter, not harder, right?" Ellis said, as he returned Marcus' laughter.

* * * *

Ellis turned off the clock radio, just as the deejay was screaming some gibberish about the next episode of *Chickenman* that would air later in the day. He dressed and left the house just past seven, about ten minutes later than he normally left for the trip to St. Louis to pick up his company van and its load of the day's deliveries. But Ellis had decided he wasn't going to make the deliveries today. Instead, he had made up his mind to head north. Ellis had decided that today he was going to be more like his dad, Judy, than what he had been posing as, his pop, Ollie. Today, Friday June 9, 1967, Ellis had decided that he was going to become his own man.

An hour and a half into the drive, Ellis had pulled into the parking lot shared by *Grandma Emma's Kitchen* and *Toby's Two Wheelers* in Palmyra. Both were businesses that he was familiar with from traveling his daily delivery route. It was nearing nine in the morning, and Ellis needed to replenish the space abandoned by the previous night's sausage pizza. In other words, he was starving. *Grandma Emma's* featured the best homemade biscuits and gravy on the western side of the Mississippi River. At least that seemed the consensus of the regulars who traveled the U.S. 61 trail between St. Louis and Iowa. The small establishment was always packed during breakfast hours. They also did a healthy amount of lunch business but would close at two each afternoon. Ellis assumed that *Grandma Emma* (and there really was a Grandma Emma) was surely an early bird who preferred shutting down well before sunset. For all her morning success, she was not interested in serving meals beyond her plentiful breakfasts and relatively light lunches.

Ellis was at the counter enjoying a rare treat of steak and eggs, along with his customary biscuits and gravy. He had decided to splurge a little this morning, adding the steak and eggs. It was a two-dollar upcharge over the normal $1.25 for the simple biscuit and gravy breakfast, which included a strong bottomless cup of coffee. But today was a special day, and Ellis had decided to go all out. He heard the empty stool next to him scoot back and he looked to see Toby Youngblood, from the bike shop next door, straddling the seat to his right.

"Morning, Toby," Ellis nodded. He had gotten to know Toby a little since starting the newest (pot delivery) phase of his employment with Max. He normally delivered a couple of pounds of Missouri Gold to Toby on Fridays for his weekend sales and personal consumption.

"Morning Ellis. How's it hanging?" Toby offered his standard greeting that was afforded everyone, male or female, hardened biker or local Methodist minister. Toby's was an unwavering personality; he didn't change for anyone. He was a very straightforward, what you saw was what you got type of person. "Saw you walking in, but I didn't see the van, looked like you came from that black Ford out there. Usually, you come see me before having your breakfast, just made me curious, you know?"

"Yeah, well about that Toby," Ellis stammered a bit. He should have known better than coming to *Grandma Emma's* if he wasn't going to be dropping product next door for Toby. "I, uh, I don't have your stuff today."

"Why not?" Toby's question was direct.

"I'm not going to be delivering anymore. I quit my job today, Toby. I'm sorry." Ellis was a little nervous about the response he would receive. He somewhat knew the man, but had never had cause to see him angry, and didn't know how he would react to not receiving his shipment today.

"Oh, well, okay Ellis." Toby seemed calm, but Ellis had watched movies in which bad guys sometimes appeared calm only to suddenly explode. "That's okay. I got enough still to last the weekend; I'll just make sure to let Max know to double up next week. Know who's taking your place, do you know?"

"No, no idea Toby," Ellis told him honestly.

"I wonder whatever happened with that kid Billy? He used to ride with Tony a lot. I always figured anything happened to Tony, he'd be next in line for the job." Toby was remembering people Ellis had never actually met. "Yeah, all of a sudden, this one Friday Tony doesn't show and then, bam, the next Friday you're here. And now you're gone. Man, lot of turnover all of a sudden, I'll say, a lot. Max is disappointing me a little."

"I'm really sorry I let you down, Toby." Ellis felt he needed to apologize again.

"Nah, it's okay, Ellis." Toby actually was demonstrating some understanding. "Hey, you're just a kid. You gotta figure your life out, it's okay." Toby stood and left, returning to his shop. Ellis suddenly felt much better, breathing a huge sigh of relief.

Forty-five minutes after his encounter with Toby Youngblood, Ellis was pulling into the driveway of his old house. As he parked, he glanced over at the rusting swing set, and once again relived the agony of the broken wrist.

As he started to open the car door, Ellis saw Max approaching from around the back of the house.

"Hey, Ellis!" Max called to him, waving with his right hand. "Glad you're here, there was a couple of things I wanted to talk to you about before I headed to the office."

This was the exact reason that Ellis had come here, rather than the office. He knew Max rarely showed up at the body shop before ten a.m.

"Come on over and have a seat in the tulips." Max motioned toward a pair of metal lawn chairs.

Alicia had the same red chairs, exactly the same, but she referred to them as her 'clam shell' chairs. Ellis assumed there must be several different monikers for this particular style of patio chair. As he walked, it struck him as odd that Max had not mentioned the fact that Ellis had arrived in his own car rather than the company van. Ellis took his seat and Max soon joined him, opening a unique plastic box, pulling out and lighting a filtered Philip Morris cigarette.

"Max, I've got something that I have to tell you," Ellis said nervously.

"I know you do Thor." Max said as he rubbed briskly between his nose and upper lip. "I got a call already this morning from my favorite Cherokee customer, Toby Youngblood. He said you disappointed him terribly this morning."

Ellis' mind wandered slightly; it had never occurred to him that Youngblood was a Native American surname.

"He didn't seem really upset, Max. He just said he would double order this week." Ellis didn't know why he was even debating the extent to which Toby had been disappointed.

"Fact is Thor, you quit on me. No warning at all. First, I get a call from St. Louis telling me you didn't show up this morning," Max held one finger in the air. "Not so bad, I had a sub sent out to make the deliveries. Second, I get the call from Youngblood, and he's telling me you're next door sloughing down breakfast. And, he says, you brought no product. Don't worry, I smoothed that over, he'll get his load in another hour, so that's all cool."

Ellis continued to listen without uttering a word. He had no defense to present except his desire to get out of the business, a reason that he so far hadn't had the opportunity to express.

"Then, the man tells me that you told him you had quit. Well funny, I'm your boss and you ain't told me that. Not a word to me, but you're out telling my customers you quit?" Max was beginning to show some anger. "You have anything to say for yourself, Thor?"

Ellis hated to be called by that name, but today was not the day to object. He needed to bite his tongue and only say what needed to be said.

"Max, I apologize for not coming right to you, but, I mean, I'm trying. That's why I came straight here to see you. I just can't do this anymore."

"I don't get it Ellis. I pay you a good wage, I promised Ollie I would take care of you and Alicia, and I do. What is the problem, Ellis?"

"It's just, it's what I do, Max. It's illegal to do what I'm doing, and I don't want to end up like Ollie did. He's dead you know; he got killed in prison." It was still hard for Ellis to talk about what had happened to Ollie.

"Yeah, I heard Ellis, and I'm sorry it happened. But you know your dad. He had a problem controlling that mouth sometimes. It wasn't unusual for his mouth to write a check that his fists couldn't cover." Max's words were hard to listen to, but even harder to doubt.

"Yeah, I know Max, but all the same, I don't think I'm cut out for this." Ellis awaited what response Max would counter with.

When Max didn't immediately speak, Ellis took the opportunity to plod on with the words he had run through his mind all morning while driving.

"Max, why didn't you tell me about Tony? Did Alicia know about him? I would guess she did, she does your books, she probably knows everything." Ellis now was feeling anger toward her. Alicia knew exactly what he was doing as an employee of Max, she knew the risk he was taking with his future. And considering the baggage he was already carrying, if she really did consider herself his mother, how could she justify allowing him work for Max?

"I'm not going to lie to you Ellis, of course she knew about Tony. She wrote his paychecks." Max laid it on the line for Ellis. "Tony was a good man, did a good job for me. But Tony got too big for his britches, always asking for more. Let's face it, I'm better off without him."

"Max, did you kill him? Is that what happened to him?" Ellis really, really wanted to know the truth.

"No, Ellis, I didn't. I liked Tony. It was the guy that he had brought on to help him. Bill was his name." Even Max didn't know why he was telling the kid so much.

"So, what happened to him, to Bill?" Ellis asked.

"Nobody knows. He killed Tony, shot the old man leaving the dump and just disappeared. He was in Tony's van. He dumped it, stole the weed that Tony had possession of and, poof, disappeared." Max pursed his lips while using his right hand to make the kissing gesture when using the word *poof*.

"That all sounds pretty reasonable, Max. But it's hard to believe. I was thinking about it a little bit while I was driving." Ellis decided to try out his own theory. "Max, it looks to me like somebody killed Tony and then shot that old man, his name was Jeremiah. Okay, so if Jeremiah doesn't get killed, which he didn't, then that means there is still a witness that can identify this unknown shooter, whether it's this guy Bill you mentioned or whoever."

Max listened quietly, with a slight smirk on his lips.

"So, Jeremiah is still alive. But then, just a few days later, he gets murdered. Now, who do you think would be responsible for that happening?" Ellis felt like that old lawyer on television, *Perry Mason*. "It's got to be the guy that shot Tony, right? Eliminating the only witness."

"Compelling argument, Thor." Max said. "So do tell me, who do you suspect? And if you have a suspect, why don't the police? I haven't read or heard of any arrests so far."

"I don't have any suspects; I'm just thinking out loud, that's all. I guess whoever is responsible did a good job of covering his tracks and making sure there was no evidence left behind." Ellis was proud of himself, hoping he had given Max some food for thought.

"Well, so much for that subject. Now I have questions for you, young Mr. Compton. I've heard that you hang out a lot with that Clemens kid. That was him that was here with you and your real dad on Sunday, wasn't it?" Max asked.

"Yeah, that was him. Why do you ask?" Ellis wondered what Max's interest was in Marcus.

"Oh, just curious. I think that's good that the two of you have been able to develop a relationship after all that happened a few years ago." After all the gruesome talk, Ellis was glad to discuss something a little more uplifting. "You know Thor, I'm not really bothered that you don't want to continue your employment, I mean I can replace you, not a problem. I just want you to know you're a big boy now and you can make decisions for yourself. I promised Ollie I'd look after you. Always remember that. I'll always try to do what is best for you."

"Thanks, Max. I appreciate that. I appreciate the fact that you take care of Alicia, too."

"You're welcome, Ellis. So, did you all enjoy your afternoon of fishing out here the other day? I had some phone calls and such I had to take care of, or I would have joined you out there." Max gave Ellis a warm smile. "When do you plan to come back and try again?"

"I don't know Max; we didn't catch anything. I think maybe that pond has been fished out."

"Maybe next time you should go to the river," Max suggested. "That thing will never get fished out."

"Funny you'd mention it because we just talked about that last night." It seemed ironic that Max would suggest something he and Marcus had just discussed. "I think we might go for the Fourth of July. We're thinking about camping out on a sandbar that Marcus knows about and doing some fishing out there."

"That sounds like a good time. That will be a good bonding experience for you guys." Max thought that sounded like a potentially compelling adventure for them. "Do you plan to have your dad make the trip with you?"

"No, at least not this time," Ellis imagined they would be cramped in the canoe they were borrowing from Marcus' friend. "We only have a single canoe, barely enough room for the two of us."

"Oh yeah, I'm sure. Well, I hope you have a good time on your camping trip." Max stood, stretching. "You'll excuse me Ellis, but I need to get to the office. Some of us do have to work."

"Once again Max, I'm sorry I let you down. I feel bad now." Ellis was suffering a bit of a guilt trip for putting Max on the spot this morning.

"No harm done, Ellis. You take care of yourself. And hey, don't let any of this stuff about Tony bother you, okay." Max gave Ellis a thumbs up as he started toward the front door.

Ellis began walking toward his car, keeping one eye on his former boss. Just as Max was reaching for the door handle, Ellis called out to him.

"Hey Max!"

"Yeah, Thor?" Max turned back smiling.

"Do you ever wear that old newsboy hat that I remember from when you used to come to see Ollie?"

"Not for a while, Ellis, why?" Max knew his newsboy hat had vanished from the dump and wondered why Ellis would suddenly remember his from five or six years ago.

"We found one the other day, Marcus thought it belonged to that fellow Jeremiah, but then I saw the initials M.S. embroidered in it." Ellis told him. "That's your initials, I thought maybe you might have lost it."

"I think the last time I saw that hat; Karen had put it in a sack of clothing donations she gave to the church or some other charitable outfit." Karen was

Max's former wife. She had faded from Max's life shortly after Alicia and Ollie had split up.

"Yeah, that thing's been gone since before she left, what six, seven years now, I guess." Max was glad to know the hat was not in the hands of the law. It was the only piece of evidence that he was aware of that could link him to any of the mess that had transpired at the dump. Max was glad he had taken care of Bill Lohman. That man had opened one hellacious can of worms.

"Good, then that means it was Jeremiah's. I'll let Marcus know." Ellis was relieved to learn that Max was no longer the owner of the hat that Marcus had found. "I guess Marcus was right, Jeremiah must have got it from a charity sale. Thanks, Max."

Ellis was pleased that he had met with Max, and they had been able to talk through his reasons for quitting. He was glad to leave with the promise that, with Ollie now gone, Max would be there for him. And it was a relief to know that they had been able to go their separate ways under good terms.

The Camping Trip

The two men were engaged in a life and death struggle. The grapple had begun on the bank of the small body of water, but when one had managed to inflict severe damage upon the other, he had forced the action into the water. His intent was obvious to the onlooker, who sat helplessly frozen in place, unable to lift a finger to intervene. The third-party witness felt a compelling urge and desperately wanted to help the injured man, but it seemed as though he was seated in a movie theater. He had no choice but to watch in silence as the action unfolded on an imaginary big screen. The entire scene was all so close, but at the same time a million miles away. What he was witnessing was real, so very, very real. And he could do nothing, absolutely nothing. The man's head once again was forced beneath the water's surface, for what surely would be the final time. Ellis was shaken when he suddenly realized he was not watching a movie but that it was he, himself that he'd seen, that he was the stranger seated on the pond's bank watching the fatal scuffle as it unfolded. He realized that he had been sitting in the grass for the entire duration of the confrontation. Inexplicably, he was no longer seeing the struggle from afar; he was suddenly a part of the action, a real live witness to a possible homicide. Time and time again, he had seen the man gasp for air as his arms flailed frantically. He had desperately thrown awkward, futile punches with few, if any, noteworthy effects on the aggressor. Finally, mercifully, the man ceased movement. His resistance had ended. The other man continued holding the motionless body down below the surface, until he was satisfied that his victim had permanently succumbed. In a few minutes, the water having calmed, the surface ripples noticeably dissipating, he finally released his grip and let the body float listlessly. He slowly trudged past the cattails that stood tall and silently erect at the water's edge. Almost, Ellis thought briefly, almost as an honor guard to the deceased on this calm day. The man was visibly exhausted and collapsed just a few feet onto the bank. He lay on his back and slowly took in deep, relaxing breaths. To Ellis, he resembled a soldier, just back from battle, thankful to have been on the side of victory. Good versus evil, with evil having been vanquished.

Ellis sat, not an arm's length from the man. But he had not been acknowledged, remaining totally ignored as the man had left the water and collapsed onto the grass. It seemed to Ellis that the man had looked directly at him, but he knew that he had gone unseen, as if the man's steely eyes had gazed completely through him. Ellis turned, wondering what was behind him that had caught the man's attention. And that's when Ellis spotted the dog. It was the first time he had seen it today, but not the first time ever. No, definitely not the first time.

Ellis awoke Monday morning, once again to his blaring clock radio and the incessant jabber of the deejay. Today the distant voice was extolling the virtues of some unknown product guaranteed to *'make your smile brighter by a mile'*. Ellis stretched and then rubbed his eyes vigorously before dropping his arms to his sides. He closed his eyes, recalling the insane recurring dream from which he had awoken. Two men fighting in the water. What could it mean? The therapist who had helped him immensely at the Missouri Training School for Boys, had been unable to pinpoint a justification or basis for the dream that had begun its manifestations shortly after his incarceration. Despite the therapist's prodding, Ellis could not name the two combatants. To the best of his recollection, the two men were faceless, their physiques generic. As hard as he tried, despite all the delving and questions asked by his therapist, Ellis could not begin to identify the two nor realize a motive for the mysterious fight highlighting the dreams. Ellis offered all he could in his sessions, describing each and every aspect of the recurring dream, providing the most intricate details possible. Almost every detail. There was one small item that Ellis withheld, an unrelated bit of information that he kept to himself for fear that its revelation would have sent him directly to a mental institution.

Determined to put the dream out of mind, Ellis jumped from bed, showered, and began gathering items for the camping trip. He already had the fishing equipment and fireworks loaded into his trunk. He still needed to pack his duffel bag with a change of clothes, a few canned goods and a scattering of odds and ends that could come in handy over the course of today and the next twenty-four hours. By nine a.m., Ellis was prepared to fill his gas tank and get on the road. Marcus was scheduled to work from seven a.m. until noon when Walt's Tire and Auto Repair would be closing early for the holiday.

* * * *

Ellis had arrived about eleven-thirty, anticipating that Marcus would join him in another thirty minutes. They had spent most of their free time for the better part of the last two weeks planning and preparing for the camping trip. Tomorrow would be the Fourth of July, and both were in anticipation of setting off fireworks later this evening. While waiting for Marcus, Ellis had some difficulty trying to relax. Despite the unseasonable heat today, Ellis had managed to drift off to sleep. Unfortunately, his brief nap had been uncomfortable and very similar to the fitful slumber of last night. The recurring dream that had been haunting him for the past three years had returned during his nap, playing out exactly as it had last night. Ellis was relieved to have been pulled from the dream by Marcus calling out to him.

"Hey, Ellis. You want to sleep or go have lunch?" Marcus asked. He opened the back door of the sedan and tossed his bag of supplies onto the seat.

"Hi Marcus," Ellis said, as cleared his mind of the leftover grogginess. "Yeah, I'm starving. I didn't have breakfast this morning so, yeah. Man, I'm hungry as all get out!"

Ellis drove to *The River's Edge Diner* and on the relatively short ride, Marcus sensed that Ellis seemed reserved. He didn't know if it was due to the fact that he had just been asleep, or if he might be mulling over a problem that was bothering him. After securing a booth in the diner and placing orders, Marcus decided to pry.

"Are you okay, Ellis?" Marcus asked. "You seem a little down today, is everything alright?"

"Yeah, yeah. I'm good Marcus," he replied.

"You sure?" Marcus hadn't seen Ellis with such a troubled look. At least not since Ollie's passing. He wondered if that might have been the root of Ellis' problem. He had seemed to handle Ollie's death well, maybe the grief had finally descended upon him.

"Can I confess something to you, Marcus?" Ellis asked. His tone seemed to suggest a touch of trepidation.

"Sure, of course, Ellis." Marcus replied.

"Okay, but promise me you won't think I'm crazy," Ellis almost pleaded. "I discussed this with my therapist while I was locked up. He helped me with a lot, but he said he wasn't an expert on dreams. He tried hard, but he never could figure out why I had these dreams or what they might mean."

"Dreams? What kinds of dreams?" Marcus had to admit to himself, this did sound interesting to him.

"Well really, not dreams. Just one dream." Ellis clarified what he meant. "I started having it not too long after I went to the training school. And I keep having it, over and over and over again. Always exactly the same, it never changes. It starts out like I'm up in the air watching everything. There're two guys fighting and one guy sitting in the grass watching and then, all of a sudden, the guy sitting in the grass is me. But it's like I'm invisible. I want to help one of them, but I don't even know who they are. I..." Marcus suddenly interrupted by finishing Ellis' story.

"The guy sitting in the grass wants to get up and help one of them," Marcus continued. "And then the stronger one holds the other guy under water until he is dead. The guy walks up onto the bank and lays down in the grass, on his back. I wanted to help, too. But I wasn't there, it was like watching a movie at *The Meridian*."

"Marcus, are you psychic?" Ellis asked, beside himself that Marcus knew precisely how the dream proceeded. "How did you know that?"

"I don't know, Ellis. I had the same dream last night. They fought on the bank and ended up in the water." Marcus was just as amazed as Ellis had been. "They didn't have faces; it was like *The Twilight Zone* or something."

"Yeah, exactly. I don't know who they were," Ellis said, almost in a questioning manner. "Their bodies were even weird; I don't know who was taller or heavier or anything."

"What about the location of the pond, Ellis? Did you recognize where it all was happening at?" Marcus asked.

"Yeah, I do Marcus. I never thought about it before." Somehow this simple detail had always escaped Ellis' notice. "It was where I used to live. It was the pond at Ollie's old place. It's where Max lives now."

"Exactly, Ellis. It's the pond we fished at with Judy a couple of weeks ago. I remember the pine trees that surrounded most of it." Marcus recalled the pond's layout very well.

"That's nuts, Marcus. I've been having that dream for three years." Ellis was truly astounded. "How is it possible for you to have the exact same dream last night?" Ellis sat, shaking his head at the astronomical odds against them not only sharing the same dream, but having the identical dream on the exact same night.

Something else occurred to Ellis, "Marcus, did you hear the voice?"

"No, I didn't hear any voice." Marcus said. "What kind of voice, what did it say?"

"The exact words were 'Do not to tempt fate. Do what you know to be right.' And that's it," Ellis told him. "I don't know what kind of voice, just like, mystical or something. It's been the same voice, same message for three years now. What do you think it could mean Marcus, any ideas?"

"No idea, none at all." Marcus was both amazed and dumbfounded. But the prospect of a mysterious voice did touch a nerve.

351

After burgers, fries, and slices of Buster's world famous (or so he claimed) rhubarb pie that Ellis had grudgingly agreed to try, the pair drove to Denny Wallace's house. There, with Denny's help, they loaded the sixteen-foot fiberglass *Old Town* canoe that Doug Wallace had graciously allowed them to borrow. With a strategically placed blanket on the roof of the sedan for protection, Ellis and Marcus carefully ran a nylon rope several times over the canoe and through the car's open windows, securely fastening it down safely. It was only a half mile drive, but neither was anxious to pony up replacement costs in the slim chance that the canoe was to be damaged.

In no time at all the canoe had been staged at the river's edge and Ellis' car properly stowed in the neighboring parking area. The two of them were soon happily rowing toward the sandbar which was located just more than two miles downstream of their launch point. It was an enjoyable cruise downstream. Marcus had not made this voyage since the previous August when he and Denny had spent Marcus' birthday camping out. He was anxious to get there, looking forward to setting off the bottle rockets and roman candles they had brought along. Marcus also thought he would like to delve into Ellis' dream a bit more. He especially wondered if there could be more to learn of the voice that Ellis professed to having heard in his dream. Additionally, Marcus had an idea in mind that he hoped to convince Ellis would be an interesting adventure for them to undertake tomorrow morning.

Upon dragging the canoe to a safe location about twenty feet up onto the sandbar, the two went about setting up their two-man green canvas pup tent and building a fire over which to cook dinner. They had brought summer sausage, green peppers, and onions to prepare for their late dinner. Ellis was new to the camping experience, but Marcus had been to the sandbar with Denny numerous times over the past couple of years and was a veteran of the routine. The two of them scoured the nearby stand of birch trees for some loose branches and came back with just what they needed to build a rough tripod, which was set it up over the fire. From the tripod, they were able to hang the old cast iron pot that Margaret had donated to the cause two summers back.

Neither being particularly hungry after the cheeseburger lunch at the diner, they had decided to hold dinner off until after they had enjoyed their private fireworks show. They put their quasi-stew on just before sundown and then started the fireworks when the sky had achieved full darkness, at the point where spectacle would be at its grandest. The roman candles were beautiful and fun, but the bottle rocket wars took the blue ribbon. They had a blast firing them from a pair of buried Coca-Cola bottles and into the river. They tried valiantly, but never quite succeeded, reaching the riverbank. By the end of the show, both young men were ready for the slow cooked meal. Afterwards they sat quietly, enjoying the fire. Marcus recommended that they keep it stoked all night. There was no concern that it would be cold, and they had purposely set up the pup tent far enough away that they would not to be affected by the fire's heat. Marcus wanted to keep the fire burning to deter any critters that may decide to act on their curiosity about the strangers who were invading their habitat.

As they sat heating marshmallows over the fire, Marcus and Ellis discussed the coincidence of their shared dream. Try as they might, neither could attach any significance to the events being played out in the dream. Aside from the shared realization that everything happened at the pond they had just visited, they could not make any type of connection. Ellis had grown up on the property and had fished the pond the entire first sixteen years of his life. He had familiarity with it, so it would only be natural that he would project it into his dream. Marcus, on the other hand, had only been there one time. However, the one visit had been just a few weeks ago, and with it being his most recent fishing expedition, that memory might have been enough to implant that suggestion into his subconscious. The inclusion of the pond in their dreams could possibly have been a simple matter of a shared suggestion, with both having a valid reason for choosing it. But the matter of the two men involved, with neither Ellis nor Marcus able to determine even the slightest of clues as to their identities, remained the sixty-four-thousand-dollar question.

The lingering issue that raised questions in Marcus' mind was the revelation that Ellis had, in each of his recurring dreams, heard a voice telling him 'Do not tempt fate. Do what you know to be right'. He had to quiz Ellis more deeply on the subject.

"Ellis, the words that the voice speaks to you, do they have any special meaning to you?" Marcus asked.

"Honestly, at first no, they meant nothing at all. It just seemed like so much gibberish, you know what I mean?" Ellis replied. "But after a while, after going to therapy for a few months, it started to make sense to me."

"Really, how come?" Marcus wanted to know Ellis' thinking.

"Well, Marcus, when I started to understand how my mind had been controlled by Ollie, I began to realize how evil the path was that he had led me down. I thought hard about some of things my therapist suggested, and it became clear to me that I had to agree with him, that with the behavior I had grown accustomed to and become comfortable with, I was just, more or less, asking for it. Without knowing it, I was begging to be punished. Marcus, my actions were in direct defiance to God and all He stands for. That was when it dawned on me that I'd been tempting fate, I had been asking for retribution." Ellis stopped to let Marcus absorb his words.

"So, you figured you had to change your behavior, right?" Marcus asked.

"Yeah, if I kept being the jerk that I was being, my life was going to continue to be crap. And I decided to listen to the second sentence, too. From now on, I do what is the right thing to do. Even when I'm told otherwise, I've finally realized that I got to stand up for myself and do what I know is right." Ellis thought about what he was saying, and then thought about the short time he had been delivering drugs while working for Max. He had struggled with what he was doing, it had been difficult to try to convince himself he wasn't doing wrong. In the end, the voice had won out. Ellis had stood up to Max and he had quit. He had stopped tempting fate, and he had done what he knew in his heart was right. Ellis looked down at his feet. He felt relieved to be telling this, sharing it with someone. In jail, he had a therapist. On the street, he basically was alone.

"It's good to cleanse, Ellis." The words that reached his brain somehow seemed distant. He instinctively looked at Marcus, who sat in the sand smiling at him.

"You think so?" Ellis said, returning the smile. "It felt good."

"What felt good?" Marcus asked.

"Cleansing, like you said."

"Cleansing what?" Marcus was confused, what Ellis was saying didn't make sense.

The voice returned. "This is not Marcus. It's time you knew, Ellis."

Ellis was looking at Marcus just as the voice was speaking. Marcus' lips were not moving, so unless he was a ventriloquist, it was obviously not Marcus he was hearing. Ellis put his hands to his ears and said, "I'm not hearing this, I'm not hearing this."

Marcus was becoming alarmed. He had never seen anyone acting like this. He was afraid that Ellis had gone stark raving mad right before his eyes. Startlingly, the reason for Ellis' disturbing conduct became crystal clear. The responsible party sat several feet behind Ellis, some ten yards away, over near the canoe. Ellis had no idea that the voice was coming from the same nemesis that, four years ago, had permanently scarred his right arm in the mausoleum.

"Ellis, I can solve one of the mysteries that has been troubling you." As the words left his mouth, a stark realization entered Marcus' mind. If Opa had spoken to Ellis, it would then follow that Ellis must hold a lifelong commitment to Marcus. He specifically remembered Cassie telling him that the caveat of her lifelong commitment was the reason Opa was able to speak to her. The key to Opa's communication had been the lifelong commitment they shared. If this were the case, this was becoming difficult to digest.

"What, Marcus, what can you solve?"

"You just heard the voice again, didn't you Ellis?" Marcus asked, as he ran the concept of commitment repeatedly through his mind.

"Yes, I did." Ellis was at a loss as to why Marcus suspected that he had heard the voice.

"Ellis, I know about the voice, and how it all works. I know who it is you're hearing." Marcus confessed. "It is going to sound crazy, but it's the truth and I'll prove it to you in a few moments."

"How do you know about the voice, Marcus? I was afraid you'd think I was insane when I told you about it." Ellis was taken back by Marcus' words.

"I know, Ellis, because it is this family thing. And I guess this is a sign that you have been accepted into the family." Marcus was about to lay it all out.

357

Ellis may or may not believe what he was about to say, but Marcus was sure he would accept the ultimate proof. "Ellis, Cassie hears the voice also."

"What?" Ellis was incredulous as he gasped his response.

"It's true. The voice you are hearing is in your head, it's not spoken. The best we can figure is it's a form of telepathic communication, it's the same thing that Cassie hears." Marcus knew he would have to handle this slowly. He thought it best to let this information sink in before continuing.

"So, you are telling Cassie hears this voice too? Does she have the dreams also, like I do?" He asked.

"No, no dreams. He just talks to her. But only when it's necessary." Marcus tried his best to go a little at a time.

"Do you hear it too, Marcus?"

"No, and I'll try to explain. Hear me out, and then I'll see if I can give you proof." Marcus took a deep breath and went on, "The voice that you had only heard in your dreams, but just came to you a few minutes ago, is the exact same voice that Cassie hears. Ellis, that is the voice of my grandfather, John Clemens. He died way back in 1934. For some reason that he has never explained, he has come back to earth to be my guardian angel. I don't know why, but he is here to look out for me. Over the last four years he has saved my life three or four times."

"That's mighty hard to believe, Marcus. If he's your guardian angel, why talk to me? I don't think I can believe this, Marcus." Ellis didn't know where the voice that he at least *thought* he heard, had come from. But it seemed so impossible that it could be the voice of an angel. "And if all of this is true, then I need proof. I need to see his face if you expect me to believe."

"Ellis, you have seen his face." Marcus said as he looked sadly into Ellis' eyes. "He once saved me from you."

"What are you saying, Marcus? I don't get it."

"Ellis, that scar on your arm. You remember where you got it, don't you?" Ellis looked at his right forearm. Of course, he remembered distinctly how he had been attacked and what had caused the scar.

Opa had moved forward and sat unnoticed at Ellis' left heel.

"Ellis, do you remember that face?" Marcus nodded toward Opa.

As he looked down at the scraggily looking dog, Ellis immediately remembered it from the mausoleum. And he simultaneously heard words echoing inside his head, "Ellis, do not tempt fate. You are here for a reason; this was planned before you were even born. Accept your fate and do what you know to be right." Ellis stood in an utter daze. The voice, a guardian angel, the truth behind his scar.

"Marcus, this is too much for one night." Ellis was at a loss for words as he stood slowly shaking his head.

"I know Ellis, I know." Marcus turned his gaze from Ellis and back down to Opa, but of course, there was no sign that Opa had ever been there. Except for the few scattered paw prints that appeared to lead off into the nearby honeysuckle, there was no evidence of his existence, aside from the memory of the two young men.

* * * *

Marcus and Ellis both awoke Tuesday morning drenched in sweat. Low cloud cover had provided a blanket effect, preserving some of the afternoon heat, resulting in warm sleeping conditions. Although they had set up their tent a fair distance away, the campfire had also contributed to miserably high overnight temperatures. An early morning quick submersion in the cooling river waters provided some satisfying relief, giving them the renewed energy to focus on the day ahead. The two snacked on beef jerky for their morning meal and discussed the plan for the remainder of the day. They had agreed not to stay too long at the campsite this morning. The two calculated that they would need to leave the sandbar no later than noon. That should allow them time to have a quick lunch at *A & W*, probably around one o'clock, before returning the canoe to Denny's father. Before heading back to Fulton, Ellis would drop Marcus at his apartment where he would enjoy a bath and possibly a nap. Later, he and Margaret would go to the Worthington's house for the annual Fourth of July fireworks party. Ellis would then have the long drive back to Fulton, where he had promised to pick up Becca and attend the fireworks show being offered by the local Kiwanis Club.

In the meantime, they were left with a window of about four hours for fun and exploration. They had originally planned to scout and investigate the eastern shoreline of the Mississippi River. But, over the course of the past few days, Marcus had been toying with a variation to that plan. He had been unsure and was hesitant to divulge to Ellis what he'd been considering. Marcus had been struggling, lacking confidence that what he wanted to do would not be a mistake. But in view of what had happened last night with Opa, Marcus had made the decision that the endeavor he had considered was worth undertaking.

After their beef jerky breakfast, Marcus informed Ellis that he had come up with a new and exciting idea to occupy their remaining morning hours. He promised Ellis that the excursion he was proposing would be fun and adventurous. When Ellis asked what exactly they would be doing, Marcus told him that he would have to reserve a full explanation for when they had reached their destination. He hoped that if the new plan did not prove fruitful, that Ellis would be satisfied to simply revert to exploring the Illinois side of the river. Without difficulty, Marcus convinced Ellis to play along, promising that, hopefully, his compliance would be well rewarded. In a joint effort, they deconstructed their campsite and prepared everything so it would all be ready to load into the canoe when they returned in a few short hours. Within thirty minutes the demobilization was completed, and the two pushed their borrowed canoe into the river and began paddling downstream, toward the Illinois shore and south of the sandbar. As they shoved off, Marcus and Ellis were oblivious to the fact that, since very early this morning, they had been under the watchful surveillance of two pairs of binoculars from the Missouri bank of the mighty river.

Marcus carefully consulted the map that had been carefully drawn, hoping that the depicted landmarks, by which he was navigating, had been presented accurately and would lead him to his desired location. About an hour into the voyage, Marcus recognized the bluffs up ahead on his left as those depicted on the map. They paddled in closer to shore and allowed the weaker current along the bank to carry them gently downstream, using the oars only to steer and stay safely away from the stronger flow a few feet out. Marcus carefully studied the bluff. He knew the foliage described on the map would have changed dramatically over the course of the past half century. Marcus silently hoped he would be able to recognize the crescent moon shape that nature had, according to his map, carved into the stone structure of the bluff centuries or perhaps even thousands of years ago. Continuing to slowly drift downstream, Marcus began to wonder if the map was truly accurate, or if he may have already passed the marker for which he had been fervently searching. Developing a fear that the crescent moon was never going to be found, Marcus had nearly given up when he realized his grandfather had not let him down. When finally spotted, the marker had not been difficult to distinguish on the face of the bluff, and Marcus was relieved and excited to give Ellis the news.

"Here it is, here it is. We need to get up on shore, right over there, next to the huge boulder by the mulberry bush." Marcus anxiously pointed toward a boulder that he estimated to be three to four feet in diameter.

They carefully landed and secured the canoe. Grabbing the pair of flashlights and a small burlap sack containing a few hand tools Marcus had wisely packed, the two started up the damp and slippery shale incline. Within moments they had found the camouflaged mouth of what appeared to be a small cave. Moving a few branches and small logs, they were presented with no more than a three-foot roughly semi-circle shaped opening in the bluff wall. Marcus knelt, shining a light inside. From what he could tell, it certainly looked as though Opa had been correct. There appeared to be a room just inside that seemed as though it opened into a larger space than the entry might have indicated. With Marcus leading the way, he and Ellis crawled through the cave entrance. Once inside the cave itself, the entrance chamber, they realized they could stand up. The room was quite large, much more so than the view from the mouth of the cave would have indicated, and it reeked of mold. Shining their flashlights around the walls, they quickly discovered the three arteries that led away from the front chamber. Marcus shined the light on the one to the far right.

"Opa said that is the one we're looking for," Marcus was confident that with the map getting them this far successfully, the rest of Opa's words would also ring true.

"And you said Opa is your grandfather, right?" Ellis asked.

"Right, my grandfather takes the shape of the dog that spoke to you last night. He visited this cave with his friend Jeremiah about fifty years ago. He drew the map that I just used to find this cave," Marcus explained.

"So, what is the purpose of being here, Marcus?"

"I'll let you know in a little bit, Ellis," Marcus replied. "I want to make sure before I tell you something that isn't true. Come on, we need to go into the passage that is on the right. Opa says to follow it to the end, there will be a room there."

Marcus led the way as they embarked on a cave journey that led them on a winding path that seemed would have no end. The musty, moldy smell was nearly unbearable as they made their way along the damp, slippery path. It felt as though they had walked half of a mile when the tunnel suddenly opened into another room, this one not quite as large as the first, at the cave's entrance. They both began scouring with their flashlights, each wanting to be the first to locate the 'X' that Opa had promised had been etched into a section of the cave's wall. Opa's promise was that the 'X' had been etched into a small section or piece of the wall that could easily be removed. Ellis was the 'first to notice the faint marking. It had only been scratched into the surface with another rock, and the etching lacked any significant penetration or depth, and after all these years wasn't much more than a chalk mark on the wall. Marcus had packed the bag of tools in anticipation of Opa's prediction being accurate. He retrieved two long bladed screwdrivers from the bag and worked them into the edges of the small section that Opa's instructions promised could be removed. Not much effort was needed for Marcus to get the block, with the aid of the screwdrivers, to slowly begin walking itself outward. When a couple of inches were protruding, Ellis grabbed ahold with his fingertips and began wiggling and pulling on the block until he was able to grab it securely with both hands and remove it from its home. As he set it on the floor, Marcus looked inside the opening. He was not disappointed by his discovery.

"My God, Opa. You were not joking when you said it was a treasure map, were you?" Marcus questioned aloud. "Take a look, Ellis."

Marcus stepped back to allow Ellis a peek. "Oh Geez, Marcus! How many are there do you think?"

"I don't know. Can you count them?"

"Maybe," Ellis commenced trying to count. The gold bars were not stacked very neatly. Ellis knew gold bars were heavy and wondered how someone was able to reach through this relatively small hole to stack them. He guessed the block he had removed was a couple of feet tall and wide, it certainly was heavy. "I'm not sure if I counted correctly, but it looks like twenty-two or twenty-three. I might have doubled up on one or two, it's kind of hard the way they're stacked up in there. What are you going to do with them, Marcus? That will be a big job getting them out of there and to your apartment or the bank or wherever you're going to take them."

"I don't know, Ellis. I might have to see my friend Deputy Daniels and get his advice about what to do." Marcus was astounded at what they had found. "I guess I can't do anything right now, though."

"Why not?" Ellis would like to have started removing them today, before someone else found them.

"Because I found the treasure map and a letter from my grandfather in the document binder that you opened for me. I need to have you open it again, too, so I can put them back." It had dawned on Marcus that the items had to be returned to the binder or he might run into legal problems down the road. "And besides, I can't legally open that thing until I'm eighteen, and it has to be in front of a lawyer to be legal and everything."

"Good point, Marcus." Ellis was disheartened, but knew Marcus was right. "Hey, they've been hiding safely back there for fifty years, what will two more hurt, right? Plus, we know where they are now, we can check on them every once in a while."

"Ellis, when I turn eighteen and open that binder legally, I'm splitting the gold with you." Ellis was floored by Marcus' announcement.

"Why? Why would you do that, Marcus?" Ellis absolutely couldn't believe Marcus' generosity.

"Because. I guess two reasons. You're a Clemens, not by your name, but you are by blood, for one. And for the other, Opa spoke to you. He can't even talk to me. Opa told Cassie the only people he was allowed to talk to were people that shared a lifelong commitment with me. He only talks to you and Cassie." Marcus knew that reason number two was the driving force behind his decision.

"Well, thank you, Marcus." Ellis said. "I'll be in your debt for the rest of my life. Thank you. And don't worry, I don't mind waiting two years. I've got experience at it. I can do two years standing on my head."

They talked a little longer, mostly about what they would do with the fortune they would be collecting in another two years, before replacing the stone and heading back toward the cave's entrance. Upon crawling back out of the cave, they carefully replaced all the camouflage they had removed upon their arrival. They made their way carefully back down the incline to the canoe. They looked around, both hoping no one had seen them enter or exit the cave, boarded the canoe, and began the long arduous trip back. The paddling was difficult, as they were working their way upstream against the current. Marcus wondered how hard this must have been for Opa and Jeremiah fifty years ago. He imagined that they were probably floating on some type of homemade raft that would not have been nearly as hydrodynamic as the fiberglass canoe they were now in.

It was quite a bit beyond the planned noon hour when they arrived back on the sandbar. They pulled the canoe partially upon onto the sand, enough that it couldn't float away. Fortunately, they had prepared everything for loading beforehand, and it took them less than fifteen minutes to pack the canoe. They were just about to shove it back into the water when they were interrupted by two rugged looking strangers that Marcus was positive he had never seen before. They approached from the brush, almost from the identical position where they had tied and secured the canoe last night. One of them had raised their attention by calling out Marcus' name. Marcus did not have an earthly clue as to why or how they knew his name. He definitely had no idea of their identity. As they walked toward Marcus and Ellis, they both raised pistols toward the two young campers. Marcus froze, his heart feeling as though it would explode straight out of his chest.

"Hey, long time no see, Thor. How ya been?" To the amazement of Marcus, one of the strangers had greeted Ellis. The words stung all the way to the pit of his stomach. Fearing the absolute worse, wondering if he had been duped into making the biggest mistake of his lifetime, Marcus looked toward Ellis in total and complete confusion. Cassie's warning from Opa played through his mind on an endless looping reel. *'It's starting again. Evil is afoot. Be careful who you trust.'*

When Ellis opened his mouth, Marcus heard the words that seemed to cut the absolute deepest.

"Hi, Mooch, how you doing Hondo?"

Full Circle

Marcus stood in utter amazement. Ellis knew these people. *What in the world is going on here?* Marcus asked himself. Marcus was second guessing himself like he never had in his young life. *I trusted Ellis, I treated him like a brother. I've told him everything. He knows about the stocks; he knows about the footlocker. He just saw the gold bars, he knows exactly where they are hidden, he knows how to access them, he even knows exactly how many there are. How could I have trusted him? Why didn't I trust Cassie's judgement? Or her parents'? They didn't trust Ellis, didn't want him around Cassie at all. Why? Why? Why?* Marcus' mind was racing, asking a myriad of questions. He wondered how Ellis knew these men and how they knew Ellis.

"What happened to you, Thor?" Hondo asked. "We got some doofus coming out bringing the dope now, ain't as much fun as you always were."

"Yeah, we miss you kid," Mooch added. "We were worried about you; you know after what happened to Tony and all."

369

"I quit. That life just doesn't sit well with me, you know?" Ellis said, in explanation. "So, if you don't mind me asking, what's with the guns?"

"Yeah, well, Max wants to see your boy here. I guess he's got some property that Max is missing." Mooch began offering to Ellis exactly what was happening here. "We got a little motorboat on the other side of the island, right through the brush there," Mooch pointed in the direction from which he and Hondo had first appeared, "maybe fifty yards that way."

"We're gonna take your buddy here with us. You worked for Max; you know how this stuff it goes." Hondo added. "And Max wants you to tag along, said he wants to talk to you about something."

"Hey, maybe he wants to get you back into your old job." Mooch said.

Ellis was pretty sure he knew what Max wanted to discuss and it wasn't his old job. He had let slip about the documents that Marcus was inheriting from Mark Twain. Since running his mouth, remorse had eaten at him and he had felt guilt over his stupidity. Max had briefly mentioned to him that Ollie might have been right after all. He was sure that Max intended to enlist him in yet another plan to steal Marcus' inheritance.

"I'll help you row your canoe back and give you a hand loading it back up on your car, Thor. Then you can follow us out to Max's place." Ellis knew the words being uttered by Mooch were neither an invitation nor suggestion. They constituted an order that he dare not refuse.

"Okay guys." Ellis was resigned to letting them take Marcus. He would just have to play along and try to come up with a way to get himself and Marcus out of this jam.

Hondo continued to hold Marcus at gunpoint as they trudged through the brush and past a gathering of black willow and birch trees growing on the eastern side of the sandbar. Prompted by a sharp nudge, Marcus quickly boarded the two-man motorized dinghy that had transported Hondo and Mooch to the sandbar. Meanwhile, on the west bank of the island, Mooch had holstered his pistol prior to joining Ellis in the canoe.

Hondo and the motorboat arrived well ahead of the canoe. As they waited for Mooch and Ellis, Marcus attempted to start a conversation.

"So, you guys know Ellis because he was your drug dealer?" He asked.

"No kid, he ain't no dealer. Max is the hot dog. Thor there, he just picked up loads of pot down in the city and then he drove around making deliveries and such. He's like the Encyclopedia Britannica guy, you know, just going door to door." Hondo tried to clarify to Marcus what Ellis had actually done in Max's employ. "No, no, he ain't the encyclopedia guy, he's like the Fuller Brush guy." Hondo started laughing hysterically. "He loads his little suitcase and then he goes door to door selling his wares." More laughter, followed by a more serious tone. "Nah, kid, Thor ain't no dealer. He don't buy and sell nothing. Just a delivery boy that's all."

371

"Why do you call him Thor? I've never heard him called that before." Marcus was stumped by the unfamiliar nickname.

"He got that in the slammer, so I hear," Hondo reminded Marcus of his friend Denny, he was quite a jabberbox. Afforded enough time, he could probably learn every detail of Hondo's life.

"Where did you get your nickname?" Marcus asked.

"Kind of embarrassing really, kid." Hondo said. "I rode a Honda back when I was about your age. And I got called Honda Boy for a while. But then I got myself a Harley Panhead in '57, and so they couldn't really call me that name no more, so it kinda evolved into Hondo."

"What about Mooch? Where did that come from?"

Hondo laughed. "Just what it sounds like, all through high school years, and even now, that's all he does is mooch off people. Food, money, whatever; always moochin'. Don't be surprised if he asks you for a buck before the day is out."

Finally, Ellis and Mooch came into view. Marcus had managed to relax a little bit while waiting and talking with Hondo but seeing the approach of Ellis and Hondo's partner certainly increased his degree of apprehension. Marcus abruptly recalled Ellis telling him about the newsboy hat, saying that Max Schofield's initials were beneath the inside flap. The sudden remembrance, combined with the knowledge of Mooch's remark that Marcus had something belonging to Max, forced him to consider that he might indeed have reason to worry. He had originally thought the hat belonged to Jeremiah, but now more details were coming back to him. It occurred to him that the black Mustang, that he and Cassie had seen leaving the dump on the day of Jeremiah's murder, was definitely a match to the one he'd seen in front of the workshop on the day they had fished on Max's property. He wished Cassie had been along, she had memorized the plate number and could have verified if the plates were one and the same. But then again, Cassie did report the plate number to the authorities. If it did match, the police would have already known that by now. Nothing seemed to make sense. Marcus couldn't imagine any connection whatsoever between Max Schofield and Jeremiah, but the possibility was clearly evident that Max could have been the person responsible for killing Jeremiah.

With the canoe loaded onto the Ford's roof and safely tied down, Ellis drove off, having promised to go directly to the Schofield residence. Mooch and Hondo got Max's dinghy onto its trailer and, with Marcus in the middle of the pickup truck's bench seat, left the boat launch about fifteen minutes later. As the truck pulled away, a familiar four-legged friend of Marcus stood perched near an aged tree stump, having studied the activity with interest.

Driving west on Highway 16, Ellis was jolted when he noticed the virtual image of red flashing lights in his rearview mirror. Spying a mailbox just ahead on the right, he knew a driveway should be either next to it or directly across the road. This was rural Missouri, and mailboxes were always located on the main road and at the end of a driveway. Ellis pulled into a farmer's long gravel driveway, turned off the ignition and waited as the deputy approached on foot.

"You appear to have been in a hurry there, son," said the deputy. Ellis was familiar with a few of the Lewis County deputies. He had received his share of speeding tickets back when he was living in Monticello. Deputy Martin, who had pulled him over today, was one with whom he was not familiar.

"Yes sir, I guess I was in a hurry." The deputy took Ellis' driver's license and returned to his cruiser to check for wants and warrants. In the meantime, Ellis sat in his car, rapidly running scenarios through his mind as he struggled with what he should do. When Deputy Martin returned, Ellis had decided to follow Opa's advice and do what he believed to be right. He had done enough lying, had practiced and participated in enough deceit in his short lifetime. Ellis told the deputy the real reason he was speeding. He explained that his cousin, Marcus Clemens, had been kidnapped. He further informed the deputy that he feared that Marcus' life could be in danger. His hope was that Deputy Martin would go to Max's house and somehow be able to free Marcus from his captors. Deputy Martin asked if he knew the address where Marcus was being held and when Ellis was able to recite it, the deputy quickly scribbled it down in his pocket notebook.

"Alright, Mr. Compton. This is how things are going to go. When I get back to my car, I'm immediately calling for backup and proceeding to this man's property. I expect you to return home to Fulton, and I mean right now." Deputy Martin spoke in a dead serious, no-nonsense tone. "I had better not see you at the site, this could end up turning ugly, and you have absolutely no reason to be involved. This could be dangerous. Am I understood?"

"Yes sir, I understand, I'll go home right now." Ellis agreed.

The deputy returned to his cruiser, backing up slightly before making a U-turn in the driveway, and speeding off, with lights and siren engaged, in a westward direction on Highway 16. Ellis remained seated in his car for another twenty minutes, repeating Opa's words over and over in his mind. *Do what you know to be right. Do what you know to be right.*

* * * *

Cassie sat on her porch swing, watching clouds roll by, as she awaited Marcus' arrival. It had been a couple of days since she'd seen him and was anxious. He had told her he should be there by two in the afternoon, assuming that Ellis would agree to drop him off, and it was now almost a quarter of two. She silently wondered how the camping trip had gone. She had never been camping and was in no hurry to try it. She preferred the comfort of her bed. Cassie couldn't begin to imagine sleeping on the hard ground and worrying about mosquitos, not to mention all the other flying and crawling insects. The mere thought caused her to shiver. Thank you, but no thank you.

Her daydreams were interrupted by a familiar voice, *"Cassie."*

She instinctively looked to her left, where Opa sat occupying his customary position in the front yard. When he spoke, he was always situated just to the left and a little in front of the swing.

"Call Mitchell right away." Opa's voice projected a sense of urgency. *"Marcus has been taken. I can't do this all on my own. You must send Mitchell to the same house where they held you. Now, Cassie. There is no time to waste."* For the first time, Opa did not wander away. He simply vanished into thin air. With Cassie looking directly at him, *poof,* he disappeared. Cassie ran to her bedroom and pulled out her diary. Thankfully, she had insisted that Marcus give her Deputy Daniels' home number, just in case. Racing to the parlor, she frantically dialed the number. Fortunately, Mitchell was home, enjoying the holiday off, and answered on the second ring.

"Mitchell, this is Cassie Worthington. I hope you remember me."

"Yes, Cassie, of course I remember you. How are you?" Mitch Daniels had always been kind to Cassie, he felt an attachment after rescuing her from the grasp of Oliver Compton.

"Mitchell, Marcus has been kidnapped and his life is in danger. I need you to help him, please save him."

"Wait, wait, Cassie. Marcus Clemens was kidnapped? By whom? When? Where did this happen?" Mitchell threw the questions out rapid fire, but Cassie didn't know the answers.

"The only thing I can tell you is he is being held in the same house where you found me the night that they took me. That's all I know." Cassie didn't want to talk, she wanted Mitchell to get in his car and go help Marcus.

"I remember the house, Ollie Compton's old place, but Cassie, I need to know more. I need information to have deputies sent out there." Mitch needed more to go on, to justify mobilizing any on-duty officers.

"No, Mitchell. No deputies. It has to be you. He said it had to be you."

"Who said that Cassie? Who said it had to be me?" Mitch asked.

Cassie was stuck, she had nothing to go on, only what Opa had told her. And of course, she could not doubt Opa's word, not for an instant. "Mitchell, I can't tell you that. If you can save Marcus, I promise we'll discuss it tomorrow. But right now, please believe what I tell you and go save him, please!" Her tears started flowing uncontrollably. "Please, Mitchell, please."

"Alright, Cassie. Get yourself under control. I'll drive out there and see what is happening. I promise you; I will call you as soon as I know Marcus is safe, okay?" Mitch Daniels hung up the phone and ran to the bedroom to change into his uniform and grab his weapon, holster and identification. Heading to his cruiser, he considered calling for backup, but knew he did not have enough information nor the necessary justification to direct any personnel to the scene.

* * * *

On the drive to Max Schofield's property. Lyle Martin had accepted the hard truth that he had allowed himself to get into something that he had not planned for and was ill-prepared to handle. He was extremely concerned with where this situation was going to lead. His original involvement had only been to help facilitate a small pot ring. He had done it to earn a few dollars on the side, to score a bit of recreational marijuana. But things had begun to spiral. With the first murder at the dump, everyone had been fortunate that he had been the responding officer. Being first on the scene allowed him to remove some of the evidence, to set the stage to make it look like it perhaps had just been an argument between two men that had ended under unfortunate circumstances. He had managed to cloud the scene enough that no suspects had been identified, there had been no substantial leads, and the case appeared to be one that would perpetually remain cold.

When Deputy Martin arrived, lights and siren extinguished moments before leaving the highway to avoid unwarranted attention, he parked in front of the workshop. He saw Hondo and Mooch smoking off to the side and around the corner of the garage's roll-up door. He recognized them as members of *The Brood,* but only because of his own involvement with Max's enterprise. They were two of Max's most trusted henchmen, always ready and willing to do his bidding. Max used them for a multitude of tasks. They acted as collection agents and provided muscle whenever needed, for both his legitimate and illegitimate businesses. Their official and legal employment was at the body shop, where both held job titles of auto mechanics. Lyle approached with two basic questions.

"Word is you two kidnapped a kid. True or false?" Martin unloaded question number one.

"Good, Lyle, I'm good, thanks for asking," Mooch responded in a sarcastic tone. "You don't greet old friends before you start asking questions? Are you in an official capacity or is this Max's business?"

"Right now, it's Max's business." It may have been unofficial, but Lyle still wanted answers. "Is the kid in there?" Lyle asked nodding toward the workshop.

"Yeah, he's in there," Hondo offered the first response. "He's fine, he ain't hurt or nothing. Max wanted him brought about because of when he did that old man at the dump, he left his hat laying there. I guess the kid here found it, so now we gotta get it back so Max don't get fingered. Got it?"

"Yeah, got it. Where is Max, anyway?" Lyle had decided he needed to have a sit down with him.

"He's over at the pond, waiting for Thor to get here. He was following us; I don't know what's taking him so long." Hondo had answered question number two, as well.

"Don't hold your breath, I just stopped him twenty minutes ago. Told him to go home." Lyle Martin was glad he'd sent the boy home.

"Boss ain't gonna like that, he wanted to talk to him." Mooch offered this tidbit of information.

"Too bad." Lyle went back to his cruiser and drove toward the pond.

Lyle Martin got out and walked up the small incline that led to the pond. He crested the top of the bank and spied Max sitting in a lawn chair, rod and reel in hand, the cork on his line about twenty feet out gently bobbing up and down.

"Hey, Max, we need to talk." Lyle said as he approached.

Max looked up, a slight expression of surprise on his face.

"Say, there Lyle, can't say I was expecting you today. I was expecting somebody else was going to be out here to talk to me." Max had a pleasant smile on his face.

"Max, this is getting out of hand, I didn't sign up for this." Lyle said.

"Really, Lyle? You didn't sign up for this? I got news for you Deputy Dawg. The first dime I paid you, the first joint I handed you, you signed up for whatever I needed you for. Get used to it, Bucko." Max turned back to the water, looking across the cattails toward the other side of the pond. That's when he saw the beady eyes glaring back at him. And this was not the first time. It had been almost daily, at different places, and to Max, it seemed like all the time. He'd seen it outside the body shop, at the edge of the woods in his backyard, even when he'd parked at the dump and gone into the old man's shack, it had been sitting there, next to the old man's wicker chair under a tree. Beady eyes, always watching. *That damned dog.* It seemed to be everywhere, constantly watching.

"I can't do it anymore, Max. I quit. I can't risk my career like this. Pot was one thing, small time.

But murder? Kidnapping? What do you plan on doing with that kid, Max?" Lyle Martin couldn't deal with it anymore.

"Okay, Deputy Dawg. You don't want to do it anymore? I certainly can't force you now, can I?" Max continued looking across the pond.

"No, Max, you can't." Lyle said firmly. He turned, intending to return to his patrol car.

"I guess if you don't want to work," Max muttered almost sounding as if he was talking to himself. "Then you no longer have any value, do you?"

Lyle Martin didn't catch the mumbled words. He stopped and turned back, intending to ask what he had said. Before he could even focus on Max, he both heard the shot and simultaneously felt the unmistakable sting of the .22 caliber bullet piercing his stomach. As he fell to the ground, Lyle fumbled for his service revolver. But before he could grab ahold of his gun, Max had pounced on him. When Lyle's hand did find the holster, he realized it had already been emptied. The Colt revolver had been pulled from its holster and thrown harmlessly to the side. Max delivered a series of punches to Lyle's head and face. Then, just as he had done with Bill Lohman, Max dragged Lyle's battered and badly injured carcass into the water and began forcefully shoving his head beneath the surface. Lyle flailed his arms in a futile attempt to defend himself, trying to get his head out of the water. He had served in the military and was trained in self-defense, but all the training in the world is ultimately useless after taking a bullet to the upper abdomen and being pummeled about the head repeatedly. Despite attempting a series of punches, after a few moments, and with his lungs filling with muddy, silty water, Lyle Martin succumbed. Max recognized the limpness, just as he had with Bill Lohman. He trudged from the water and up onto the incline of the grassy bank, where he collapsed in sheer exhaustion. He rolled over, lying on his bank and with his eyes closed, began taking deep and calming breaths.

* * * *

Ellis pulled up to the front of the workshop. Hondo stood outside, calmly smoking a cigarette. Ellis got out of his car and walked toward him.

"About time you got here Thor. Where you been?" Hondo asked.

"Got pulled over for speeding. Took forever to get the ticket and get away from his speeching and scolding. Where's Marcus?" Ellis needed to know what they had done with him.

"In the workshop, he's fine. Waiting for Max to come talk to him."

"Well, where's Max?" Ellis needed to talk to Max before he got to Marcus.

"Over to the pond I expect. I think he's over there shooting bullfrogs. I heard a gunshot or two from over there," said Hondo.

Ellis broke into a sprint, racing to the pond as fast as he could. As he ran, he saw the deputy's cruiser parked in the Indiangrass. He prayed that the cruiser was Deputy Martin's car and that the gunshots Hondo had heard were those of the deputy putting an end to Max Schofield forever.

Ellis climbed the incline and stood at the top of the bank, taking in the scene before him. It was his recurring dream, laid out in full view. Now he was able to identify the men fighting in the dream. The man floating in the water face down was in a deputy's uniform. It must be Deputy Martin. The man lying in the grass he recognized instantly as Max Schofield. As Ellis stood, continuing to eye the carnage before him, the reality of Marcus' fate came into focus. Max wanted that stupid hat, he could not allow that evidence to remain out there. And after he got it, Ellis knew, Max was going to kill Marcus. No doubt about it. If he left Marcus alive, Max would end up in prison. It was a simple fact; he could not leave any witnesses. Just as he had eliminated Marcus' friend Jeremiah, he would do the same with Marcus. Ellis saw the gun, a revolver, which was just lying there in the grass. It seemed huge and looked vaguely familiar. Ellis thought it reminded him of the gun that was holstered at Deputy Martin's side. It had garnered his attention during the traffic stop. Sitting in his car, it had been right there, almost at eye level while the officer had stood inspecting Ellis' driver's license. He could only assume that Max had stripped it from Deputy Martin as they fought. Ellis picked it up quietly and forced it into the top of his jeans, at the small of his back.

"Max are you insane?" Ellis called out to him.

Max continued to lie in the grass, eyes remaining closed. Max was always calm, always in control of every situation.

"Is that you, Thor?" Max asked. "I've been expecting you."

"What did you do, Max?" Ellis asked, knowing he would not be afforded a straightforward answer.

"Thor, I've been thinking about something. Remember when you told me about those stocks that Clemens kid was going to be getting from that Twain character?" Ellis could kick himself for being so stupid, for mentioning that to Max. At the time he spoke, he knew in his heart that Max was no good, but somehow Ellis still believed he could be trusted. Little did he know at the time. "Well, I've been thinking about it, Thor," Max went on, "and by God, I think Ollie was right. I'm pretty darn sure if that kid were to somehow meet an unfortunate end, that you Ellis Compton, aka Jude Allensworth, would be the rightful heir to that fortune. Look, my boy. I'm in a unique position to help you. Well, for half the bounty, mind you. A partnership. What do you say, Thor?"

Ellis pulled the revolver from the back of his jeans and stood, legs spread and facing in the general direction of Max, who still lay nonchalantly in the grass, but now with his eyes trained on Lyle Martin's service weapon.

"Max, you're just as crazy as Ollie, and you deserve the same that he got." Ellis firmly stood his ground as Max coolly got to his feet.

"Kid I doubt you even know how to use that. And besides, don't you wonder if I didn't already empty the chambers?" Despite standing a good thirty feet away, Max suddenly, unexpectedly tried to bullrush Ellis. Head lowered, he began running uphill, charging at Ellis.

"You should never have crossed a Clemens, Max." Ellis fired one .38 caliber round from the Colt police revolver. The bullet entered just left of and a few inches above the center of Max's chest and he collapsed in a lifeless heap.

"You're nothing but an animal Max Schofield." Ellis said as he walked toward him. "And you deserve to be put down like one." Ellis grabbed Max by the ankles and dragged him back to the water's edge.

Ellis stood over the top of Max and said, "Oh, by the way Max, Ollie used to bring me out here to shoot bullfrogs and beer cans when I was a kid. And yeah, I checked the cylinder to make sure it was loaded before I challenged you."

Ellis tossed the revolver down near the water's edge and then, just to be certain, he grabbed Max again by the ankles, dragging him into the muddy water. As he was being pulled, Max felt enormous pressure in his chest and struggled to take in air. He had seen Ellis looking down at him, speaking, but everything had gone silent. Everything except for an excited barking, and Max knew without seeing. *That stupid damned dog.* Three feet removed from the safety of the bank, and not far from Lyle Martin, Max was facing the heavens as Ellis gently pushed down on his shoulders, making sure he was fully submerged. He could see Max appearing to look straight up into the cloudless sky, eyes wide open and lifeless. Ellis waited a few more brief seconds before relaxing his grip. He couldn't believe he had just killed Max Schofield.

As he started to leave the cursed water, Ellis saw Opa at the top of the bank. He smiled when Opa's voice spoke inside his head, *"You have done well, Ellis. You have done what you knew to be right. Go now, help Marcus."*

As he walked back toward the house, Ellis saw another deputy's cruiser pull into the driveway and park next his Ford. When he arrived at the workshop entrance a deputy was checking the prone body of Hondo for a pulse. Ellis stepped closer and saw that Hondo's throat had been horribly gashed, ripped open it seemed. He then saw Deputy Daniels' nametag.

"You are Mitch Daniels, Marcus' friend?" Ellis asked, offering his hand. "I'm Ellis Compton, his cousin."

"Nice to meet you." Mitch answered, ignoring Ellis' outstretched hand. "Do you know where Marcus is?"

"Inside, I was told."

They entered the workshop, Mitchell first with gun drawn. They saw Marcus right away, bound, gagged, and tethered to a support column. Ellis recognized Mooch on the floor, having suffered the same gory fate as Hondo. Mitch raced to Marcus' side, first pulling out the gag, and then setting about releasing his bindings.

"Are you alright Marcus?" Mitch Daniels, of course, was deeply concerned for Marcus' safety.

"Yes Mitch. I'm fine, thank you for helping me." Marcus was incredibly grateful that Mitch had come to his rescue. "How did you know I was here? Did Ellis send you?"

"No, Marcus, Cassie called me at home and told me you had been kidnapped and were here, at Ollie Compton's place."

"How did she know I'd been kidnapped and where I was?" Marcus looked at Ellis inquisitively.

"Wasn't me, Marcus. I sent another deputy over here to try to save you." Ellis was going to have to inform Deputy Daniels about the fate of his fellow officer. "I sent Deputy Martin, but now he's dead. His car is over by the pond. That's where his body is too, it's out there, floating in the pond, alongside Max Schofield."

"Let me call for some reinforcements and notify the coroner's office, then we'll go to this pond and start sorting things out." The three of them went out into the sunshine. While Mitchell was gone to his car, Ellis asked Marcus what in blazes had happened at the workshop.

"It was Opa. I know he got the one inside, and it looks like he attacked this one too. It's just like he did you, Ellis." Marcus explained to him. "Only difference was he went for your arm. He went for their throats."

Ellis breathed a sigh of relief. "I'm sure glad he didn't go for my throat, Marcus."

"Me too, Ellis," Marcus agreed. "But I think there's a reason he didn't want to kill you."

"Why? What's the reason?" Ellis asked.

"Because you couldn't die Ellis. There was a plan for you. You had to be stopped to save me, but you couldn't die. There were plans for you." Marcus said with all earnestness.

Deputy Daniels motioned for them to join him in his car. Ellis climbed in back while Marcus rode shotgun. The car cut through the Indiangrass and parked next to Lyle Martin's abandoned cruiser. After parking the car, Mitchell Daniels looked at Marcus expecting answers and explanations.

"Okay, Mitch. Here is what happened." Marcus went into great detail about finding the hat at the scene of Jeremiah's murder and the resulting kidnapping. Mitch could understand the reason why Max - if he had been the one to shoot Jeremiah - would have wanted to recover the hat.

"What about the two bodies back there, Marcus? You were there, what happened to them?" Mitchell had never seen anything quite like what he saw at the workshop.

"I only saw the one inside the shop, Mitch." Marcus knew what he was about to say would be met with skepticism. "It was a German Shepherd. The guy had been teasing and aggravating this dog, maybe it was his or belonged to the guy Max, I don't know. I guess the dog got mad and attacked him. Then it went out the open door and I heard barking and growling. I guess it attacked that guy, too."

Mitchell thought the story sounded a bit far-fetched, but he had seen the wounds. The violence that he'd seen evidence of did appear to have been consistent with that type of attack.

The three of them exited the car and began climbing the incline.

"So, Ellis, we're going to find two more bodies here in the water, one of which you admit responsibility for. Am I correct?"

"Yes, sir." While back in the car, Ellis had explained how Max had tried to convince him to help revive Ollie's old scheme to get rid of Marcus in order to claim the Mark Twain inheritance. He told Mitchell how things had transpired. He described finding the deputy's gun, how he had refused to assist in the plan against Marcus, and Max rushing to attack him. He told Mitchell how he had shot Max in self-defense and admitted to getting him into the water and making sure Max had died.

As they were about to crest the pond's bank, Mitchell ordered Marcus to stay behind while he and Ellis went ahead to investigate. There was no point in Marcus unnecessarily witnessing another gruesome scene. As they reached the top of the bank, Mitchell could clearly see his fellow deputy, now partially submerged, and still floating face down, about eight feet from the bank. In the meantime, Ellis instantly noticed that Max was no longer in the water, and informed Mitchell that Max's body was not where he had left it a short time ago. Max now lay more up on the grassy bank, with only the lower part of his legs still in the water. He was flat on his back, right arm draped across his chest.

With gun now drawn, Mitchell said, "You must not have finished the job, Ellis. It appears you might have left him still alive. It looks like he managed to almost get out before he died."

The two approached the lifeless form. As they neared, Ellis suddenly remembered that after he had shot Max, he had carelessly dropped the weapon somewhere in the immediate area, right there on the bank. He looked across to the other side of Max, where he thought it may have been before he had begun dragging Max into the water. Unexpectedly, Ellis spotted the gun in Max's bloody right hand, raised ever so slightly, but he'd seen it too late. He tried to warn Mitchell, but before he could utter a single sound, the muzzle briefly flashed and searing pain rushed through Ellis' body. Mitchell fired two rapid shots in response, leaving no doubt that Max Schofield was no more. Racing over to the corpse, Mitchell grabbed the Colt from the grass, throwing it a safe distance away. He returned to Ellis' side, dropping to his knees. He immediately started looking for the wound, desperately tearing at the white tee shirt that was now coated in crimson.

Having heard gunfire followed by eerie silence; Marcus had come running. From the top of the bank, he could see Mitchell from behind, down on his knees and sitting back on his heels. Marcus stopped running, standing in numbing shock, when he clearly saw him. Ellis had been propped up onto Mitchell's lap and seemed to stare, with unfocused eyes, at the heavens above. It struck Marcus that Ellis looked content. He wondered if his cousin was at peace.

Marcus simultaneously had a ghastly flashback to a teenaged girl in a colorful polka dancer's dress. He imagined the top of her outfit had been a pristine white when Zofia Wozniak had gotten dressed, preparing to attend her club meeting, before it had been unceremoniously coated in blood.

His eyes flooded with tears as Marcus stared at the beautiful white clouds slowly making their way across the sky. He thought of Opa, who had once again protected him and wondered why Ellis had not been gifted a guardian angel.

James E. Anderson

Epilogue

Three months have now passed since the July Fourth insanity. During the course of their investigation, law enforcement had discovered what had presented as a freshly dug and hastily covered mound located just northeast of the pond on Max Schofield's property. Further examination revealed a shallow grave containing the body of a young man named Bill Lohman. It was discovered that Lohman, who had hailed from St. Louis, apparently had initially been beaten severely and had ultimately drowned before being unceremoniously buried. Although almost certainly connected to the other deaths of the day, the case of Bill Lohman would remain unsolved. Officials were left with no evidence, leads, witnesses, nor suspects. Unfortunately, there had been no final satisfactory solution to Jeremiah's murder either, although Marcus and Cassie had determined, at least in their court of opinion, that Max Schofield had been guilty.

In regard to Deputy Lyle Martin, he was celebrated as a fallen hero. Investigators speculated that he had suspected Max Schofield's involvement in the murder of Jeremiah Paige and had unfortunately been killed while trying to conduct an interview of the subject. Even though that determination threw shade on Max Schofield, substantial evidence was never discovered to connect him with Jeremiah. The existence of the newsboy hat containing Max's initials proved to be purely circumstantial and essentially meant nothing at all. The deaths of Ellis Compton and Max Schofield were cut and dried. Mitch had witnessed Ellis being shot, and Max's shooting by Ellis had been ruled justifiable. The deaths of the two men who had been attacked by the dog were reported as accidental. The assumption was that the attacking dog had been owned by Max Schofield, although Mitch Daniels later told Marcus that there was never anything found to support that assumption. No collars or leashes, no dog food, no food or water bowls, and no veterinary records anywhere in the county. Everything seemed to be explained or excused away, the entire case all bundled and tied up nicely, legally speaking. But Marcus Clemens was aware of the truth, or at least most of it.

* * * *

Marcus and Cassie had returned to her house from church and then taken Marcus' relatively new prized possession over to Randolph Park to while away the afternoon. With a little help from Chester and Louie, the 1959 Nash Metropolitan was now in tiptop condition. Luckily, they had been able to repair its inefficient heater, for it had been needed today. The first Sunday of October was chilly, and they had wisely brought along a woolen blanket to throw across their laps as they sat on the park bench watching the ducks. Observimg ducks as they frolicked in the pond at Randolph Park had been a beloved pastime of Cassie's that dated back to their first visit together to the park in 1963. Early fall, as it turned out, was a good time of year to indulge. Marcus had studied up on the habits of Cassie's favorite fowl. He had learned that by living on the banks of the Mississippi River they were in the middle of *The Mississippi Flyway*, the migratory route of over 300 species of birds. Early October was a happy time for Cassie; now was when the blue-winged teal were making a temporary stopover. They could be expected to visit for a short time, but by November they will have moved further south.

The two had been sitting for an hour or so, with Cassie leaning her beanie covered head against Marcus' right shoulder. Cassie's pixie cut had begun growing back out and, to Marcus' delight, her red hair was now sporadically visible around the hat's fringes. Their topic of conversation had evolved from the migrating fowl to family.

"How is Cousin Judy doing, Marcus? Has he been by to see you since we saw him on Labor Day?" Cassie asked.

"I guess I forgot to tell you, he stopped by the apartment last Saturday while I was at work. But Mama was gone, she was working at the restaurant. I don't know why he bothered. He knows she works on weekends. So, since she wasn't home, he stopped by Walt's just to say hi. He took the Metro for a spin. He didn't like it; it was too small he said. Plus, it wasn't fast enough." Marcus laughed at Judy's overall evaluation but had to agree that his only complaint so far had been the car's low top end. The speedometer went to eighty, but that milestone was unattainable.

"I guess not, compared to that race car he drives." Cassie laughed, too. But then, more seriously, she asked, "How is he doing with the loss of Ellis?"

"I don't know he hasn't talked about him with me." Marcus thought about Judy's overall demeanor. "I don't know Cassie, he used to always be pretty upbeat, but now he does seem a little quieter and more reserved. But, I mean, I guess that would only be normal, wouldn't it?"

Both returned to relative silence as they sat relaxing. Until they had discussed Ellis and Judy, the day could not have gone any more perfectly. They were both taken by surprise when an old friend suddenly appeared, apparently to visit and chat. Over the past three months, they had seen him from a distance, but this is the first time he had approached since the Fourth of July.

"Hello Opa," Cassie said as she reached down to ruffle his ears. "What brings you around?"

The voice was silent, but she heard it just the same.

"I thought it was time to express my sympathy for what happened to Ellis. Marcus should know that Ellis did as he should, he did not tempt fate, he did not shrink from his calling."

Cassie related the message to Marcus.

"Opa, I think I deserve some answers." There were several things that Marcus wanted to know. "Why did Ellis have to die? Why couldn't you save him? Why didn't you intervene?"

"Tell him, Cassie, that he has received these answers before. I am Marcus' guardian angel. I cannot save anyone else from their fate. As for why Ellis had to die, I do not have that answer. The book is already written, the plans are already made. Ellis had debts that were owed, and he balanced his books. Ease your minds by knowing that in the end, Ellis did as he knew was right. He had a part that he was born to play, and in the end he played it flawlessly."

Hearing and accepting what Cassie was relaying, Marcus had one more question, "I thought Cassie was the only person you could speak to. How were you able to speak to Ellis?"

"Commitment Marcus. I've explained it to you. Ellis had a lifelong commitment to you. From the moment he made his commitment to you, he never wavered, it continued until the end of his life. I must leave now, but I have a message that I need Marcus to deliver. My nephew Jude is devastated over the loss of Ellis. He hurts badly. Marcus must deliver this message to him; tell him it is an anonymous message that he must take to heart. The words will be painful for him, but he must hear them. Marcus, tell him to remember these eleven words – This Is All Your Fault, Jude. You Are Responsible for Ellis."

Opa turned and walked away.

www.ingramcontent.com/pod-product-compliance
Lightning Source LLC
Chambersburg PA
CBHW021127260626
47169CB00005B/1482